THE WORLD'S CLASSICS

YOUTH, HEART OF DARKNESS, THE END OF THE TETHER

JOSEPH CONRAD was born Józef Teodor Konrad Korzeniowski in the Russian part of Poland in 1857. His parents were punished by the Russians for their Polish nationalist activities and both died while Conrad was still a child. In 1874 he left Poland for France and in 1878 began a career with the British merchant navy. He spent nearly twenty years as a sailor and did not begin writing novels until he was approaching forty. He became a British citizen in 1886 and settled permanently in England after his marriage to Jessie George in 1896.

Conrad is a writer of extreme subtlety and sophistication; works such as *Heart of Darkness*, *Lord Jim*, and *Nostromo* display technical complexities which have established Conrad as one of the first English 'Modernists'. He is also noted for the unprecedented vividness with which he communicates a pessimist's view of man's personal and social destiny in such works as *The Secret Agent*, *Under Western Eyes*, and *Victory*. Despite the immediate critical recognition that they received in his life-time Conrad's major novels did not sell, and he lived in relative poverty until the commercial success of *Chance* (1913) secured for him a wider public and an assured income. In 1923 he visited America, with great acclaim, and he was offered a knighthood (which he declined) shortly before his death in 1924. Since then his reputation has steadily grown and he is now seen as a writer who revolutionized the English novel and was arguably the most important single innovator of the twentieth century.

ROBERT KIMBROUGH is Professor of English at the University of Wisconsin-Madison (USA). Although the emphasis of his research, teaching, and publication is in the Renaissance, he has published critical editions of Conrad and James: *The Heart of Darkness* (1963, rev. 1971) and *The Nigger of the 'Narcissus'* (1979); *The Turn of the Screw* (1966).

THE WORLD'S CLASSICS

JOSEPH CONRAD

Youth
Heart of Darkness
The End of the Tether

Edited with an introduction by
ROBERT KIMBROUGH

Oxford   New York
OXFORD UNIVERSITY PRESS
1984

Oxford University Press, Walton Street, Oxford OX2 6DP

London New York Toronto
Delhi Bombay Calcutta Madras Karachi
Kuala Lumpur Singapore Hong Kong Tokyo
Nairobi Dar es Salaam Cape Town
Melbourne Auckland

and associated companies in
Beirut Berlin Ibadan Mexico City Nicosia

Oxford is a trade mark of Oxford University Press

Introduction, Notes, Glossary © Robert Kimbrough 1984
Select Bibliography, Chronology © John Batchelor 1983

British Library Cataloguing in Publication Data
Conrad, Joseph
Youth; Heart of darkness; The end of the
tether.—(The World's classics)
I. Title   II. Kimbrough, Robert
823'.912 [F]   PR6005.04
ISBN 0-19-281626-8

Library of Congress Cataloging in Publication Data
Conrad, Joseph, 1857–1924.
Youth; Heart of darkness; The end of the tether.
(The World's classics)
Bibliography: p.
I. Kimbrough, Robert.   II. Title: Youth.
III. Title: Heart of darkness.   IV. Title: End of the
tether.   V. Series.
PR6005.04A6 1984   823'.912   84–840
ISBN 0-19-281626-8 (pbk.)

Printed in Great Britain by
Hazell Watson & Viney Limited,
Aylesbury, Bucks

CONTENTS

INTRODUCTION

I

IN THE year of his death (1924), Joseph Conrad said that the three stories in *Youth: A Narrative; and Two Other Stories* (1902)—'Youth', 'Heart of Darkness', and 'The End of the Tether'—represent the three ages of man— youth, maturity, and age. The comment is helpful, but only in a general, introductory way, even if supported by the relative length of each story: 'Youth' is about 13,000 words, 'Heart of Darkness', about 38,000, and 'The End of the Tether', about 47,000—Conrad's longest. (His shortest novel, *The Nigger of the 'Narcissus'* (1897) is about 54,000 words.) In fact, the very first sentence in Conrad's 1917 Preface states that 'the three stories in this volume lay no claim to unity of artistic purpose'. Conrad did not set out to write about three separate periods of life; he wrote about life from three separate points of view, using three separate techniques—even though the first two are told by the same man, Marlow.

Not 'The End of the Tether', but *Lord Jim*, in the form of a short story ('Lord Jim'), was to have been the third piece for a volume contracted in 1898 by the Edinburgh publisher, William Blackwood. 'Youth' and 'Heart of Darkness' had first appeared in *Blackwood's Magazine* (*Maga*) in 1897 and 1899, as had *Lord Jim* in 1899–1900 (and as would 'The End of the Tether'). Upon completion *Lord Jim* had proved too long for inclusion as a short story and was published separately as a novel in 1900. Before the third story had been received, however, the first two stories had been set in print for the single volume. Thus,

Conrad still had to provide about 40,000 words in order to fulfil his contract to complete the book.

Had *Lord Jim* remained short enough to be entitled 'Lord Jim' the resulting volume could have been entitled *Marlow*, because Marlow, that friend of the anonymous narrator of 'Youth', 'Heart of Darkness', and *Lord Jim*, is actually the principal narrator within all three. Thus, all three are *about* Marlow as well as *by* Marlow. But in writing 'The End of the Tether' to complete *Youth: A Narrative; and Two Other Stories*, Conrad chose not to evoke Marlow, possibly because to do so would draw too much attention to the many ways that 'The End of the Tether' is a kind of recasting of Lord Jim's story, which Marlow had already recounted.

Conrad's 1917 Preface to the *Youth* volume of 1902 remains the best introduction to Marlow and to the three stories in that volume—and, of course, in this: hence, readers might well wish to turn to Conrad's 'Author's Note' at this point. There Conrad places the composition of the stories between the two critically acknowledged landmarks of his early career as a writer, *The Nigger of the 'Narcissus'* (1897) and *Nostromo* (1904). He tells us that each of the three stories is based in part on his own experience:

'Youth' is a feat of memory. It is a record of experience; but that experience, in its facts... begins and ends in myself. 'Heart of Darkness' is experience, too; but it is experience pushed a little (and only very little) beyond the actual facts of the case... 'The End of the Tether' is a story of sea-life... the pages of that story—a fair half of the book—are also the product of experience.

For the details of Conrad's experiences as the second mate on the barque *Palestine* in 1881–2 ('Youth'), as the captain of a steamer on the Congo in 1890 ('Heart of Darkness') and as the first mate of the *Vidar* in 1888 ('The End of the

Tether'), the reader should consult Roger Tennant's 1981 biography and Norman Sherry's excellent volumes on Conrad's Eastern and Western worlds (see the headnote to the Notes, p. 341). When Conrad was forthright enough to say that 'all art is autobiographical or it is nothing', he did not mean that all art is biography. Indeed, he made it abundantly clear in a letter to his young friend Richard Curle in 1921 that scholarly, critical 'explicitness is fatal to art'. Hence, the Notes in this present volume do not link details of fiction to details of life. Indeed, the proper degree of scholarly, critical reserve that we should adopt is exemplified by Conrad himself in his remarks on Marlow, that 'most discreet, understanding man'.

Conrad rightly laughs at those of us who debate whether Marlow is or is not Conrad. Clearly, Marlow is both, at the same time that he is neither. Marlow is, in the Elizabethan sense, an invention—something come across, something happened upon, something uncovered—something discovered in the very process of writing. Hence, we need not doubt that 'Marlow and I came together in the casual manner of those health-resort acquaintances which sometimes ripen into friendships', that Marlow 'haunts my hours of solitude', and that 'as we part at the end of a tale I am never sure that it may not be for the last time' (this was written in 1917, four years after *Chance*, which turned out to be the fourth and last of the Marlow stories). Because of the imaginative source of Marlow within Conrad, we can appreciate the warmth and humour in Conrad's 'Yet I don't think that either of us would much care to survive the other.'

II

The special appeal of 'Youth' is that it simultaneously celebrates and laughs at young ideas and acts, that it is

simultaneously sentimental and world-weary. This simul-
taneity, this mix, could not be achieved without Marlow.
Had the story been told in the first-person during or
immediately after the events, the egoism of youth—the
self-congratulation, the self-centredness, the self-glorifica-
tion: in short, the romanticism of youth—would have been
so central that the story would have sounded a single-
noted effect, either of celebration or of derision. Or, had
the story been told in a restricted third-person, either past
or present tense, the effect, again, would be either/or:
either of sentimentality or of embittered disillusionment.
But with Marlow, a character within someone else's narrative telling his own story from a recollective point of view,
all of the either/or's disappear. Marlow can laugh at
himself for having been foolhardy, stupid, and limited in
vision; nevertheless, it was Marlow himself who was
adventurous, brave, and guided by idealistic patterns
superimposed on the world. As a result, Marlow's report
has integrity, wholeness, truth.

Between Marlow and us is the anonymous narrator
who, like his four friends, 'began life in the merchant
service'. To him, then, life at sea 'is life itself'. This
statement prepares us for Marlow's 'You fellows know
there are those voyages that seem ordered for the illustration of life, that might stand for a symbol of existence'.
And at forty-two, Marlow looks back twenty years to
recount his initiation into life, his movement from youth to
manhood.

To the young Marlow, the *Judea* (with its simplistic
motto of an arrested adolescence: 'Do or Die' ['Death
Before Dishonour', 'Better Dead Than Red', 'Love It or
Leave It']) was 'the endeavour, the test, the trial of life',
and his journey ends with 'the thought that I had been
tried in that ship and had come out pretty well... I did not
know how good a man I was till then'. In present perspec-

tive, however, before he gets wine-soaked sentimental at the end, Marlow can clear-sightedly say of his adventure, 'It was like an absurd dream'. The narrator, too, cynically concludes that the life of youth is 'the romance of illusions'. But because of the invention of Marlow, Conrad can rightly claim to have captured in 'Youth' a double-layered 'mood of wistful regret, or reminiscent tenderness', which is life in a larger perspective than that merely of past time or present.

III

Once invented in 'Youth', Marlow allowed Conrad to turn to his deeply traumatic, cataclysmically catalytic venture into Africa and to convert the experience into art. While a lot of autobiography is deeply hidden in 'Heart of Darkness', there is only surface biography because here, in addition to Marlow, we are given Kurtz. 'Youth' is double-layered; 'Heart of Darkness' is multi-layered. Question: When Kurtz utters 'The horror! The horror!' what do you think that Conrad thought that the narrator thought that Marlow thought that Kurtz thought? The answer to that question lies not in Conrad's biography, but is found at the heart of this dark story—or, it resides as well in the darkness surrounding the heart of the story, for all referents point inward and outward at the same time, which is the way symbols work on us.

In 'Youth', through Marlow, Conrad turned from his previous technique of straightforward single-layered narrative to one that was indirect and double. Still, the tensions, the potential ambiguities, were contained within the dimensions of Marlow's original experience. With the addition of Kurtz's experience, Conrad is able to add a symbolic dimension to his earlier narrative technique. In the surviving manuscript version of the story, Conrad included an episode that describes Marlow's arrival at the seat of colonial government within the estuary of the River Congo. Marlow says in part:

'I had heard enough in Europe about its advanced state of civilization; the papers, nay the very paper vendors in the sepulchral city were boasting about the steam tramway and the hotel—especially the hotel. I beheld that wonder. *It was like a symbol at the gate.* It stood alone, a grey high cube of iron with two tiers of galleries outside towering above one of those ruinous-looking fore-shores you come upon at home in out-of-the-way places where refuse is thrown out. To make the resemblance complete it wanted only a drooping post bearing a board with the legend: rubbish shot here, and *the symbol* would have had the clearness of the naked truth.' [emphasis added]

The passage never got into print; perhaps the symbolism of this mock sepulchral city linking Europe with Africa was too blatant, too naked. But the repetition of the word 'symbol' indicates that Conrad realized that he was bringing a new kind of writing into 'Heart of Darkness'. Where his earlier narratives were primarily objective, descriptive, and thematically clear, 'Heart of Darkness' is also interior, suggestively analytic, and highly psychological. Indeed, Conrad realized that in comparison to 'Youth', 'Heart of Darkness' is 'written in another mood'; the 'sombre theme had to be given a sinister resonance, a tonality of its own, a continued vibration' and the result is 'like another art altogether'.

While 'Heart of Darkness' is the story of the story of Marlow's venture up the Congo River to Stanley Falls, Marlow's interest (to the regret of the reporting narrator) is centred in Kurtz:

'I don't want to bother you much with what happened to me personally', he began, showing in his remark the weakness of many tellers of tales who seem so often unaware of what their audience would best like to hear; 'yet to understand the effect of it on me you ought to know how I got out there, what I saw, how I went up that river to the place where I first met the poor chap.'

Hence, it is Kurtz's story that Marlow is telling, even before he and we meet Kurtz. But Marlow's story is the mediating story between the inner one of Kurtz's invasion of the so-called Belgian Congo and the outer story that Conrad is telling of Europe's invasion of Africa. Without Kurtz's story, 'Heart of Darkness' would, like 'Youth', be a simultaneous celebration of self and satire of society. But with Kurtz the reverberations and implications multiply, for Kurtz is the central symbol.

All of Europe, we are told, contributed to the making of Kurtz—Europe: safe, civilized, scheduled, masculine, literate, Christian, and dead. Kurtz, a European 'Knight', sets out on a crusade to win the hearts and minds of a lesser people, ignorant of the degree to which Africa is dangerous, wild, timeless, feminine, unfettered by letters, religious, and vibrant. His love turns to rape when he discovers how unfitted he is to master the magnificent vitality of a natural world. The difference between Europe and Africa is the difference between two secondary symbols: the European woman who has helped to puff up Kurtz's pride and the African woman who has helped to deflate him.

The Intended (nameless, intended for someone else, not herself) is totally protected (helpless), rhetorically programmed (words without matter), nun-like in her adoration (sexually repressed), living in black, in a place of darkness, in a pre-Eliot City of the Dead, in the wasteland of modern Europe. She, like Europe, is primarily exterior, for the simple black garment hides nothing.

The Native Woman is Africa, all interior, in spite of her lavish mode of dress. While Kurtz is male, white, bald, oral, unrestrained, the native woman is female, black, stunningly coiffured, emotive, and restrained. Here, in part, is her introduction:

'She walked with measured steps, draped in striped and fringed cloths, with a slight jingle and flash of barbarous ornaments... She was savage and superb, wild-eyed, and magnificent; there was something ominous and stately in her deliberate progress. And in the hush that had fallen suddenly upon the whole sorrowful land, the immense wilderness, the colossal body of the fecund and mysterious life seemed to look at her, pensive, as though it had been looking at the image of its own tenebrous and passionate soul.'

Africa, yes, but she is also Tellus Mater, Amazon, Dido, and a type of Venus. Kurtz is clearly a kind of Mars. While this does not mean that the arrows shot through the pilot-house door come from their son Cupid, these arrows are, however, a fine example of the phallic futility of their relationship, which has none of the creativity and bonding of love, only love's hate and anger. Kurtz's lustful exploitation of her, then, is rape, just as were his raids in the lake region, just as was the fantastic invasion of Africa by Christian, capitalistic Western civilization and its discontents.

Marlow's story links these inner and outer stories. In a sense, Marlow exploits the exploiters in order to carry out his boyhood dream of going to Africa, where there was 'one river especially, a mighty big river, that you could see on the map, with its head in the sea, its body at rest curving afar over a vast country, and its tail lost in the depths of the land. And as I looked at the map of it in a shop-window, it fascinated me as a snake would a bird—a silly little bird... The snake had charmed me.' The snake and the bird, age-old phallic symbols, set up the motif of sexual encounter. Recalling the map on the office wall in the sepulchral city, Marlow says, 'I was going into the yellow. Dead in the centre. And the river was there—

'fascinating—deadly—like a snake.' And as he departed in his French steamer he 'felt as though, instead of going to the centre of a continent, I were about to set off for the centre of the earth'.

Thus the river is a phallus within the vulva of Africa, the head of the penis touching the womb, the heart, the inner darkness. But the river itself is a vulva, mouth open to the sea, inviting the sexually excited scavenger birds of Europe. The snake swallowing its own tail is the sign of fulfilment, of perfection, of androgynous wholeness, because penis and vulva circle continuously. But in 'Heart of Darkness' the phallus of Europe enters the snake's mouth, moves inward to the heart of darkness, reaches climax, and is disgorged. Phallic futility, vaginal pain—no fulfilment, no content.

During Marlow's trip to Africa, the coast line was 'smiling, frowning, inviting, grand, mean, insipid, or savage, and always mute with an air of whispering, Come and find out'. This female image is counterpointed by the masculine surf: 'The voice of the surf heard now and then was a positive pleasure, like the speech of a brother. It was something natural, that had its reason, that had a meaning', as did the native men who came out to the ship in canoes: 'they had bone, muscle, a wild vitality, and intense energy of movement, that was as natural and true as the surf along their coast'—a surf that is a 'dangerous surf, as if Nature herself had tried to ward off intruders'.

Within this self-contained, positive, masculine-feminine context, we get a symbol of the intruders in the French man-of-war, 'her ensign drooped limp like a rag', 'shelling the bush' from 'long six-inch guns' sticking out of its low hull:

'In the empty immensity of earth, sky, and water, there she was, incomprehensible, firing into a continent. Pop, would go one of the six-inch guns; a small flame would dart and vanish, a little white smoke would disappear, a tiny projectile would give a feeble screech—and nothing happened. Nothing could happen. There was a touch of insanity in the proceeding, a sense of lugubrious drollery in the sight.'

Interestingly, these guns were 'ten-inch' in manuscript, 'eight-inch' in *Blackwood's Magazine*, and are 'six-inch' here in the *Youth* volume; 'inch', of course, refers to muzzle/bore diameter, but the association of diminishing size to male sexual pride, fear, and fantasy is obvious.

Fittingly, when Marlow first hears the high explosives used in clearing for the railroad that will connect the Lower and Central Stations, he is reminded of the French phallic futility: 'a heavy and dull detonation shook the ground, a puff of smoke came out of the cliff and that was all. No change appeared on the face of the rock. They were building a railway. The cliff was not in the way or anything; but this objectless blasting was all the work going on... Another report from the cliff made me think suddenly of that ship of war I had seen firing into a continent.'

After fifteen days and two hundred miles of tramping, Marlow gets from the Lower to the Central Station. The cockiness of the manager and the impotence of his underlings are caught at once: 'They wandered here and there with their absurd long staves in their hands, like a lot of faithless pilgrims bewitched inside a rotten fence... And outside, the silent wilderness surrounding this cleared speck on the earth struck me as something great and invincible.' This phallic futility and failed interaction is followed up by the invasion, the infliction, the visitation by the Eldorado Exploring Expedition, and Marlow overhears one night snatches of conversation between the manager and his uncle, the leader of the Expedition:

'I saw him extend his short flipper of an arm for a gesture that took in the forest, the creek, the mud, the river—seemed to beckon with a dishonouring flourish before the sunlit face of the land a treacherous appeal to the lurking death, to the hidden evil, to the profound darkness of its heart. The high stillness confronted these two figures with its ominous patience, waiting for the passing away of a fantastic invasion.'

At this point, Conrad's manuscript reads: 'The thick voice was swallowed up, the confident gesture was lost in the high stillness... with its ominous air [of] patient waiting', and cancelled is a comparison of the voice and gesture to 'bursting shells' and 'blasted rocks'.

The central sexual experience of the book is the trip up the river by the men aboard that symbol of Western civilization, the steamboat, which is here simultaneously a phallus penetrating the river-vulva and semen carrying sterile sperm within the river-phallus moving up to the mouth of the womb of Africa. This adventure to attempt to 'rescue' Kurtz culminates in a sexual explosion of nature's fog and man's smoke, of natural noises and man-made ones, of arrows and bullets. What more appropriate than to find the Russian fool at the Inner Station, for the fool is another age-old phallic symbol: folly resides in the head of the penis; the folly of folly, folly within folly.

The whole experience is given context by a passage spoken by Marlow before he describes this ascent into the heart of darkness. Ostensibly for the benefit of his immediate audience, but actually for ours, he asks: 'Do you see the story? Do you see anything? It seems to me I am trying to tell you a dream—making a vain attempt, because no relation of a dream can convey the dream-sensation, that commingling of absurdity, surprise, and bewilderment in a tremor of struggling revolt, that notion of being captured by the incredible which is the very essence of dreams.' The description of the passage up river 'as we penetrated deeper and deeper into the heart of darkness' *is* a dream narrative, a prose poem, that must be read aloud, slowly in order for the sensuality of the experience to be felt: from p. 92—'Going up that river was like travelling back to the earliest beginnings of the world, when vegetation rioted on the earth and the big trees were kings'—to p. 96—'They howled and leaped, and spun, and made horrid faces; but what thrilled you was just the thought of their humanity—like yours—the thought of your remote kinship with this wild and passionate uproar.'

The manuscript of the story tells us that comprehension of the wilderness could not come to the travellers because they were merely passing by. True comprehension could come only 'by conquest—or by surrender'. Kurtz came to a full knowledge both ways, by conquest and surrender: 'The wilderness had patted him on the head, and, behold, it was like a ball—an ivory ball; it had caressed him, and—lo!—he had withered; it had taken him, loved him, embraced him, got into his veins, consumed his flesh, and sealed his soul to its own by the inconceivable ceremonies of some devilish initiation. He was its spoiled and pampered favourite.' In his sexually spent condition, Kurtz looks like Red Cross Knight, also the victim of his own sexual pride. But the native woman is not Duessa, and the Intended is not Una. Rather, the reverse, for when Kurtz conquered and surrendered to the Native Woman he discovered Truth. It is not the Intended, but the African, 'wild and gorgeous', to whom Marlow refers when he says Kurtz 'had conquered one soul in the world that was neither rudimentary nor tainted with self-seeking'. It is she to whom Kurtz tries to return at night, and Marlow is appalled: 'I tried to break the spell—the heavy, mute spell of the wilderness—that seemed to draw him to its pitiless breast by the awakening of forgotten and brutal instincts, by the memory of gratified and monstrous passions.' These are Marlow's words, and those who would have us believe that this is Conrad speaking as well are misrepresenting Kurtz, who, in spite of Marlow's and Conrad's reactions to his sexual experiences, has learned all there is to learn about *Love and Will* before Rollo May, with a debt to Schopenhauer, wrote about the demonic within us. When the steamer is leaving, the woman returns, puts out her hands, and screams something. Marlow asks Kurtz if he understands: 'He kept on looking out past me with fiery, longing eyes, with a mingled expression of *wistfulness* and *hate*... "Do I not?"' he said slowly, gasping, as if the words had been torn out of him by a supernatural power' (emphasis added).

When Kurtz says 'The horror! The horror!' rhetoric and reality come together; Europe and Africa, the Intended and the African, collide. Kurtz realizes that all he has been nurtured to believe in, to operate from, is a sham; hence, a horror. The primal nature of nature is also, *to him*, a horror, because he has been stripped of his own culture and stands both literally and figuratively naked before another; he has been exposed to desire but cannot comprehend it through some established framework. That which we cannot understand we stand over; that which we cannot embrace, we reject; that which we cannot love, we hate. To Kurtz, Europe and Africa have both become nightmares—'The horror! The horror!'—and it is between these nightmares that Marlow must make his choice.

Meditating on his own brush with death, Marlow wonders if he could have reached the insight and self-discovery that Kurtz obtained through his exposure to the timeless world of love and hate:

'He had summed up—he had judged. "The horror!" He was a remarkable man. After all, this was the expression of some sort of belief; it had candour, it had conviction, it had a vibrating note of revolt in its whisper, it had the appalling face of a glimpsed truth—the strange commingling of *desire* and *hate*... It was an affirmation, a moral victory paid for by innumerable defeats, by abominable terrors, by abominable satisfactions. But it was a victory!' [emphasis added]

Because of his total self- and sexual knowledge, Kurtz could never go back to his Intended—the agony of this realization informs his repeated 'horror'. Such as he had become would overwhelm the male-sheltered, carefully cultured, literally manufactured woman. Her repressed sexuality, further battened down by her mourning, is part of Kurtz's horror. On the one hand he experienced lust unleashed—through carnal knowledge of Africa coming into self-knowledge of his European hollowness—but he is rendered unable to share that knowledge. To do so would be to inflict rape and slaughter merely of a different kind in a different place in the world. And for Marlow to have indicated to the Intended the way Kurtz lived and died would have been to carry out that rape and slaughter.

Conrad set up the ironic contrast between the two women through the painting by Kurtz that he left behind at the Central Station. The picture represented 'a woman, draped and blindfolded, carrying a lighted torch. The background was sombre—almost black. The movement of the woman was stately, and the effect of the torchlight on the face was sinister.' Europe in Africa—the torch will be quenched, the blind woman swallowed whole. Marlow did not really lie, for the last words Kurtz pronounced were in partial reference to his symbolic model for his symbolic picture.

Marlow knows that the Intended could not stand up to (understand) the raw truth as discovered by Kurtz, could never stand up to (understand) the Native Woman. Marlow neatly sums up the tragic relationship that was created among these three people:

'She put out her arms as if after a retreating figure, stretching

them back and with clasped pale hands across the fading and
narrow sheen of the window. "Never see him!" I saw him clearly
enough then. I shall see this eloquent phantom as long as I live,
and I shall see her too, a tragic and familiar shade, resembling in
this gesture another one, tragic also, and bedecked with powerless charms, stretching bare brown arms over the glitter of the
infernal stream, the stream of darkness.'

Empty words, empty gestures. Europe and Africa. Each
is a Heart of Darkness. A choice of nightmares.

IV

After 'Heart of Darkness', Conrad began 'Lord Jim: A
Sketch', to be the third story in that volume of three to be
published by Blackwood; but 'Jim' went on to fill thirteen
instalments in *Blackwood's Magazine* and became the
novel, *Lord Jim*. In all that space, Marlow tells us no more
of Africa or of any personal aftermath. Indirectly, however, *Lord Jim* is a minute examination of 'a choice of
nightmares' such as Marlow faced on a small scale and
Kurtz on a large. Although five stories came between *Lord
Jim* and 'The End of the Tether', when Conad sat down in
1902 to settle his account with Blackwood, the question of
'a choice of nightmares' and the resulting psychological
evaluation of its consequences returned to haunt Conrad,
but now without his familiar, his attendant spirit, Marlow.

While no claim can be made that 'The End of the Tether'
achieves the artistic wholeness or creates the dramatic
impact of either of the first two stories, to judge it solely in
comparison with 'Youth' and 'Heart of Darkness' is a
mistake—and is misleading. While 'The End of the Tether'
may seem to complete a pattern of youth–maturity–age
among the three stories, it cannot be read as a 'sequel' to
the first two, if only because it does not utilize the
technique of a character-narrator. Yet, within the third

person narration of 'The End of the Tether' there is marvellous indirection at work, both in technique and tone. Critics complain that the story is too long, too vague, too sentimental; but these complaints arise only when Conrad's technique—his painter's style—and his tone— his creation of an urbane, ironic voice worthy of Henry James—are not comprehended. To understand 'The End of the Tether' one must be willing to take second looks, to view both broadly and up close. What one discovers is that the story is sketched broadly, but filled with minute dots and strokes—the technique is layered, and understanding must come from unlayering. The whole is accomplished through patient, ironic indirection—and the least discovery is the discovery of Captain Whalley's blindness, referred to as early as the first three paragraphs of the story, but indirectly.

The major discovery is that Captain Whalley is none of the persons any of the on-looking world thinks he is, including Whalley. A blind man blind to himself. Possibly his daughter Ivy, his romanticized 'fair maid', measured him for the completely simple soul he is—but children have a built-in tendency to make such an assessment. But no one, not even the narrator, makes the assessment directly: that is left to the reader.

In 'Youth' and 'Heart of Darkness' we are forced by the narrator into the hands of Marlow and are compelled to listen to him for the clues and codes, signs and symbols of significance. If we come to 'The End of the Tether' expecting to be charmed by the ancient magic of a story-teller, we shall be disappointed. This is no oral discourse; it is literate—highly sophisticated and removed. The appeal is not based primarily in the story line, but in the effects of interplay of character. Very little happens in the less-than-two days of the story. Even the melodramatic climax is undercut: Massy the owner is bailed out and Ivy receives her inheritance—unless lawyers are inept or corrupt. Whalley was incapable of working out either that he will save others when he commits suicide to escape the ignominy of a lost reputation, or that his reputation is so firmly established that his stupidity in trying to hide his blindness, had it been revealed at a board of inquiry, would have been interpreted as a noble, heroic endeavour.

Although there is no aural pun in Whalley/whale, there is a visual one, which is reinforced by Sterne's discovery by means of analogy of the Captain's blindness: the Pilot Serang is to Whalley as a pilot-fish is to a whale. And like a whale, Whalley is large and magnificent in appearance, at home only at sea, and has attributed to his simple mammalian brain all sorts of mysterious wisdom and dignity— Moby Dick with a white beard.

Conrad's sea-fiction and his essays on his fellowship with the craft are filled with tributes to the simple souls of seamen. Possibly the archetypal one is Old Singleton of the *Narcissus*. But Whalley is not a simple Singleton; he is a simpleton—and Conrad seems to have been aware of the possibility of the accusation of betrayal in his drawing of the portrait of his Captain. In his Preface, Conrad tells us that '"The End of the Tether" is a story of sea-life *in a rather special way*; and the most intimate thing I can say of it is this; that having lived that life fully, amongst its men, its thoughts and sensations, I have found it possible, *without the slightest misgiving, in all sincerity of heart and peace of conscience*, to conceive the existence of Captain Whalley's personality and to relate the manner of his end' (emphasis added). Even if one does not agree that here Conrad protests too much, at least his assertions lead us to the basic irony of the story—the elevated Whalley is less the man the lesser persons look up to: the jolly, assured Ned Eliot; the paranoid, puny Massy; the self-contained, but racially intimidated Serang; the self-destructive opportunist Sterne; the Byronic romantic Van Wyk. Each of these is painted in small strokes, slowly, through indirect discourse, interior monologue, and deduced implications of reported dialogue. As a group they are unified by their reactions to Whalley: each reads Whalley from the point of view of his own defective character; each reads into him; each has a psychological need to see him for what he is not. But not Ivy, who clings and kills.

Ivy may 'kill' her father, but the fault is not hers: 'He had named her Ivy because of the sound of the word, and *obscurely* fascinated by a *vague* asssociation of ideas' (emphasis added). Here the narrator is at work; he, not Whalley, understands the ego that hears the 'I' in Ivy and who knows that while Ivy clings and kills, it is also tough and hearty. Its roots are firmly planted. Through the narrator we can absorb the ironies and recognize the further one of the father tethering himself to the child.

There are two ends to a tether, one fixed and one free, as free as the length of the tether. One end of the tether is Ivy, the other is Whalley. Because Ivy is the fixed end, she is the tether holding the father, whose end ends the hold of the tether. In this sense, the end of the tether is the ending of his life and his ending is finally only the end or destiny of his life: dust to dust. But end as purpose takes us back to the other end, Ivy, the support of whom has been the sole end of Whalley's life. But in the final analysis, Ivy is not really the particular motivating force in Whalley's life: supporting her merely gives an overall end or purpose to Whalley's life. He gave up his 'fair maid' three times: through marriage, through the sale of the *Fair Maid*, through suicide.

But these variations on the meaning of the title come only after reading the story. In its initial, primary sense, the title means Whalley's getting free from the bind of the contract with Massy; this is the primary relevance of Conrad's words 'the manner of his end' (just quoted): Whalley's suicide frees him from the tether of the contract.

The bold extent of Conrad's use of ironies is found in the fact that he allows Whalley twice to use the titular phrase without any awareness of irony. In the midst of the apparent resolution of the two-day story—when Massy states that Whalley will get exposed, that the ship is lost, and that the insurance will not be paid—the narrator says: 'Captain Whalley did not move. True! Ivy's money. Gone in the wreck. Again he had a flash of insight. He was indeed at the end of his tether.'

The great insight is that he must kill himself. The 'indeed' is not loaded with multiple significance *for him*; it is a simple confirmation of the 'insight' he had had before this voyage, when he composed and left with the lawyer the letter delivered to Ivy upon his death in which he had, in effect, said, 'I really don't know what to do in my predicament; I am at my wit's end'. Quite literally, any solution lies *beyond* his comprehension. Whalley has always had a short hold on life—his comprehension does not reach beyond a fixed, measured, absolute length. The irony rings out in the narrator's report of the indirect, interior monologue, just quoted above, 'True!'

The James-like irony of the subdued narrator is apparent on every page of 'The End of the Tether' once the reader is alerted to its presence. Nowhere is this irony more withering than in the last paragraph of the story— which ends, 'she felt she had loved him after all'. Small wonder that of the three tales in *Youth* (1902) Henry James liked only 'The End of the Tether'.

V

In the texts of these stories, Conrad's use of the three dots of ellipsis to indicate interruptions has been quietly regularized, but substantive departures from the copytext for this series have been acknowledged in the Notes. Because all three stories refer to the sea, to ships, and to boats, the Notes are followed by a general Glossary of nautical terms.

ROBERT KIMBROUGH

University of Wisconsin-Madison

SELECT BIBLIOGRAPHY

DENT'S Collected Edition, 1946—(based on the Uniform Edition, 1923–8) has all Conrad's works except for *The Inheritors* and *The Nature of a Crime* (which are largely Ford Madox Ford's), *The Sisters* and the dramatizations. *Congo Diary and Other Uncollected Pieces* (ed. Zdzisław Najder, 1978) contains Conrad's Congo notebooks, *The Sisters*, *The Nature of a Crime* and other pieces.

The most important editions of Conrad's letters are as follows: William Blackburn (ed.), *Joseph Conrad: Letters to William Blackwood and David J. Meldrum* (1958), G. Jean-Aubry, *Joseph Conrad: Life and Letters* (1927), Zdzisław Najder (ed.), *Conrad's Polish Background: Letters to and from Polish Friends* (1964), C. T. Watts (ed.), *Joseph Conrad's Letters to R. B. Cunninghame Graham* (1969). There are further collections of letters edited by Richard Curle (1928), Edward Garnett (1928), J. A. Gee and P. J. Sturm (1940), D. B. J. Randall (1968) and G. Jean-Aubry (1930).

There are many biographies and personal memoirs of Conrad; the most important memoirs are those by Jessie Conrad (1926 and 1935), Richard Curle (1928) and Ford Madox Ford (1924), and there are futher memoirs by Borys Conrad (1970) and John Conrad (1981). The best biographies of Conrad are those by Jocelyn Baines (1960), G. Jean-Aubry (1957), Bernard Meyer (a 'Psychoanalytic' biography, 1967) and Roger Tennant (1981), and there are large critical biographies by Frederick Karl (1979) and Ian Watt (*Conrad in the Nineteenth Century*, 1980).

There are biographically related studies which make substantial use of background or manuscript material of which the most important are J. D. Gordan, *Joseph Conrad: The Making of a Novelist* (1941), Norman Sherry, *Conrad's Eastern World* (1966) and *Conrad's Western World* (1971). There are further relevant studies by Jerry Allen (1965), Edward Crankshaw (1930), Richard Curle (1914), R. R. Hodges (1967), R. L. Mégroz (1931),

Gustav Morf (1930 and 1976), J. H. Retinger (1941) and Norman Sherry (1972).

A very large number of critical books have now been published on Conrad. The ones to be most strongly recommended are Jacques Berthoud, *Joseph Conrad: The Major Phase* (1978), H. M. Daleski, *Joseph Conrad: The Way of Dispossession* (1977), A. J. Guerard, *Conrad the Novelist* (1958), Jeremy Hawthorn, *Joseph Conrad: Language and Fictional Self-Consciousness* (1979) and E. K. Hay, *The Political Novels of Jospeh Conrad* (1963). There are other studies of interest by C. B. Cox (1974), Avrom Fleishman (1967), Douglas Hewitt (1952), Bruce Johnson (1971), Paul Kirschner (1968), and Thomas Moser (1957). There are important essays on Conrad in Graham Hough, *Image and Experience* (1960), J. Hillis Miller, *Poets of Reality* (1966), and Norman Sherry (ed.), *Conrad: The Critical Heritage* (1973) and *Joseph Conrad: A Commemoration* (1976).

A CHRONOLOGY OF JOSEPH CONRAD

1857   3 December: Born Józef Teodor Konrad Korzeniowski, of Polish parents in the Ukraine.

1861   His father, poet and translator Apollo Korzeniowski, arrested for patriotic conspiracy.

1862   Conrad's parents exiled to Vologda, Russia; their son accompanies them.

1865   Death of his mother.

1869   Death of Apollo Korzeniowski in Kraków; Conrad comes under the protection of his uncle, Tadeusz Borbrowski.

1874   Leaves Poland for Marseilles to become a trainee seaman with the French merchant navy.

1876   As a 'steward' on the *Sainte-Antoine*, becomes acquainted with Dominic Cervoni (who appears in *The Mirror of the Sea* and *The Arrow of Gold* and is the source for Nostromo, and Peyrol in *The Rover*).

1877   Possibly involved in smuggling arms to the Spanish 'Carlists' from Marseilles.

1878   March: Shoots himself in the chest in Marseilles but is not seriously injured; as a direct result of this suicide attempt his uncle clears his debts. April: Joins his first British ship, the *Mavis*, and later in the same year joins *The Skimmer of the Sea*. Would have become liable for Russian military service if he had stayed with the French merchant navy.

1886   Becomes a British citizen and passes the examination for a Master's certificate.

1887   Is injured on the *Highland Forest* and hospitalized in Singapore.

1887–8   Gets to know the Malay archipelago as an officer of the *Vidar*.

1888   Master of the *Otago*, his only command.

1889   Resigns from the *Otago*, settles briefly in London and begins to write *Almayer's Folly*. Begins a lasting friendship with Marguerite Poradowska.

1890   Works in the Belgian Congo for the Société Anonyme pour le Commerce du Haut-Congo.

1891–3   His pleasantest experience at sea, as an officer of the *Torrens*; meets John Galsworthy, who is among the passengers and becomes a loyal friend.

1893   Autumn: Meets Jessie George.

1894   February: Death of Tadeusz Bobrowski. October: *Almayer's Folly* accepted by Unwin. Meets Edward Garnett, Unwin's reader and an influential literary friend.

1895   *Almayer's Folly* published.

1896   *An Outcast of the Islands* published. Becomes acquainted with H. G. Wells. 24 March: marriage to Jessie George. Begins work on *The Rescue*.

1897   *The Nigger of the 'Narcissus'* published. Meets Henry James and R. B. Cunninghame Graham (to be a close friend and the source for Gould in *Nostromo*).

1898   *Tales of Unrest* ('Karain', 'The Idiots', 'An Outpost of Progress', 'The Return', 'The Lagoon') published. Enters into collaboration with Ford Madox Ford (then Hueffer). Takes over from Ford the lease of a Kentish farmhouse, 'The Pent'. Friendship with Stephen Crane. Borys Conrad born.

1898–9   'Heart of Darkness' serialized in *Blackwood's*.

1899   J. B. Pinker becomes Conrad's literary agent.

1899–1900   *Lord Jim* serialized in *Blackwood's*.

1900   Stephen Crane dies. *Lord Jim* published as a book.

1901   *The Inheritors* (collaboration with Ford) published.

1902 *Youth: A Narrative; and Two Other Stories* ('Youth', 'Heart of Darkness', 'The End of the Tether') published.

1903 *Typhoon: And Other Stories* ('Typhoon', 'Amy Foster', 'Falk', 'Tomorrow') and *Romance* (collaboration with Ford) published.

1904 Jessie Conrad injures her knees and is partially disabled for life. *Nostromo* published.

1906 Meets Arthur Marwood, who becomes his closest friend. John Conrad born. *The Mirror of the Sea* published.

1907 The Conrads move to The Someries, Luton Hoo. *The Secret Agent* published.

1908 *A Set of Six* ('Gaspar Ruiz', 'The Informer', 'The Brute', 'An Anarchist', 'The Duel', 'Il Conde') published.

1909 Quarrels with Ford over his contributions to *The English Review*. The Conrads move to a cottage at Aldington, near 'The Pent'.

1910 Completion of *Under Western Eyes* accompanied by a nervous breakdown; Conrad lies in bed holding 'converse with the characters' of the novel. On his recovery the Conrads move to Capel House, Orlestone.

1911 *Under Western Eyes* published.

1912 *A Personal Record* and *'Twixt Land and Sea* ('A Smile of Fortune', 'The Secret Sharer', 'Freya of the Seven Isles') published.

1913 *Chance* published.

1914 *Chance* has good sales, especially in America; the earlier work now finds a larger public. The Conrads visit Poland and are nearly trapped by the outbreak of war.

1915 *Within the Tides* ('The Planter of Malata', 'The Partner', 'The Inn of the Two Witches') and *Victory* published.

1917 *The Shadow-Line* published. Conrad begins to write Author's Notes for a collected edition of his works.

AUTHOR'S NOTE

THE three stories in this volume lay no claim to
unity of artistic purpose. The only bond between
them is that of the time in which they were written.
They belong to the period immediately following the
publication of the "Nigger of the Narcissus," and preceding the first conception of "Nostromo," two books
which, it seems to me, stand apart and by themselves
in the body of my work. It is also the period during
which I contributed to *Maga;* a period dominated
by "Lord Jim" and associated in my grateful memory
with the late Mr. William Blackwood's encouraging and
helpful kindness.

"Youth" was not my first contribution to *Maga.*
It was the second. But that story marks the first
appearance in the world of the man Marlow, with
whom my relations have grown very intimate in the
course of years. The origins of that gentleman (nobody as far as I know had ever hinted that he was anything but that)—his origins have been the subject of
some literary speculation of, I am glad to say, a friendly
nature.

One would think that I am the proper person to
throw a light on the matter; but in truth I find that it
isn't so easy. It is pleasant to remember that nobody
had charged him with fraudulent purposes or looked
down on him as a charlatan; but apart from that he was
supposed to be all sorts of things: a clever screen, a mere
device, a "personator," a familiar spirit, a whispering
"dæmon." I myself have been suspected of a meditated plan for his capture.

That is not so. I made no plans. The man Marlow and I came together in the casual manner of those health-resort acquaintances which sometimes ripen into friendships. This one has ripened. For all his assertiveness in matters of opinion he is not an intrusive person. He haunts my hours of solitude, when, in silence, we lay our heads together in great comfort and harmony; but as we part at the end of a tale I am never sure that it may not be for the last time. Yet I don't think that either of us would care much to survive the other. In his case, at any rate, his occupation would be gone and he would suffer from that extinction, because I suspect him of some vanity. I don't mean vanity in the Solomonian sense. Of all my people he's the one that has never been a vexation to my spirit. A most discreet, understanding man. . . .

Even before appearing in book-form "Youth" was very well received. It lies on me to confess at last, and this is as good a place for it as another, that I have been all my life—all my two lives—the spoiled adopted child of Great Britain and even of the Empire; for it was Australia that gave me my first command. I break out into this declaration not because of a lurking tendency to megalomania, but, on the contrary, as a man who has no very notable illusions about himself. I follow the instincts of vain-glory and humility natural to all mankind. For it can hardly be denied that it is not their own deserts that men are most proud of, but rather of their prodigious luck, of their marvellous fortune: of that in their lives for which thanks and sacrifices must be offered on the altars of the inscrutable gods.

"Heart of Darkness" also received a certain amount of notice from the first; and of its origins this much may be said: it is well known that curious men go prying into all sorts of places (where they have no business) and come out of them with all kinds of spoil. This story, and one other, not in this volume, are all the spoil I brought out from the centre of Africa, where, really, I had no sort of business. More ambitious in its scope and longer in the telling, "Heart of Darkness" is quite as authentic in fundamentals as "Youth." It is, obviously, written in another mood. I won't characterize the mood precisely, but anybody can see that it is anything but the mood of wistful regret, of reminiscent tenderness.

One more remark may be added. "Youth" is a feat of memory. It is a record of experience; but that experience, in its facts, in its inwardness and in its outward colouring, begins and ends in myself. "Heart of Darkness" is experience, too; but it is experience pushed a little (and only very little) beyond the actual facts of the case for the perfectly legitimate, I believe, purpose of bringing it home to the minds and bosoms of the readers. There it was no longer a matter of sincere colouring. It was like another art altogether. That sombre theme had to be given a sinister resonance, a tonality of its own, a continued vibration that, I hoped, would hang in the air and dwell on the ear after the last note had been struck.

After saying so much there remains the last tale of the book, still untouched. "The End of the Tether" is a story of sea-life in a rather special way; and the most intimate thing I can say of it is this; that having lived that life fully, amongst its men, its thoughts and sensations, I have found it possible, without the slightest misgiving, in all sincerity of heart and peace of conscience, to conceive the existence of Captain Whalley's personality and to relate the manner of his end. This statement acquires some force from the circumstance

that the pages of that story—a fair half of the book—
are also the product of experience. That experience
belongs (like "Youth's") to the time before I ever
thought of putting pen to paper. As to its "reality,"
that is for the readers to determine. One had to pick
up one's facts here and there. More skill would have
made them more real and the whole composition more
interesting. But here we are approaching the veiled
region of artistic values which it would be improper and
indeed dangerous for me to enter. I have looked over
the proofs, have corrected a misprint or two, have
changed a word or two—and that's all. It is not very
likely that I shall ever read "The End of the Tether"
again. No more need be said. It accords best with
my feelings to part from Captain Whalley in affectionate silence.

J. C.

1917.

YOUTH: A NARRATIVE

> '...but the Dwarf answered:
> "No, something human is
> dearer to me than the wealth of
> the world."'
>
> Grimm's Tales

To
My Wife

YOUTH

THIS could have occurred nowhere but in England, where men and sea interpenetrate, so to speak—the sea entering into the life of most men, and the men knowing something or everything about the sea, in the way of amusement, of travel, or of bread-winning.

We were sitting round a mahogany table that reflected the bottle, the claret-glasses, and our faces as we leaned on our elbows. There was a director of companies, an accountant, a lawyer, Marlow, and myself. The director had been a *Conway* boy,* the accountant had served four years at sea, the lawyer—a fine crusted Tory, High Churchman, the best of old fellows, the soul of honour—had been chief officer in the P. & O.* service in the good old days when mail-boats were square-rigged at least on two masts, and used to come down the China Sea before a fair monsoon with stun'-sails set alow and aloft. We all began life in the merchant service. Between the five of us there was the strong bond of the sea, and also the fellowship of the craft, which no amount of enthusiasm for yachting, cruising, and so on can give, since one is only the amusement of life and the other is life itself.

Marlow (at least I think that is how he spelt his name) told the story, or rather the chronicle, of a voyage:—

"Yes, I have seen a little of the Eastern seas; but what I remember best is my first voyage there. You fellows know there are those voyages that seem ordered

3

for the illustration of life, that might stand for a symbol of existence. You fight, work, sweat, nearly kill yourself, sometimes do kill yourself, trying to accomplish something—and you can't. Not from any fault of yours. You simply can do nothing, neither great nor little—not a thing in the world—not even marry an old maid, or get a wretched 600-ton cargo of coal to its port of destination.

"It was altogether a memorable affair. It was my first voyage to the East, and my first voyage as second mate; it was also my skipper's first command. You'll admit it was time. He was sixty if a day; a little man, with a broad, not very straight back, with bowed shoulders and one leg more bandy than the other, he had that queer twisted-about appearance you see so often in men who work in the fields. He had a nut-cracker face —chin and nose trying to come together over a sunken mouth—and it was framed in iron-gray fluffy hair, that looked like a chin-strap of cotton-wool sprinkled with coal-dust. And he had blue eyes in that old face of his, which were amazingly like a boy's, with that candid expression some quite common men preserve to the end of their days by a rare internal gift of simplicity of heart and rectitude of soul. What induced him to accept me was a wonder. I had come out of a crack Australian clipper, where I had been third officer, and he seemed to have a prejudice against crack clippers as aristocratic and high-toned. He said to me, 'You know, in this ship you will have to work.' I said I had to work in every ship I had ever been in. 'Ah, but this is different, and you gentlemen out of them big ships; . . . but there! I dare say you will do. Join to-morrow.'

"I joined to-morrow. It was twenty-two years ago; and I was just twenty. How time passes! It was one of the happiest days of my life. Fancy! Second mate for the first time—a really responsible officer! I wouldn't have thrown up my new billet for a fortune. The mate looked me over carefully. He was also an old chap, but of another stamp. He had a Roman nose, a snow-white, long beard, and his name was Mahon, but he insisted that it should be pronounced Mann. He was well connected; yet there was something wrong with his luck, and he had never got on.

"As to the captain, he had been for years in coasters, then in the Mediterranean, and last in the West Indian trade. He had never been round the Capes. He could just write a kind of sketchy hand, and didn't care for writing at all. Both were thorough good seamen of course, and between those two old chaps I felt like a small boy between two grandfathers.

"The ship also was old. Her name was the *Judea*. Queer name, isn't it? She belonged to a man Wilmer, Wilcox—some name like that; but he has been bankrupt and dead these twenty years or more, and his name don't matter. She had been laid up in Shadwell basin for ever so long. You may imagine her state. She was all rust, dust, grime—soot aloft, dirt on deck. To me it was like coming out of a palace into a ruined cottage. She was about 400 tons, had a primitive windlass, wooden latches to the doors, not a bit of brass about her, and a big square stern. There was on it, below her name in big letters, a lot of scrollwork, with the gilt off, and some sort of a coat of arms, with the motto 'Do or Die' underneath. I remember it took my fancy immensely. There was a touch of romance in it, something that made me love the old thing—something that appealed to my youth!

"We left London in ballast—sand ballast—to load a cargo of coal in a northern port for Bankok. Bankok!

I thrilled. I had been six years at sea, but had only seen Melbourne and Sydney, very good places, charming places in their way—but Bankok!

"We worked out of the Thames under canvas, with a North Sea pilot on board. His name was Jermyn, and he dodged all day long about the galley drying his handkerchief before the stove. Apparently he never slept. He was a dismal man, with a perpetual tear sparkling at the end of his nose, who either had been in trouble, or was in trouble, or expected to be in trouble— couldn't be happy unless something went wrong. He mistrusted my youth, my common-sense, and my seamanship, and made a point of showing it in a hundred little ways. I dare say he was right. It seems to me I knew very little then, and I know not much more now; but I cherish a hate for that Jermyn to this day.

"We were a week working up as far as Yarmouth* Roads, and then we got into a gale—the famous October gale of twenty-two years ago. It was wind, lightning, sleet, snow, and a terrific sea. We were flying light, and you may imagine how bad it was when I tell you we had smashed bulwarks and a flooded deck. On the second night she shifted her ballast into the lee bow, and by that time we had been blown off somewhere on the Dogger Bank.* There was nothing for it but go below with shovels and try to right her, and there we were in that vast hold, gloomy like a cavern, the tallow dips stuck and flickering on the beams, the gale howling above, the ship tossing about like mad on her side; there we all were, Jermyn, the captain, every one, hardly able to keep our feet, engaged on that gravedigger's work, and trying to toss shovelfuls of wet sand up to wind-ward. At every tumble of the ship you could see vaguely in the dim light men falling down with a great flourish of shovels. One of the ship's boys (we had two), impressed by the weirdness of the scene, wept as if his heart would break. We could hear him blubbering somewhere in the shadows.

"On the third day the gale died out, and by-and-by a north-country tug picked us up. We took sixteen days in all to get from London to the Tyne!* When we got into dock we had lost our turn for loading, and they hauled us off to a tier*where we remained for a month. Mrs. Beard (the captain's name was Beard) came from Colchester to see the old man. She lived on board. The crew of runners had left, and there remained only the officers, one boy and the steward, a mulatto who answered to the name of Abraham. Mrs. Beard was an old woman, with a face all wrinkled and ruddy like a winter apple, and the figure of a young girl. She caught sight of me once, sewing on a button, and insisted on having my shirts to repair. This was something different from the captains' wives I had known on board crack clippers. When I brought her the shirts, she said: 'And the socks? They want mending, I am sure, and John's—Captain Beard's—things are all in order now. I would be glad of something to do.' Bless the old woman. She overhauled my outfit for me, and meantime I read for the first time *Sartor Resartus**and Burnaby's *Ride to Khiva*.* I didn't understand much of the first then; but I remember I preferred the soldier to the philosopher at the time; a preference which life has only confirmed. One was a man, and the other was either more—or less. However, they are both dead and Mrs. Beard is dead, and youth, strength, genius, thoughts, achievements, simple hearts—all dies. . . . No matter.

"They loaded us at last. We shipped a crew. Eight able seamen and two boys. We hauled off one evening to the buoys at the dock-gates, ready to go out,

and with a fair prospect of beginning the voyage next
day. Mrs. Beard was to start for home by a late train.
When the ship was fast we went to tea. We sat rather
silent through the meal—Mahon, the old couple, and I.
I finished first, and slipped away for a smoke, my cabin
being in a deck-house just against the poop. It was
high water, blowing fresh with a drizzle; the double
dock-gates were opened, and the steam-colliers were
going in and out in the darkness with their lights burning bright, a great plashing of propellers, rattling of
winches, and a lot of hailing on the pier-heads. I
watched the procession of head-lights gliding high and
of green lights gliding low in the night, when suddenly
a red gleam flashed at me, vanished, came into view
again, and remained. The fore-end of a steamer loomed
up close. I shouted down the cabin, 'Come up, quick!'
and then heard a startled voice saying afar in the dark,
'Stop her, sir.' A bell jingled. Another voice cried
warningly, 'We are going right into that barque, sir.'
The answer to this was a gruff 'All right,' and the next
thing was a heavy crash as the steamer struck a glancing
blow with the bluff of her bow about our fore-rigging.
There was a moment of confusion, yelling, and running
about. Steam roared. Then somebody was heard
saying, 'All clear, sir.' . . . 'Are you all right?'
asked the gruff voice. I had jumped forward to see the
damage, and hailed back, 'I think so.' 'Easy astern,'
said the gruff voice. A bell jingled. 'What steamer is
that?' screamed Mahon. By that time she was no
more to us than a bulky shadow manœuvring a little
way off. They shouted at us some name—a woman's
name, Miranda or Melissa—or some such thing. 'This
means another month in this beastly hole,' said Mahon
to me, as we peered with lamps about the splintered bulwarks and broken braces. 'But where's the captain?'

"We had not heard or seen anything of him all that time. We went aft to look. A doleful voice arose hailing somewhere in the middle of the dock, '*Judea* ahoy!' . . . How the devil did he get there? . . . 'Hallo!' we shouted. 'I am adrift in our boat without oars,' he cried. A belated water-man offered his services, and Mahon struck a bargain with him for half-a-crown to tow our skipper alongside; but it was Mrs. Beard that came up the ladder first. They had been floating about the dock in that mizzly cold rain for nearly an hour. I was never so surprised in my life.

"It appears that when he heard my shout 'Come up' he understood at once what was the matter, caught up his wife, ran on deck, and across, and down into our boat, which was fast to the ladder. Not bad for a sixty-year-old. Just imagine that old fellow saving heroically in his arms that old woman—the woman of his life. He set her down on a thwart, and was ready to climb back on board when the painter came adrift somehow, and away they went together. Of course in the confusion we did not hear him shouting. He looked abashed. She said cheerfully, 'I suppose it does not matter my losing the train now?' 'No, Jenny—you go below and get warm,' he growled. Then to us: 'A sailor has no business with a wife—I say. There I was, out of the ship. Well, no harm done this time. Let's go and look at what that fool of a steamer smashed.'

"It wasn't much, but it delayed us three weeks. At the end of that time, the captain being engaged with his agents, I carried Mrs. Beard's bag to the railway-station and put her all comfy into a third-class carriage. She lowered the window to say, 'You are a good young man. If you see John—Captain Beard—without his muffler at night, just remind him from me to keep his throat well wrapped up.' 'Certainly, Mrs. Beard,' I

said. 'You are a good young man; I noticed how
attentive you are to John—to Captain——' The train
pulled out suddenly; I took my cap off to the old
woman: I never saw her again. . . . Pass the
bottle.

"We went to sea next day. When we made that
start for Bankok we had been already three months out
of London. We had expected to be a fortnight or so—
at the outside.

"It was January, and the weather was beautiful—the
beautiful sunny winter weather that has more charm
than in the summer-time, because it is unexpected, and
crisp, and you know it won't, it can't, last long. It's
like a windfall, like a godsend, like an unexpected piece
of luck.

"It lasted all down the North Sea, all down Channel;
and it lasted till we were three hundred miles or so to
the westward of the Lizards: then the wind went round
to the sou'west and began to pipe up. In two days it
blew a gale. The *Judea*, hove to, wallowed on the
Atlantic like an old candle-box. It blew day after day:
it blew with spite, without interval, without mercy,
without rest. The world was nothing but an immensity
of great foaming waves rushing at us, under a sky low
enough to touch with the hand and dirty like a smoked
ceiling. In the stormy space surrounding us there was
as much flying spray as air. Day after day and night
after night there was nothing round the ship but the
howl of the wind, the tumult of the sea, the noise of
water pouring over her deck. There was no rest for her
and no rest for us. She tossed, she pitched, she stood on
her head, she sat on her tail, she rolled, she groaned, and
we had to hold on while on deck and cling to our bunks
when below, in a constant effort of body and worry of
mind.

"One night Mahon spoke through the small window of my berth. It opened right into my very bed, and I was lying there sleepless, in my boots, feeling as though I had not slept for years, and could not if I tried. He said excitedly—

"'You got the sounding-rod in here, Marlow? I can't get the pumps to suck. By God! it's no child's play.'

"I gave him the sounding-rod and lay down again, trying to think of various things—but I thought only of the pumps. When I came on deck they were still at it, and my watch relieved at the pumps. By the light of the lantern brought on deck to examine the sounding-rod I caught a glimpse of their weary, serious faces. We pumped all the four hours. We pumped all night, all day, all the week—watch and watch. She was working herself loose, and leaked badly—not enough to drown us at once, but enough to kill us with the work at the pumps. And while we pumped the ship was going from us piecemeal: the bulwarks went, the stanchions were torn out, the ventilators smashed, the cabin-door burst in. There was not a dry spot in the ship. She was being gutted bit by bit. The long-boat changed, as if by magic, into matchwood where she stood in her gripes. I had lashed her myself, and was rather proud of my handiwork, which had withstood so long the malice of the sea. And we pumped. And there was no break in the weather. The sea was white like a sheet of foam, like a caldron of boiling milk; there was not a break in the clouds, no—not the size of a man's hand— no, not for so much as ten seconds. There was for us no sky, there were for us no stars, no sun, no universe— nothing but angry clouds and an infuriated sea. We pumped watch and watch, for dear life; and it seemed to last for months, for years, for all eternity, as though we had been dead and gone to a hell for sailors. We forgot the day of the week, the name of the month, what year it was, and whether we had ever been ashore. The sails blew away, she lay broadside on under a weather-cloth, the ocean poured over her, and we did not care. We turned those handles, and had the eyes of idiots. As soon as we had crawled on deck I used to take a round turn with a rope about the men, the pumps, and the mainmast, and we turned, we turned incessantly, with the water to our waists, to our necks, over our heads. It was all one. We had forgotten how it felt to be dry.

"And there was somewhere in me the thought: By Jove! this is the deuce of an adventure—something you read about; and it is my first voyage as second mate—and I am only twenty—and here I am lasting it out as well as any of these men, and keeping my chaps up to the mark. I was pleased. I would not have given up the experience for worlds. I had moments of exultation. Whenever the old dismantled craft pitched heavily with her counter high in the air, she seemed to me to throw up, like an appeal, like a defiance, like a cry to the clouds without mercy, the words written on her stern: 'Judea, London. Do or Die.'

"O youth! The strength of it, the faith of it, the imagination of it! To me she was not an old rattle-trap carting about the world a lot of coal for a freight—to me she was the endeavour, the test, the trial of life. I think of her with pleasure, with affection, with regret—as you would think of someone dead you have loved. I shall never forget her. . . . Pass the bottle.

"One night when tied to the mast, as I explained, we were pumping on, deafened with the wind, and without spirit enough in us to wish ourselves dead, a heavy sea crashed aboard and swept clean over us. As soon as I got my breath I shouted, as in duty bound, 'Keep on, boys!' when suddenly I felt something hard floating on deck strike the calf of my leg. I made a grab at it and missed. It was so dark we could not see each other's faces within a foot—you understand.

"After that thump the ship kept quiet for a while, and the thing, whatever it was, struck my leg again. This time I caught it—and it was a saucepan. At first, being stupid with fatigue and thinking of nothing but the pumps, I did not understand what I had in my hand. Suddenly it dawned upon me, and I shouted, 'Boys, the house on deck is gone. Leave this, and let's look for the cook.'

"There was a deck-house forward, which contained the galley, the cook's berth, and the quarters of the crew. As we had expected for days to see it swept away, the hands had been ordered to sleep in the cabin —the only safe place in the ship. The steward, Abraham, however, persisted in clinging to his berth, stupidly, like a mule—from sheer fright I believe, like an animal that won't leave a stable falling in an earth-quake. So we went to look for him. It was chancing death, since once out of our lashings we were as exposed as if on a raft. But we went. The house was shattered as if a shell had exploded inside. Most of it had gone overboard—stove, men's quarters, and their property, all was gone; but two posts, holding a portion of the bulkhead to which Abraham's bunk was attached, re-mained as if by a miracle. We groped in the ruins and came upon this, and there he was, sitting in his bunk, surrounded by foam and wreckage, jabbering cheerfully to himself. He was out of his mind; completely and for ever mad, with this sudden shock coming upon the fag-end of his endurance. We snatched him up, lugged him aft, and pitched him head-first down the cabin companion. You understand there was no time to carry him down with infinite precautions and wait to see how he got on. Those below would pick him up at the bottom of the stairs all right. We were in a hurry to go back to the pumps. That business could not wait. A bad leak is an inhuman thing.

"One would think that the sole purpose of that fiendish gale had been to make a lunatic of that poor devil of a mulatto. It eased before morning, and next day the sky cleared, and as the sea went down the leak took up. When it came to bending a fresh set of sails the crew demanded to put back—and really there was nothing else to do. Boats gone, decks swept clean, cabin gutted, men without a stitch but what they stood in, stores spoiled, ship strained. We put her head for home, and—would you believe it? The wind came east right in our teeth. It blew fresh, it blew continuously. We had to beat up every inch of the way, but she did not leak so badly, the water keeping comparatively smooth. Two hours' pumping in every four is no joke —but it kept her afloat as far as Falmouth.*

"The good people there live on casualties of the sea, and no doubt were glad to see us. A hungry crowd of shipwrights sharpened their chisels at the sight of that carcass of a ship. And, by Jove! they had pretty pickings off us before they were done. I fancy the owner was already in a tight place. There were delays. Then it was decided to take part of the cargo out and caulk her topsides. This was done, the repairs finished, cargo reshipped; a new crew came on board, and we went out—for Bankok. At the end of a week we were back again. The crew said they weren't going to Bankok—a hundred and fifty days' passage—in a something hooker that wanted pumping eight hours out of the twenty-four; and the nautical papers inserted again the little paragraph: '*Judea*. Barque. Tyne to Bankok; coals; put back to Falmouth leaky and with crew refusing duty.'

"There were more delays—more tinkering. The owner came down for a day, and said she was as right as a little fiddle. Poor old Captain Beard looked like the ghost of a Geordie* skipper—through the worry and humiliation of it. Remember he was sixty, and it was his first command. Mahon said it was a foolish business, and would end badly. I loved the ship more than ever, and wanted awfully to get to Bankok. To Bankok! Magic name, blessed name. Mesopotamia wasn't a patch on it. Remember I was twenty, and it was my first second-mate's billet, and the East was waiting for me.

"We went out and anchored in the outer roads with a fresh crew—the third. She leaked worse than ever. It was as if those confounded shipwrights had actually made a hole in her. This time we did not even go outside. The crew simply refused to man the windlass.

"They towed us back to the inner harbour, and we became a fixture, a feature, an institution of the place. People pointed us out to visitors as 'That 'ere barque that's going to Bankok—has been here six months—put back three times.' On holidays the small boys pulling about in boats would hail, '*Judea*, ahoy!' and if a head showed above the rail shouted, 'Where you bound to?— Bankok?' and jeered. We were only three on board. The poor old skipper mooned in the cabin. Mahon undertook the cooking, and unexpectedly developed all a Frenchman's genius for preparing nice little messes.* I looked languidly after the rigging. We became citizens of Falmouth. Every shopkeeper knew us. At

the barber's or tobacconist's they asked familiarly,
'Do you think you will ever get to Bankok?' Meantime the owner, the underwriters, and the charterers
squabbled amongst themselves in London, and our pay
went on. . . . Pass the bottle.

"It was horrid. Morally it was worse than pumping
for life. It seemed as though we had been forgotten by
the world, belonged to nobody, would get nowhere; it
seemed that, as if bewitched, we would have to live for
ever and ever in that inner harbour, a derision and a by-
word to generations of long-shore loafers and dishonest
boatmen. I obtained three months' pay and a five days'
leave, and made a rush for London. It took me a day to
get there and pretty well another to come back—but three
months' pay went all the same. I don't know what I
did with it. I went to a music-hall, I believe, lunched,
dined, and supped in a swell place in Regent Street, and
was back to time, with nothing but a complete set of
Byron's works and a new railway rug to show for three
months' work. The boat-man who pulled me off to the
ship said: 'Hallo! I thought you had left the old
thing. *She* will never get to Bankok.' 'That's all *you*
know about it,' I said, scornfully—but I didn't like that
prophecy at all.

"Suddenly a man, some kind of agent to somebody,
appeared with full powers. He had grog-blossoms*all
over his face, an indomitable energy, and was a jolly
soul. We leaped into life again. A hulk came alongside, took our cargo, and then we went into dry dock to
get our copper stripped. No wonder she leaked. The
poor thing, strained beyond endurance by the gale, had,
as if in disgust, spat out all the oakum of her lower
seams. She was recaulked, new coppered, and made as
tight as a bottle. We went back to the hulk and reshipped our cargo.

"Then, on a fine moonlight night, all the rats left the ship.

"We had been infested with them. They had destroyed our sails, consumed more stores than the crew, affably shared our beds and our dangers, and now, when the ship was made seaworthy, concluded to clear out. I called Mahon to enjoy the spectacle. Rat after rat appeared on our rail, took a last look over his shoulder, and leaped with a hollow thud into the empty hulk. We tried to count them, but soon lost the tale. Mahon said: 'Well, well! don't talk to me about the intelligence of rats. They ought to have left before, when we had that narrow squeak from foundering. There you have the proof how silly is the superstition about them. They leave a good ship for an old rotten hulk, where there is nothing to eat, too, the fools! . . . I don't believe they know what is safe or what is good for them, any more than you or I.'

"And after some more talk we agreed that the wisdom of rats had been grossly overrated, being in fact no greater than that of men.

"The story of the ship was known, by this, all up the Channel from Land's End* to the Forelands,* and we could get no crew on the south coast. They sent us one all complete from Liverpool, and we left once more—for Bankok.

"We had fair breezes, smooth water right into the tropics, and the old *Judea* lumbered along in the sunshine. When she went eight knots everything cracked aloft, and we tied our caps to our heads; but mostly she strolled on at the rate of three miles an hour. What could you expect? She was tired—that old ship. Her youth was where mine is—where yours is—you fellows who listen to this yarn; and what friend would throw your years and your weariness in your face? We didn't

grumble at her.   To us aft, at least, it seemed as though
we had been born in her, reared in her, had lived in her
for ages, had never known any other ship.   I would just
as soon have abused the old village church at home for
not being a cathedral.

"And for me there was also my youth to make me
patient.   There was all the East before me, and all
life, and the thought that I had been tried in that ship
and had come out pretty well.   And I thought of men of
old who, centuries ago, went that road in ships that
sailed no better, to the land of palms, and spices, and
yellow sands, and of brown nations ruled by kings more
cruel than Nero the Roman, and more splendid than
Solomon the Jew.   The old bark lumbered on, heavy
with her age and the burden of her cargo, while I lived
the life of youth in ignorance and hope.   She lumbered
on through an interminable procession of days; and the
fresh gilding flashed back at the setting sun, seemed to
cry out over the darkening sea the words painted on
her stern, '*Judea*, London.   Do or Die.'

"Then we entered the Indian Ocean and steered
northerly for Java Head.* The winds were light.
Weeks slipped by.   She crawled on, do or die, and
people at home began to think of posting us as overdue.

"One Saturday evening, I being off duty, the men
asked me to give them an extra bucket of water or so—
for washing clothes.   As I did not wish to screw on the
fresh-water pump so late, I went forward whistling, and
with a key in my hand to unlock the forepeak scuttle,
intending to serve the water out of a spare tank we kept
there.

"The smell down below was as unexpected as it was
frightful.   One would have thought hundreds of
paraffin-lamps had been flaring and smoking in that
hole for days.   I was glad to get out.   The man with

me coughed and said, 'Funny smell, sir.' I answered negligently, 'It's good for the health they say,' and walked aft.

"The first thing I did was to put my head down the square of the midship ventilator. As I lifted the lid a visible breath, something like a thin fog, a puff of faint haze, rose from the opening. The ascending air was hot, and had a heavy, sooty, paraffiny smell. I gave one sniff, and put down the lid gently. It was no use choking myself. The cargo was on fire.

"Next day she began to smoke in earnest. You see it was to be expected, for though the coal was of a safe kind, that cargo had been so handled, so broken up with handling, that it looked more like smithy coal than anything else. Then it had been wetted—more than once. It rained all the time we were taking it back from the hulk, and now with this long passage it got heated, and there was another case of spontaneous combustion.

"The captain called us into the cabin. He had a chart spread on the table, and looked unhappy. He said, 'The coast of West Australia is near, but I mean to proceed to our destination. It is the hurricane month, too; but we will just keep her head for Bankok, and fight the fire. No more putting back anywhere, if we all get roasted. We will try first to stifle this 'ere damned combustion by want of air.'

"We tried. We battened down everything, and still she smoked. The smoke kept coming out through imperceptible crevices; it forced itself through bulkheads and covers; it oozed here and there and everywhere in slender threads, in an invisible film, in an incomprehensible manner. It made its way into the cabin, into the forecastle; it poisoned the sheltered places on the deck, it could be sniffed as high as the mainyard. It was clear that if the smoke came out the air came in. This was disheartening. This combustion refused to be stifled.

"We resolved to try water, and took the hatches off. Enormous volumes of smoke, whitish, yellowish, thick, greasy, misty, choking, ascended as high as the trucks. All hands cleared out aft. Then the poisonous cloud blew away, and we went back to work in a smoke that was no thicker now than that of an ordinary factory chimney.

"We rigged the force-pump, got the hose along, and by-and-by it burst. Well, it was as old as the ship—a prehistoric hose, and past repair. Then we pumped with the feeble head-pump, drew water with buckets, and in this way managed in time to pour lots of Indian Ocean into the main hatch. The bright stream flashed in sunshine, fell into a layer of white crawling smoke, and vanished on the black surface of coal. Steam ascended mingling with the smoke. We poured salt water as into a barrel without a bottom. It was our fate to pump in that ship, to pump out of her, to pump into her; and after keeping water out of her to save ourselves from being drowned, we frantically poured water into her to save ourselves from being burnt.

"And she crawled on, do or die, in the serene weather. The sky was a miracle of purity, a miracle of azure. The sea was polished, was blue, was pellucid, was sparkling like a precious stone, extending on all sides, all round to the horizon—as if the whole terrestrial globe had been one jewel, one colossal sapphire, a single gem fashioned into a planet. And on the lustre of the great calm waters the *Judea* glided imperceptibly, enveloped in languid and unclean vapours, in a lazy cloud that drifted to leeward, light and slow; a pestiferous cloud defiling the splendour of sea and sky.

"All this time of course we saw no fire. The cargo smouldered at the bottom somewhere. Once Mahon, as we were working side by side, said to me with a queer smile: 'Now, if she only would spring a tidy leak—like that time when we first left the Channel—it would put a stopper on this fire. Wouldn't it?' I remarked irrelevantly, 'Do you remember the rats?'

"We fought the fire and sailed the ship too as carefully as though nothing had been the matter. The steward cooked and attended on us. Of the other twelve men, eight worked while four rested. Everyone took his turn, captain included. There was equality, and if not exactly fraternity, then a deal of good feeling. Sometimes a man, as he dashed a bucketful of water down the hatchway, would yell out, 'Hurrah for Bankok!' and the rest laughed. But generally we were taciturn and serious—and thirsty. Oh! how thirsty! And we had to be careful with the water. Strict allowance. The ship smoked, the sun blazed. . . . Pass the bottle.

"We tried everything. We even made an attempt to dig down to the fire. No good, of course. No man could remain more than a minute below. Mahon, who went first, fainted there, and the man who went to fetch him out did likewise. We lugged them out on deck. Then I leaped down to show how easily it could be done. They had learned wisdom by that time, and contented themselves by fishing for me with a chainhook tied to a broom-handle, I believe. I did not offer to go and fetch up my shovel, which was left down below.

"Things began to look bad. We put the long-boat into the water. The second boat was ready to swing out. We had also another, a 14-foot thing, on davits aft, where it was quite safe.

"Then, behold, the smoke suddenly decreased. We redoubled our efforts to flood the bottom of the ship. In two days there was no smoke at all. Everybody was on the broad grin. This was on a Friday. On Saturday no work, but sailing the ship of course, was done. The men washed their clothes and their faces for the first time in a fortnight, and had a special dinner given them. They spoke of spontaneous combustion with contempt, and implied *they* were the boys to put out combustions. Somehow we all felt as though we each had inherited a large fortune. But a beastly smell of burning hung about the ship. Captain Beard had hollow eyes and sunken cheeks. I had never noticed so much before how twisted and bowed he was. He and Mahon prowled soberly about hatches and ventilators, sniffing. It struck me suddenly poor Mahon was a very, very old chap. As to me, I was as pleased and proud as though I had helped to win a great naval battle. O! Youth!

"The night was fine. In the morning a homeward-bound ship passed us hull down—the first we had seen for months; but we were nearing the land at last, Java Head being about 190 miles off, and nearly due north.

"Next day it was my watch on deck from eight to twelve. At breakfast the captain observed, 'It's wonderful how that smell hangs about the cabin.' About ten, the mate being on the poop, I stepped down on the main-deck for a moment. The carpenter's bench stood abaft the mainmast: I leaned against it sucking at my pipe, and the carpenter, a young chap, came to talk to me. He remarked, 'I think we have done very well, haven't we?' and then I perceived with annoyance the fool was trying to tilt the bench. I said curtly, 'Don't, Chips,' and immediately became aware of a queer sensation, of an absurd delusion,—I seemed somehow to be in the air. I heard all round me like a pent-up breath released—as if a thousand giants simultaneously had said Phoo!—and felt a dull concussion which made my ribs ache suddenly. No doubt about it—I was in the air, and my body was describing a short parabola. But short as it was, I had the time to think several thoughts in, as far as I can remember, the following order: 'This can't be the carpenter— What is it?—Some accident—Submarine volcano?— Coals, gas!—By Jove! we are being blown up—Everybody's dead—I am falling into the after-hatch—I see fire in it.'

"The coal-dust suspended in the air of the hold had glowed dull-red at the moment of the explosion. In the twinkling of an eye, in an infinitesimal fraction of a second since the first tilt of the bench, I was sprawling full length on the cargo. I picked myself up and scrambled out. It was quick like a rebound. The deck was a wilderness of smashed timber, lying crosswise like trees in a wood after a hurricane; an immense curtain of solid rags waved gently before me—it was the mainsail blown to strips. I thought, The masts will be toppling over directly; and to get out of the way bolted on all-fours towards the poop-ladder. The first person I saw was Mahon, with eyes like saucers, his mouth open, and the long white hair standing straight on end round his head like a silver halo. He was just about to go down when the sight of the main-deck stirring, heaving up, and changing into splinters before his eyes, petrified him on the top step. I stared at him in unbelief, and he stared at me with a queer kind of shocked curiosity. I did not know that I had no hair, no eyebrows, no eyelashes, that my young moustache was burnt off, that my face was black, one cheek laid open, my nose cut, and my chin bleeding. I had lost my cap, one of my slippers, and my shirt was torn to rags. Of all this I was not aware. I was amazed to see the ship still afloat, the poop-deck whole—and, most of all, to see anybody alive. Also the peace of the sky and the serenity of the sea were distinctly surprising. I suppose I expected to see them convulsed with horror. . . . Pass the bottle.

"There was a voice hailing the ship from somewhere —in the air, in the sky—I couldn't tell. Presently I saw the captain—and he was mad. He asked me eagerly, 'Where's the cabin-table?' and to hear such a question was a frightful shock. I had just been blown up, you understand, and vibrated with that experience, —I wasn't quite sure whether I was alive. Mahon began to stamp with both feet and yelled at him, 'Good God! don't you see the deck's blown out of her?' I found my voice, and stammered out as if conscious of some gross neglect of duty, 'I don't know where the cabin-table is.' It was like an absurd dream.

"Do you know what he wanted next? Well, he wanted to trim the yards. Very placidly, and as if lost in thought, he insisted on having the foreyard squared. 'I don't know if there's anybody alive,' said Mahon, almost tearfully. 'Surely,' he said, gently, 'there will be enough left to square the foreyard.'

"The old chap, it seems, was in his own berth winding up the chronometers, when the shock sent him spinning. Immediately it occurred to him—as he said afterwards —that the ship had struck something, and ran out into the cabin. There, he saw, the cabin-table had vanished somewhere. The deck being blown up, it had fallen down into the lazarette of course. Where we had our breakfast that morning he saw only a great hole in the floor. This appeared to him so awfully mysterious, and impressed him so immensely, that what he saw and heard after he got on deck were mere trifles in comparison. And, mark, he noticed directly the wheel deserted and his barque off her course—and his only thought was to get that miserable, stripped, undecked, smouldering shell of a ship back again with her head pointing at her port of destination. Bankok! That's what he was after. I tell you this quiet, bowed, bandy-legged, almost deformed little man was immense in the singleness of his idea and in his placid ignorance of our agitation. He motioned us forward with a commanding gesture, and went to take the wheel himself.

"Yes; that was the first thing we did—trim the yards of that wreck! No one was killed, or even disabled, but everyone was more or less hurt. You should have seen them! Some were in rags, with black faces, like coal-heavers, like sweeps, and had bullet heads that seemed closely cropped, but were in fact singed to the skin. Others, of the watch below, awakened by being shot out from their collapsing bunks, shivered incessantly, and kept on groaning even as we went about our work. But they all worked. That crew of Liverpool hard cases had in them the right stuff. It's my experience they always have. It is the sea that gives it—the vastness, the loneliness surrounding their dark stolid souls. Ah! Well! we stumbled, we crept, we fell, we barked our shins on the wreckage, we hauled. The masts stood, but we did not know how much they might be charred down below. It was nearly calm, but a long swell ran from the west and made her roll. They might go at any moment. We looked at them with apprehension. One could not foresee which way they would fall.

"Then we retreated aft and looked about us. The deck was a tangle of planks on edge, of planks on end, of splinters, of ruined woodwork. The masts rose from that chaos like big trees above a matted undergrowth.

The interstices of that mass of wreckage were full of
something whitish, sluggish, stirring—of something that
was like a greasy fog. The smoke of the invisible fire
was coming up again, was trailing, like a poisonous
thick mist in some valley choked with dead wood.
Already lazy wisps were beginning to curl upwards
amongst the mass of splinters. Here and there a piece
of timber, stuck upright, resembled a post. Half of a
fife-rail had been shot through the foresail, and the sky
made a patch of glorious blue in the ignobly soiled canvas. A portion of several boards holding together had
fallen across the rail, and one end protruded overboard,
like a gangway leading upon nothing, like a gangway
leading over the deep sea, leading to death—as if
inviting us to walk the plank at once and be done with
our ridiculous troubles. And still the air, the sky—a
ghost, something invisible was hailing the ship.

"Someone had the sense to look over, and there was
the helmsman, who had impulsively jumped overboard,
anxious to come back. He yelled and swam lustily like
a merman, keeping up with the ship. We threw him a
rope, and presently he stood amongst us streaming with
water and very crestfallen. The captain had surrendered the wheel, and apart, elbow on rail and chin in
hand, gazed at the sea wistfully. We asked ourselves,
What next? I thought, Now, this is something like.
This is great. I wonder what will happen. O youth!

"Suddenly Mahon sighted a steamer far astern.
Captain Beard said, 'We may do something with her
yet.' We hoisted two flags, which said in the international language of the sea, 'On fire. Want immediate assistance.' The steamer grew bigger rapidly,
and by-and-by spoke with two flags on her foremast, 'I
am coming to your assistance.'

"In half an hour she was abreast, to windward, within

hail, and rolling slightly, with her engines stopped.
We lost our composure, and yelled all together with
excitement, 'We've been blown up'. A man in a white
helmet, on the bridge, cried, 'Yes! All right! all right!'
and he nodded his head, and smiled, and made soothing
motions with his hand as though at a lot of frightened
children. One of the boats dropped in the water,
and walked towards us upon the sea with her long
oars. Four Calashes*pulled a swinging stroke. This
was my first sight of Malay seamen.* I've known
them since, but what struck me then was their un-
concern: they came alongside, and even the bowman
standing up and holding to our main-chains with the
boat-hook did not deign to lift his head for a glance.
I thought people who had been blown up deserved
more attention.

"A little man, dry like a chip and agile like a monkey,
clambered up. It was the mate of the steamer. He
gave one look, and cried, 'O boys—you had better quit.'

"We were silent. He talked apart with the captain
for a time,—seemed to argue with him. Then they
went away together to the steamer.

"When our skipper came back we learned that the
steamer was the *Somerville*, Captain Nash, from West
Australia to Singapore *via* Batavia*with mails, and that
the agreement was she should tow us to Anjer* or
Batavia, if possible, where we could extinguish the fire
by scuttling, and then proceed on our voyage—to
Bankok! The old man seemed excited. 'We will do
it yet,' he said to Mahon, fiercely. He shook his fist at
the sky. Nobody else said a word.

"At noon the steamer began to tow. She went ahead
slim and high, and what was left of the *Judea* followed
at the end of seventy fathom of tow-rope,—followed her
swiftly like a cloud of smoke with mast-heads pro-

truding above. We went aloft to furl the sails. We
coughed on the yards, and were careful about the
bunts. Do you see the lot of us there, putting a neat
furl on the sails of that ship doomed to arrive nowhere?
There was not a man who didn't think that at any moment the masts would topple over. From aloft we
could not see the ship for smoke, and they worked carefully, passing the gaskets with even turns. 'Harbour
furl—aloft there!' cried Mahon from below.

"You understand this? I don't think one of those
chaps expected to get down in the usual way. When
we did I heard them saying to each other, 'Well, I
thought we would come down overboard, in a lump—
sticks and all—blame me if I didn't.' 'That's what I
was thinking to myself,' would answer wearily another
battered and bandaged scarecrow. And, mind, these
were men without the drilled-in habit of obedience. To
an onlooker they would be a lot of profane scallywags
without a redeeming point. What made them do it—
what made them obey me when I, thinking consciously
how fine it was, made them drop the bunt of the foresail
twice to try and do it better? What? They had no
professional reputation—no examples, no praise. It
wasn't a sense of duty; they all knew well enough how to
shirk, and laze, and dodge—when they had a mind to
it—and mostly they had. Was it the two pounds ten
a-month that sent them there? They didn't think
their pay half good enough. No; it was something in
them, something inborn and subtle and everlasting. I
don't say positively that the crew of a French or German merchantman wouldn't have done it, but I doubt
whether it would have been done in the same way.
There was a completeness in it, something solid like a
principle, and masterful like an instinct—a disclosure of
something secret—of that hidden something, that gift of

good or evil that makes racial difference, that shapes the fate of nations.

"It was that night at ten that, for the first time since we had been fighting it, we saw the fire. The speed of the towing had fanned the smouldering destruction. A blue gleam appeared forward, shining below the wreck of the deck. It wavered in patches, it seemed to stir and creep like the light of a glowworm. I saw it first, and told Mahon. 'Then the game's up,' he said. 'We had better stop this towing, or she will burst out suddenly fore and aft before we can clear out.' We set up a yell; rang bells to attract their attention; they towed on. At last Mahon and I had to crawl forward and cut the rope with an axe. There was no time to cast off the lashings. Red tongues could be seen licking the wilderness of splinters under our feet as we made our way back to the poop.

"Of course they very soon found out in the steamer that the rope was gone. She gave a loud blast of her whistle, her lights were seen sweeping in a wide circle, she came up ranging close along-side, and stopped. We were all in a tight group on the poop looking at her. Every man had saved a little bundle or a bag. Suddenly a conical flame with a twisted top shot up forward and threw upon the black sea a circle of light, with the two vessels side by side and heaving gently in its centre. Captain Beard had been sitting on the gratings still and mute for hours, but now he rose slowly and advanced in front of us, to the mizzen-shrouds. Captain Nash hailed: 'Come along! Look sharp. I have mail-bags on board. I will take you and your boats to Singapore.'

"'Thank you! No!' said our skipper. 'We must see the last of the ship.'

"'I can't stand by any longer,' shouted the other. 'Mails—you know.'

"'Ay! ay! We are all right.'

"'Very well! I'll report you in Singapore. . . . Good-bye!'

"He waved his hand. Our men dropped their bundles quietly. The steamer moved ahead, and passing out of the circle of light, vanished at once from our sight, dazzled by the fire which burned fiercely. And then I knew that I would see the East first as commander of a small boat. I thought it fine; and the fidelity to the old ship was fine. We should see the last of her. Oh, the glamour of youth! Oh, the fire of it, more dazzling than the flames of the burning ship, throwing a magic light on the wide earth, leaping audaciously to the sky, presently to be quenched by time, more cruel, more pitiless, more bitter than the sea—and like the flames of the burning ship surrounded by an impenetrable night.

*   *   *   *   *   *

"The old man warned us in his gentle and inflexible way that it was part of our duty to save for the under-writers as much as we could of the ship's gear. Accordingly we went to work aft, while she blazed forward to give us plenty of light. We lugged out a lot of rub-bish. What didn't we save? An old barometer fixed with an absurd quantity of screws nearly cost me my life: a sudden rush of smoke came upon me, and I just got away in time. There were various stores, bolts of canvas, coils of rope; the poop looked like a marine bazaar, and the boats were lumbered to the gunwales. One would have thought the old man wanted to take as much as he could of his first command with him. He was very, very quiet, but off his balance evidently. Would you believe it? He wanted to take a length of old stream-cable and a kedge-anchor with him in the long-boat. We said, 'Ay, ay, sir,' deferentially, and on

the quiet let the things slip overboard. The heavy
medicine-chest went that way, two bags of green coffee,
tins of paint—fancy, paint!—a whole lot of things.
Then I was ordered with two hands into the boats to
make a stowage and get them ready against the time it
would be proper for us to leave the ship.

"We put everything straight, stepped the long-boat's
mast for our skipper, who was to take charge of her, and
I was not sorry to sit down for a moment. My face felt
raw, every limb ached as if broken, I was aware of all
my ribs, and would have sworn to a twist in the backbone. The boats, fast astern, lay in a deep shadow, and
all around I could see the circle of the sea lighted by the
fire. A gigantic flame arose forward straight and clear.
It flared fierce, with noises like the whirr of wings, with
rumbles as of thunder. There were cracks, detonations,
and from the cone of flame the sparks flew upwards, as
man is born to trouble, to leaky ships, and to ships that
burn.

"What bothered me was that the ship, lying broadside to the swell and to such wind as there was—a mere
breath—the boats would not keep astern where they
were safe, but persisted, in a pig-headed way boats have,
in getting under the counter and then swinging alongside. They were knocking about dangerously and
coming near the flame, while the ship rolled on them,
and, of course, there was always the danger of the masts
going over the side at any moment. I and my two
boat-keepers kept them off as best we could, with oars
and boat-hooks; but to be constantly at it became exasperating, since there was no reason why we should not
leave at once. We could not see those on board, nor
could we imagine what caused the delay. The boat-
keepers were swearing feebly, and I had not only my
share of the work but also had to keep at it two men

who showed a constant inclination to lay themselves down and let things slide.

"At last I hailed, 'On deck there,' and someone looked over. 'We're ready here,' I said. The head disappeared, and very soon popped up again. 'The captain says, All right, sir, and to keep the boats well clear of the ship.'

"Half an hour passed. Suddenly there was a frightful racket, rattle, clanking of chain, hiss of water, and millions of sparks flew up into the shivering column of smoke that stood leaning slightly above the ship. The cat-heads had burned away, and the two red-hot anchors had gone to the bottom, tearing out after them two hundred fathom of red-hot chain. The ship trembled, the mass of flame swayed as if ready to collapse, and the fore top-gallant-mast fell. It darted down like an arrow of fire, shot under, and instantly leaping up within an oar's-length of the boats, floated quietly, very black on the luminous sea. I hailed the deck again. After some time a man in an unexpectedly cheerful but also muffled tone, as though he had been trying to speak with his mouth shut, informed me, 'Coming directly, sir,' and vanished. For a long time I heard nothing but the whirr and roar of the fire. There were also whistling sounds. The boats jumped, tugged at the painters, ran at each other playfully, knocked their sides together, or, do what we would, swung in a bunch against the ship's side. I couldn't stand it any longer, and swarming up a rope, clambered aboard over the stern.

"It was as bright as day. Coming up like this, the sheet of fire facing me was a terrifying sight, and the geat seemed hardly bearable at first. On a settee cushion dragged out of the cabin Captain Beard, his legs drawn up and one arm under his head, slept with

the light playing on him. Do you know what the rest
were busy about? They were sitting on deck right aft,
round an open case, eating bread and cheese and drinking bottled stout.

"On the background of flames twisting in fierce
tongues above their heads they seemed at home like
salamanders, and looked like a band of desperate
pirates. The fire sparkled in the whites of their eyes,
gleamed on patches of white skin seen through the torn
shirts. Each had the marks as of a battle about him—
bandaged heads, tied-up arms, a strip of dirty rag round
a knee—and each man had a bottle between his legs and
a chunk of cheese in his hand. Mahon got up. With
his handsome and disreputable head, his hooked profile,
his long white beard, and with an uncorked bottle in his
hand, he resembled one of those reckless sea-robbers of
old making merry amidst violence and disaster. 'The
last meal on board,' he explained solemnly. 'We had
nothing to eat all day, and it was no use leaving all this.'
He flourished the bottle and indicated the sleeping
skipper. 'He said he couldn't swallow anything, so I
got him to lie down,' he went on; and as I stared, 'I
don't know whether you are aware, young fellow, the
man had no sleep to speak of for days—and there will be
dam' little sleep in the boats.' 'There will be no boats
by-and-by if you fool about much longer,' I said, indignantly. I walked up to the skipper and shook him
by the shoulder. At last he opened his eyes, but did
not move. 'Time to leave her, sir,' I said quietly.

"He got up painfully, looked at the flames, at the
sea sparkling round the ship, and black, black as ink
farther away; he looked at the stars shining dim through
a thin veil of smoke in a sky black, black as Erebus.

"'Youngest first,' he said.

"And the ordinary seaman, wiping his mouth with

the back of his hand, got up, clambered over the taffrail, and vanished. Others followed. One, on the point of going over, stopped short to drain his bottle, and with a great swing of his arm flung it at the fire. 'Take this!' he cried.

"The skipper lingered disconsolately, and we left him to commune alone for a while with his first command. Then I went up again and brought him away at last. It was time. The ironwork on the poop was hot to the touch.

"Then the painter of the long-boat was cut, and the three boats, tied together, drifted clear of the ship. It was just sixteen hours after the explosion when we abandoned her. Mahon had charge of the second boat, and I had the smallest—the 14-foot thing. The long-boat would have taken the lot of us; but the skipper said we must save as much property as we could—for the underwriters—and so I got my first command. I had two men with me, a bag of biscuits, a few tins of meat, and a breaker of water. I was ordered to keep close to the long-boat, that in case of bad weather we might be taken into her.

"And do you know what I thought? I thought I would part company as soon as I could. I wanted to have my first command all to myself. I wasn't going to sail in a squadron if there were a chance for independent cruising. I would make land by myself. I would beat the other boats. Youth! All youth! The silly, charming, beautiful youth.

"But we did not make a start at once. We must see the last of the ship. And so the boats drifted about that night, heaving and setting on the swell. The men dozed, waked, sighed, groaned. I looked at the burning ship.

"Between the darkness of earth and heaven she was

burning fiercely upon a disc of purple sea shot by the blood-red play of gleams; upon a disc of water glittering and sinister. A high, clear flame, an immense and lonely flame, ascended from the ocean, and from its summit the black smoke poured continuously at the sky. She burned furiously; mournful and imposing like a funeral pile kindled in the night, surrounded by the sea, watched over by the stars. A magnificent death had come like a grace, like a gift, like a reward to that old ship at the end of her laborious days. The surrender of her weary ghost to the keeping of stars and sea was stirring like the sight of a glorious triumph. The masts fell just before daybreak, and for a moment there was a burst and turmoil of sparks that seemed to fill with flying fire the night patient and watchful, the vast night lying silent upon the sea. At daylight she was only a charred shell, floating still under a cloud of smoke and bearing a glowing mass of coal within.

"Then the oars were got out, and the boats forming in a line moved round her remains as if in procession —the long-boat leading. As we pulled across her stern a slim dart of fire shot out viciously at us, and suddenly she went down, head first, in a great hiss of steam. The unconsumed stern was the last to sink; but the paint had gone, had cracked, had peeled off, and there were no letters, there was no word, no stubborn device that was like her soul, to flash at the rising sun her creed and her name.

"We made our way north. A breeze sprang up, and about noon all the boats came together for the last time. I had no mast or sail in mine, but I made a mast out of a spare oar and hoisted a boat-awning for a sail, with a boat-hook for a yard. She was certainly over-masted, but I had the satisfaction of knowing that with the wind aft I could beat the other two. I had to wait for them.

Then we all had a look at the captain's chart, and, after
a sociable meal of hard bread and water, got our last
instructions. These were simple: steer north, and
keep together as much as possible. 'Be careful with
that jury-rig, Marlow,' said the captain; and Mahon, as
I sailed proudly past his boat, wrinkled his curved nose
and hailed, 'You will sail that ship of yours under water,
if you don't look out, young fellow.' He was a malicious
old man—and may the deep sea where he sleeps now
rock him gently, rock him tenderly to the end of time!

"Before sunset a thick rain-squall passed over the
two boats, which were far astern, and that was the last
I saw of them for a time. Next day I sat steering my
cockle-shell—my first command—with nothing but
water and sky around me. I did sight in the afternoon
the upper sails of a ship far away, but said nothing, and
my men did not notice her. You see I was afraid she
might be homeward bound, and I had no mind to turn
back from the portals of the East. I was steering for
Java—another blessed name—like Bankok, you know.
I steered many days.

"I need not tell you what it is to be knocking about
in an open boat. I remember nights and days of calm,
when we pulled, we pulled, and the boat seemed to
stand still, as if bewitched within the circle of the sea
horizon. I remember the heat, the deluge of rain-
squalls that kept us baling for dear life (but filled our
water-cask), and I remember sixteen hours on end with
a mouth dry as a cinder and a steering-oar over the
stern to keep my first command head on to a breaking
sea. I did not know how good a man I was till then. I
remember the drawn faces, the dejected figures of my
two men, and I remember my youth and the feeling that
will never come back any more—the feeling that I could
last for ever, outlast the sea, the earth, and all men; the

deceitful feeling that lures us on to joys, to perils, to love, to vain effort—to death; the triumphant conviction of strength, the heat of life in the handful of dust, the glow in the heart that with every year grows dim, grows cold, grows small, and expires—and expires, too soon, too soon—before life itself.

"And this is how I see the East. I have seen its secret places and have looked into its very soul; but now I see it always from a small boat, a high outline of mountains, blue and afar in the morning; like faint mist at noon; a jagged wall of purple at sunset. I have the feel of the oar in my hand, the vision of a scorching blue sea in my eyes. And I see a bay, a wide bay, smooth as glass and polished like ice, shimmering in the dark. A red light burns far off upon the gloom of the land, and the night is soft and warm. We drag at the oars with aching arms, and suddenly a puff of wind, a puff faint and tepid and laden with strange odours of blossoms, of aromatic wood, comes out of the still night —the first sigh of the East on my face. That I can never forget. It was impalpable and enslaving, like a charm, like a whispered promise of mysterious delight.

"We had been pulling this finishing spell for eleven hours. Two pulled, and he whose turn it was to rest sat at the tiller. We had made out the red light in that bay and steered for it, guessing it must mark some small coasting port. We passed two vessels, outlandish and high-sterned, sleeping at anchor, and, approaching the light, now very dim, ran the boat's nose against the end of a jutting wharf. We were blind with fatigue. My men dropped the oars and fell off the thwarts as if dead. I made fast to a pile. A current rippled softly. The scented obscurity of the shore was grouped into vast masses, a density of colossal clumps of vegetation, probably—mute and fantastic shapes. And at their foot the semicircle of a beach gleamed faintly, like an illusion. There was not a light, not a stir, not a sound. The mysterious East faced me, perfumed like a flower, silent like death, dark like a grave.

"And I sat weary beyond expression, exulting like a conqueror, sleepless and entranced as if before a profound, a fateful enigma.

"A splashing of oars, a measured dip reverberating on the level of water, intensified by the silence of the shore into loud claps, made me jump up. A boat, a European boat, was coming in. I invoked the name of the dead; I hailed: *Judea* ahoy! A thin shout answered.

"It was the captain. I had beaten the flagship by three hours, and I was glad to hear the old man's voice again, tremulous and tired. 'Is it you, Marlow?' 'Mind the end of that jetty, sir,' I cried.

"He approached cautiously, and brought up with the deep-sea lead-line which we had saved—for the underwriters. I eased my painter and fell alongside. He sat, a broken figure at the stern, wet with dew, his hands clasped in his lap. His men were asleep already. 'I had a terrible time of it,' he murmured. 'Mahon is behind—not very far.' We conversed in whispers, in low whispers, as if afraid to wake up the land. Guns, thunder, earthquakes would not have awakened the men just then.

"Looking round as we talked, I saw away at sea a bright light travelling in the night. 'There's a steamer passing the bay,' I said. She was not passing, she was entering, and she even came close and anchored. 'I wish,' said the old man, 'you would find out whether she is English. Perhaps they could give us a passage somewhere.' He seemed nervously anxious. So by dint of punching and kicking I started one of my men into a state of somnambulism, and giving him an oar, took another and pulled towards the lights of the steamer.

"There was a murmur of voices in her, metallic hollow clangs of the engine-room, footsteps on the deck. Her ports shone, round like dilated eyes. Shapes moved about, and there was a shadowy man high up on the bridge. He heard my oars.

"And then, before I could open my lips, the East spoke to me, but it was in a Western voice. A torrent of words was poured into the enigmatical, the fateful silence; outlandish, angry words, mixed with words and even whole sentences of good English, less strange but even more surprising. The voice swore and cursed violently; it riddled the solemn peace of the bay by a volley of abuse. It began by calling me Pig, and from that went crescendo into unmentionable adjectives— in English. The man up there raged aloud in two languages, and with a sincerity in his fury that almost convinced me I had, in some way, sinned against the harmony of the universe. I could hardly see him, but began to think he would work himself into a fit.

"Suddenly he ceased, and I could hear him snorting and blowing like a porpoise. I said—

"'What steamer is this, pray?'

"'Eh? What's this? And who are you?'

"'Castaway crew of an English barque burnt at sea. We came here to-night. I am the second mate. The captain is in the long-boat, and wishes to know if you would give us a passage somewhere.'

"'Oh, my goodness! I say. . . . This is the *Celestial* from Singapore on her return trip. I'll arrange with your captain in the morning, . . . and, . . . I say, . . . did you hear me just now?'

"'I should think the whole bay heard you.'

"'I thought you were a shore-boat. Now, look here

—this infernal lazy scoundrel of a caretaker has gone to
sleep again—curse him. The light is out, and I nearly
ran foul of the end of this damned jetty. This is the
third time he plays me this trick. Now, I ask you, can
anybody stand this kind of thing? It's enough to drive
a man out of his mind. I'll report him. . . . I'll
get the Assistant Resident to give him the sack,
by . . . ! See—there's no light. It's out, isn't
it? I take you to witness the light's out. There
should be a light, you know. A red light on the——'

"'There was a light,' I said, mildly.

"'But it's out, man! What's the use of talking like
this? You can see for yourself it's out—don't you?
If you had to take a valuable steamer along this God-
forsaken coast you would want a light, too. I'll kick
him from end to end of his miserable wharf. You'll see
if I don't. I will——'

"'So I may tell my captain you'll take us?' I broke
in.

"'Yes, I'll take you. Good-night,' he said, brusquely.

"I pulled back, made fast again to the jetty, and then
went to sleep at last. I had faced the silence of the
East. I had heard some of its language. But when I
opened my eyes again the silence was as complete as
though it had never been broken. I was lying in a
flood of light, and the sky had never looked so far, so
high, before. I opened my eyes and lay without moving.

"And then I saw the men of the East—they were
looking at me. The whole length of the jetty was full
of people. I saw brown, bronze, yellow faces, the black
eyes, the glitter, the colour of an Eastern crowd. And
all these beings stared without a murmur, without a
sigh, without a movement. They stared down at the
boats, at the sleeping men who at night had come to

them from the sea. Nothing moved. The fronds of
palms stood still against the sky. Not a branch stirred
along the shore, and the brown roofs of hidden houses
peeped through the green foliage, through the big leaves
that hung shining and still like leaves forged of heavy
metal. This was the East of the ancient navigators, so
old, so mysterious, resplendent and sombre, living and
unchanged, full of danger and promise. And these
were the men. I sat up suddenly. A wave of movement passed through the crowd from end to end, passed
along the heads, swayed the bodies, ran along the jetty
like a ripple on the water, like a breath of wind on a
field—and all was still again. I see it now—the wide
sweep of the bay, the glittering sands, the wealth of
green infinite and varied, the sea blue like the sea of a
dream, the crowd of attentive faces, the blaze of vivid
colour—the water reflecting it all, the curve of the
shore, the jetty, the high-sterned outlandish craft
floating still, and the three boats with the tired men
from the West sleeping, unconscious of the land and the
people and of the violence of sunshine. They slept
thrown across the thwarts, curled on bottom-boards, in
the careless attitudes of death. The head of the old
skipper, leaning back in the stern of the long-boat, had
fallen on his breast, and he looked as though he would
never wake. Farther out old Mahon's face was up-
turned to the sky, with the long white beard spread out
on his breast, as though he had been shot where he sat
at the tiller; and a man, all in a heap in the bows of the
boat, slept with both arms embracing the stem-head and
with his cheek laid on the gunwale. The East looked
at them without a sound.

"I have known its fascination since; I have seen
the mysterious shores, the still water, the lands of brown
nations, where a stealthy Nemesis lies in wait, pursues,

overtakes so many of the conquering race, who are proud of their wisdom, of their knowledge, of their strength. But for me all the East is contained in that vision of my youth. It is all in that moment when I opened my young eyes on it. I came upon it from a tussle with the sea—and I was young—and I saw it looking at me. And this is all that is left of it! Only a moment; a moment of strength, of romance, of glamour —of youth! . . . A flick of sunshine upon a strange shore, the time to remember, the time for a sigh, and— good-bye!—Night—Good-bye . . . !"

He drank.

"Ah! The good old time—the good old time. Youth and the sea. Glamour and the sea! The good, strong sea, the salt, bitter sea, that could whisper to you and roar at you and knock your breath out of you."

He drank again.

"By all that's wonderful it is the sea, I believe, the sea itself—or is it youth alone? Who can tell? But you here—you all had something out of life: money, love—whatever one gets on shore—and, tell me, wasn't that the best time, that time when we were young at sea; young and had nothing, on the sea that gives nothing, except hard knocks—and sometimes a chance to feel your strength—that only—what you all regret?"

And we all nodded at him: the man of finance, the man of accounts, the man of law, we all nodded at him over the polished table that like a still sheet of brown water reflected our faces, lined, wrinkled; our faces marked by toil, by deceptions, by success, by love; our weary eyes looking still, looking always, looking anxiously for something out of life, that while it is expected is already gone—has passed unseen, in a sigh, in a flash—together with the youth, with the strength, with the romance of illusions.

HEART OF DARKNESS

HEART OF DARKNESS

I

THE *Nellie*, a cruising yawl, swung to her anchor without a flutter of the sails, and was at rest. The flood had made, the wind was nearly calm, and being bound down the river, the only thing for it was to come to and wait for the turn of the tide.

The sea-reach of the Thames stretched before us like the beginning of an interminable waterway. In the offing the sea and the sky were welded together without a joint, and in the luminous space the tanned sails of the barges drifting up with the tide seemed to stand still in red clusters of canvas sharply peaked, with gleams of varnished spirits. A haze rested on the low shores that ran out to sea in vanishing flatness. The air was dark above Gravesend,* and farther back still seemed condensed into a mournful gloom, brooding motionless over the biggest, and the greatest, town on earth.

The Director of Companies was our captain and our host. We four affectionately watched his back as he stood in the bows looking to seaward. On the whole river there was nothing that looked half so nautical. He resembled a pilot, which to a seaman is trustworthiness personified. It was difficult to realize his work was not out there in the luminous estuary, but behind him, within the brooding gloom.

Between us there was, as I have already said somewhere, the bond of the sea. Besides holding our hearts together through long periods of separation, it had the

effect of making us tolerant of each other's yarns—and
even convictions. The Lawyer—the best of old fellows
—had, because of his many years and many virtues, the
only cushion on deck, and was lying on the only rug.
The Accountant had brought out already a box of
dominoes, and was toying architecturally with the
bones. Marlow sat cross-legged right aft, leaning
against the mizzen-mast. He had sunken cheeks, a
yellow complexion, a straight back, an ascetic aspect,
and, with his arms dropped, the palms of hands outwards, resembled an idol. The director, satisfied the
anchor had good hold, made his way aft and sat down
amongst us. We exchanged a few words lazily. Afterwards there was silence on board the yacht. For some
reason or other we did not begin that game of dominoes.
We felt meditative, and fit for nothing but placid
staring. The day was ending in a serenity of still and
exquisite brilliance. The water shone pacifically; the
sky, without a speck, was a benign immensity of un-
stained light; the very mist on the Essex marshes was
like a gauzy and radiant fabric, hung from the wooded
rises inland, and draping the low shores in diaphanous
folds. Only the gloom to the west, brooding over the
upper reaches, became more sombre every minute, as if
angered by the approach of the sun.

And at last, in its curved and imperceptible fall, the
sun sank low, and from glowing white changed to a dull
red without rays and without heat, as if about to go out
suddenly, stricken to death by the touch of that gloom
brooding over a crowd of men.

Forthwith a change came over the waters, and the
serenity became less brilliant but more profound. The
old river in its broad reach rested unruffled at the decline of day, after ages of good service done to the race
that peopled its banks, spread out in the tranquil

dignity of a waterway leading to the uttermost ends of the earth. We looked at the venerable stream not in the vivid flush of a short day that comes and departs for ever, but in the august light of abiding memories. And indeed nothing is easier for a man who has, as the phrase goes, "followed the sea" with reverence and affection, than to evoke the great spirit of the past upon the lower reaches of the Thames. The tidal current runs to and fro in its unceasing service, crowded with memories of men and ships it had borne to the rest of home or to the battles of the sea. It had known and served all the men of whom the nation is proud, from Sir Francis Drake to Sir John Franklin,* knights all, titled and untitled—the great knights-errant of the sea. It had borne all the ships whose names are like jewels flashing in the night of time, from the *Golden Hind* returning with her round flanks full of treasure, to be visited by the Queen's Highness and thus pass out of the gigantic tale, to the *Erebus* and *Terror*, bound on other conquests—and that never returned. It had known the ships and the men. They had sailed from Deptford, from Greenwich, from Erith*—the adventurers and the settlers; kings' ships and the ships of men on 'Change;* captains, admirals, the dark "interlopers"* of the Eastern trade, and the commissioned "generals" of East India fleets. Hunters for gold or pursuers of fame, they all had gone out on that stream, bearing the sword, and often the torch, messengers of the might within the land, bearers of a spark from the sacred fire. What greatness had not floated on the ebb of that river into the mystery of an unknown earth! . . . The dreams of men, the seed of commonwealths, the germs of empires.

The sun set; the dusk fell on the stream, and lights began to appear along the shore. The Chapman lighthouse, a three-legged thing erect on a mud-flat, shone strongly. Lights of ships moved in the fairway—a great stir of lights going up and going down. And farther west on the upper reaches the place of the monstrous town was still marked ominously on the sky, a brooding gloom in sunshine, a lurid glare under the stars.

"And this also," said Marlow suddenly, "has been one of the dark places of the earth."

He was the only man of us who still "followed the sea." The worst that could be said of him was that he did not represent his class. He was a seaman, but he was a wanderer, too, while most seamen lead, if one may so express it, a sedentary life. Their minds are of the stay-at-home order, and their home is always with them—the ship; and so is their country—the sea. One ship is very much like another, and the sea is always the same. In the immutability of their surroundings the foreign shores, the foreign faces, the changing immensity of life, glide past, veiled not by a sense of mystery but by a slightly disdainful ignorance; for there is nothing mysterious to a seaman unless it be the sea itself, which is the mistress of his existence and as inscrutable as Destiny. For the rest, after his hours of work, a casual stroll or a casual spree on shore suffices to unfold for him the secret of a whole continent, and generally he finds the secret not worth knowing. The yarns of seamen have a direct simplicity, the whole meaning of which lies within the shell of a cracked nut. But Marlow was not typical (if his propensity to spin yarns be excepted), and to him the meaning of an episode was not inside like a kernel but outside, enveloping the tale which brought it out only as a glow brings out a haze, in the likeness of one of these misty halos that sometimes are made visible by the spectral illumination of moonshine.

His remark did not seem at all surprising. It was just like Marlow. It was accepted in silence. No one took the trouble to grunt even; and presently he said, very slow—

"I was thinking of very old times, when the Romans first came here, nineteen hundred years ago—the other day. . . . Light came out of this river since—you say Knights? Yes; but it is like a running blaze on a plain, like a flash of lightning in the clouds. We live in the flicker—may it last as long as the old earth keeps rolling! But darkness was here yesterday. Imagine the feelings of a commander of a fine—what d'ye call 'em?—trireme in the Mediterranean, ordered suddenly to the north; run overland across the Gauls in a hurry; put in charge of one of these craft the legionaries—a wonderful lot of handy men they must have been, too—used to build, apparently by the hundred, in a month or two, if we may believe what we read. Imagine him here—the very end of the world, a sea the colour of lead, a sky the colour of smoke, a kind of ship about as rigid as a concertina—and going up this river with stores, or orders, or what you like. Sand-banks, marshes, forests, savages,—precious little to eat fit for a civilized man, nothing but Thames water to drink. No Falernian wine here, no going ashore. Here and there a military camp lost in a wilderness, like a needle in a bundle of hay—cold, fog, tempests, disease, exile, and death,—death skulking in the air, in the water, in the bush. They must have been dying like flies here. Oh, yes—he did it. Did it very well, too, no doubt, and without thinking much about it either, except afterwards to brag of what he had gone through in his time, perhaps. They were men enough to face the darkness. And perhaps he was cheered by keeping his eye on a chance of promotion to the fleet at Ravenna by-and-by, if he had good friends in Rome and survived the awful climate. Or think of a decent young citizen in a toga—perhaps too much dice, you know—coming out here in the train of some prefect, or tax-gatherer, or trader even, to mend his fortunes. Land in a swamp, march through the woods, and in some inland post feel the savagery, the utter savagery, had closed round him,—all that mysterious life of the wilderness that stirs in the forest, in the jungles, in the hearts of wild men. There's no initiation either into such mysteries. He has to live in the midst of the incomprehensible, which is also detestable. And it has a fascination, too, that goes to work upon him. The fascination of the abomination—you know, imagine the growing regrets, the longing to escape, the powerless disgust, the surrender, the hate."

He paused.

"Mind," he began again, lifting one arm from the elbow, the palm of the hand outwards, so that, with his legs folded before him, he had the pose of a Buddha preaching in European clothes and without a lotus-flower—"Mind, none of us would feel exactly like this. What saves us is efficiency—the devotion to efficiency. But these chaps were not much account, really. They were no colonists; their administration was merely a squeeze, and nothing more, I suspect. They were conquerors, and for that you want only brute force—nothing to boast of, when you have it, since your strength is just an accident arising from the weakness of others. They grabbed what they could get for the sake of what was to be got. It was just robbery with violence, aggravated murder on a great scale, and men going at it blind—as is very proper for those who tackle a darkness. The conquest of the earth, which mostly means the taking it away from those who have a different complexion or slightly flatter noses than ourselves, is not a

pretty thing when you look into it too much. What
redeems it is the idea only. An idea at the back of it;
not a sentimental pretence but an idea; and an unsel-
fish belief in the idea—something you can set up, and
bow down before, and offer a sacrifice to. . . ."

He broke off. Flames glided in the river, small green
flames, red flames, white flames, pursuing, overtaking,
joining, crossing each other—then separating slowly
or hastily. The traffic of the great city went on in the
deepening night upon the sleepless river. We looked
on, waiting patiently—there was nothing else to do till
the end of the flood; but it was only after a long silence,
when he said, in a hesitating voice, "I suppose you
fellows remember I did once turn fresh-water sailor for
a bit," that we knew we were fated, before the ebb began
to run, to hear about one of Marlow's inconclusive
experiences.

"I don't want to bother you much with what happened to me personally," he began, showing in this remark the weakness of many tellers of tales who seem so
often unaware of what their audience would best like to
hear; "yet to understand the effect of it on me you
ought to know how I got out there, what I saw, how I
went up that river to the place where I first met the
poor chap. It was the farthest point of navigation and
the culminating point of my experience. It seemed
somehow to throw a kind of light on everything about
me—and into my thoughts. It was sombre enough,
too—and pitiful—not extraordinary in any way—not
very clear either. No, not very clear. And yet it
seemed to throw a kind of light.

"I had then, as you remember, just returned to
London after a lot of Indian Ocean, Pacific, China Seas
—a regular dose of the East—six years or so, and I was
loafing about, hindering you fellows in your work and

invading your homes, just as though I had got a heavenly mission to civilize you. It was very fine for a time, but after a bit I did get tired of resting. Then I began to look for a ship—I should think the hardest work on earth. But the ships wouldn't even look at me. And I got tired of that game, too.

"Now when I was a little chap I had a passion for maps. I would look for hours at South America, or Africa, or Australia, and lose myself in all the glories of exploration. At that time there were many blank spaces on the earth, and when I saw one that looked particularly inviting on a map (but they all look that) I would put my finger on it and say, When I grow up I will go there. The North Pole was one of these places, I remember. Well, I haven't been there yet, and shall not try now. The glamour's off. Other places were scattered about the Equator, and in every sort of latitude all over the two hemispheres. I have been in some of them, and . . . well, we won't talk about that. But there was one yet—the biggest, the most blank, so to speak—that I had a hankering after.

"True, by this time it was not a blank space any more. It had got filled since my boyhood with rivers and lakes and names. It had ceased to be a blank space of delightful mystery—a white patch for a boy to dream gloriously over. It had become a place of darkness. But there was in it one river especially, a mighty big river, that you could see on the map, resembling an immense snake uncoiled, with its head in the sea, its body at rest curving afar over a vast country, and its tail lost in the depths of the land. And as I looked at the map of it in a shop-window, it fascinated me as a snake would a bird—a silly little bird. Then I remembered there was a big concern, a Company for trade on that river. Dash it all! I thought to myself,

they can't trade without using some kind of craft on
that lot of fresh water—steamboats! Why shouldn't
I try to get charge of one? I went on along Fleet
Street, but could not shake off the idea. The snake had
charmed me.

"You understand it was a Continental concern, that
Trading society; but I have a lot of relations living on
the Continent, because it's cheap and not so nasty as it
looks, they say.

"I am sorry to own I began to worry them. This
was already a fresh departure for me. I was not used
to get things that way, you know. I always went my
own road and on my own legs where I had a mind to go.
I wouldn't have believed it of myself; but, then—you
see—I felt somehow I must get there by hook or by
crook. So I worried them. The men said 'My dear
fellow,' and did nothing. Then—would you believe
it?—I tried the women. I, Charlie Marlow, set the
women to work—to get a job. Heavens! Well, you
see, the notion drove me. I had an aunt, a dear
enthusiastic soul. She wrote: 'It will be delightful.
I am ready to do anything, anything for you. It is a
glorious idea. I know the wife of a very high personage
in the Administration, and also a man who has lots of
influence with,' etc., etc. She was determined to make
no end of fuss to get me appointed skipper of a river
steamboat, if such was my fancy.

"I got my appointment—of course; and I got it very
quick. It appears the Company had received news that
one of their captains had been killed in a scuffle with the
natives. This was my chance, and it made me the
more anxious to go. It was only months and months
afterwards, when I made the attempt to recover what
was left of the body, that I heard the original quarrel
arose from a misunderstanding about some hens. Yes,

two black hens. Fresleven—that was the fellow's
name, a Dane—thought himself wronged somehow in
the bargain, so he went ashore and started to hammer
the chief of the village with a stick. Oh, it didn't surprise me in the least to hear this, and at the same time to
be told that Fresleven was the gentlest, quietest creature that ever walked on two legs. No doubt he was;
but he had been a couple of years already out there
engaged in the noble cause, you know, and he probably felt the need at last of asserting his self-respect
in some way. Therefore he whacked the old nigger
mercilessly, while a big crowd of his people watched
him, thunderstruck, till some man—I was told the
chief's son—in desperation at hearing the old chap yell,
made a tentative jab with a spear at the white man—
and of course it went quite easy between the shoulder-
blades. Then the whole population cleared into the
forest, expecting all kinds of calamities to happen,
while, on the other hand, the steamer Fresleven commanded left also in a bad panic, in charge of the engineer, I believe. Afterwards nobody seemed to trouble
much about Fresleven's remains, till I got out and
stepped into his shoes. I couldn't let it rest, though;
but when an opportunity offered at last to meet my
predecessor, the grass growing through his ribs was tall
enough to hide his bones. They were all there. The
supernatural being had not been touched after he fell.
And the village was deserted, the huts gaped black,
rotting, all askew within the fallen enclosures. A
calamity had come to it, sure enough. The people had
vanished. Mad terror had scattered them, men,
women, and children, through the bush, and they had
never returned. What became of the hens I don't know
either. I should think the cause of progress got them,
anyhow. However, through this glorious affair I got

my appointment, before I had fairly begun to hope for it.

"I flew around like mad to get ready, and before forty-eight hours I was crossing the Channel to show myself to my employers, and sign the contract. In a very few hours I arrived in a city that always makes me think of a whited sepulchre. Prejudice no doubt. I had no difficulty in finding the Company's offices. It was the biggest thing in the town, and everybody I met was full of it. They were going to run an over-sea empire, and make no end of coin by trade.

"A narrow and deserted street in deep shadow, high houses, innumerable windows with venetian blinds, a dead silence, grass sprouting between the stones, imposing carriage archways right and left, immense double doors standing ponderously ajar. I slipped through one of these cracks, went up a swept and ungarnished staircase, as arid as a desert, and opened the first door I came to. Two women, one fat and the other slim, sat on straw-bottomed chairs, knitting black wool. The slim one got up and walked straight at me—still knitting with down-cast eyes—and only just as I began to think of getting out of her way, as you would for a somnambulist, stood still, and looked up. Her dress was as plain as an umbrella-cover, and she turned round without a word and preceded me into a waiting-room. I gave my name, and looked about. Deal table in the middle, plain chairs all round the walls, on one end a large shining map, marked with all the colours of a rainbow. There was a vast amount of red—good to see at any time, because one knows that some real work is done in there, a deuce of a lot of blue, a little green, smears of orange, and, on the East Coast, a purple patch, to show where the jolly pioneers of progress drink the jolly lager-beer. However, I wasn't going

into any of these. I was going into the yellow. Dead
in the centre. And the river was there—fascinating—
deadly—like a snake. Ough! A door opened, a white-
haired secretarial head, but wearing a compassionate
expression, appeared, and a skinny forefinger beckoned
me into the sanctuary. Its light was dim, and a heavy
writing-desk squatted in the middle. From behind that
structure came out an impression of pale plumpness in a
frock-coat. The great man himself. He was five feet
six, I should judge, and had his grip on the handle-end
of ever so many millions. He shook hands, I fancy,
murmured vaguely, was satisfied with my French.
Bon voyage.

"In about forty-five seconds I found myself again in
the waiting-room with the compassionate secretary,
who, full of desolation and sympathy, made me sign
some document. I believe I undertook amongst other
things not to disclose any trade secrets. Well, I am not
going to.

"I began to feel slightly uneasy. You know I am
not used to such ceremonies, and there was something
ominous in the atmosphere. It was just as though I
had been let into some conspiracy—I don't know—
something not quite right; and I was glad to get out.
In the outer room the two women knitted black wool
feverishly. People were arriving, and the younger one
was walking back and forth introducing them. The
old one sat on her chair. Her flat cloth slippers were
propped up on a foot-warmer, and a cat reposed on her
lap. She wore a starched white affair on her head, had
a wart on one cheek, and silver-rimmed spectacles hung
on the tip of her nose. She glanced at me above the
glasses. The swift and indifferent placidity of that
look troubled me. Two youths with foolish and cheery
countenances were being piloted over, and she threw at

them the same quick glance of unconcerned wisdom. She seemed to know all about them and about me, too. An eerie feeling came over me. She seemed uncanny and fateful. Often far away there I thought of these two, guarding the door of Darkness, knitting black wool as for a warm pall, one introducing, introducing continuously to the unknown, the other scrutinizing the cheery and foolish faces with unconcerned old eyes. *Ave !** Old knitter of black wool. *Morituri te salutant.** Not many of those she looked at ever saw her again—not half, by a long way.

"There was yet a visit to the doctor. 'A simple formality,' assured me the secretary, with an air of taking an immense part in all my sorrows. Accordingly a young chap wearing his hat over the left eyebrow, some clerk I suppose,—there must have been clerks in the business, though the house was as still as a house in a city of the dead—came from somewhere up-stairs, and led me forth. He was shabby and careless, with ink-stains on the sleeves of his jacket, and his cravat was large and billowy, under a chin shaped like the toe of an old boot. It was a little too early for the doctor, so I proposed a drink, and thereupon he developed a vein of joviality. As we sat over our vermuths he glorified the Company's business, and by-and-by I expressed casually my surprise at him not going out there. He became very cool and collected all at once. 'I am not such a fool as I look, quoth Plato to his disciples,' he said sententiously, emptied his glass with great resolution, and we rose.

"The old doctor felt my pulse, evidently thinking of something else the while. 'Good, good for there,' he mumbled, and then with a certain eagerness asked me whether I would let him measure my head. Rather surprised, I said Yes, when he produced a thing like

calipers and got the dimensions back and front and
every way, taking notes carefully. He was an un-
shaven little man in a threadbare coat like a gaberdine,
with his feet in slippers, and I thought him a harmless
fool. 'I always ask leave, in the interests of science, to
measure the crania of those going out there,' he said.
'And when they come back, too?' I asked. 'Oh, I
never see them,' he remarked; 'and, moreover, the
changes take place inside, you know.' He smiled, as if
at some quiet joke. 'So you are going out there.
Famous. Interesting, too.' He gave me a searching
glance, and made another note. 'Ever any madness in
your family?' he asked, in a matter-of-fact tone. I felt
very annoyed. 'Is that question in the interests of
science, too?' 'It would be,' he said, without taking
notice of my irritation, 'interesting for science to watch
the mental changes of individuals, on the spot, but . . .'
'Are you an alienist?'* I interrupted. 'Every doctor
should be—a little,' answered that original, imperturb-
ably. 'I have a little theory which you Messieurs who
go out there must help me to prove. This is my share
in the advantages my country shall reap from the possession of such a magnificent dependency. The mere
wealth I leave to others. Pardon my questions, but
you are the first Englishman coming under my observation . . .' I hastened to assure him I was not in
the least typical. 'If I were,' said I, 'I wouldn't be
talking like this with you.' 'What you say is rather
profound, and probably erroneous,' he said, with a
laugh. 'Avoid irritation more than exposure to the
sun. Adieu. How do you English say, eh? Good-
bye. Ah! Good-bye. Adieu. In the tropics one
must before everything keep calm.' . . . He lifted
a warning forefinger. . . . '*Du calme, du calme.
Adieu.*'

"One thing more remained to do—say good-bye to my excellent aunt. I found her triumphant. I had a cup of tea—the last decent cup of tea for many days— and in a room that most soothingly looked just as you would expect a lady's drawing-room to look, we had a long quiet chat by the fireside. In the course of these confidences it became quite plain to me I had been represented to the wife of the high dignitary, and good- ness knows to how many more people besides, as an exceptional and gifted creature—a piece of good fortune for the Company—a man you don't get hold of every day. Good heavens! and I was going to take charge of a two-penny-half-penny river-steamboat with a penny whistle attached! It appeared, however, I was also one of the Workers, with a capital—you know. Some- thing like an emissary of light, something like a lower sort of apostle. There had been a lot of such rot let loose in print and talk just about that time, and the excellent woman, living right in the rush of all that humbug, got carried off her feet. She talked about 'weaning those ignorant millions from their horrid ways,' till, upon my word, she made me quite un- comfortable. I ventured to hint that the Company was run for profit.

"'You forget, dear Charlie, that the labourer is worthy of his hire,' she said, brightly. It's queer how out of touch with truth women are. They live in a world of their own, and there had never been anything like it, and never can be. It is too beautiful altogether, and if they were to set it up it would go to pieces before the first sunset. Some confounded fact we men have been living contentedly with ever since the day of creation would start up and knock the whole thing over.

"After this I got embraced, told to wear flannel, be sure to write often, and so on—and I left. In the

street—I don't know why—a queer feeling came to me
that I was an impostor. Odd thing that I, who used
to clear out for any part of the world at twenty-four
hours' notice, with less thought than most men give to
the crossing of a street, had a moment—I won't say of
hesitation, but of startled pause, before this commonplace affair. The best way I can explain it to you is by
saying that, for a second or two, I felt as though, instead of going to the centre of a continent, I were about
to set off for the centre of the earth.

"I left in a French steamer, and she called in every
blamed port they have out there, for, as far as I could
see, the sole purpose of landing soldiers and custom-
house officers. I watched the coast. Watching a coast
as it slips by the ship is like thinking about an enigma.
There it is before you—smiling, frowning, inviting,
grand, mean, insipid, or savage, and always mute
with an air of whispering, Come and find out. This
one was almost featureless, as if still in the making,
with an aspect of monotonous grimness. The edge of a
colossal jungle, so dark-green as to be almost black,
fringed with white surf, ran straight, like a ruled line,
far, far away along a blue sea whose glitter was blurred
by a creeping mist. The sun was fierce, the land seemed
to glisten and drip with steam. Here and there grayish-
whitish specks showed up clustered inside the white
surf, with a flag flying above them perhaps. Settle-
ments some centuries old, and still no bigger than pin-
heads on the untouched expanse of their background.
We pounded along, stopped, landed soldiers; went on,
landed custom-house clerks to levy toll in what looked
like a God-forsaken wilderness, with a tin shed and a
flag-pole lost in it; landed more soldiers—to take care
of the custom-house clerks, presumably. Some, I heard,
got drowned in the surf; but whether they did or not,

nobody seemed particularly to care. They were just
flung out there, and on we went. Every day the coast
looked the same, as though we had not moved; but we
passed various places—trading places—with names
like Gran' Bassam, Little Popo; names that seemed to
belong to some sordid farce acted in front of a sinister
back-cloth. The idleness of a passenger, my isolation
amongst all these men with whom I had no point of
contact, the oily and languid sea, the uniform sombre-
ness of the coast, seemed to keep me away from the
truth of things, within the toil of a mournful and senseless delusion. The voice of the surf heard now and
then was a positive pleasure, like the speech of a
brother. It was something natural, that had its reason,
that had a meaning. Now and then a boat from the
shore gave one a momentary contact with reality. It
was paddled by black fellows. You could see from afar
the white of their eyeballs glistening. They shouted,
sang; their bodies streamed with perspiration; they had
faces like grotesque masks—these chaps; but they had
bone, muscle, a wild vitality, an intense energy of
movement, that was as natural and true as the surf
along their coast. They wanted no excuse for being
there. They were a great comfort to look at. For a
time I would feel I belonged still to a world of straightforward facts; but the feeling would not last long.
Something would turn up to scare it away. Once, I
remember, we came upon a man-of-war anchored off the
coast. There wasn't even a shed there, and she was
shelling the bush. It appears the French had one of
their wars going on thereabouts. Her ensign drooped*
limp like a rag; the muzzles of the long six-inch guns
stuck out all over the low hull; the greasy, slimy swell
swung her up lazily and let her down, swaying her thin
masts. In the empty immensity of earth, sky, and

water, there she was, incomprehensible, firing into a continent. Pop, would go one of the six-inch guns; a small flame would dart and vanish, a little white smoke would disappear, a tiny projectile would give a feeble screech— and nothing happened. Nothing could happen. There was a touch of insanity in the proceeding, a sense of lugubrious drollery in the sight; and it was not dissipated by somebody on board assuring me earnestly there was a camp of natives—he called them enemies!— hidden out of sight somewhere.

"We gave her her letters (I heard the men in that lonely ship were dying of fever at the rate of three a-day) and went on. We called at some more places with farcical names, where the merry dance of death and trade goes on in a still and earthy atmosphere as of an overheated catacomb; all along the formless coast bordered by dangerous surf, as if Nature herself had tried to ward off intruders; in and out of rivers, streams of death in life, whose banks were rotting into mud, whose waters, thickened into slime, invaded the contorted mangroves, that seemed to writhe at us in the extremity of an impotent despair. Nowhere did we stop long enough to get a particularized impression, but the general sense of vague and oppressive wonder grew upon me. It was like a weary pilgrimage amongst hints for nightmares.

"It was upward of thirty days before I saw the mouth of the big river. We anchored off the seat of the government. But my work would not begin till some two hundred miles farther on. So as soon as I could I made a start for a place thirty miles higher up.

"I had my passage on a little sea-going steamer. Her captain was a Swede, and knowing me for a seaman, invited me on the bridge. He was a young man, lean, fair, and morose, with lanky hair and a shuffling gait.

As we left the miserable little wharf, he tossed his head
contemptuously at the shore. 'Been living there?' he
asked. I said, 'Yes.' 'Fine lot these government
chaps—are they not?' he went on, speaking English with
great precision and considerable bitterness. 'It is
funny what some people will do for a few francs a-
month. I wonder what becomes of that kind when it
goes up country?' I said to him I expected to see that
soon. 'So-o-o!' he exclaimed. He shuffled athwart,
keeping one eye ahead vigilantly. 'Don't be too
sure,' he continued. 'The other day I took up a man
who hanged himself on the road. He was a Swede,
too.' 'Hanged himself! Why, in God's name?' I
cried. He kept on looking out watchfully. 'Who
knows? The sun too much for him, or the country perhaps.'

"At last we opened a reach. A rocky cliff appeared,
mounds of turned-up earth by the shore, houses on a
hill, others with iron roofs, amongst a waste of excavations, or hanging to the declivity. A continuous
noise of the rapids above hovered over this scene of
inhabited devastation. A lot of people, mostly black
and naked, moved about like ants. A jetty projected
into the river. A blinding sunlight drowned all this at
times in a sudden recrudescence of glare. 'There's
your Company's station,' said the Swede, pointing to
three wooden barrack-like structures on the rocky slope.
'I will send your things up. Four boxes did you say?
So. Farewell.'

"I came upon a boiler wallowing in the grass, then
found a path leading up the hill. It turned aside for
the boulders, and also for an undersized railway-truck
lying there on its back with its wheels in the air. One
was off. The thing looked as dead as the carcass of
some animal. I came upon more pieces of decaying

machinery, a stack of rusty rails. To the left a clump of trees made a shady spot, where dark things seemed to stir feebly. I blinked, the path was steep. A horn tooted to the right, and I saw the black people run. A heavy and dull detonation shook the ground, a puff of smoke came out of the cliff, and that was all. No change appeared on the face of the rock. They were building a railway. The cliff was not in the way or anything; but this objectless blasting was all the work going on.

"A slight clinking behind me made me turn my head. Six black men advanced in a file, toiling up the path. They walked erect and slow, balancing small baskets full of earth on their heads, and the clink kept time with their footsteps. Black rags were wound round their loins, and the short ends behind waggled to and fro like tails. I could see every rib, the joints of their limbs were like knots in a rope; each had an iron collar on his neck, and all were connected together with a chain whose bights swung between them, rhythmically clinking. Another report from the cliff made me think suddenly of that ship of war I had seen firing into a continent. It was the same kind of ominous voice; but these men could by no stretch of imagination be called enemies. They were called criminals, and the outraged law, like the bursting shells, had come to them, an insoluble mystery from the sea. All their meagre breasts panted together, the violently dilated nostrils quivered, the eyes stared stonily up-hill. They passed me within six inches, without a glance, with that complete, deathlike indifference of unhappy savages. Behind this raw matter one of the reclaimed, the product of the new forces at work, strolled despondently, carrying a rifle by its middle. He had a uniform jacket with one button off, and seeing a white man on the path, hoisted his weapon to his shoulder with alacrity. This

was simple prudence, white men being so much alike at
a distance that he could not tell who I might be. He
was speedily reassured, and with a large, white, rascally
grin, and a glance at his charge, seemed to take me into
partnership in his exalted trust. After all, I also was
a part of the great cause of these high and just proceedings.

"Instead of going up, I turned and descended to the
left. My idea was to let that chain-gang get out of
sight before I climbed the hill. You know I am not
particularly tender; I've had to strike and to fend off.
I've had to resist and to attack sometimes—that's only
one way of resisting—without counting the exact cost,
according to the demands of such sort of life as I had
blundered into. I've seen the devil of violence, and the
devil of greed, and the devil of hot desire; but, by all the
stars! these were strong, lusty, red-eyed devils, that
swayed and drove men—men, I tell you. But as I
stood on this hillside, I foresaw that in the blinding
sunshine of that land I would become acquainted with a
flabby, pretending, weak-eyed devil of a rapacious and
pitiless folly. How insidious he could be, too, I was
only to find out several months later and a thousand
miles farther. For a moment I stood appalled, as
though by a warning. Finally I descended the hill,
obliquely, towards the trees I had seen.

"I avoided a vast artificial hole somebody had been
digging on the slope, the purpose of which I found it
impossible to divine. It wasn't a quarry or a sandpit,
anyhow. It was just a hole. It might have been
connected with the philanthropic desire of giving the
criminals something to do. I don't know. Then I
nearly fell into a very narrow ravine, almost no more
than a scar in the hillside. I discovered that a lot of
imported drainage-pipes for the settlement had been

tumbled in there. There wasn't one that was not broken. It was a wanton smash-up. At last I got under the trees. My purpose was to stroll into the shade for a moment; but no sooner within than it seemed to me I had stepped into the gloomy circle of some Inferno. The rapids were near, and an uninterrupted, uniform, headlong, rushing noise filled the mournful stillness of the grove, where not a breath stirred, not a leaf moved, with a mysterious sound—as though the tearing pace of the launched earth had suddenly become audible.

"Black shapes crouched, lay, sat between the trees leaning against the trunks, clinging to the earth, half coming out, half effaced within the dim light, in all the attitudes of pain, abandonment, and despair. Another mine on the cliff went off, followed by a slight shudder of the soil under my feet. The work was going on. The work! And this was the place where some of the helpers had withdrawn to die.

"They were dying slowly—it was very clear. They were not enemies, they were not criminals, they were nothing earthly now,—nothing but black shadows of disease and starvation, lying confusedly in the greenish gloom. Brought from all the recesses of the coast in all the legality of time contracts, lost in uncongenial surroundings, fed on unfamiliar food, they sickened, became inefficient, and were then allowed to crawl away and rest. These moribund shapes were free as air—and nearly as thin. I began to distinguish the gleam of the eyes under the trees. Then, glancing down, I saw a face near my hand. The black bones reclined at full length with one shoulder against the tree, and slowly the eyelids rose and the sunken eyes looked up at me, enormous and vacant, a kind of blind, white flicker in the depths of the orbs, which died out slowly. The man seemed young—almost a boy—but you know with them it's hard to tell. I found nothing else to do but to offer him one of my good Swede's ship's biscuits I had in my pocket. The fingers closed slowly on it and held —there was no other movement and no other glance. He had tied a bit of white worsted* round his neck— Why? Where did he get it? Was it a badge—an ornament—a charm—a propitiatory act? Was there any idea at all connected with it? It looked startling round his black neck, this bit of white thread from beyond the seas.

"Near the same tree two more bundles of acute angles sat with their legs drawn up. One, with his chin propped on his knees, stared at nothing, in an intoler- able and appalling manner: his brother phantom rested its forehead, as if overcome with a great weari- ness; and all about others were scattered in every pose of contorted collapse, as in some picture of a massacre or a pestilence. While I stood horror-struck, one of these creatures rose to his hands and knees, and went off on all-fours towards the river to drink. He lapped out of his hand, then sat up in the sunlight, crossing his shins in front of him, and after a time let his woolly head fall on his breastbone.

"I didn't want any more loitering in the shade, and I made haste towards the station. When near the buildings I met a white man, in such an unexpected elegance of get-up that in the first moment I took him for a sort of vision. I saw a high starched collar, white cuffs, a light alpaca jacket, snowy trousers, a clear necktie, and varnished boots. No hat. Hair parted, brushed, oiled, under a green-lined parasol held in a big white hand. He was amazing, and had a penholder be- hind his ear.

"I shook hands with this miracle, and I learned he

was the Company's chief accountant, and that all the book-keeping was done at this station. He had come out for a moment, he said, 'to get a breath of fresh air.' The expression sounded wonderfully odd, with its suggestion of sedentary desk-life. I wouldn't have mentioned the fellow to you at all, only it was from his lips that I first heard the name of the man who is so indissolubly connected with the memories of that time. Moreover, I respected the fellow. Yes; I respected his collars, his vast cuffs, his brushed hair. His appearance was certainly that of a hairdresser's dummy; but in the great demoralization of the land he kept up his appearance. That's backbone. His starched collars and got-up shirt-fronts were achievements of character. He had been out nearly three years; and, later, I could not help asking him how he managed to sport such linen. He had just the faintest blush, and said modestly, 'I've been teaching one of the native women about the station. It was difficult. She had a distaste for the work.' Thus this man had verily accomplished something. And he was devoted to his books, which were in apple-pie order.

"Everything else in the station was in a muddle, —heads, things, buildings. Strings of dusty niggers with splay feet arrived and departed; a stream of manufactured goods, rubbishy cottons, beads, and brass-wire sent* into the depths of darkness, and in return came a precious trickle of ivory.

"I had to wait in the station for ten days—an eternity. I lived in a hut in the yard, but to be out of the chaos I would sometimes get into the accountant's office. It was built of horizontal planks, and so badly put together that, as he bent over his high desk, he was barred from neck to heels with narrow strips of sunlight. There was no need to open the big shutter to see.

It was hot there, too; big flies buzzed fiendishly, and did not sting, but stabbed. I sat generally on the floor, while, of faultless appearance (and even slightly scented), perching on a high stool, he wrote, he wrote. Sometimes he stood up for exercise. When a truckle-bed with a sick man (some invalid agent from up-country) was put in there, he exhibited a gentle annoyance. 'The groans of this sick person,' he said, 'distract my attention. And without that it is extremely difficult to guard against clerical errors in this climate.'

"One day he remarked, without lifting his head, 'In the interior you will no doubt meet Mr. Kurtz.' On my asking who Mr. Kurtz was, he said he was a first-class agent; and seeing my disappointment at this information, he added slowly, laying down his pen, 'He is a very remarkable person.' Further questions elicited from him that Mr. Kurtz was at present in charge of a trading post, a very important one, in the true ivory-country, at 'the very bottom of there. Sends in as much ivory as all the others put to-gether . . .' He began to write again. The sick man was too ill to groan. The flies buzzed in a great peace.

"Suddenly there was a growing murmur of voices and a great tramping of feet. A caravan had come in. A violent babble of uncouth sounds burst out on the other side of the planks. All the carriers were speaking together, and in the midst of the uproar the lamentable voice of the chief agent was heard 'giving it up' tearfully for the twentieth time that day. . . . He rose slowly. 'What a frightful row,' he said. He crossed the room gently to look at the sick man, and returning, said to me, 'He does not hear.' 'What! Dead?' I asked, startled. 'No, not yet,' he answered, with great composure. Then, alluding with a toss of the head to the tumult in the station-yard, 'When one has got to make correct entries, one comes to hate those savages—hate them to the death.' He remained thoughtful for a moment. 'When you see Mr. Kurtz,' he went on, 'tell him from me that everything here'—he glanced at the desk—'is very satisfactory. I don't like to write to him—with those messengers of ours you never know who may get hold of your letter—at that Central Station.' He stared at me for a moment with his mild, bulging eyes. 'Oh, he will go far, very far,' he began again. 'He will be a somebody in the Administration before long. They, above—the Council in Europe, you know—mean him to be.'

"He turned to his work. The noise outside had ceased, and presently in going out I stopped at the door. In the steady buzz of flies the homeward-bound agent was lying flushed and insensible; the other, bent over his books, was making correct entries of perfectly correct transactions; and fifty feet below the doorstep I could see the still tree-tops of the grove of death.

"Next day I left that station at last, with a caravan of sixty men, for a two-hundred-mile tramp.

"No use telling you much about that. Paths, paths, everywhere; a stamped-in network of paths spreading over the empty land, through long grass, through burnt grass, through thickets, down and up chilly ravines, up and down stony hills ablaze with heat; and a solitude, a solitude, nobody, not a hut. The population had cleared out a long time ago. Well, if a lot of mysterious niggers armed with all kinds of fearful weapons suddenly took to travelling on the road between Deal* and Gravesend, catching the yokels right and left to carry heavy loads for them, I fancy every farm and cottage thereabouts would get empty very soon. Only here the dwellings were gone, too. Still I passed through several abandoned villages. There's something pathetically childish in the ruins of grass walls. Day after day, with the stamp and shuffle of sixty pair of bare feet behind me, each pair under a 60-lb. load. Camp, cook, sleep, strike camp, march. Now and then a carrier dead in harness, at rest in the long grass near the path, with an empty water-gourd and his long staff lying by his side. A great silence around and above. Perhaps on some quiet night the tremor of far-off drums, sinking, swelling, a tremor vast, faint; a sound weird, appealing, suggestive, and wild—and perhaps with as profound a meaning as the sound of bells in a Christian country. Once a white man in an unbuttoned uniform, camping on the path with an armed escort of lank Zanzibaris,* very hospitable and festive—not to say drunk. Was looking after the upkeep of the road, he declared. Can't say I saw any road or any upkeep, unless the body of a middle-aged negro, with a bullet-hole in the forehead, upon which I absolutely stumbled three miles farther on, may be considered as a permanent improvement. I had a white companion, too, not a bad chap, but rather too fleshy and with the exasperating habit of fainting on the hot hillsides, miles away from the least bit of shade and water. Annoying, you know, to hold your own coat like a parasol over a man's head while he is coming-to. I couldn't help asking him once what he meant by coming there at all. 'To make money, of course. What do you think?' he said, scornfully. Then he got fever, and had to be carried in a hammock slung under a pole. As he weighed sixteen stone* I had no end of rows with the carriers. They jibbed, ran away, sneaked off with their loads in the night—quite a mutiny. So, one evening, I made a speech in English with gestures, not one of which was lost to the sixty pairs of eyes before me, and the next morning I started the hammock off in front all right. An hour afterwards I came upon the whole concern wrecked in a bush—man, hammock, groans, blankets, horrors. The heavy pole had skinned his poor nose. He was very anxious for me to kill somebody, but there wasn't the shadow of a carrier near. I remember the old doctor,—'It would be interesting for science to watch the mental changes of individuals, on the spot.' I felt I was becoming scientifically interesting. However, all that is to no purpose. On the fifteenth day I came in sight of the big river again, and hobbled into the Central Station. It was on a back water surrounded by scrub and forest, with a pretty border of smelly mud on one side, and on the three others enclosed by a crazy fence of rushes. A neglected gap was all the gate it had, and the first glance at the place was enough to let you see the flabby devil was running that show. White men with long staves in their hands appeared languidly from amongst the buildings, strolling up to take a look at me, and then retired out of sight somewhere. One of them, a stout, excitable chap with black moustaches, informed me with great volubility and many digressions, as soon as I told him who I was, that my steamer was at the bottom of the river. I was thunderstruck. What, how, why? Oh, it was 'all right.' The 'manager himself' was there. All quite correct. 'Everybody had behaved splendidly! splendidly!'—'you must,' he said in agitation, 'go and see the general manager at once. He is waiting!'

"I did not see the real significance of that wreck at once. I fancy I see it now. but I am not sure—not at all. Certainly the affair was too stupid—when I think of it—to be altogether natural. Still. . . . But at the moment it presented itself simply as a confounded nuisance. The steamer was sunk. They had started two days before in a sudden hurry up the river with the manager on board, in charge of some volunteer skipper, and before they had been out three hours they tore the bottom out of her on stones, and she sank near the south bank. I asked myself what I was to do there, now my boat was lost. As a matter of fact, I had plenty to do in fishing my command out of the river. I had to set about it the very next day. That, and the repairs when I brought the pieces to the station, took some months.

"My first interview with the manager was curious. He did not ask me to sit down after my twenty-mile walk that morning. He was commonplace in complexion, in feature, in manners, and in voice. He was of middle size and of ordinary build. His eyes, of the usual blue, were perhaps remarkably cold, and he certainly could make his glance fall on one as trenchant and heavy as an axe. But even at these times the rest of his person seemed to disclaim the intention. Otherwise there was only an indefinable, faint expression of his lips, something stealthy—a smile—not a smile—I remember it, but I can't explain. It was unconscious, this smile was, though just after he had said something it got intensified for an instant. It came at the end of his speeches like a seal applied on the words to make the meaning of the commonest phrase appear absolutely inscrutable. He was a common trader, from his youth up employed in these parts—nothing more. He was obeyed, yet he inspired neither love nor fear, nor even respect. He inspired uneasiness. That was it! Uneasiness. Not a definite mistrust—just uneasiness—nothing more. You have no idea how effective such a . . . a . . . faculty can be. He had no genius for organizing, for initiative, or for order even. That was evident in such things as the deplorable state

of the station.   He had no learning, and no intelligence.
His position had come to him—why?   Perhaps because
he was never ill.   .   .   .   He had served three terms of
three years out there.   .   .   .   Because triumphant
health in the general rout of constitutions is a kind of
power in itself.   When he went home on leave he rioted
on a large scale—pompously.   Jack ashore—with a
difference—in externals only.   This one could gather
from his casual talk.   He originated nothing, he could
keep the routine going—that's all.   But he was great.
He was great by this little thing that it was impossible
to tell what could control such a man.   He never gave
that secret away.   Perhaps there was nothing within
him.   Such a suspicion made one pause—for out there
there were no external checks.   Once when various
tropical diseases had laid low almost every 'agent' in the
station, he was heard to say, 'Men who come out here
should have no entrails.'   He sealed the utterance with
that smile of his, as though it had been a door opening
into a darkness he had in his keeping.   You fancied you
had seen things—but the seal was on.   When annoyed
at meal-times by the constant quarrels of the white
men about precedence, he ordered an immense round
table to be made, for which a special house had to be
built.   This was the station's mess-room.   Where he
sat was the first place—the rest were nowhere.   One
felt this to be his unalterable conviction.   He was
neither civil nor uncivil.   He was quiet.   He allowed
his 'boy'—an overfed young negro from the coast—to
treat the white men, under his very eyes, with provoking
insolence.

"He began to speak as soon as he saw me.   I had
been very long on the road.   He could not wait.   Had
to start without me.   The up-river stations had to be
relieved.   There had been so many delays already that

he did not know who was dead and who was alive, and how they got on—and so on, and so on. He paid no attention to my explanations, and, playing with a stick of sealing-wax, repeated several times that the situation was 'very grave, very grave.' There were rumours that a very important station was in jeopardy, and its chief, Mr. Kurtz, was ill. Hoped it was not true. Mr. Kurtz was. . . . I felt weary and irritable. Hang Kurtz, I thought. I interrupted him by saying I had heard of Mr. Kurtz on the coast. 'Ah! So they talk of him down there,' he murmured to himself. Then he began again, assuring me Mr. Kurtz was the best agent he had, an exceptional man, of the greatest importance to the Company; therefore I could understand his anxiety. He was, he said, 'very, very uneasy.' Certainly he fidgeted on his chair a good deal, exclaimed, 'Ah, Mr. Kurtz!' broke the stick of sealing-wax and seemed dumfounded by the accident. Next thing he wanted to know 'how long it would take to' . . . I interrupted him again. Being hungry, you know, and kept on my feet, too, I was getting savage. 'How could I tell?' I said. 'I hadn't even seen the wreck yet—some months, no doubt.' All this talk seemed to me so futile. 'Some months,' he said. 'Well, let us say three months before we can make a start. Yes. That ought to do the affair.' I flung out of his hut (he lived all alone in a clay hut with a sort of verandah) muttering to myself my opinion of him. He was a chattering idiot. Afterwards I took it back when it was borne in upon me startlingly with what extreme nicety he had estimated the time requisite for the 'affair.'

"I went to work the next day, turning, so to speak, my back on that station. In that way only it seemed to me I could keep my hold on the redeeming facts of life. Still, one must look about sometimes; and then I saw this station, these men strolling aimlessly about in the sunshine of the yard. I asked myself sometimes what it all meant. They wandered here and there with their absurd long staves in their hands, like a lot of faithless pilgrims bewitched inside a rotten fence. The word 'ivory' rang in the air, was whispered, was sighed. You would think they were praying to it. A taint of imbecile rapacity blew through it all, like a whiff from some corpse. By Jove! I've never seen anything so unreal in my life. And outside, the silent wilderness surrounding this cleared speck on the earth struck me as something great and invincible, like evil or truth, waiting patiently for the passing away of this fantastic invasion.

"Oh, these months! Well, never mind. Various things happened. One evening a grass shed full of calico, cotton prints, beads, and I don't know what else, burst into a blaze so suddenly that you would have thought the earth had opened to let an avenging fire consume all that trash. I was smoking my pipe quietly by my dismantled steamer, and saw them all cutting capers in the light, with their arms lifted high, when the stout man with moustaches came tearing down to the river, a tin pail in his hand, assured me that everybody was 'behaving splendidly, splendidly,' dipped about a quart of water and tore back again. I noticed there was a hole in the bottom of his pail.

"I strolled up. There was no hurry. You see the thing had gone off like a box of matches. It had been hopeless from the very first. The flame had leaped high, driven everybody back, lighted up everything—and collapsed. The shed was already a heap of embers glowing fiercely. A nigger was being beaten near by. They said he had caused the fire in some way; be that as it may, he was screeching most horribly. I saw him, later, for several days, sitting in a bit of shade looking very sick and trying to recover himself: afterwards he arose and went out—and the wilderness without a sound took him into its bosom again. As I approached the glow from the dark I found myself at the back of two men, talking. I heard the name of Kurtz pronounced, then the words, 'take advantage of this unfortunate accident.' One of the men was the manager. I wished him a good evening. 'Did you ever see anything like it—eh? it is incredible,' he said, and walked off. The other man remained. He was a first-class agent, young, gentlemanly, a bit reserved, with a forked little beard and a hooked nose. He was stand-offish with the other agents, and they on their side said he was the manager's spy upon them. As to me, I had hardly ever spoken to him before. We got into talk, and by-and-by we strolled away from the hissing ruins. Then he asked me to his room, which was in the main building of the station. He struck a match, and I perceived that this young aristocrat had not only a silver-mounted dressing-case but also a whole candle all to himself. Just at that time the manager was the only man supposed to have any right to candles. Native mats covered the clay walls; a collection of spears, assegais,* shields, knives was hung up in trophies. The business intrusted to this fellow was the making of bricks—so I had been informed; but there wasn't a fragment of a brick anywhere in the station, and he had been there more than a year—waiting. It seems he could not make bricks without something, I don't know what—straw maybe. Anyways, it could not be found there, and as it was not likely to be sent from Europe, it did not appear clear to me what he was waiting for. An act of special creation perhaps. However, they were all waiting—all the sixteen or twenty pilgrims of them—for something; and upon my word it did not seem an uncongenial occupation, from the way they took it, though the only thing that ever came to them was disease—as far as I could see. They beguiled the time by backbiting and intriguing against each other in a foolish kind of way. There was an air of plotting about that station, but nothing came of it, of course. It was as unreal as everything else—as the philanthropic pretence of the whole concern, as their talk, as their government, as their show of work. The only real feeling was a desire to get appointed to a trading-post where ivory was to be had, so that they could earn percentages. They intrigued and slandered and hated each other only on that account,—but as to effectually lifting a little finger—oh, no. By heavens! there is something after all in the world allowing one man to steal a horse while another must not look at a halter. Steal a horse straight out. Very well. He has done it. Perhaps he can ride. But there is a way of looking at a halter that would provoke the most charitable of saints into a kick.

"I had no idea why he wanted to be sociable, but as we chatted in there it suddenly occurred to me the fellow was trying to get at something—in fact, pumping me. He alluded constantly to Europe, to the people I was supposed to know there—putting leading questions as to my acquaintances in the sepulchral city, and so on. His little eyes glittered like mica discs—with curiosity—though he tried to keep up a bit of superciliousness. At first I was astonished, but very soon I became awfully curious to see what he would find out from me. I couldn't possibly imagine what I had in me to make it worth his while. It was very pretty to see how he baffled himself, for in truth my body was full only of chills, and my head had nothing in it but that wretched steamboat business. It was evident he took me for a perfectly shameless prevaricator. At last he got angry, and, to conceal a movement of furious annoyance, he yawned. I rose. Then I noticed a small sketch in oils, on a panel, representing a woman, draped and blindfolded, carrying a lighted torch. The background was sombre—almost black. The movement of the woman was stately, and the effect of the torch-light on the face was sinister.

"It arrested me, and he stood by civilly, holding an empty half-pint champagne bottle (medical comforts) with the candle stuck in it. To my question he said Mr. Kurtz had painted this—in this very station more than a year ago—while waiting for means to go to his trading-post. 'Tell me, pray,' said I, 'who is this Mr. Kurtz?'

"'The chief of the Inner Station,' he answered in a short tone, looking away. 'Much obliged,' I said, laughing. 'And you are the brickmaker of the Central Station. Everyone knows that.' He was silent for a while. 'He is a prodigy,' he said at last. 'He is an emissary of pity, and science, and progress, and devil knows what else. We want,' he began to declaim suddenly, 'for the guidance of the cause intrusted to us by Europe, so to speak, higher intelligence, wide sympathies, a singleness of purpose.' 'Who says that?' I asked. 'Lots of them,' he replied. 'Some even write that; and so *he* comes here, a special being, as you ought to know.' 'Why ought I to know?' I interrupted, really surprised. He paid no attention. 'Yes. To-day he is chief of the best station, next year he will be assistant-manager, two years more and . . . but I daresay you know what he will be in two years' time. You are of the new gang— the gang of virtue. The same people who sent him specially also recommended you. Oh, don't say no. I've my own eyes to trust.' Light dawned upon me. My dear aunt's influential acquaintances were pro-

ducing an unexpected effect upon that young man. I
nearly burst into a laugh. 'Do you read the Company's
confidential correspondence?' I asked. He hadn't a
word to say. It was great fun. 'When Mr. Kurtz,' I
continued, severely, 'is General Manager, you won't have
the opportunity.'

"He blew the candle out suddenly, and we went outside. The moon had risen. Black figures strolled about
listlessly, pouring water on the glow, whence proceeded a
sound of hissing; steam ascended in the moonlight, the
beaten nigger groaned somewhere. 'What a row the
brute makes!' said the indefatigable man with the
moustaches, appearing near us. 'Serve him right.
Transgression—punishment—bang! Pitiless,   pitiless.
That's the only way. This will prevent all conflagrations
for the future. I was just telling the manager. . . .'
He noticed my companion, and became crestfallen all at
once. 'Not in bed yet,' he said, with a kind of servile
heartiness; 'it's so natural. Ha! Danger—agitation.'
He vanished. I went on to the river-side, and the other
followed me. I heard a scathing murmur at my ear,
'Heap of muffs—go to.' The pilgrims could be seen in
knots gesticulating, discussing. Several had still their
staves in their hands. I verily believe they took these
sticks to bed with them. Beyond the fence the forest
stood up spectrally in the moonlight, and through the
dim stir, through the faint sounds of that lamentable
courtyard, the silence of the land went home to one's
very heart—its mystery, its greatness, the amazing
reality of its concealed life. The hurt nigger moaned
feebly somewhere near by, and then fetched a deep sigh
that made me mend my pace away from there. I felt a
hand introducing itself under my arm. 'My dear sir,'
said the fellow, 'I don't want to be misunderstood, and
especially by you, who will see Mr. Kurtz long before I

can have that pleasure. I wouldn't like him to get a false idea of my disposition. . . .'

"I let him run on, this papier-maché Mephistopheles, and it seemed to me that if I tried I could poke my fore-finger through him, and would find nothing inside but a little loose dirt, maybe. He, don't you see, had been planning to be assistant-manager by-and-by under the present man, and I could see that the coming of that Kurtz had upset them both not a little. He talked precipitately, and I did not try to stop him. I had my shoulders against the wreck of my steamer, hauled up on the slope like a carcass of some big river animal. The smell of mud, of primeval mud, by Jove! was in my nostrils, the high stillness of primeval forest was before my eyes; there were shiny patches on the black creek. The moon had spread over everything a thin layer of silver—over the rank grass, over the mud, upon the wall of matted vegetation standing higher than the wall of a temple, over the great river I could see through a sombre gap glittering, glittering, as it flowed broadly by without a murmur. All this was great, expectant, mute, while the man jabbered about himself. I wondered whether the stillness on the face of the immensity looking at us two were meant as an appeal or as a menace. What were we who had strayed in here? Could we handle that dumb thing, or would it handle us? I felt how big, how con-foundedly big, was that thing that couldn't talk, and perhaps was deaf as well. What was in there? I could see a little ivory coming out from there, and I had heard Mr. Kurtz was in there. I had heard enough about it, too—God knows! Yet somehow it didn't bring any image with it—no more than if I had been told an angel or a fiend was in there. I believed it in the same way one of you might believe there are inhabitants in the planet Mars. I knew once a Scotch sailmaker who

was certain, dead sure, there were people in Mars. If
you asked him for some idea how they looked and
behaved, he would get shy and mutter something about
'walking on all-fours.' If you as much as smiled, he
would—though a man of sixty—offer to fight you. I
would not have gone so far as to fight for Kurtz, but
I went for him near enough to a lie. You know I
hate, detest, and can't bear a lie, not because I am
straighter than the rest of us, but simply because it
appals me. There is a taint of death, a flavour of
mortality in lies—which is exactly what I hate and detest
in the world—what I want to forget. It makes me
miserable and sick, like biting something rotten would do.
Temperament, I suppose. Well, I went near enough to
it by letting the young fool there believe anything he
liked to imagine as to my influence in Europe. I became
in an instant as much of a pretence as the rest of the
bewitched pilgrims. This simply because I had a notion
it somehow would be of help to that Kurtz whom at the
time I did not see—you understand. He was just a word
for me. I did not see the man in the name any more
than you do. Do you see him? Do you see the story?
Do you see anything? It seems to me I am trying to
tell you a dream—making a vain attempt, because no
relation of a dream can convey the dream-sensation, that
commingling of absurdity, surprise, and bewilderment in
a tremor of struggling revolt, that notion of being
captured by the incredible which is of the very essence of
dreams. . . ."

He was silent for a while.

". . . No, it is impossible; it is impossible to convey the life-sensation of any given epoch of one's existence—that which makes its truth, its meaning—its
subtle and penetrating essence. It is impossible. We
live, as we dream—alone. . . ."

He paused again as if reflecting, then added—

"Of course in this you fellows see more than I could then. You see me, whom you know. . . ."

It had become so pitch dark that we listeners could hardly see one another. For a long time already he, sitting apart, had been no more to us than a voice. There was not a word from anybody. The others might have been asleep, but I was awake. I listened, I listened on the watch for the sentence, for the word, that would give me the clue to the faint uneasiness inspired by this narrative that seemed to shape itself without human lips in the heavy night-air of the river.

". . . Yes—I let him run on," Marlow began again, "and think what he pleased about the powers that were behind me. I did! And there was nothing behind me! There was nothing but that wretched, old, mangled steamboat I was leaning against, while he talked fluently about 'the necessity for every man to get on.' 'And when one comes out here, you conceive, it is not to gaze at the moon.' Mr. Kurtz was a 'universal genius,' but even a genius would find it easier to work with 'adequate tools—intelligent men.' He did not make bricks—why, there was a physical impossibility in the way—as I was well aware; and if he did secretarial work for the manager, it was because 'no sensible man rejects wantonly the confidence of his superiors.' Did I see it? I saw it. What more did I want? What I really wanted was rivets, by heaven! Rivets. To get on with the work—to stop the hole. Rivets I wanted. There were cases of them down at the coast—cases—piled up—burst—split! You kicked a loose rivet at every second step in that station yard on the hillside. Rivets had rolled into the grove of death. You could fill your pockets with rivets for the trouble of stooping down—and there wasn't one rivet to be found where it was wanted. We had plates that would do, but nothing to fasten them with. And every week the messenger, a lone negro, letter-bag on shoulder and staff in hand, left our station for the coast. And several times a week a coast caravan came in with trade goods—ghastly glazed calico that made you shudder only to look at it, glass beads value about a penny a quart, confounded spotted cotton handkerchiefs. And no rivets. Three carriers could have brought all that was wanted to set that steamboat afloat.

"He was becoming confidential now, but I fancy my unresponsive attitude must have exasperated him at last, for he judged it necessary to inform me he feared neither God nor devil, let alone any mere man. I said I could see that very well, but what I wanted was a certain quantity of rivets—and rivets were what really Mr. Kurtz wanted, if he had only known it. Now letters went to the coast every week. . . . 'My dear sir,' he cried, 'I write from dictation.' I demanded rivets. There was a way—for an intelligent man. He changed his manner; became very cold, and suddenly began to talk about a hippopotamus; wondered whether sleeping on board the steamer (I stuck to my salvage night and day) I wasn't disturbed. There was an old hippo that had the bad habit of getting out on the bank and roaming at night over the station grounds. The pilgrims used to turn out in a body and empty every rifle they could lay hands on at him. Some even had sat up o' nights for him. All this energy was wasted, though. 'That animal has a charmed life,' he said; 'but you can say this only of brutes in this country. No man—you apprehend me?—no man here bears a charmed life.' He stood there for a moment in the moonlight with his delicate hooked nose set a little askew, and his mica eyes glittering without a wink, then, with a curt Good-

night, he strode off. I could see he was disturbed and
considerably puzzled, which made me feel more hope-
ful than I had been for days. It was a great comfort to
turn from that chap to my influential friend, the battered,
twisted, ruined, tin-pot steamboat. I clambered on
board. She rang under my feet like an empty Huntley
& Palmer biscuit-tin kicked along a gutter; she was
nothing so solid in make, and rather less pretty in shape,
but I had expended enough hard work on her to make me
love her. No influential friend would have served me
better. She had given me a chance to come out a bit—
to find out what I could do. No, I don't like work. I
had rather laze about and think of all the fine things
that can be done. I don't like work—no man does—but
I like what is in the work,—the chance to find yourself.
Your own reality—for yourself, not for others—what no
other man can ever know. They can only see the mere
show, and never can tell what it really means.

"I was not surprised to see somebody sitting aft,
on the deck, with his legs dangling over the mud. You
see I rather chummed with the few mechanics there were
in that station, whom the other pilgrims naturally
despised—on account of their imperfect manners, I suppose. This was the foreman—a boiler-maker by trade—
a good worker. He was a lank, bony, yellow-faced man,
with big intense eyes. His aspect was worried, and his
head was as bald as the palm of my hand; but his hair in
falling seemed to have stuck to his chin, and had prospered in the new locality, for his beard hung down to his
waist. He was a widower with six young children (he
had left them in charge of a sister of his to come out
there), and the passion of his life was pigeon-flying. He
was an enthusiast and a connoisseur. He would rave
about pigeons. After work hours he used sometimes to
come over from his hut for a talk about his children and

his pigeons; at work, when he had to crawl in the mud under the bottom of the steamboat, he would tie up that beard of his in a kind of white serviette*he brought for the purpose. It had loops to go over his ears. In the evening he could be seen squatted on the bank rinsing that wrapper in the creek with great care, then spreading it solemnly on a bush to dry.

"I slapped him on the back and shouted 'We shall have rivets!' He scrambled to his feet exclaiming 'No! Rivets!' as though he couldn't believe his ears. Then in a low voice, 'You . . . eh?' I don't know why we behaved like lunatics. I put my finger to the side of my nose and nodded mysteriously. 'Good for you!' he cried, snapped his fingers above his head, lifting one foot. I tried a jig. We capered on the iron deck. A frightful clatter came out of that hulk, and the virgin forest on the other bank of the creek sent it back in a thundering roll upon the sleeping station. It must have made some of the pilgrims sit up in their hovels. A dark figure obscured the lighted doorway of the manager's hut, vanished, then, a second or so after, the doorway itself vanished, too. We stopped, and the silence driven away by the stamping of our feet flowed back again from the recesses of the land. The great wall of vegetation, an exuberant and entangled mass of trunks, branches, leaves, boughs, festoons, motionless in the moonlight, was like a rioting invasion of soundless life, a rolling wave of plants, piled up, crested, ready to topple over the creek, to sweep every little man of us out of his little existence. And it moved not. A deadened burst of mighty splashes and snorts reached us from afar, as though an ichthyosaurus* had been taking a bath of glitter in the great river. 'After all,' said the boiler-maker in a reasonable tone, 'why shouldn't we get the rivets?' Why not, indeed! I did not know of any reason why we shouldn't. 'They'll come in three weeks,' I said, confidently.

"But they didn't. Instead of rivets there came an invasion, an infliction, a visitation. It came in sections during the next three weeks, each section headed by a donkey carrying a white man in new clothes and tan shoes, bowing from that elevation right and left to the impressed pilgrims. A quarrelsome band of footsore sulky niggers trod on the heels of the donkey; a lot of tents, camp-stools, tin boxes, white cases, brown bales would be shot down in the courtyard, and the air of mystery would deepen a little over the muddle of the station. Five such instalments came, with their absurd air of disorderly flight with the loot of innumerable outfit shops and provision stores, that, one would think, they were lugging, after a raid, into the wilderness for equitable division. It was an inextricable mess of things decent in themselves but that human folly made look like spoils of thieving.

"This devoted band called itself the Eldorado Exploring Expedition, and I believe they were sworn to secrecy. Their talk, however, was the talk of sordid buccaneers: it was reckless without hardihood, greedy without audacity, and cruel without courage; there was not an atom of foresight or of serious intention in the whole batch of them, and they did not seem aware these things are wanted for the work of the world. To tear treasure out of the bowels of the land was their desire, with no more moral purpose at the back of it than there is in burglars breaking into a safe. Who paid the expenses of the noble enterprise I don't know; but the uncle of our manager was leader of that lot.

"In exterior he resembled a butcher in a poor neighbourhood, and his eyes had a look of sleepy cunning. He carried his fat paunch with ostentation on his short

legs, and during the time his gang infested the station
spoke to no one but his nephew. You could see these
two roaming about all day long with their heads close
together in an everlasting confab.

"I had given up worrying myself about the rivets.
One's capacity for that kind of folly is more limited than
you would suppose. I said Hang!—and let things slide.
I had plenty of time for meditation, and now and then I
would give some thought to Kurtz. I wasn't very
interested in him. No. Still, I was curious to see
whether this man, who had come out equipped with
moral ideas of some sort, would climb to the top after all
and how he would set about his work when there."

II

"ONE evening as I was lying flat on the deck of my steamboat, I heard voices approaching—and there were the nephew and the uncle strolling along the bank. I laid my head on my arm again, and had nearly lost myself in a doze, when somebody said in my ear, as it were: 'I am as harmless as a little child, but I don't like to be dictated to. Am I the manager—or am I not? I was ordered to send him there. It's incredible.' . . . I became aware that the two were standing on the shore alongside the forepart of the steamboat, just below my head. I did not move; it did not occur to me to move: I was sleepy. 'It *is* unpleasant,' grunted the uncle. 'He has asked the Administration to be sent there,' said the other, 'with the idea of showing what he could do; and I was instructed accordingly. Look at the influence that man must have. Is it not frightful?' They both agreed it was frightful, then made several bizarre remarks: 'Make rain and fine weather—one man—the Council—by the nose'—bits of absurd sentences that got the better of my drowsiness, so that I had pretty near the whole of my wits about me when the uncle said, 'The climate may do away with this difficulty for you. Is he alone there?' 'Yes,' answered the manager; 'he sent his assistant down the river with a note to me in these terms: "Clear this poor devil out of the country, and don't bother sending more of that sort. I had rather be alone than have the kind of men you can dispose of with me." It was more than a year ago. Can you imagine such impudence!' 'Anything since then?' asked the other, hoarsely.

'Ivory,' jerked the nephew; 'lots of it—prime sort—lots—most annoying, from him.' 'And with that?' questioned the heavy rumble. 'Invoice,' was the reply fired out, so to speak. Then silence. They had been talking about Kurtz.

"I was broad awake by this time, but, lying perfectly at ease, remained still, having no inducement to change my position. 'How did that ivory come all this way?' growled the elder man, who seemed very vexed. The other explained that it had come with a fleet of canoes in charge of an English half-caste clerk Kurtz had with him; that Kurtz had apparently intended to return himself, the station being by that time bare of goods and stores, but after coming three hundred miles, had suddenly decided to go back, which he started to do alone in a small dugout with four paddlers, leaving the half-caste to continue down the river with the ivory. The two fellows there seemed astounded at anybody attempting such a thing. They were at a loss for an adequate motive. As to me, I seemed to see Kurtz for the first time. It was a distinct glimpse: the dugout, four paddling savages, and the lone white man turning his back suddenly on the headquarters, on relief, on thoughts of home—perhaps; setting his face towards the depths of the wilderness, towards his empty and desolate station. I did not know the motive. Perhaps he was just simply a fine fellow who stuck to his work for its own sake. His name, you understand, had not been pronounced once. He was 'that man.' The half-caste, who, as far as I could see, had conducted a difficult trip with great prudence and pluck, was invariably alluded to as 'that scoundrel.' The 'scoundrel' had reported that the 'man' had been very ill—had recovered imperfectly. . . . The two below me moved away then a few paces, and strolled back and forth at some little distance. I heard:

'Military post—doctor—two hundred miles—quite alone now—unavoidable delays—nine months—no news—strange rumours.' They approached again, just as the manager was saying, 'No one, as far as I know, unless a species of wandering trader—a pestilential fellow, snapping ivory from the natives.' Who was it they were talking about now? I gathered in snatches that this was some man supposed to be in Kurtz's district, and of whom the manager did not approve. 'We will not be free from unfair competition till one of these fellows is hanged for an example,' he said. 'Certainly,' grunted the other; 'get him hanged! Why not? Anything—anything can be done in this country. That's what I say; nobody here, you understand, *here*, can endanger your position. And why? You stand the climate—you outlast them all. The danger is in Europe; but there before I left I took care to——' They moved off and whispered, then their voices rose again. 'The extraordinary series of delays is not my fault. I did my best.' The fat man sighed. 'Very sad.' 'And the pestiferous absurdity of his talk,' continued the other; 'he bothered me enough when he was here. "Each station should be like a beacon on the road towards better things, a centre for trade of course, but also for humanizing, improving, instructing." Conceive you—that ass! And he wants to be manager! No, it's——' Here he got choked by excessive indignation, and I lifted my head the least bit. I was surprised to see how near they were—right under me. I could have spat upon their hats. They were looking on the ground, absorbed in thought. The manager was switching his leg with a slender twig: his sagacious relative lifted his head. 'You have been well since you came out this time?' he asked. The other gave a start. 'Who? I? Oh! Like a charm—like a charm. But the rest—oh, my goodness!

All sick. They die so quick, too, that I haven't the time to send them out of the country—it's incredible!' 'H'm. Just so,' grunted the uncle. 'Ah! my boy, trust to this—I say, trust to this.' I saw him extend his short flipper of an arm for a gesture that took in the forest, the creek, the mud, the river,—seemed to beckon with a dishonouring flourish before the sunlit face of the land a treacherous appeal to the lurking death, to the hidden evil, to the profound darkness of its heart. It was so startling that I leaped to my feet and looked back at the edge of the forest, as though I had expected an answer of some sort to that black display of confidence. You know the foolish notions that come to one sometimes. The high stillness confronted these two figures with its ominous patience, waiting for the passing away of a fantastic invasion.

"They swore aloud together—out of sheer fright, I believe—then pretending not to know anything of my existence, turned back to the station. The sun was low; and leaning forward side by side, they seemed to be tugging painfully uphill their two ridiculous shadows of unequal length, that trailed behind them slowly over the tall grass without bending a single blade.

"In a few days the Eldorado Expedition went into the patient wilderness, that closed upon it as the sea closes over a diver. Long afterwards the news came that all the donkeys were dead. I know nothing as to the fate of the less valuable animals. They, no doubt, like the rest of us, found what they deserved. I did not inquire. I was then rather excited at the prospect of meeting Kurtz very soon. When I say very soon I mean it comparatively. It was just two months from the day we left the creek when we came to the bank below Kurtz's station.

"Going up that river was like travelling back to the earliest beginnings of the world, when vegetation rioted on the earth and the big trees were kings. An empty stream, a great silence, an impenetrable forest. The air was warm, thick, heavy, sluggish. There was no joy in the brilliance of sunshine. The long stretches of the waterway ran on, deserted, into the gloom of over-shadowed distances. On silvery sandbanks hippos and alligators sunned themselves side by side. The broadening waters flowed through a mob of wooded islands; you lost your way on that river as you would in a desert, and butted all day long against shoals, trying to find the channel, till you thought yourself bewitched and cut off for ever from everything you had known once—somewhere—far away—in another existence perhaps. There were moments when one's past came back to one, as it will sometimes when you have not a moment to spare to yourself; but it came in the shape of an unrestful and noisy dream, remembered with wonder amongst the overwhelming realities of this strange world of plants, and water, and silence. And this stillness of life did not in the least resemble a peace. It was the stillness of an implacable force brooding over an inscrutable intention. It looked at you with a vengeful aspect. I got used to it afterwards; I did not see it any more; I had no time. I had to keep guessing at the channel; I had to discern, mostly by inspiration, the signs of hidden banks; I watched for sunken stones; I was learning to clap my teeth smartly before my heart flew out, when I shaved by a fluke some infernal sly old snag that would have ripped the life out of the tin-pot steamboat and drowned all the pilgrims; I had to keep a look-out for the signs of dead wood we could cut up in the night for next day's steam-ing. When you have to attend to things of that sort, to the mere incidents of the surface, the reality—the reality, I tell you—fades. The inner truth is hidden—luckily, luckily. But I felt it all the same; I felt often its mysterious stillness watching me at my monkey tricks, just as it watches you fellows performing on your respective tight-ropes for—what is it? half-a-crown a tumble——"

"Try to be civil, Marlow," growled a voice, and I knew there was at least one listener awake besides myself.

"I beg your pardon. I forgot the heartache which makes up the rest of the price. And indeed what does the price matter, if the trick be well done? You do your tricks very well. And I didn't do badly either, since I managed not to sink that steamboat on my first trip. It's a wonder to me yet. Imagine a blindfolded man set to drive a van over a bad road. I sweated and shivered over that business considerably, I can tell you. After all, for a seaman, to scrape the bottom of the thing that's supposed to float all the time under his care is the unpardonable sin. No one may know of it, but you never forget the thump—eh? A blow on the very heart. You remember it, you dream of it, you wake up at night and think of it—years after—and go hot and cold all over. I don't pretend to say that steamboat floated all the time. More than once she had to wade for a bit, with twenty cannibals splashing around and pushing. We had enlisted some of these chaps on the way for a crew. Fine fellows—cannibals—in their place. They were men one could work with, and I am grateful to them. And, after all, they did not eat each other before my face: they had brought along a provision of hippo-meat which went rotten, and made the mystery of the wilderness stink in my nostrils. Phoo! I can sniff it now. I had the manager on board and three or four pilgrims with their staves—all complete. Sometimes we came upon a station close by the bank, clinging to the skirts of the unknown, and the white men rushing out of a tumble-down hovel, with great gestures of joy and surprise and welcome, seemed very strange—had the appearance of being held there captive by a spell. The word ivory would ring in the air for a while—and on we went again into the silence, along empty reaches, round the still bends, between the high walls of our winding way, reverberating in hollow claps the ponderous beat of the stern-wheel. Trees, trees, millions of trees, massive, immense, running up high; and at their foot, hugging the bank against the stream, crept the little begrimed steamboat, like a sluggish beetle crawling on the floor of a lofty portico. It made you feel very small, very lost, and yet it was not altogether depressing, that feeling. After all, if you were small, the grimy beetle crawled on—which was just what you wanted it to do. Where the pilgrims imagined it crawled to I don't know. To some place where they expected to get something, I bet! For me it crawled towards Kurtz—exclusively; but when the steam-pipes started leaking we crawled very slow. The reaches opened before us and closed behind, as if the forest had stepped leisurely across the water to bar the way for our return. We penetrated deeper and deeper into the heart of darkness. It was very quiet there. At night sometimes the roll of drums behind the curtain of trees would run up the river and remain sustained faintly, as if hovering in the air high over our heads, till the first break of day. Whether it meant war, peace, or prayer we could not tell. The dawns were heralded by the descent· of a chill stillness; the wood-cutters slept, their fires burned low; the snapping of a twig would make you start. We were wanderers on prehistoric earth, on an earth that wore the aspect of an unknown planet. We could have fancied ourselves the first of men taking possession of an accursed inheritance, to be subdued at the cost of profound anguish and of excessive toil. But

suddenly, as we struggled round a bend, there would be
a glimpse of rush walls, of peaked grass-roofs, a burst
of yells, a whirl of black limbs, a mass of hands clapping,
of feet stamping, of bodies swaying, of eyes rolling, under
the droop of heavy and motionless foliage. The steamer
toiled along slowly on the edge of a black and incomprehensible frenzy. The prehistoric man was cursing us,
praying to us, welcoming us—who could tell? We were
cut off from the comprehension of our surroundings; we
glided past like phantoms, wondering and secretly
appalled, as sane men would be before an enthusiastic
outbreak in a madhouse. We could not understand because we were too far and could not remember, because
we were travelling in the night of first ages, of those ages
that are gone, leaving hardly a sign—and no memories.

"The earth seemed unearthly. We are accustomed to
look upon the shackled form of a conquered monster, but
there—there you could look at a thing monstrous and
free. It was unearthly, and the men were—— No,
they were not inhuman. Well, you know, that was the
worst of it—this suspicion of their not being inhuman.
It would come slowly to one. They howled and leaped,
and spun, and made horrid faces; but what thrilled you
was just the thought of their humanity—like yours—the
thought of your remote kinship with this wild and
passionate uproar. Ugly. Yes, it was ugly enough;
but if you were man enough you would admit to yourself that there was in you just the faintest trace of a response to the terrible frankness of that noise, a dim suspicion of there being a meaning in it which you—you so
remote from the night of first ages—could comprehend.
And why not? The mind of man is capable of anything
—because everything is in it, all the past as well as all
the future. What was there after all? Joy, fear,
sorrow, devotion, valour, rage—who can tell?—but truth

—truth stripped of its cloak of time. Let the fool gape and shudder—the man knows, and can look on without a wink. But he must at least be as much of a man as these on the shore. He must meet that truth with his own true stuff—with his own inborn strength. Principles won't do. Acquisitions, clothes, pretty rags—rags that would fly off at the first good shake. No; you want a deliberate belief. An appeal to me in this fiendish row—is there? Very well; I hear; I admit, but I have a voice, too, and for good or evil mine is the speech that cannot be silenced. Of course, a fool, what with sheer fright and fine sentiments, is always safe. Who's that grunting? You wonder I didn't go ashore for a howl and a dance? Well, no—I didn't. Fine sentiments, you say? Fine sentiments, be hanged! I had no time. I had to mess about with white-lead and strips of woollen blanket helping to put bandages on those leaky steam-pipes—I tell you. I had to watch the steering, and circumvent those snags, and get the tin-pot along by hook or by crook. There was surface-truth enough in these things to save a wiser man. And between whiles I had to look after the savage who was fireman. He was an improved specimen; he could fire up a vertical boiler. He was there below me, and, upon my word, to look at him was as edifying as seeing a dog in a parody of breeches and a feather hat, walking on his hind-legs. A few months of training had done for that really fine chap. He squinted at the steam-gauge and at the water-gauge with an evident effort of intrepidity—and he had filed teeth, too, the poor devil, and the wool of his pate shaved into queer patterns, and three ornamental scars on each of his cheeks. He ought to have been clapping his hands and stamping his feet on the bank, instead of which he was hard at work, a thrall to strange witchcraft, full of improving knowledge. He was useful because he had been instructed; and what he knew was this—that should the water in that transparent thing disappear, the evil spirit inside the boiler would get angry through the greatness of his thirst, and take a terrible vengeance. So he sweated and fired up and watched the glass fearfully (with an impromptu charm, made of rags, tied to his arm, and a piece of polished bone, as big as a watch, stuck flatways through his lower lip), while the wooded banks slipped past us slowly, the short noise was left behind, the interminable miles of silence—and we crept on, towards Kurtz. But the snags were thick, the water was treacherous and shallow, the boiler seemed indeed to have a sulky devil in it, and thus neither that fireman nor I had any time to peer into our creepy thoughts.

"Some fifty miles below the Inner Station we came upon a hut of reeds, an inclined and melancholy pole, with the unrecognizable tatters of what had been a flag of some sort flying from it, and a neatly stacked wood-pile. This was unexpected. We came to the bank, and on the stack of firewood found a flat piece of board with some faded pencil-writing on it. When deciphered it said: 'Wood for you. Hurry up. Approach cautiously.' There was a signature, but it was illegible—not Kurtz— a much longer word. Hurry up. Where? Up the river? 'Approach cautiously.' We had not done so. But the warning could not have been meant for the place where it could be only found after approach. Something was wrong above. But what—and how much? That was the question. We commented adversely upon the imbecility of that telegraphic style. The bush around said nothing, and would not let us look very far, either. A torn curtain of red twill hung in the doorway of the hut, and flapped sadly in our faces. The dwelling was dismantled; but we could see a white man had lived there not very long ago. There remained a rude table—a plank on two posts; a heap of rubbish reposed in a dark corner, and by the door I picked up a book. It had lost its covers, and the pages had been thumbed into a state of extremely dirty softness; but the back had been lovingly stitched afresh with white cotton thread, which looked clean yet. It was an extraordinary find. Its title was, *An Inquiry into some Points of Seamanship*, by a man Tower, Towson—some such name—Master in his Majesty's Navy. The matter looked dreary reading enough, with illustrative diagrams and repulsive tables of figures, and the copy was sixty years·old. I handled this amazing antiquity with the greatest possible tenderness, lest it should dissolve in my hands. Within, Towson or Towser was inquiring earnestly into the breaking strain of ships' chains and tackle, and other such matters. Not a very enthralling book; but at the first glance you could see there a singleness of intention, an honest concern for the right way of going to work, which made these humble pages, thought out so many years ago, luminous with another than a professional light. The simple old sailor, with his talk of chains and purchases, made me forget the jungle and the pilgrims in a delicious sensation of having come upon something unmistakably real. Such a book being there was wonderful enough; but still more astounding were the notes pencilled in the margin, and plainly referring to the text. I couldn't believe my eyes! They were in cipher! Yes, it looked like cipher. Fancy a man lugging with him a book of that description into this nowhere and studying it—and making notes—in cipher at that! It was an extravagant mystery.

"I had been dimly aware for some time of a worrying noise, and when I lifted my eyes I saw the wood-pile was gone, and the manager, aided by all the pilgrims, was shouting at me from the river-side. I slipped the book into my pocket. I assure you to leave off reading was

like tearing myself away from the shelter of an old and
solid friendship.

"I started the lame engine ahead. 'It must be this
miserable trader—this intruder,' exclaimed the manager,
looking back malevolently at the place we had left. 'He
must be English,' I said. 'It will not save him from
getting into trouble if he is not careful,' muttered the
manager darkly. I observed with assumed innocence
that no man was safe from trouble in this world.

"The current was more rapid now, the steamer seemed
at her last gasp, the stern-wheel flopped languidly, and I
caught myself listening on tiptoe for the next beat of
the float,* for in sober truth I expected the wretched
thing to give up every moment. It was like watching the
last flickers of a life. But still we crawled. Sometimes I
would pick out a tree a little way ahead to measure our
progress towards Kurtz by, but I lost it invariably before
we got abreast. To keep the eyes so long on one thing
was too much for human patience. The manager displayed a beautiful resignation. I fretted and fumed and
took to arguing with myself whether or no I would talk
openly with Kurtz; but before I could come to any con-
clusion it occurred to me that my speech or my silence,
indeed any action of mine, would be a mere futility.
What did it matter what any one knew or ignored?
What did it matter who was manager? One gets sometimes such a flash of insight. The essentials of this
affair lay deep under the surface, beyond my reach, and
beyond my power of meddling.

"Towards the evening of the second day we judged
ourselves about eight miles from Kurtz's station. I
wanted to push on; but the manager looked grave, and
told me the navigation up there was so dangerous that it
would be advisable, the sun being very low already, to
wait where we were till next morning. Moreover, he

pointed out that if the warning to approach cautiously were to be followed, we must approach in daylight—not at dusk, or in the dark. This was sensible enough. Eight miles meant nearly three hours' steaming for us, and I could also see suspicious ripples at the upper end of the reach. Nevertheless, I was annoyed beyond expression at the delay, and most unreasonably, too, since one night more could not matter much after so many months. As we had plenty of wood, and caution was the word, I brought up in the middle of the stream. The reach was narrow, straight, with high sides like a railway cutting. The dusk came gliding into it long before the sun had set. The current ran smooth and swift, but a dumb immobility sat on the banks. The living trees, lashed together by the creepers and every living bush of the undergrowth, might have been changed into stone, even to the slenderest twig, to the lightest leaf. It was not sleep—it seemed unnatural, like a state of trance. Not the faintest sound of any kind could be heard. You looked on amazed, and began to suspect yourself of being deaf—then the night came suddenly, and struck you blind as well. About three in the morning some large fish leaped, and the loud splash made me jump as though a gun had been fired. When the sun rose there was a white fog, very warm and clammy, and more blinding than the night. It did not shift or drive; it was just there, standing all round you like something solid. At eight or nine, perhaps, it lifted as a shutter lifts. We had a glimpse of the towering multitude of trees, of the immense matted jungle, with the blazing little ball of the sun hanging over it—all perfectly still—and then the white shutter came down again, smoothly, as if sliding in greased grooves. I ordered the chain, which we had begun to heave in, to be paid out again. Before it stopped running with a muffled rattle, a cry, a very loud cry, as of infinite desolation, soared slowly in the opaque air. It ceased. A complaining clamour, modulated in savage discords, filled our ears. The sheer unexpectedness of it made my hair stir under my cap. I don't know how it struck the others: to me it seemed as though the mist itself had screamed, so suddenly, and apparently from all sides at once, did this tumultuous and mournful uproar arise. It culminated in a hurried outbreak of almost intolerably excessive shrieking, which stopped short, leaving us stiffened in a variety of silly attitudes, and obstinately listening to the nearly as appalling and excessive silence. 'Good God! What is the meaning——' stammered at my elbow one of the pilgrims,—a little fat man, with sandy hair and red whiskers, who wore sidespring boots, and pink pyjamas tucked into his socks. Two others remained open-mouthed a whole minute, then dashed into the little cabin, to rush out incontinently and stand darting scared glances, with Winchesters at 'ready' in their hands. What we could see was just the steamer we were on, her outlines blurred as though she had been on the point of dissolving, and a misty strip of water, perhaps two feet broad, around her—and that was all. The rest of the world was nowhere, as far as our eyes and ears were concerned. Just nowhere. Gone, disappeared; swept off without leaving a whisper or a shadow behind.

"I went forward, and ordered the chain to be hauled in short, so as to be ready to trip the anchor and move the steamboat at once if necessary. 'Will they attack?' whispered an awed voice. 'We will be all butchered in this fog,' murmured another. The faces twitched with the strain, the hands trembled slightly, the eyes forgot to wink. It was very curious to see the contrast of expressions of the white men and of the black fellows of our crew, who were as much strangers to that part of the river as we, though their homes were only eight hundred miles away. The whites, of course greatly discomposed, had besides a curious look of being painfully shocked by such an outrageous row. The others had an alert, naturally interested expression; but their faces were essentially quiet, even those of the one or two who grinned as they hauled at the chain. Several exchanged short, grunting phrases, which seemed to settle the matter to their satisfaction. Their headman, a young, broad-chested black, severely draped in dark-blue fringed cloths, with fierce nostrils and his hair all done up artfully in oily ringlets, stood near me. 'Aha!' I said, just for good fellowship's sake. 'Catch 'im,' he snapped, with a bloodshot widening of his eyes and a flash of sharp teeth—'catch 'im. Give 'im to us.' 'To you, eh?' I asked; 'what would you do with them?' 'Eat 'im!' he said, curtly, and, leaning his elbow on the rail, looked out into the fog in a dignified and profoundly pensive attitude. I would no doubt have been properly horrified, had it not occurred to me that he and his chaps must be very hungry: that they must have been growing increasingly hungry for at least this month past. They had been engaged for six months (I don't think a single one of them had any clear idea of time, as we at the end of countless ages have. They still belonged to the beginnings of time—had no inherited experience to teach them as it were), and of course, as long as there was a piece of paper written over in accordance with some farcical law or other made down the river, it didn't enter anybody's head to trouble how they would live. Certainly they had brought with them some rotten hippo-meat, which couldn't have lasted very long, anyway, even if the pilgrims hadn't, in the midst of a shocking hullabaloo, thrown a considerable quantity of it overboard. It looked like a high-handed proceeding; but it was really a case of legitimate self-defence. You

can't breathe dead hippo waking, sleeping, and eating,
and at the same time keep your precarious grip on existence. Besides that, they had given them every week
three pieces of brass wire, each about nine inches long;
and the theory was they were to buy their provisions
with that currency in river-side villages. You can see
how *that* worked. There were either no villages, or the
people were hostile, or the director, who like the rest of us
fed out of tins, with an occasional old he-goat thrown in,
didn't want to stop the steamer for some more or less
recondite reason. So, unless they swallowed the wire
itself, or made loops of it to snare the fishes with, I don't
see what good their extravagant salary could be to them.
I must say it was paid with a regularity worthy of a
large and honourable trading company. For the rest,
the only thing to eat—though it didn't look eatable in
the least—I saw in their possession was a few lumps of
some stuff like half-cooked dough, of a dirty lavender
colour, they kept wrapped in leaves, and now and then
swallowed a piece of, but so small that it seemed done
more for the looks of the thing than for any serious purpose of sustenance. Why in the name of all the gnawing
devils of hunger they didn't go for us—they were thirty
to five—and have a good tuck in for once, amazes me
now when I think of it. They were big powerful men,
with not much capacity to weigh the consequences, with
courage, with strength, even yet, though their skins
were no longer glossy and their muscles no longer hard.
And I saw that something restraining, one of those human secrets that baffle probability, had come into play
there. I looked at them with a swift quickening of
interest—not because it occurred to me I might be
eaten by them before very long, though I own to you
that just then I perceived—in a new light, as it were—
how unwholesome the pilgrims looked, and I hoped, yes,

I positively hoped, that my aspect was not so—what shall I say?—so—unappetizing: a touch of fantastic vanity which fitted well with the dream-sensation that pervaded all my days at that time. Perhaps I had a little fever, too. One can't live with one's finger everlastingly on one's pulse. I had often 'a little fever,' or a little touch of other things—the playful paw-strokes of the wilderness, the preliminary trifling before the more serious onslaught which came in due course. Yes; I looked at them as you would on any human being, with a curiosity of their impulses, motives, capacities, weaknesses, when brought to the test of an inexorable physical necessity. Restraint! What possible restraint? Was it superstition, disgust, patience, fear—or some kind of primitive honour? No fear can stand up to hunger, no patience can wear it out, disgust simply does not exist where hunger is; and as to superstition, beliefs, and what you may call principles, they are less than chaff in a breeze. Don't you know the devilry of lingering starvation, its exasperating torment, its black thoughts, its sombre and brooding ferocity? Well, I do. It takes a man all his inborn strength to fight hunger properly. It's really easier to face bereavement, dishonour, and the perdition of one's soul—than this kind of prolonged hunger. Sad, but true. And these chaps, too, had no earthly reason for any kind of scruple. Restraint! I would just as soon have expected restraint from a hyena prowling amongst the corpses of a battlefield. But there was the fact facing me—the fact dazzling, to be seen, like the foam on the depths of the sea, like a ripple on an unfathomable enigma, a mystery greater—when I thought of it—than the curious, inexplicable note of desperate grief in this savage clamour that had swept by us on the river-bank, behind the blind whiteness of the fog.

"Two pilgrims were quarrelling in hurried whispers as to which bank. 'Left.' 'No, no; how can you? Right, right, of course.' 'It is very serious,' said the manager's voice behind me; 'I would be desolated if anything should happen to Mr. Kurtz before we came up.' I looked at him, and had not the slightest doubt he was sincere. He was just the kind of man who would wish to preserve appearances. That was his restraint. But when he muttered something about going on at once, I did not even take the trouble to answer him. I knew, and he knew, that it was impossible. Were we to let go our hold of the bottom, we would be absolutely in the air—in space. We wouldn't be able to tell where we were going to—whether up or down stream, or across—till we fetched against one bank or the other,—and then we wouldn't know at first which it was. Of course I made no move. I had no mind for a smash-up. You couldn't imagine a more deadly place for a shipwreck. Whether drowned at once or not, we were sure to perish speedily in one way or another. 'I authorize you to take all the risks,' he said, after a short silence. 'I refuse to take any,' I said, shortly; which was just the answer he expected, though its tone might have surprised him. 'Well, I must defer to your judgment. You are captain,' he said, with marked civility. I turned my shoulder to him in sign of my appreciation, and looked into the fog. How long would it last? It was the most hopeless look-out. The approach to this Kurtz grubbing for ivory in the wretched bush was beset by as many dangers as though he had been an enchanted princess sleeping in a fabulous castle. 'Will they attack, do you think?' asked the manager, in a confidential tone.

"I did not think they would attack, for several obvious reasons. The thick fog was one. If they left the bank in their canoes they would get lost in it, as we would

be if we attempted to move.   Still, I had also judged the
jungle of both banks quite impenetrable—and yet eyes
were in it, eyes that had seen us.   The river-side bushes
were certainly very thick; but the undergrowth behind
was evidently penetrable.   However, during the short
lift I had seen no canoes anywhere in the reach—
certainly not abreast of the steamer.   But what made
the idea of attack inconceivable to me was the nature of
the noise—of the cries we had heard.   They had not the
fierce character boding of immediate hostile intention.
Unexpected, wild, and violent as they had been, they
had given me an irresistible impression of sorrow.   The
glimpse of the steamboat had for some reason filled those
savages with unrestrained grief.   The danger, if any,
I expounded, was from our proximity to a great human
passion let loose.   Even extreme grief may ultimately
vent itself in violence—but more generally takes the
form of apathy. . . .

"You should have seen the pilgrims stare!   They had
no heart to grin, or even to revile me: but I believe they
thought me gone mad—with fright, maybe.   I delivered
a regular lecture.   My dear boys, it was no good bother-
ing.   Keep a look-out?   Well, you may guess I watched
the fog for the signs of lifting as a cat watches a mouse;
but for anything else our eyes were of no more use to us
than if we had been buried miles deep in a heap of
cotton-wool.   It felt like it, too—choking, warm, stifling.
Besides, all I said, though it sounded extravagant, was
absolutely true to fact.   What we afterwards alluded to
as an attack was really an attempt at repulse.   The
action was very far from being aggressive—it was not
even defensive, in the usual sense: it was undertaken
under the stress of desperation, and in its essence was
purely protective.

"It developed itself, I should say, two hours after

the fog lifted, and its commencement was at a spot, roughly speaking, about a mile and a half below Kurtz's station. We had just floundered and flopped round a bend, when I saw an islet, a mere grassy hummock of bright green, in the middle of the stream. It was the only thing of the kind; but as we opened the reach more, I perceived it was the head of a long sandbank, or rather of a chain of shallow patches stretching down the middle of the river. They were discoloured, just awash, and the whole lot was seen just under the water, exactly as a man's backbone is seen running down the middle of his back under the skin. Now, as far as I did see, I could go to the right or to the left of this. I didn't know either channel, of course. The banks looked pretty well alike, the depth appeared the same; but as I had been informed the station was on the west side, I naturally headed for the western passage.

"No sooner had we fairly entered it than I became aware it was much narrower than I had supposed. To the left of us there was the long uninterrupted shoal, and to the right a high, steep bank heavily overgrown with bushes. Above the bush the trees stood in serried* ranks. The twigs overhung the current thickly, and from distance to distance a large limb of some tree projected rigidly over the stream. It was then well on in the afternoon, the face of the forest was gloomy, and a broad strip of shadow had already fallen on the water. In this shadow we steamed up—very slowly, as you may imagine. I sheered her well inshore—the water being deepest near the bank, as the sounding-pole informed me.

"One of my hungry and forbearing friends was sounding in the bows just below me. This steamboat was exactly like a decked scow. On the deck, there were two little teak-wood houses, with doors and windows. The boiler was in the fore-end, and the machinery right

astern. Over the whole there was a light roof, supported on stanchions. The funnel projected through
that roof, and in front of the funnel a small cabin built
of light planks served for a pilot-house. It contained a
couch, two camp-stools, a loaded Martini-Henry*leaning
in one corner, a tiny table, and the steering-wheel. It
had a wide door in front and a broad shutter at each
side. All these were always thrown open, of course. I
spent my days perched up there on the extreme fore-
end of that roof, before the door. At night I slept, or
tried to, on the couch. An athletic black belonging to
some coast tribe, and educated by my poor predecessor,
was the helmsman. He sported a pair of brass earrings,
wore a blue cloth wrapper from the waist to the ankles,
and thought all the world of himself. He was the most
unstable kind of fool I had ever seen. He steered with
no end of a swagger while you were by; but if he lost
sight of you, he became instantly the prey of an abject funk, and would let that cripple of a steamboat get
the upper hand of him in a minute.

"I was looking down at the sounding-pole, and feeling
much annoyed to see at each try a little more of it stick
out of that river, when I saw my poleman give up the
business suddenly, and stretch himself flat on the deck,
without even taking the trouble to haul his pole in. He
kept hold on it though, and it trailed in the water. At
the same time the fireman, whom I could also see below
me, sat down abruptly before his furnace and ducked his
head. I was amazed. Then I had to look at the river
mighty quick, because there was a snag in the fairway.
Sticks, little sticks, were flying about—thick: they were
whizzing before my nose, dropping below me, striking
behind me against my pilot-house. All this time the
river, the shore, the woods, were very quiet—perfectly
quiet. I could only hear the heavy splashing thump of

the stern-wheel and the patter of these things. We cleared the snag clumsily. Arrows, by Jove! We were being shot at! I stepped in quickly to close the shutter on the land-side. That fool-helmsman, his hands on the spokes, was lifting his knees high, stamping his feet, champing his mouth, like a reined-in horse. Confound him! And we were staggering within ten feet of the bank. I had to lean right out to swing the heavy shutter, and I saw a face amongst the leaves on the level with my own, looking at me very fierce and steady; and then suddenly, as though a veil had been removed from my eyes, I made out, deep in the tangled gloom, naked breasts, arms, legs, glaring eyes,—the bush was swarming with human limbs in movement, glistening, of bronze colour. The twigs shook, swayed, and rustled, the arrows flew out of them, and then the shutter came to. 'Steer her straight,' I said to the helmsman. He held his head rigid, face forward; but his eyes rolled, he kept on, lifting and setting down his feet gently, his mouth foamed a little. 'Keep quiet!' I said in a fury. I might just as well have ordered a tree not to sway in the wind. I darted out. Below me there was a great scuffle of feet on the iron deck; confused exclamations; a voice screamed, 'Can you turn back?' I caught sight of a V-shaped ripple on the water ahead. What? Another snag! A fusillade burst out under my feet. The pilgrims had opened with their Winchesters, and were simply squirting lead into that bush. A deuce of a lot of smoke came up and drove slowly forward. I swore at it. Now I couldn't see the ripple or the snag either. I stood in the doorway, peering, and the arrows came in swarms. They might have been poisoned, but they looked as though they wouldn't kill a cat. The bush began to howl. Our wood-cutters raised a warlike whoop; the report of a rifle just at my back deafened me. I glanced over my shoulder, and the pilot-house was yet full of noise and smoke when I made a dash at the wheel. The fool-nigger had dropped everything, to throw the shutter open and let off that Martini-Henry. He stood before the wide opening, glaring, and I yelled at him to come back, while I straightened the sudden twist out of that steamboat. There was no room to turn even if I had wanted to, the snag was somewhere very near ahead in that confounded smoke, there was no time to lose, so I just crowded her into the bank—right into the bank, where I knew the water was deep.

"We tore slowly along the overhanging bushes in a whirl of broken twigs and flying leaves. The fusillade below stopped short, as I had foreseen it would when the squirts got empty. I threw my head back to a glinting whizz that traversed the pilot-house, in at one shutter-hole and out at the other. Looking past that mad helmsman, who was shaking the empty rifle and yelling at the shore, I saw vague forms of men running bent double, leaping, gliding, distinct, incomplete, evanes-cent. Something big appeared in the air before the shutter, the rifle went overboard, and the man stepped back swiftly, looked at me over his shoulder in an extraor-dinary, profound, familiar manner, and fell upon my feet. The side of his head hit the wheel twice, and the end of what appeared a long cane clattered round and knocked over a little camp-stool. It looked as though after wrenching that thing from somebody ashore he had lost his balance in the effort. The thin smoke had blown away, we were clear of the snag, and looking ahead I could see that in another hundred yards or so I would be free to sheer off, away from the bank; but my feet felt so very warm and wet that I had to look down. The man had rolled on his back and stared straight up at

me; both his hands clutched that cane.   It was the shaft
of a spear that, either thrown or lunged through the opening, had caught him in the side just below the ribs; the
blade had gone in out of sight, after making a frightful
gash; my shoes were full; a pool of blood lay very still,
gleaming dark-red under the wheel; his eyes shone with
an amazing lustre.   The fusillade burst out again. , He
looked at me anxiously, gripping the spear like something precious, with an air of being afraid I would try to
take it away from him.   I had to make an effort to free
my eyes from his gaze and attend to the steering.   With
one hand I felt above my head for the line of the steam
whistle, and jerked out screech after screech hurriedly.
The tumult of angry and warlike yells was checked
instantly, and then from the depths of the woods went
out such a tremulous and prolonged wail of mournful
fear and utter despair as may be imagined to follow the
flight of the last hope from the earth.   There was a
great commotion in the bush; the shower of arrows
stopped, a few dropping shots rang out sharply—then
silence, in which the languid beat of the stern-wheel
came plainly to my ears.   I put the helm hard a-star-
board at the moment when the pilgrim in pink pyjamas,
very hot and agitated, appeared in the doorway.   'The
manager sends me——' he began in an official tone, and
stopped short.   'Good God!' he said, glaring at the
wounded man.

"We two whites stood over him, and his lustrous and
inquiring glance enveloped us both. , I declare it looked
as though he would presently put to us some question in
an understandable language; but he died without utter-
ing a sound, without moving a limb, without twitching
a muscle.   Only in the very last moment, as though in
response to some sign we could not see, to some whisper
we could not hear, he frowned heavily, and that frown

gave to his black death-mask an inconceivably sombre, brooding, and menacing expression. The lustre of inquiring glance faded swiftly into vacant glassiness. 'Can you steer?' I asked the agent eagerly. He looked very dubious; but I made a grab at his arm, and he understood at once I meant him to steer whether or no. To tell you the truth, I was morbidly anxious to change my shoes and socks. 'He is dead,' murmured the fellow, immensely impressed. 'No doubt about it,' said I, tugging like mad at the shoe-laces. 'And by the way, I suppose Mr. Kurtz is dead as well by this time.'

"For the moment that was the dominant thought. There was a sense of extreme disappointment, as though I had found out I had been striving after something altogether without a substance. I couldn't have been more disgusted if I had travelled all this way for the sole purpose of talking with Mr. Kurtz. Talking with. . . . I flung one shoe overboard, and became aware that that was exactly what I had been looking forward to—a talk with Kurtz. I made the strange discovery that I had never imagined him as doing, you know, but as discoursing. I didn't say to myself, 'Now I will never see him,' or 'Now I will never shake him by the hand,' but, 'now I will never hear him.' The man presented himself as a voice. Not of course that I did not connect him with some sort of action. Hadn't I been told in all the tones of jealousy and admiration that he had collected, bartered, swindled, or stolen more ivory than all the other agents together? That was not the point. The point was in his being a gifted creature, and that of all his gifts the one that stood out preëminently, that carried with it a sense of real presence, was his ability to talk, his words— the gift of expression, the bewildering, the illuminating, the most exalted and the most contemptible, the pulsat-

ing stream of light, or the deceitful flow from the heart
of an impenetrable darkness.

"The other shoe went flying unto the devil-god of
that river. I thought, By Jove! it's all over. We are
too late; he has vanished—the gift has vanished, by
means of some spear, arrow, or club. I will never hear
that chap speak after all,—and my sorrow had a startling extravagance of emotion, even such as I had noticed
in the howling sorrow of these savages in the bush. I
couldn't have felt more of lonely desolation somehow,
had I been robbed of a belief or had missed my destiny
in life. . . . Why do you sigh in this beastly way,
somebody? Absurd? Well, absurd. Good Lord!
mustn't a man ever—— Here, give me some tobacco." . . .

There was a pause of profound stillness, then a match
flared, and Marlow's lean face appeared, worn, hollow,
with downward folds and dropped eyelids, with an
aspect of concentrated attention; and as he took vigorous draws at his pipe, it seemed to retreat and advance
out of the night in the regular flicker of the tiny flame.
The match went out.

"Absurd!" he cried. "This is the worst of trying to
tell. . . . Here you all are, each moored with two
good addresses, like a hulk with two anchors, a butcher
round one corner, a policeman round another, excellent appetites, and temperature normal—you hear—
normal from year's end to year's end. And you say,
Absurd! Absurd be—exploded! Absurd! My dear
boys, what can you expect from a man who out of sheer
nervousness had just flung overboard a pair of new
shoes! Now I think of it, it is amazing I did not shed
tears. I am, upon the whole, proud of my fortitude. I
was cut to the quick at the idea of having lost the in-
estimable privilege of listening to the gifted Kurtz.

Of course I was wrong. The privilege was waiting for me. Oh, yes, I heard more than enough. And I was right, too. A voice. He was very little more than a voice. And I heard—him—it—this voice—other voices—all of them were so little more than voices—and the memory of that time itself lingers around me, impalpable, like a dying vibration of one immense jabber, silly, atrocious, sordid, savage, or simply mean, without any kind of sense. Voices, voices—even the girl herself—now——"

He was silent for a long time.

"I laid the ghost of his gifts at last with a lie," he began, suddenly. "Girl! What? Did I mention a girl? Oh, she is out of it—completely. They—the women I mean—are out of it—should be out of it. We must help them to stay in that beautiful world of their own, lest ours gets worse. Oh, she had to be out of it. You should have heard the disinterred body of Mr. Kurtz saying, 'My Intended.' You would have perceived directly then how completely she was out of it. And the lofty frontal bone of Mr. Kurtz! They say the hair goes on growing sometimes, but this—ah—specimen, was impressively bald. The wilderness had patted him on the head, and, behold, it was like a ball—an ivory ball; it had caressed him, and—lo!—he had withered; it had taken him, loved him, embraced him, got into his veins, consumed his flesh, and sealed his soul to its own by the inconceivable ceremonies of some devilish initiation. He was its spoiled and pampered favourite. Ivory? I should think so. Heaps of it, stacks of it. The old mud shanty was bursting with it. You would think there was not a single tusk left either above or below the ground in the whole country. 'Mostly fossil,' the manager had remarked, disparagingly. It was no more fossil than I am; but they call it fossil when it is dug up. It appears these niggers do bury the tusks sometimes—but evidently they couldn't bury this parcel deep enough to save the gifted Mr. Kurtz from his fate. We filled the steamboat with it, and had to pile a lot on the deck. Thus he could see and enjoy as long as he could see, because the appreciation of this favour had remained with him to the last. You should have heard him say, 'My ivory.' Oh yes, I heard him. 'My Intended, my ivory, my station, my river, my——' everything belonged to him. It made me hold my breath in expectation of hearing the wilderness burst into a prodigious peal of laughter that would shake the fixed stars in their places. Everything belonged to him—but that was a trifle. The thing was to know what he belonged to, how many powers of darkness claimed him for their own. That was the reflection that made you creepy all over. It was impossible—it was not good for one either—trying to imagine. He had taken a high seat amongst the devils of the land—I mean literally. You can't understand. How could you?—with solid pavement under your feet, surrounded by kind neighbours ready to cheer you or to fall on you, stepping delicately between the butcher and the policeman, in the holy terror of scandal and gallows and lunatic asylums—how can you imagine what particular region of the first ages a man's untrammelled feet may take him into by the way of solitude—utter solitude without a policeman—by the way of silence—utter silence, where no warning voice of a kind neighbour can be heard whispering of public opinion? These little things make all the great difference. When they are gone you must fall back upon your own innate strength, upon your own capacity for faithfulness. Of course you may be too much of a fool to go wrong—too dull even to know you are being assaulted by the powers of

darkness. I take it, no fool ever made a bargain for his
soul with the devil: the fool is too much of a fool, or the
devil too much of a devil—I don't know which. Or you
may be such a thunderingly exalted creature as to be
altogether deaf and blind to anything but heavenly
sights and sounds. Then the earth for you is only a
standing place—and whether to be like this is your loss
or your gain I won't pretend to say. But most of us
are neither one nor the other. The earth for us is a
place to live in, where we must put up with sights, with
sounds, with smells, too, by Jove!—breathe dead hippo,
so to speak, and not be contaminated. And there, don't
you see? your strength comes in, the faith in your
ability for the digging of unostentatious holes to bury
the stuff in—your power of devotion, not to yourself,
but to an obscure, back-breaking business. And that's
difficult enough. Mind, I am not trying to excuse or
even explain—I am trying to account to myself for—
for—Mr. Kurtz—for the shade of Mr. Kurtz. This
initiated wraith from the back of Nowhere honoured me
with its amazing confidence before it vanished altogether. This was because it could speak English to
me. The original Kurtz had been educated partly in
England, and—as he was good enough to say himself—
his sympathies were in the right place. His mother was
half-English, his father was half-French. All Europe
contributed to the making of Kurtz; and by-and-by I
learned that, most appropriately, the International
Society for the Suppression of Savage Customs had
intrusted him with the making of a report, for its future
guidance. And he had written it, too. I've seen it.
I've read it. It was eloquent, vibrating with eloquence,
but too high-strung, I think. Seventeen pages of close
writing he had found time for! But this must have
been before his—let us say—nerves, went wrong, and

caused him to preside at certain midnight dances ending
with unspeakable rites, which—as far as I reluctantly
gathered from what I heard at various times—were
offered up to him—do you understand?—to Mr. Kurtz
himself. But it was a beautiful piece of writing. The
opening paragraph, however, in the light of later information, strikes me now as ominous. He began with
the argument that we whites, from the point of develop-
ment we had arrived at, 'must necessarily appear to
them [savages] in the nature of supernatural beings—
we approach them with the might as of a deity,' and so
on, and so on. 'By the simple exercise of our will we
can exert a power for good practically unbounded,' etc.
etc. From that point he soared and took me with him.
The peroration was magnificent, though difficult to
remember, you know. It gave me the notion of an
exotic Immensity ruled by an august Benevolence. It
made me tingle with enthusiasm. This was the unbounded power of eloquence—of words—of burning
noble words. There were no practical hints to interrupt
the magic current of phrases, unless a kind of note at the
foot of the last page, scrawled evidently much later, in
an unsteady hand, may be regarded as the exposition of
a method. It was very simple, and at the end of that
moving appeal to every altruistic sentiment it blazed at
you, luminous and terrifying, like a flash of lightning in
a serene sky: 'Exterminate all the brutes!' The curious part was that he had apparently forgotten all about
that valuable postscriptum, because, later on, when he
in a sense came to himself, he repeatedly entreated me
to take good care of 'my pamphlet' (he called it), as it
was sure to have in the future a good influence upon his
career. I had full information about all these things,
and, besides, as it turned out, I was to have the care of
his memory. I've done enough for it to give me the

indisputable right to lay it, if I choose, for an everlasting rest in the dust-bin of progress, amongst all the
sweepings and, figuratively speaking, all the dead cats
of civilization. But then, you see, I can't choose. He
won't be forgotten. Whatever he was, he was not
common. He had the power to charm or frighten rudimentary souls into an aggravated witch-dance in his
honour; he could also fill the small souls of the pilgrims
with bitter misgivings: he had one devoted friend at
least, and he had conquered one soul in the world that
was neither rudimentary nor tainted with self-seeking.
No; I can't forget him, though I am not prepared to
affirm the fellow was exactly worth the life we lost in
getting to him. I missed my late helmsman awfully,—
I missed him even while his body was still lying in the
pilot-house. Perhaps you will think it passing strange
this regret for a savage who was no more account than a
grain of sand in a black Sahara. Well, don't you see,
he had done something, he had steered; for months I had
him at my back—a help—an instrument. It was a kind
of partnership. He steered for me—I had to look after
him, I worried about his deficiencies, and thus a subtle
bond had been created, of which I only became aware
when it was suddenly broken. And the intimate pro-
fundity of that look he gave me when he received his hurt
remains to this day in my memory—like a claim of distant kinship affirmed in a supreme moment.

"Poor fool! If he had only left that shutter alone.
He had no restraint, no restraint—just like Kurtz—a
tree swayed by the wind. As soon as I had put on a
dry pair of slippers, I dragged him out, after first jerking
the spear out of his side, which operation I confess I per-
formed with my eyes shut tight. His heels leaped together over the little door-step; his shoulders were
pressed to my breast; I hugged him from behind

desperately. Oh! he was heavy, heavy; heavier than
any man on earth, I should imagine. Then without
more ado I tipped him overboard. The current
snatched him as though he had been a wisp of grass, and
I saw the body roll over twice before I lost sight of it for
ever. All the pilgrims and the manager were then con-
gregated on the awning-deck about the pilot-house,
chattering at each other like a flock of excited magpies,
and there was a scandalized murmur at my heartless
promptitude. What they wanted to keep that body
hanging about for I can't guess. Embalm it, maybe.
But I had also heard another, and a very ominous, murmur on the deck below. My friends the wood-cutters
were likewise scandalized, and with a better show of
reason—though I admit that the reason itself was quite
inadmissible. Oh, quite! I had made up my mind
that if my late helmsman was to be eaten, the fishes
alone should have him. He had been a very second-
rate helmsman while alive, but now he was dead he
might have become a first-class temptation, and possibly
cause some startling trouble. Besides, I was anxious to
take the wheel, the man in pink pyjamas showing himself a hopeless duffer at the business.

"This I did directly the simple funeral was over.
We were going half-speed, keeping right in the middle
of the stream, and I listened to the talk about me. They
had given up Kurtz, they had given up the station;
Kurtz was dead, and the station had been burnt—and
so on—and so on. The red-haired pilgrim was beside
himself with the thought that at least this poor Kurtz
had been properly avenged. 'Say! We must have
made a glorious slaughter of them in the bush. Eh?
What do you think? Say?' He positively danced,
the bloodthirsty little gingery beggar. And he had
nearly fainted when he saw the wounded man! I could

not help saying, 'You made a glorious lot of smoke, anyhow.' I had seen, from the way the tops of the bushes
rustled and flew, that almost all the shots had gone too
high. You can't hit anything unless you take aim and
fire from the shoulder; but these chaps fired from the hip
with their eyes shut. The retreat, I maintained—and I
was right—was caused by the screeching of the steam-
whistle. Upon this they forgot Kurtz, and began to
howl at me with indignant protests.

"The manager stood by the wheel murmuring con-
fidentially about the necessity of getting well away down
the river before dark at all events, when I saw in the
distance a clearing on the river-side and the outlines of
some sort of building. 'What's this?' I asked. He
clapped his hands in wonder. 'The station!' he cried.
I edged in at once, still going half-speed.

"Through my glasses I saw the slope of a hill inter-
spersed with rare trees and perfectly free from undergrowth. A long decaying building on the summit was
half buried in the high grass; the large holes in the
peaked roof gaped black from afar; the jungle and the
woods made a background. There was no enclosure or
fence of any kind; but there had been one apparently,
for near the house half-a-dozen slim posts remained in a
row, roughly trimmed, and with their upper ends ornamented with round carved balls. The rails, or whatever there had been between, had disappeared. Of
course the forest surrounded all that. The river-bank
was clear, and on the water-side I saw a white man
under a hat like a cart-wheel beckoning persistently
with his whole arm. Examining the edge of the forest
above and below, I was almost certain I could see movements—human forms gliding here and there. I steamed
past prudently, then stopped the engines and let her
drift down. The man on the shore began to shout,

urging us to land. 'We have been attacked,' screamed the manager. 'I know—I know. It's all right,' yelled back the other, as cheerful as you please. 'Come along. It's all right. I am glad.'

"His aspect reminded me of something I had seen—something funny I had seen somewhere. As I manœuvred to get alongside, I was asking myself, 'What does this fellow look like?' Suddenly I got it. He looked like a harlequin. His clothes had been made of some stuff that was brown holland probably, but it was covered with patches all over, with bright patches, blue, red, and yellow,—patches on the back, patches on the front, patches on elbows, on knees; coloured binding around his jacket, scarlet edging at the bottom of his trousers; and the sunshine made him look extremely gay and wonderfully neat withal, because you could see how beautifully all this patching had been done. A beardless, boyish face, very fair, no features to speak of, nose peeling, little blue eyes, smiles and frowns chasing each other over that open countenance like sunshine and shadow on a wind-swept plain. 'Look out, captain!' he cried; 'there's a snag lodged in here last night.' What! Another snag? I confess I swore shamefully. I had nearly holed my cripple, to finish off that charming trip. The harlequin on the bank turned his little pug-nose up to me. 'You English?' he asked, all smiles. 'Are you?' I shouted from the wheel. The smiles vanished, and he shook his head as if sorry for my disappointment. Then he brightened up. 'Never mind!' he cried, encouragingly. 'Are we in time?' I asked. 'He is up there,' he replied, with a toss of the head up the hill, and becoming gloomy all of a sudden. His face was like the autumn sky, overcast one moment and bright the next.

"When the manager, escorted by the pilgrims, all

of them armed to the teeth, had gone to the house this chap came on board. 'I say, I don't like this. These natives are in the bush,' I said. He assured me earnestly it was all right. 'They are simple people,' he added; 'well, I am glad you came. It took me all my time to keep them off.' 'But you said it was all right,' I cried. 'Oh, they meant no harm,' he said; and as I stared he corrected himself, 'Not exactly.' Then vivaciously, 'My faith, your pilot-house wants a clean up!' In the next breath he advised me to keep enough steam on the boiler to blow the whistle in case of any trouble. 'One good screech will do more for you than all your rifles. They are simple people,' he repeated. He rattled away at such a rate he quite overwhelmed me. He seemed to be trying to make up for lots of silence, and actually hinted, laughing, that such was the case. 'Don't you talk with Mr. Kurtz?' I said. 'You don't talk with that man—you listen to him,' he exclaimed with severe exaltation. 'But now——' He waved his arm, and in the twinkling of an eye was in the uttermost depths of despondency. In a moment he came up again with a jump, possessed himself of both my hands, shook them continuously, while he gabbled: 'Brother sailor . . . honour . . . pleasure . . . delight . . . introduce myself . . . Russian . . . son of an arch-priest . . . Government of Tambov . . . What? Tobacco! English tobacco; the excellent English tobacco! Now, that's brotherly. Smoke? Where's a sailor that does not smoke?'

"The pipe soothed him, and gradually I made out he had run away from school, had gone to sea in a Russian ship; ran away again; served some time in English ships; was now reconciled with the arch-priest. He made a point of that. 'But when one is young one must see things, gather experience, ideas; enlarge the mind.'

'Here!' I interrupted. 'You can never tell! Here I met Mr. Kurtz,' he said, youthfully solemn and reproachful. I held my tongue after that. It appears he had persuaded a Dutch trading-house on the coast to fit him out with stores and goods, and had started for the interior with a light heart, and no more idea of what would happen to him than a baby. He had been wandering about that river for nearly two years alone, cut off from everybody and everything. 'I am not so young as I look. I am twenty-five,' he said. 'At first old Van Shuyten would tell me to go to the devil,' he narrated with keen enjoyment; 'but I stuck to him, and talked and talked, till at last he got afraid I would talk the hind-leg off his favourite dog, so he gave me some cheap things and a few guns, and told me he hoped he would never see my face again. Good old Dutchman, Van Shuyten. I've sent him one small lot of ivory a year ago, so that he can't call me a little thief when I get back. I hope he got it. And for the rest I don't care. I had some wood stacked for you. That was my old house. Did you see?'

"I gave him Towson's book. He made as though he would kiss me, but restrained himself. 'The only book I had left, and I thought I had lost it,' he said, looking at it ecstatically. 'So many accidents happen to a man going about alone, you know. Canoes get upset sometimes—and sometimes you've got to clear out so quick when the people get angry.' He thumbed the pages. 'You made notes in Russian?' I asked. He nodded. 'I thought they were written in cipher,' I said. He laughed, then became serious. 'I had lots of trouble to keep these people off,' he said. 'Did they want to kill you?' I asked. 'Oh, no!' he cried, and checked himself. 'Why did they attack us?' I pursued. He hesitated, then said shamefacedly, 'They don't want him to go.' 'Don't they?' I said, curiously. He nodded a nod full of mystery and wisdom. 'I tell you,' he cried, 'this man has enlarged my mind.' He opened his arms wide, staring at me with his little blue eyes that were perfectly round."

"I LOOKED at him, lost in astonishment. There he was before me, in motley, as though he had absconded from a troupe of mimes, enthusiastic, fabulous. His very existence was improbable, inexplicable, and altogether bewildering. He was an insoluble problem. It was inconceivable how he had existed, how he had succeeded in getting so far, how he had managed to remain—why he did not instantly disappear. 'I went a little farther,' he said, 'then still a little farther—till I had gone so far that I don't know how I'll ever get back. Never mind. Plenty time. I can manage. You take Kurtz away quick—quick—I tell you.' The glamour of youth enveloped his particoloured rags, his destitution, his loneliness, the essential desolation of his futile wanderings. For months—for years—his life hadn't been worth a day's purchase; and there he was gallantly, thoughtlessly alive, to all appearance indestructible solely by the virtue of his few years and of his unreflecting audacity. I was seduced into something like admiration—like envy. Glamour urged him on, glamour kept him unscathed. He surely wanted nothing from the wilderness but space to breathe in and to push on through. His need was to exist, and to move onwards at the greatest possible risk, and with a maximum of privation. If the absolutely pure, uncalculating, unpractical spirit of adventure had ever ruled a human being, it ruled this be-patched youth. I almost envied him the possession of this modest and clear flame. It seemed to have consumed all thought of self so completely, that even while he was talking to you, you forgot that it was he—the man before your eyes—who had gone through these things. I did not envy him his devotion to Kurtz, though. He had not meditated over it. It came to him, and he accepted it with a sort of eager fatalism. I must say that to me it appeared about the most dangerous thing in every way he had come upon so far.

"They had come together unavoidably, like two ships becalmed near each other, and lay rubbing sides at last. I suppose Kurtz wanted an audience, because on a certain occasion, when encamped in the forest, they had talked all night, or more probably Kurtz had talked. 'We talked of everything,' he said, quite transported at the recollection. 'I forgot there was such a thing as sleep. The night did not seem to last an hour. Everything! Everything! . . . Of love, too.' 'Ah, he talked to you of love!' I said, much amused. 'It isn't what you think,' he cried, almost passionately. 'It was in general. He made me see things—things.'

"He threw his arms up. We were on deck at the time, and the headman of my wood-cutters, lounging near by, turned upon him his heavy and glittering eyes. I looked around, and I don't know why, but I assure you that never, never before, did this land, this river, this jungle, the very arch of this blazing sky, appear to me so hopeless and so dark, so impenetrable to human thought, so pitiless to human weakness. 'And, ever since, you have been with him, of course?' I said.

"On the contrary. It appears their intercourse had been very much broken by various causes. He had, as he informed me proudly, managed to nurse Kurtz through two illnesses (he alluded to it as you would to some risky feat), but as a rule Kurtz wandered alone, far in the depths of the forest. 'Very often coming to this station, I had to wait days and days before he would turn up,' he said. 'Ah, it was worth waiting for!—sometimes.' 'What was he doing? exploring or what?' I asked. 'Oh, yes, of course;' he had discovered lots of villages, a lake, too—he did not know exactly in what direction; it was dangerous to inquire too much—but mostly his expeditions had been for ivory. 'But he had no goods to trade with by that time,' I objected. 'There's a good lot of cartridges left even yet,' he answered, looking away. 'To speak plainly, he raided the country,' I said. He nodded. 'Not alone, surely!' He muttered something about the villages round that lake. 'Kurtz got the tribe to follow him, did he?' I suggested. He fidgeted a little. 'They adored him,' he said. The tone of these words was so extraordinary that I looked at him searchingly. It was curious to see his mingled eagerness and reluctance to speak of Kurtz. The man filled his life, occupied his thoughts, swayed his emotions. 'What can you expect?' he burst out; 'he came to them with thunder and lightning, you know—and they had never seen anything like it—and very terrible. He could be very terrible. You can't judge Mr. Kurtz as you would an ordinary man. No, no, no! Now—just to give you an idea—I don't mind telling you, he wanted to shoot me, too, one day—but I don't judge him.' 'Shoot you!' I cried. 'What for?' 'Well, I had a small lot of ivory the chief of that village near my house gave me. You see I used to shoot game for them. Well, he wanted it, and wouldn't hear reason. He declared he would shoot me unless I gave him the ivory and then cleared out of the country, because he could do so, and had a fancy for it, and there was nothing on earth to prevent him killing whom he jolly well pleased. And it was true, too. I gave him the ivory. What did I care!

But I didn't clear out. No, no. I couldn't leave him. I had to be careful, of course, till we got friendly again for a time. He had his second illness then. Afterwards I had to keep out of the way; but I didn't mind. He was living for the most part in those villages on the lake. When he came down to the river, sometimes he would take to me, and sometimes it was better for me to be careful. This man suffered too much. He hated all this, and somehow he couldn't get away. When I had a chance I begged him to try and leave while there was time; I offered to go back with him. And he would say yes, and then he would remain; go off on another ivory hunt; disappear for weeks; forget himself amongst these people—forget himself—you know.' 'Why! he's mad,' I said. He protested indignantly. Mr. Kurtz couldn't be mad. If I had heard him talk, only two days ago, I wouldn't dare hint at such a thing. . . . I had taken up my binoculars while we talked, and was looking at the shore, sweeping the limit of the forest at each side and at the back of the house. The consciousness of there being people in that bush, so silent, so quiet—as silent and quiet as the ruined house on the hill—made me uneasy. There was no sign on the face of nature of this amazing tale that was not so much told as suggested to me in desolate exclamations, completed by shrugs, in interrupted phrases, in hints ending in deep sighs. The woods were unmoved, like a mask—heavy, like the closed door of a prison—they looked with their air of hidden knowledge, of patient expectation, of unapproachable silence. The Russian was explaining to me that it was only lately that Mr. Kurtz had come down to the river, bringing along with him all the fighting men of that lake tribe. He had been absent for several months—getting himself adored, I suppose—and had come down un-

expectedly, with the intention to all appearance of
making a raid either across the river or down stream.
Evidently the appetite for more ivory had got the better
of the—what shall I say?—less material aspirations.
However he had got much worse suddenly. 'I heard
he was lying helpless, and so I came up—took my
chance,' said the Russian. 'Oh, he is bad, very bad.'
I directed my glass to the house. There were no signs
of life, but there was the ruined roof, the long mud wall
peeping above the grass, with three little square win-
dow-holes, no two of the same size; all this brought
within reach of my hand, as it were. And then I made
a brusque movement, and one of the remaining posts
of that vanished fence leaped up in the field of my glass.
You remember I told you I had been struck at the
distance by certain attempts at ornamentation, rather
remarkable in the ruinous aspect of the place. Now I
had suddenly a nearer view, and its first result was to
make me throw my head back as if before a blow. Then
I went carefully from post to post with my glass, and I
saw my mistake. These round knobs were not ornamental but symbolic; they were expressive and puzzling,
striking and disturbing—food for thought and also for
the vultures if there had been any looking down from the
sky; but at all events for such ants as were industrious
enough to ascend the pole. They would have been even
more impressive, those heads on the stakes, if their
faces had not been turned to the house. Only one, the
first I had made out, was facing my way. I was not so
shocked as you may think. The start back I had given
was really nothing but a movement of surprise. I had
expected to see a knob of wood there, you know. I
returned deliberately to the first I had seen—and there
it was, black, dried, sunken, with closed eyelids,—a
head that seemed to sleep at the top of that pole, and,

with the shrunken dry lips showing a narrow white line of the teeth, was smiling, too, smiling continuously at some endless and jocose dream of that eternal slumber.

"I am not disclosing any trade secrets. In fact, the manager said afterwards that Mr. Kurtz's methods had ruined the district. I have no opinion on that point, but I want you clearly to understand that there was nothing exactly profitable in these heads being there. They only showed that Mr. Kurtz lacked restraint in the gratification of his various lusts, that there was something wanting in him—some small matter which, when the pressing need arose, could not be found under his magnificent eloquence. Whether he knew of this deficiency himself I can't say. I think the knowledge came to him at last—only at the very last. But the wilderness had found him out early, and had taken on him a terrible vengeance for the fantastic invasion. I think it had whispered to him things about himself which he did not know, things of which he had no conception till he took counsel with this great solitude—and the whisper had proved irresistibly fascinating. It echoed loudly within him because he was hollow at the core. . . . I put down the glass, and the head that had appeared near enough to be spoken to seemed at once to have leaped away from me into inaccessible distance.

"The admirer of Mr. Kurtz was a bit crestfallen. In a hurried, indistinct voice he began to assure me he had not dared to take these—say, symbols—down. He was not afraid of the natives; they would not stir till Mr. Kurtz gave the word. His ascendancy was extraordinary. The camps of these people surrounded the place, and the chiefs came every day to see him. They would crawl. . . . 'I don't want to know anything of the ceremonies used when approaching

Mr. Kurtz,' I shouted.   Curious, this feeling that came
over me that such details would be more intolerable
than those heads drying on the stakes under Mr. Kurtz's
windows.   After all, that was only a savage sight, while
I seemed at one bound to have been transported into
some lightless region of subtle horrors, where pure, un-
complicated savagery was a positive relief, being something that had a right to exist—obviously—in the
sunshine.   The young man looked at me with surprise.
I suppose it did not occur to him that Mr. Kurtz was
no idol of mine.   He forgot I hadn't heard any of these
splendid monologues on, what was it? on love, justice,
conduct of life—or what not.   If it had come to crawling before Mr. Kurtz, he crawled as much as the veriest
savage of them all.   I had no idea of the conditions, he
said: these heads were the heads of rebels.   I shocked
him excessively by laughing.   Rebels!   What would
be the next definition I was to hear?   There had been
enemies, criminals, workers—and these were rebels.
Those rebellious heads looked very subdued to me on
their sticks.   'You don't know how such a life tries a
man like Kurtz,' cried Kurtz's last disciple.   'Well, and
you?' I said.   'I! I! I am a simple man.   I have
no great thoughts.   I want nothing from anybody.
How can you compare me to? . . .' His feelings
were too much for speech, and suddenly he broke down.
'I don't understand,' he groaned.   'I've been doing my
best to keep him alive, and that's enough.   I had no
hand in all this.   I have no abilities.   There hasn't
been a drop of medicine or a mouthful of invalid food
for months here.   He was shamefully abandoned.   A
man like this, with such ideas.   Shamefully!   Shamefully! I—I—haven't slept for the last ten nights... .'

"His voice lost itself in the calm of the evening.   The
long shadows of the forest had slipped down hill while

we talked, had gone far beyond the ruined hovel, beyond the symbolic row of stakes. All this was in the gloom, while we down there were yet in the sunshine, and the stretch of the river abreast of the clearing glittered in a still and dazzling splendour, with a murky and overshadowed bend above and below. Not a living soul was seen on the shore. The bushes did not rustle.

"Suddenly round the corner of the house a group of men appeared, as though they had come up from the ground. They waded waist-deep in the grass, in a compact body, bearing an improvised stretcher in their midst. Instantly, in the emptiness of the landscape, a cry arose whose shrillness pierced the still air like a sharp arrow flying straight to the very heart of the land; and, as if by enchantment, streams of human beings—of naked human beings—with spears in their hands, with bows, with shields, with wild glances and savage movements, were poured into the clearing by the dark-faced and pensive forest. The bushes shook, the grass swayed for a time, and then everything stood still in attentive immobility.

"'Now, if he does not say the right thing to them we are all done for,' said the Russian at my elbow. The knot of men with the stretcher had stopped, too, half-way to the steamer, as if petrified. I saw the man on the stretcher sit up, lank and with an uplifted arm, above the shoulders of the bearers. 'Let us hope that the man who can talk so well of love in general will find some particular reason to spare us this time,' I said. I resented bitterly the absurd danger of our situation, as if to be at the mercy of that atrocious phantom had been a dishonouring necessity. I could not hear a sound, but through my glasses I saw the thin arm extended commandingly, the lower jaw moving, the eyes of that apparition shining darkly far in its bony head that nodded with grotesque jerks. Kurtz—Kurtz—that means short in German—don't it? Well, the name was as true as everything else in his life—and death. He looked at least seven feet long. His covering had fallen off, and his body emerged from it pitiful and appalling as from a winding-sheet. I could see the cage of his ribs all astir, the bones of his arm waving. It was as though an animated image of death carved out of old ivory had been shaking its hand with menaces at a motionless crowd of men made of dark and glittering bronze. I saw him open his mouth wide—it gave him a weirdly voracious aspect, as though he had wanted to swallow all the air, all the earth, all the men before him. A deep voice reached me faintly. He must have been shouting. He fell back suddenly. The stretcher shook as the bearers staggered forward again, and almost at the same time I noticed that the crowd of savages was vanishing without any perceptible movement of retreat, as if the forest that had ejected these beings so suddenly had drawn them in again as the breath is drawn in a long aspiration.

"Some of the pilgrims behind the stretcher carried his arms—two shot-guns, a heavy rifle, and a light revolver-carbine—the thunderbolts of that pitiful Jupiter. The manager bent over him murmuring as he walked beside his head. They laid him down in one of the little cabins—just a room for a bedplace and a camp-stool or two, you know. We had brought his belated correspondence, and a lot of torn envelopes and open letters littered his bed. His hand roamed feebly amongst these papers. I was struck by the fire of his eyes and the composed languor of his expression. It was not so much the exhaustion of disease. He did not seem in pain. This shadow looked satiated and calm, as though for the moment it had had its fill of all the emotions.

"He rustled one of the letters, and looking straight in my face said, 'I am glad.' Somebody had been writing to him about me. These special recommendations were turning up again. The volume of tone he emitted without effort, almost without the trouble of moving his lips, amazed me. A voice! a voice! It was grave, profound, vibrating, while the man did not seem capable of a whisper. However, he had enough strength in him—factitious no doubt—to very nearly make an end of us, as you shall hear directly.

"The manager appeared silently in the doorway; I stepped out at once and he drew the curtain after me. The Russian, eyed curiously by the pilgrims, was staring at the shore. I followed the direction of his glance.

"Dark human shapes could be made out in the distance, flitting indistinctly against the gloomy border of the forest, and near the river two bronze figures, leaning on tall spears, stood in the sunlight under fantastic head-dresses of spotted skins, warlike and still in statuesque repose. And from right to left along the lighted shore moved a wild and gorgeous apparition of a woman.

"She walked with measured steps, draped in striped and fringed cloths, treading the earth proudly, with a slight jingle and flash of barbarous ornaments. She carried her head high; her hair was done in the shape of a helmet; she had brass leggings to the knee, brass wire gauntlets to the elbow, a crimson spot on her tawny cheek, innumerable necklaces of glass beads on her neck; bizarre things, charms, gifts of witch-men, that hung about her, glittered and trembled at every step. She must have had the value of several elephant tusks upon her. She was savage and superb, wild-eyed and

magnificent; there was something ominous and stately
in her deliberate progress. And in the hush that had
fallen suddenly upon the whole sorrowful land, the
immense wilderness, the colossal body of the fecund
and mysterious life seemed to look at her, pensive, as
though it had been looking at the image of its own
tenebrous and passionate soul.

"She came abreast of the steamer, stood still, and
faced us. Her long shadow fell to the water's edge.
Her face had a tragic and fierce aspect of wild sorrow
and of dumb pain mingled with the fear of some struggling, half-shaped resolve. She stood looking at us
without a stir, and like the wilderness itself, with an air
of brooding over an inscrutable purpose. A whole
minute passed, and then she made a step forward. There
was a low jingle, a glint of yellow metal, a sway of
fringed draperies, and she stopped as if her heart had
failed her. The young fellow by my side growled. The
pilgrims murmured at my back. She looked at us all
as if her life had depended upon the unswerving steadiness of her glance. Suddenly she opened her bared
arms and threw them up rigid above her head, as
though in an uncontrollable desire to touch the sky,
and at the same time the swift shadows darted out on
the earth, swept around on the river, gathering the
steamer into a shadowy embrace. A formidable silence
hung over the scene.

"She turned away slowly, walked on, following the
bank, and passed into the bushes to the left. Once
only her eyes gleamed back at us in the dusk of the
thickets before she disappeared.

"'If she had offered to come aboard I really think
I would have tried to shoot her,' said the man of patches,
nervously. 'I had been risking my life every day for
the last fortnight to keep her out of the house. She

got in one day and kicked up a row about those miserable rags I picked up in the storeroom to mend my clothes with. I wasn't decent. At least it must have been that, for she talked like a fury to Kurtz for an hour, pointing at me now and then. I don't understand the dialect of this tribe. Luckily for me, I fancy Kurtz felt too ill that day to care, or there would have been mischief. I don't understand. . . . No— it's too much for me. Ah, well, it's all over now.'

"At this moment I heard Kurtz's deep voice behind the curtain: 'Save me!—save the ivory, you mean. Don't tell me. Save *me!* Why, I've had to save you. You are interrupting my plans now. Sick! Sick! Not so sick as you would like to believe. Never mind. I'll carry my ideas out yet—I will return. I'll show you what can be done. You with your little peddling notions—you are interfering with me. I will return. I. . . .'

"The manager came out. He did me the honour to take me under the arm and lead me aside. 'He is very low, very low,' he said. He considered it necessary to sigh, but neglected to be consistently sorrowful. 'We have done all we could for him—haven't we? But there is no disguising the fact, Mr. Kurtz has done more harm than good to the Company. He did not see the time was not ripe for vigorous action. Cautiously, cautiously—that's my principle. We must be cautious yet. The district is closed to us for a time. Deplorable! Upon the whole, the trade will suffer. I don't deny there is a remarkable quantity of ivory—mostly fossil. We must save it, at all events—but look how precarious the position is—and why? Because the method is unsound.' 'Do you,' said I, looking at the shore, 'call it "unsound method?"' 'Without doubt,' he exclaimed, hotly. 'Don't you?' . . .

'No method at all,' I murmured after a while.
'Exactly,' he exulted. 'I anticipated this. Shows
a complete want of judgment. It is my duty to point
it out in the proper quarter.' 'Oh,' said I, 'that fellow
—what's his name?—the brickmaker, will make a read-
able report for you.' He appeared confounded for a
moment. It seemed to me I had never breathed an
atmosphere so vile, and I turned mentally to Kurtz for
relief—positively for relief. 'Nevertheless I think Mr.
Kurtz is a remarkable man,' I said with emphasis. He
started, dropped on me a cold heavy glance, said very
quietly, 'he *was*,' and turned his back on me. My
hour of favour was over; I found myself lumped along
with Kurtz as a partisan of methods for which the time
was not ripe: I was unsound! Ah! but it was something
to have at least a choice of nightmares.

"I had turned to the wilderness really, not to Mr.
Kurtz, who, I was ready to admit, was as good as buried.
And for a moment it seemed to me as if I also were
buried in a vast grave full of unspeakable secrets. I
felt an intolerable weight oppressing my breast, the
smell of the damp earth, the unseen presence of vic-
torious corruption, the darkness of an impenetrable
night. . . . The Russian tapped me on the shoulder. I heard him mumbling and stammering something about 'brother seaman—couldn't conceal—knowledge of matters that would affect Mr. Kurtz's reputation.' I waited. For him evidently Mr. Kurtz was
not in his grave; I suspect that for him Mr. Kurtz was
one of the immortals. 'Well!' said I at last, 'speak out.
As it happens, I am Mr. Kurtz's friend—in a way.'

"He stated with a good deal of formality that had
we not been 'of the same profession,' he would have
kept the matter to himself without regard to consequences. 'He suspected there was an active ill will

towards him on the part of these white men that——'
'You are right,' I said, remembering a certain conversation I had overheard. 'The manager thinks you ought to be hanged.' He showed a concern at this intelligence which amused me at first. 'I had better get out of the way quietly,' he said, earnestly. 'I can do no more for Kurtz now, and they would soon find some excuse. What's to stop them? There's a military post three hundred miles from here.' 'Well, upon my word,' said I, 'perhaps you had better go if you have any friends amongst the savages near by.' 'Plenty,' he said. 'They are simple people—and I want nothing, you know.' He stood biting his lip, then: 'I don't want any harm to happen to these whites here, but of course I was thinking of Mr. Kurtz's reputation—but you are a brother seaman and——' 'All right,' said I, after a time. 'Mr. Kurtz's reputation is safe with me.' I did not know how truly I spoke.

"He informed me, lowering his voice, that it was Kurtz who had ordered the attack to be made on the steamer. 'He hated sometimes the idea of being taken away—and then again. . . . But I don't understand these matters. I am a simple man. He thought it would scare you away—that you would give it up, thinking him dead. I could not stop him. Oh, I had an awful time of it this last month.' 'Very well,' I said. 'He is all right now.' 'Ye-e-es,' he muttered, not very convinced apparently. 'Thanks,' said I; 'I shall keep my eyes open.' 'But quiet—eh?' he urged, anxiously. 'It would be awful for his reputation if anybody here——' I promised a complete discretion with great gravity. 'I have a canoe and three black fellows waiting not very far. I am off. Could you give me a few Martini-Henry cartridges?' I could, and did, with proper secrecy. He helped himself, with a wink at me, to a handful of my tobacco. 'Between sailors—you know—good English tobacco.' At the door of the pilot-house he turned round—'I say, haven't you a pair of shoes you could spare?' He raised one leg. 'Look.' The soles were tied with knotted strings sandal-wise under his bare feet. I rooted out an old pair, at which he looked with admiration before tucking it under his left arm. One of his pockets (bright red) was bulging with cartridges, from the other (dark blue) peeped 'Towson's Inquiry,' etc., etc. He seemed to think himself excellently well equipped for a renewed encounter with the wilderness. 'Ah! I'll never, never meet such a man again. You ought to have heard him recite poetry—his own, too, it was, he told me. Poetry!' He rolled his eyes at the recollection of these delights. 'Oh, he enlarged my mind!' 'Good-bye,' said I. He shook hands and vanished in the night. Sometimes I ask myself whether I had ever really seen him—whether it was possible to meet such a phenomenon! . . .

"When I woke up shortly after midnight his warning came to my mind with its hint of danger that seemed, in the starred darkness, real enough to make me get up for the purpose of having a look round. On the hill a big fire burned, illuminating fitfully a crooked corner of the station-house. One of the agents with a picket of a few of our blacks, armed for the purpose, was keeping guard over the ivory; but deep within the forest, red gleams that wavered, that seemed to sink and rise from the ground amongst confused columnar shapes of intense blackness, showed the exact position of the camp where Mr. Kurtz's adorers were keeping their uneasy vigil. The monotonous beating of a big drum filled the air with muffled shocks and a lingering vibration. A steady droning sound of many men chanting each to himself some weird incantation came out from the black, flat wall of the woods as the humming of bees comes out of a hive, and had a strange narcotic effect upon my half-awake senses. I believe I dozed off leaning over the rail, till an abrupt burst of yells, an overwhelming outbreak of a pent-up and mysterious frenzy, woke me up in a bewildered wonder. It was cut short all at once, and the low droning went on with an effect of audible and soothing silence. I glanced casually into the little cabin. A light was burning within, but Mr. Kurtz was not there.

"I think I would have raised an outcry if I had believed my eyes. But I didn't believe them at first—the thing seemed so impossible. The fact is I was completely unnerved by a sheer blank fright, pure abstract terror, unconnected with any distinct shape of physical danger. What made this emotion so overpowering was—how shall I define it?—the moral shock I received, as if something altogether monstrous, intolerable to thought and odious to the soul, had been thrust upon me unexpectedly. This lasted of course the merest fraction of a second, and then the usual sense of commonplace, deadly danger, the possibility of a sudden onslaught and massacre, or something of the kind, which I saw impending, was positively welcome and composing. It pacified me, in fact, so much, that I did not raise an alarm.

"There was an agent buttoned up inside an ulster* and sleeping on a chair on deck within three feet of me. The yells had not awakened him; he snored very slightly; I left him to his slumbers and leaped ashore. I did not betray Mr. Kurtz—it was ordered I should never betray him—it was written I should be loyal to the nightmare of my choice. I was anxious to deal with this shadow by myself alone,—and to this day I don't know why I was so jealous of sharing with any one the peculiar blackness of that experience.

"As soon as I got on the bank I saw a trail—a broad trail through the grass. I remember the exultation with which I said to myself, 'He can't walk—he is crawling on all-fours—I've got him.' The grass was wet with dew. I strode rapidly with clenched fists. I fancy I had some vague notion of falling upon him and giving him a drubbing. I don't know. I had some imbecile thoughts. The knitting old woman with the cat obtruded herself upon my memory as a most improper person to be sitting at the other end of such an affair. I saw a row of pilgrims squirting lead in the air out of Winchesters held to the hip. I thought I would never get back to the steamer, and imagined myself living alone and unarmed in the woods to an advanced age. Such silly things—you know. And I remember I confounded the beat of the drum with the beating of my heart, and was pleased at its calm regularity.

"I kept to the track though—then stopped to listen. The night was very clear; a dark blue space, sparkling with dew and starlight, in which black things stood very still. I thought I could see a kind of motion ahead of me. I was strangely cocksure of everything that night. I actually left the track and ran in a wide semicircle (I verily believe chuckling to myself) so as to get in front of that stir, of that motion I had seen— if indeed I had seen anything. I was circumventing Kurtz as though it had been a boyish game.

"I came upon him, and, if he had not heard me coming, I would have fallen over him, too, but he got up in time. He rose, unsteady, long, pale, indistinct, like a vapour exhaled by the earth, and swayed slightly, misty and silent before me; while at my back the fires loomed between the trees, and the murmur of many voices issued from the forest. I had cut him off cleverly; but when actually confronting him I seemed to come to my senses, I saw the danger in its right proportion. It was by no means over yet. Suppose he began to shout? Though he could hardly stand, there was still plenty of vigour in his voice. 'Go away—hide yourself,' he said, in that profound tone. It was very awful. I glanced back. We were within thirty yards from the nearest fire. A black figure stood up, strode on long black legs, waving long black arms, across the glow. It had horns—antelope horns, I think—on its head. Some sorcerer, some witch-man, no doubt: it looked fiend-like enough. 'Do you know what you are doing?' I whispered. 'Perfectly,' he answered, raising his voice for that single word: it sounded to me far off and yet loud, like a hail through a speaking-trumpet. If he makes a row we are lost, I thought to myself. This clearly was not a case for fisticuffs, even apart from the very natural aversion I had to beat that Shadow—this wandering and tormented thing. 'You will be lost,' I said—'utterly lost.' One gets sometimes such a flash of inspiration, you know. I did say the right thing, though indeed he could not have been more irretrievably lost than he was at this very moment, when the foundations of our intimacy were being laid—to endure—to endure—even to the end—even beyond.

"'I had immense plans,' he muttered irresolutely. 'Yes,' said I; 'but if you try to shout I'll smash your head with——' There was not a stick or a stone near. 'I will throttle you for good,' I corrected myself. 'I was on the threshold of.great things,' he pleaded, in a voice of longing, with a wistfulness of tone that made my blood run cold. 'And now for this stupid scoundrel——' 'Your success in Europe is assured in any

case,' I affirmed, steadily. I did not want to have the
throttling of him, you understand—and indeed it would
have been very little use for any practical purpose. I
tried to break the spell—the heavy, mute spell of the
wilderness—that seemed to draw him to its pitiless
breast by the awakening of forgotten and brutal
instincts, by the memory of gratified and monstrous
passions. This alone, I was convinced, had driven him
out to the edge of the forest, to the bush, towards the
gleam of fires, the throb of drums, the drone of weird
incantations; this alone had beguiled his unlawful soul
beyond the bounds of permitted aspirations. And,
don't you see, the terror of the position was not in being
knocked on the head—though I had a very lively sense
of that danger, too—but in this, that I had to deal with
a being to whom I could not appeal in the name of
anything high or low. I had, even like the niggers, to
invoke him—himself—his own exalted and incredible
degradation. There was nothing either above or below
him, and I knew it. He had kicked himself loose of
the earth. Confound the man! he had kicked the
very earth to pieces. He was alone, and I before him
did not know whether I stood on the ground or floated
in the air. I've been telling you what we said—repeating the phrases we pronounced—but what's the
good? They were common everyday words—the familiar, vague sounds exchanged on every waking day of
life. But what of that? They had behind them, to my
mind, the terrific suggestiveness of words heard in
dreams, of phrases spoken in nightmares. Soul! If
anybody had ever struggled with a soul, I am the man.
And I wasn't arguing with a lunatic either. Believe
me or not, his intelligence was perfectly clear—concentrated, it is true, upon himself with horrible intensity, yet clear; and therein was my only chance—

barring, of course, the killing him there and then, which
wasn't so good, on account of unavoidable noise. But
his soul was mad. Being alone in the wilderness, it had
looked within itself, and, by heavens! I tell you, it
had gone mad. I had—for my sins, I suppose—to go
through the ordeal of looking into it myself. No
eloquence could have been so withering to one's belief
in mankind as his final burst of sincerity. He struggled with himself, too. I saw it,—I heard it. I saw
the inconceivable mystery of a soul that knew no restraint, no faith, and no fear, yet struggling blindly
with itself. I kept my head pretty well; but when I
had him at last stretched on the couch, I wiped my
forehead, while my legs shook under me as though I
had carried half a ton on my back down that hill. And
yet I had only supported him, his bony arm clasped
round my neck—and he was not much heavier than
a child.

"When next day we left at noon, the crowd, of whose
presence behind the curtain of trees I had been acutely
conscious all the time, flowed out of the woods again,
filled the clearing, covered the slope with a mass of
naked, breathing, quivering, bronze bodies. I steamed
up a bit, then swung downstream, and two thousand
eyes followed the evolutions of the splashing, thumping, fierce river-demon beating the water with its
terrible tail and breathing black smoke into the air. In
front of the first rank, along the river, three men, plastered with bright red earth from head to foot, strutted
to and fro restlessly. When we came abreast again,
they faced the river, stamped their feet, nodded their
horned heads, swayed their scarlet bodies; they shook
towards the fierce river-demon a bunch of black feath-
ers, a mangy skin with a pendent tail—something that
looked like a dried gourd; they shouted periodically

together strings of amazing words that resembled no sounds of human language; and the deep murmurs of the crowd, interrupted suddenly, were like the responses of some satanic litany.

"We had carried Kurtz into the pilot-house: there was more air there. Lying on the couch, he stared through the open shutter. There was an eddy in the mass of human bodies, and the woman with helmeted head and tawny cheeks rushed out to the very brink of the stream. She put out her hands, shouted something, and all that wild mob took up the shout in a roaring chorus of articulated, rapid, breathless utterance.

"'Do you understand this?' I asked.

"He kept on looking out past me with fiery, longing eyes, with a mingled expression of wistfulness and hate. He made no answer, but I saw a smile, a smile of indefinable meaning, appear on his colourless lips that a moment after twitched convulsively. 'Do I not?' he said slowly, gasping, as if the words had been torn out of him by a supernatural power.

"I pulled the string of the whistle, and I did this because I saw the pilgrims on deck getting out their rifles with an air of anticipating a jolly lark. At the sudden screech there was a movement of abject terror through that wedged mass of bodies. 'Don't! don't you frighten them away,' cried someone on deck disconsolately. I pulled the string time after time. They broke and ran, they leaped, they crouched, they swerved, they dodged the flying terror of the sound. The three red chaps had fallen flat, face down on the shore, as though they had been shot dead. Only the barbarous and superb woman did not so much as flinch, and stretched tragically her bare arms after us over the sombre and glittering river.

"And then that imbecile crowd down on the deck started their little fun, and I could see nothing more for smoke.

"The brown current ran swiftly out of the heart of darkness, bearing us down towards the sea with twice the speed of our upward progress; and Kurtz's life was running swiftly, too, ebbing, ebbing out of his heart into the sea of inexorable time. The manager was very placid, he had no vital anxieties now, he took us both in with a comprehensive and satisfied glance: the 'affair' had come off as well as could be wished. I saw the time approaching when I would be left alone of the party of 'unsound method.' The pilgrims looked upon me with disfavour. I was, so to speak, numbered with the dead. It is strange how I accepted this unforeseen partnership, this choice of nightmares forced upon me in the tenebrous land invaded by these mean and greedy phantoms.

"Kurtz discoursed. A voice! a voice! It rang deep to the very last. It survived his strength to hide in the magnificent folds of eloquence the barren darkness of his heart. Oh, he struggled! he struggled! The wastes of his weary brain were haunted by shadowy images now—images of wealth and fame revolving obsequiously round his unextinguishable gift of noble and lofty expression. My Intended, my station, my career, my ideas—these were the subjects for the occasional utterances of elevated sentiments. The shade of the original Kurtz frequented the bedside of the hollow sham, whose fate it was to be buried presently in the mould of primeval earth. But both the diabolic love and the unearthly hate of the mysteries it had penetrated fought for the possession of that soul satiated with primitive emotions, avid of lying fame, of sham distinction, of all the appearances of success and power.

"Sometimes he was contemptibly childish. He desired to have kings meet him at railway-stations on his return from some ghastly Nowhere, where he intended to accomplish great things. 'You show them you have in you something that is really profitable, and then there will be no limits to the recognition of your ability,' he would say. 'Of course you must take care of the motives—right motives—always.' The long reaches that were like one and the same reach, monotonous bends that were exactly alike, slipped past the steamer with their multitude of secular*trees looking patiently after this grimy fragment of another world, the forerunner of change, of conquest, of trade, of massacres, of blessings. I looked ahead—piloting. 'Close the shutter,' said Kurtz suddenly one day; 'I can't bear to look at this.' I did so. There was a silence. 'Oh, but I will wring your heart yet!' he cried at the invisible wilderness.

"We broke down—as I had expected—and had to lie up for repairs at the head of an island. This delay was the first thing that shook Kurtz's confidence. One morning he gave me a packet of papers and a photograph—the lot tied together with a shoe-string. 'Keep this for me,' he said. 'This noxious fool' (meaning the manager) 'is capable of prying into my boxes when I am not looking.' In the afternoon I saw him. He was lying on his back with closed eyes, and I withdrew quietly, but I heard him mutter, 'Live rightly, die, die. . . .' I listened. There was nothing more. Was he rehearsing some speech in his sleep, or was it a fragment of a phrase from some newspaper article? He had been writing for the papers and meant to do so again, 'for the furthering of my ideas. It's a duty.'

"His was an impenetrable darkness. I looked at him as you peer down at a man who is lying at the bottom of a precipice where the sun never shines. But I had not much time to give him, because I was helping the engine-driver to take to pieces the leaky cylinders, to straighten a bent connecting-rod, and in other such matters. I lived in an infernal mess of rust, filings, nuts, bolts, spanners, hammers, ratchet-drills—things I abominate, because I don't get on with them. I tended the little forge we fortunately had aboard; I toiled wearily in a wretched scrap-heap—unless I had the shakes too bad to stand.

"One evening coming in with a candle I was startled to hear him say a little tremulously, 'I am lying here in the dark waiting for death.' The light was within a foot of his eyes. I forced myself to murmur, 'Oh, nonsense!' and stood over him as if transfixed.

"Anything approaching the change that came over his features I have never seen before, and hope never to see again. Oh, I wasn't touched. I was fascinated. It was as though a veil had been rent. I saw on that ivory face the expression of sombre pride, of ruthless power, of craven terror—of an intense and hopeless despair. Did he live his life again in every detail of desire, temptation, and surrender during that supreme moment of complete knowledge? He cried in a whisper at some image, at some vision—he cried out twice, a cry that was no more than a breath—

"'The horror! The horror!'

"I blew the candle out and left the cabin. The pilgrims were dining in the mess-room, and I took my place opposite the manager, who lifted his eyes to give me a questioning glance, which I successfully ignored.

He leaned back, serene, with that peculiar smile of his sealing the unexpressed depths of his meanness. A continuous shower of small flies streamed upon the lamp, upon the cloth, upon our hands and faces. Suddenly the manager's boy put his insolent black head in the doorway, and said in a tone of scathing contempt—

"'Mistah Kurtz—he dead.'

"All the pilgrims rushed out to see. I remained, and went on with my dinner. I believe I was considered brutally callous. However, I did not eat much. There was a lamp in there—light, don't you know—and outside it was so beastly, beastly dark. I went no more near the remarkable man who had pronounced a judgment upon the adventures of his soul on this earth. The voice was gone. What else had been there? But I am of course aware that next day the pilgrims buried something in a muddy hole.

"And then they very nearly buried me.

"However, as you see, I did not go to join Kurtz there and then. I did not. I remained to dream the nightmare out to the end, and to show my loyalty to Kurtz once more. Destiny. My destiny! Droll thing life is—that mysterious arrangement of merciless logic for a futile purpose. The most you can hope from it is some knowledge of yourself—that comes too late—a crop of unextinguishable regrets. I have wrestled with death. It is the most unexciting contest you can imagine. It takes place in an impalpable grayness, with nothing underfoot, with nothing around, without spectators, without clamour, without glory, without the great desire of victory, without the great fear of defeat, in a sickly atmosphere of tepid scepticism, without much belief in your own right, and still less in that of your adversary. If such is the form of ultimate wisdom, then life is a greater riddle than some of us think

it to be. I was within a hair's-breadth of the last
opportunity for pronouncement, and I found with
humiliation that probably I would have nothing to
say. This is the reason why I affirm that Kurtz was
a remarkable man. He had something to say. He
said it. Since I had peeped over the edge myself,
I understand better the meaning of his stare, that
could not see the flame of the candle, but was wide
enough to embrace the whole universe, piercing enough
to penetrate all the hearts that beat in the darkness.
He had summed up—he had judged. 'The horror!'
He was a remarkable man. After all, this was the expression of some sort of belief; it had candour, it had
conviction, it had a vibrating note of revolt in its whisper, it had the appalling face of a glimpsed truth—
the strange commingling of desire and hate. And it is
not my own extremity I remember best—a vision of
grayness without form filled with physical pain, and a
careless contempt for the evanescence of all things—
even of this pain itself. No! It is his extremity that
I seem to have lived through. True, he had made
that last stride, he had stepped over the edge, while I
had been permitted to draw back my hesitating foot.
And perhaps in this is the whole difference; perhaps all
the wisdom, and all truth, and all sincerity, are just
compressed into that inappreciable moment of time
in which we step over the threshold of the invisible.
Perhaps! I like to think my summing-up would not
have been a word of careless contempt. Better his
cry—much better. It was an affirmation, a moral victory paid for by innumerable defeats, by abominable terrors, by abominable satisfactions. But it was
a victory! That is why I have remained loyal to
Kurtz to the last, and even beyond, when a long
time after I heard once more, not his own voice, but

the echo of his magnificent eloquence thrown to me from a soul as translucently pure as a cliff of crystal.

"No, they did not bury me, though there is a period of time which I remember mistily, with a shuddering wonder, like a passage through some inconceivable world that had no hope in it and no desire. I found myself back in the sepulchral city resenting the sight of people hurrying through the streets to filch a little money from each other, to devour their infamous cookery, to gulp their unwholesome beer, to dream their insignificant and silly dreams. They trespassed upon my thoughts. They were intruders whose knowledge of life was to me an irritating pretence, because I felt so sure they could not possibly know the things I knew. Their bearing, which was simply the bearing of commonplace individuals going about their business in the assurance of perfect safety, was offensive to me like the outrageous flauntings of folly in the face of a danger it is unable to comprehend. I had no particular desire to enlighten them, but I had some difficulty in restraining myself from laughing in their faces, so full of stupid importance. I daresay I was not very well at that time. I tottered about the streets—there were various affairs to settle—grinning bitterly at perfectly respectable persons. I admit my behaviour was inexcusable, but then my temperature was seldom normal in these days. My dear aunt's endeavours to 'nurse up my strength' seemed altogether beside the mark. It was not my strength that wanted nursing, it was my imagination that wanted soothing. I kept the bundle of papers given me by Kurtz, not knowing exactly what to do with it. His mother had died lately, watched over, as I was told, by his Intended. A clean-shaved man, with an official manner and wearing gold-rimmed spectacles, called on me one day and made inquiries, at first circuitous, afterwards suavely pressing, about what he was pleased to denominate certain 'documents.' I was not surprised, because I had had two rows with the manager on the subject out there. I had refused to give up the smallest scrap out of that package, and I took the same attitude with the spectacled man. He became darkly menacing at last, and with much heat argued that the Company had the right to every bit of information about its 'territories.' And said he, 'Mr. Kurtz's knowledge of unexplored regions must have been necessarily extensive and peculiar—owing to his great abilities and to the deplorable circumstances in which he had been placed: therefore——' I assured him Mr. Kurtz's knowledge, however extensive, did not bear upon the problems of commerce or administration. He invoked then the name of science. 'It would be an incalculable loss if,' etc., etc. I offered him the report on the 'Suppression of Savage Customs,' with the postscriptum torn off. He took it up eagerly, but ended by sniffing at it with an air of contempt. 'This is not what we had a right to expect,' he remarked. 'Expect nothing else,' I said. 'There are only private letters.' He withdrew upon some threat of legal proceedings, and I saw him no more; but another fellow, calling himself Kurtz's cousin, appeared two days later, and was anxious to hear all the details about his dear relative's last moments. Incidentally he gave me to understand that Kurtz had been essentially a great musician. 'There was the making of an immense success,' said the man, who was an organist, I believe, with lank gray hair flowing over a greasy coat-collar. I had no reason to doubt his statement; and to this day I am unable to say what was Kurtz's profession, whether he ever had any—which was the greatest of his talents. I

had taken him for a painter who wrote for the papers,
or else for a journalist who could paint—but even
the cousin (who took snuff during the interview)
could not tell me what he had been—exactly. He
was a universal genius—on that point I agreed with
the old chap, who thereupon blew his nose noisily
into a large cotton handkerchief and withdrew in
senile agitation, bearing off some family letters and
memoranda without importance. Ultimately a journalist anxious to know something of the fate of his
'dear colleague' turned up. This visitor informed
me Kurtz's proper sphere ought to have been politics
'on the popular side.' He had furry straight eyebrows, bristly hair cropped short, an eye-glass on a
broad ribbon, and, becoming expansive, confessed
his opinion that Kurtz really couldn't write a bit—
'but heavens! how that man could talk. He elec-
trified large meetings. He had faith—don't you see?—
he had the faith. He could get himself to believe anything—anything. He would have been a splendid
leader of an extreme party.' 'What party?' I
asked. 'Any party,' answered the other. 'He was an
—an—extremist.' Did I not think so? I assented.
Did I know, he asked, with a sudden flash of curiosity,
'what it was that had induced him to go out there?'
'Yes,' said I, and forthwith handed him the famous
Report for publication, if he thought fit. He glanced
through it hurriedly, mumbling all the time, judged
'it would do,' and took himself off with this plunder.

"Thus I was left at last with a slim packet of letters
and the girl's portrait. She struck me as beautiful—
I mean she had a beautiful expression. I know that
the sunlight can be made to lie, too, yet one felt that
no manipulation of light and pose could have con-
veyed the delicate shade of truthfulness upon those

features. She seemed ready to listen without mental reservation, without suspicion, without a thought for herself. I concluded I would go and give her back her portrait and those letters myself. Curiosity? Yes; and also some other feeling perhaps. All that had been Kurtz's had passed out of my hands: his soul, his body, his station, his plans, his ivory, his career. There remained only his memory and his Intended—and I wanted to give that up, too, to the past, in a way—to surrender personally all that remained of him with me to that oblivion which is the last word of our common fate. I don't defend myself. I had no clear perception of what it was I really wanted. Perhaps it was an impulse of unconscious loyalty, or the fulfilment of one of these ironic necessities that lurk in the facts of human existence. I don't know. I can't tell. But I went.

"I thought his memory was like the other memories of the dead that accumulate in every man's life— a vague impress on the brain of shadows that had fallen on it in their swift and final passage; but before the high and ponderous door, between the tall houses of a street as still and decorous as a well-kept alley in a cemetery, I had a vision of him on the stretcher, opening his mouth voraciously, as if to devour all the earth with all its mankind. He lived then before me; he lived as much as he had ever lived—a shadow insatiable of splendid appearances, of frightful realities; a shadow darker than the shadow of the night, and draped nobly in the folds of a gorgeous eloquence. The vision seemed to enter the house with me—the stretcher, the phantom-bearers, the wild crowd of obedient worshippers, the gloom of the forests, the glitter of the reach between the murky bends, the beat of the drum, regular and muffled like the beating of a heart—the heart of a

conquering darkness. It was a moment of triumph for
the wilderness, an invading and vengeful rush which,
it seemed to me, I would have to keep back alone for
the salvation of another soul. And the memory of
what I had heard him say afar there, with the horned
shapes stirring at my back, in the glow of fires, within
the patient woods, those broken phrases came back to
me, were heard again in their ominous and terrifying
simplicity. I remembered his abject pleading, his
abject threats, the colossal scale of his vile desires, the
meanness, the torment, the tempestuous anguish of
his soul. And later on I seemed to see his collected
languid manner, when he said one day, 'This lot of
ivory now is really mine. The Company did not
pay for it. I collected it myself at a very great personal risk. I am afraid they will try to claim it as
theirs though. H'm. It is a difficult case. What
do you think I ought to do—resist? Eh? I want
no more than justice.' . . . He wanted no more
than justice—no more than justice. I rang the bell
before a mahogany door on the first floor, and while I
waited he seemed to stare at me out of the glassy panel
—stare with that wide and immense stare embracing,
condemning, loathing all the universe. I seemed to
hear the whispered cry, 'The horror! The horror!'

"The dusk was falling. I had to wait in a lofty
drawing-room with three long windows from floor to
ceiling that were like three luminous and bedraped
columns. The bent gilt legs and backs of the furniture shone in indistinct curves. The tall marble
fireplace had a cold and monumental whiteness. A
grand piano stood massively in a corner; with dark
gleams on the flat surfaces like a sombre and polished
sarcophagus. A high door opened—closed. I rose.

"She came forward, all in black, with a pale

head, floating towards me in the dusk. She was
in mourning. It was more than a year since his
death, more than a year since the news came; she
seemed as though she would remember and mourn
for ever. She took both my hands in hers and murmured, 'I had heard you were coming.' I noticed she
was not very young—I mean not girlish. She had a
mature capacity for fidelity, for belief, for suffering.
The room seemed to have grown darker, as if all the sad
light of the cloudy evening had taken refuge on her
forehead. This fair hair, this pale visage, this pure
brow, seemed surrounded by an ashy halo from which
the dark eyes looked out at me. Their glance was guile-
less, profound, confident, and trustful. She carried her
sorrowful head as though she were proud of that sorrow, as though she would say, I—I alone know how
to mourn for him as he deserves. But while we were
still shaking hands, such a look of awful desolation
came upon her face that I perceived she was one of
those creatures that are not the playthings of Time.
For her he had died only yesterday. And, by Jove!
the impression was so powerful that for me, too, he
seemed to have died only yesterday—nay, this very
minute. I saw her and him in the same instant of time
—his death and her sorrow—I saw her sorrow in the
very moment of his death. Do you understand? I
saw them together—I heard them together. She had
said, with a deep catch of the breath, 'I have survived'
while my strained ears seemed to hear distinctly,
mingled with her tone of despairing regret, the summing
up whisper of his eternal condemnation. I asked myself what I was doing there, with a sensation of panic in
my heart as though I had blundered into a place of
cruel and absurd mysteries not fit for a human being to
behold. She motioned me to a chair. We sat down.

I laid the packet gently on the little table, and she put her hand over it. . . . 'You knew him well,' she murmured, after a moment of mourning silence.

"'Intimacy grows quickly out there,' I said. 'I knew him as well as it is possible for one man to know another.'

"'And you admired him,' she said. 'It was impossible to know him and not to admire him. Was it?'

"'He was a remarkable man,' I said, unsteadily. Then before the appealing fixity of her gaze, that seemed to watch for more words on my lips, I went on, 'It was impossible not to——'

"'Love him,' she finished eagerly, silencing me into an appalled dumbness. 'How true! how true! But when you think that no one knew him so well as I! I had all his noble confidence. I knew him best.'

"'You knew him best,' I repeated. And perhaps she did. But with every word spoken the room was growing darker, and only her forehead, smooth and white, remained illumined by the unextinguishable light of belief and love.

"'You were his friend,' she went on. 'His friend,' she repeated, a little louder. 'You must have been, if he had given you this, and sent you to me. I feel I can speak to you—and oh! I must speak. I want you—you who have heard his last words—to know I have been worthy of him. . . . It is not pride. . . . Yes! I am proud to know I understood him better than any one on earth—he told me so himself. And since his mother died I have had no one—no one—to—to——'

"I listened. The darkness deepened. I was not even sure whether he had given me the right bundle. I rather suspect he wanted me to take care of another batch of his papers which, after his death, I saw the manager examining under the lamp. And the girl talked, easing her pain in the certitude of my sympathy; she talked as thirsty men drink. I had heard that her engagement with Kurtz had been disapproved by her people. He wasn't rich enough or something. And indeed I don't know whether he had not been a pauper all his life. He had given me some reason to infer that it was his impatience of comparative poverty that drove him out there.

"'. . . Who was not his friend who had heard him speak once?' she was saying. 'He drew men towards him by what was best in them.' She looked at me with intensity. 'It is the gift of the great,' she went on, and the sound of her low voice seemed to have the accompaniment of all the other sounds, full of mystery, desolation, and sorrow, I had ever heard—the ripple of the river, the soughing of the trees swayed by the wind, the murmurs of the crowds, the faint ring of incomprehensible words cried from afar, the whisper of a voice speaking from beyond the threshold of an eternal darkness. 'But you have heard him! You know!' she cried.

"'Yes, I know,' I said with something like despair in my heart, but bowing my head before the faith that was in her, before that great and saving illusion that shone with an unearthly glow in the darkness, in the triumphant darkness from which I could not have defended her—from which I could not even defend myself.

"'What a loss to me—to us!'—she corrected herself with beautiful generosity; then added in a murmur, 'To the world.' By the last gleams of twilight I could see the glitter of her eyes, full of tears—of tears that would not fall.

"'I have been very happy—very fortunate—very

proud,' she went on. 'Too fortunate. Too happy for a little while. And now I am unhappy for—for life.'

"She stood up; her fair hair seemed to catch all the remaining light in a glimmer of gold. I rose, too.

"'And of all this,' she went on, mournfully, 'of all his promise, and of all his greatness, of his generous mind, of his noble heart, nothing remains—nothing but a memory. You and I——'

"'We shall always remember him,' I said, hastily.

"'No!' she cried. 'It is impossible that all this should be lost—that such a life should be sacrificed to leave nothing—but sorrow. You know what vast plans he had. I knew of them, too—I could not perhaps understand—but others knew of them. Something must remain. His words, at least, have not died.'

"'His words will remain,' I said.

"'And his example,' she whispered to herself. 'Men looked up to him—his goodness shone in every act. His example——'

"'True,' I said; 'his example, too. Yes, his example. I forgot that.'

"'But I do not. I cannot—I cannot believe—not yet. I cannot believe that I shall never see him again, that nobody will see him again, never, never, never.'

"She put out her arms as if after a retreating figure, stretching them back* and with clasped pale hands across the fading and narrow sheen of the window. Never see him! I saw him clearly enough then. I shall see this eloquent phantom as long as I live, and I shall see her, too, a tragic and familiar Shade, resembling in this gesture another one, tragic also, and be-decked with powerless charms, stretching bare brown arms over the glitter of the infernal stream, the stream of darkness. She said suddenly very low, 'He died as he lived.'

"'His end,' said I, with dull anger stirring in me, 'was in every way worthy of his life.'

"'And I was not with him,' she murmured. My anger subsided before a feeling of infinite pity.

"'Everything that could be done——' I mumbled.

"'Ah, but I believed in him more than any one on earth—more than his own mother, more than—himself. He needed me! Me! I would have treasured every sigh, every word, every sign, every glance.'

"I felt like a chill grip on my chest. 'Don't,' I said, in a muffled voice.

"'Forgive me. I—I—have mourned so long in silence—in silence. . . . You were with him—to the last? I think of his loneliness. Nobody near to understand him as I would have understood. Perhaps no one to hear. . . .'

"'To the very end,' I said, shakily. 'I heard his very last words. . . .' I stopped in a fright.

"'Repeat them,' she murmured in a heart-broken tone. 'I want—I want—something—something—to —to live with.'

"I was on the point of crying at her, 'Don't you hear them?' The dusk was repeating them in a persistent whisper all around us, in a whisper that seemed to swell menacingly like the first whisper of a rising wind. 'The horror! the horror!'

"'His last word—to live with,' she insisted. 'Don't you understand I loved him—I loved him—I loved him!'

"I pulled myself together and spoke slowly.

"'The last word he pronounced was—your name.'

"I heard a light sigh and then my heart stood still, stopped dead short by an exulting and terrible cry, by the cry of inconceivable triumph and of unspeakable pain. 'I knew it—I was sure!' . . . She knew. She was sure. I heard her weeping; she had hidden her face in her hands. It seemed to me that the house would collapse before I could escape, that the heavens would fall upon my head. But nothing happened. The heavens do not fall for such a trifle. Would they have fallen, I wonder, if I had rendered Kurtz that justice which was his due? Hadn't he said he wanted only justice? But I couldn't. I could not tell her. It would have been too dark—too dark altogether. . . ."

Marlow ceased, and sat apart, indistinct and silent, in the pose of a meditating Buddha. Nobody moved for a time. "We have lost the first of the ebb," said the Director, suddenly. I raised my head. The offing was barred by a black bank of clouds, and the tranquil waterway leading to the uttermost ends of the earth flowed sombre under an overcast sky—seemed to lead into the heart of an immense darkness.

THE END OF THE TETHER

THE END OF THE TETHER

I

For a long time after the course of the steamer *Sofala**had been altered for the land, the low swampy coast had retained its appearance of a mere smudge of darkness beyond a belt of glitter. The sunrays fell violently upon the calm sea—seemed to shatter themselves upon an adamantine surface into sparkling dust, into a dazzling vapour of light that blinded the eye and wearied the brain with its unsteady brightness.

Captain Whalley did not look at it. When his Serang,* approaching the roomy cane arm-chair which he filled capably, had informed him in a low voice that the course was to be altered, he had risen at once and had remained on his feet, face forward, while the head of his ship swung through a quarter of a circle. He had not uttered a single word, not even the word to steady the helm. It was the Serang, an elderly, alert, little Malay, with a very dark skin, who murmured the order to the helmsman. And then slowly Captain Whalley sat down again in the arm-chair on the bridge and fixed his eyes on the deck between his feet.

He could not hope to see anything new upon this lane of the sea. He had been on these coasts for the last three years. From Low Cape to Malantan the distance was fifty miles, six hours' steaming for the old ship with the tide, or seven against. Then you steered straight for the land, and by-and-by three palms would appear on the sky, tall and slim, and with their di-

shevelled heads in a bunch, as if in confidential criticism
of the dark mangroves. The *Sofala* would be headed
towards the sombre strip of the coast, which at a given
moment, as the ship closed with it obliquely, would
show several clean shining fractures—the brimful
estuary of a river. Then on through a brown liquid,
three parts water and one part black earth, on and on
between the low shores, three parts black earth and one
part brackish water, the *Sofala* would plough her way
upstream, as she had done once every month for these
seven years or more, long before he was aware of her
existence, long before he had ever thought of having
anything to do with her and her invariable voyages.
The old ship ought to have known the road better than
her men, who had not been kept so long at it without
a change; better than the faithful Serang, whom he had
brought over from his last ship to keep the captain's
watch; better than he himself, who had been her captain
for the last three years only. She could always be
depended upon to make her courses. Her compasses
were never out. She was no trouble at all to take about,
as if her great age had given her knowledge, wisdom,
and steadiness. She made her landfalls to a degree
of the bearing, and almost to a minute of her allowed
time. At any moment, as he sat on the bridge without
looking up, or lay sleepless in his bed, simply by reckon-
ing the days and the hours he could tell where he was—
the precise spot of the beat. He knew it well, too, this
monotonous huckster's round, up and down the Straits;
he knew its order and its sights and its people. Malacca
to begin with, in at daylight and out at dusk, to cross
over with a rigid phosphorescent wake this highway of
the Far East. Darkness and gleams on the water, clear
stars on a black sky, perhaps the lights of a home
steamer keeping her unswerving course in the middle,

or maybe the elusive shadow of a native craft with her mat sails flitting by silently—and low land on the other side in sight at daylight. At noon the three palms of the next place of call, up a sluggish river. The only white man residing there was a retired young sailor, with whom he had become friendly in the course of many voyages. Sixty miles farther on there was another place of call, a deep bay with only a couple of houses on the beach. And so on, in and out, picking up coastwise cargo here and there, and finishing with a hundred miles' steady steaming through the maze of an archipelago of small islands up to a large native town at the end of the beat. There was a three days' rest for the old ship before he started her again in inverse order, seeing the same shores from another bearing, hearing the same voices in the same places, back again to the *Sofala's* port of registry on the great highway to the East, where he would take up a berth nearly opposite the big stone pile of the harbour office till it was time to start again on the old round of 1,600 miles and thirty days. Not a very enterprising life, this, for Captain Whalley, Henry Whalley, otherwise Daredevil Harry Whalley, of the *Condor*,* a famous clipper in her day. No. Not a very enterprising life for a man who had served famous firms, who had sailed famous ships (more than one or two of them his own); who had made famous passages, had been the pioneer of new routes and new trades; who had steered across the unsurveyed tracts of the South Seas, and had seen the sun rise on uncharted islands. Fifty years at sea, and forty out in the East ("a pretty thorough apprenticeship," he used to remark smilingly), had made him honourably known to a generation of shipowners and merchants in all the ports from Bombay clear over to where the East merges into the West upon the coast of

the two Americas. His fame remained writ, not very
large but plain enough, on the Admiralty charts. Was
there not somewhere between Australia and China a
Whalley Island and a Condor Reef? On that dangerous coral formation the celebrated clipper had hung
stranded for three days, her captain and crew throwing
her cargo overboard with one hand and with the other,
as it were, keeping off her a flotilla of savage war-canoes.
At that time neither the island nor the reef had any
official existence. Later the officers of her Majesty's
steam-vessel *Fusilier*, despatched to make a survey
of the route, recognized in the adoption of these two
names the enterprise of the man and the solidity of the
ship. Besides, as any one who cares may see, the
*General Directory**vol. ii. p. 410, begins the description
of the "Malotuor. Whalley Passage" with the words:
"This advantageous route, first discovered in 1850 by
Captain Whalley in the ship *Condor*," etc., and ends by
recommending it warmly to sailing vessels leaving the
China ports for the south in the months from December
to April inclusive.

This was the clearest gain he had out of life. Nothing could rob him of this kind of fame. The piercing
of the Isthmus of Suez, like the breaking of a dam, had
let in upon the East a flood of new ships, new men, new
methods of trade. It had changed the face of the
Eastern seas and the very spirit of their life; so that his
early experiences meant nothing whatever to the new
generation of seamen.

In those bygone days he had handled many thousands of pounds of his employers' money and of his
own; he had attended faithfully, as by law a shipmaster
is expected to do, to the conflicting interests of owners,
charterers, and underwriters. He had never lost a ship
or consented to a shady transaction; and he had lasted

well, outlasting in the end the conditions that had gone
to the making of his name. He had buried his wife
(in the Gulf of Petchili), had married off his daughter
to the man of her unlucky choice, and had lost more
than an ample competence in the crash of the notorious
Travancore and Deccan Banking Corporation, whose
downfall had shaken the East like an earthquake. And
he was sixty-seven years old.

II

His age sat lightly enough on him; and of his ruin he was not ashamed. He had not been alone to believe in the stability of the Banking Corporation. Men whose judgment in matters of finance was as expert as his seamanship had commended the prudence of his investments, and had themselves lost much money in the great failure. The only difference between him and them was that he had lost his all. And yet not his all. There had remained to him from his lost fortune a very pretty little barque, *Fair Maid*,* which he had bought to occupy his leisure of a retired sailor—"to play with," as he expressed it himself.

He had formally declared himself tired of the sea the year preceding his daughter's marriage. But after the young couple had gone to settle in Melbourne he found out that he could not make himself happy on shore. He was too much of a merchant sea-captain for mere yachting to satisfy him. He wanted the illusion of affairs; and his acquisition of the *Fair Maid* preserved the continuity of his life. He introduced her to his acquaintances in various ports as "my last command." When he grew too old to be trusted with a ship, he would lay her up and go ashore to be buried, leaving directions in his will to have the barque towed out and scuttled decently in deep water on the day of the funeral. His daughter would not grudge him the satisfaction of knowing that no stranger would handle his last command after him. With the fortune he was able to leave her, the value of a 500-ton barque was

neither here nor there. All this would be said with a
jocular twinkle in his eye: the vigorous old man had too
much vitality for the sentimentalism of regret; and a
little wistfully withal, because he was at home in life,
taking a genuine pleasure in its feelings and its pos-
sessions; in the dignity of his reputation and his wealth,
in his love for his daughter, and in his satisfaction with
the ship—the plaything of his lonely leisure.

He had the cabin arranged in accordance with his
simple ideal of comfort at sea. A big bookcase (he
was a great reader) occupied one side of his stateroom;
the portrait of his late wife, a flat bituminous oil-
painting representing the profile and one long black
ringlet of a young woman, faced his bedplace. Three
chronometers ticked him to sleep and greeted him on
waking with the tiny competition of their beats. He
rose at five every day. The officer of the morning
watch, drinking his early cup of coffee aft by the wheel,
would hear through the wide orifice of the copper ventilators all the splashings, blowings, and splutterings
of his captain's toilet. These noises would be followed
by a sustained deep murmur of the Lord's Prayer
recited in a loud earnest voice. Five minutes afterwards the head and shoulders of Captain Whalley
emerged out of the companion-hatchway. Invariably
he paused for a while on the stairs, looking all round at
the horizon; upwards at the trim of the sails; inhaling
deep draughts of the fresh air. Only then he would step
out on the poop, acknowledging the hand raised to the
peak of the cap with a majestic and benign "Good
morning to you." He walked the deck till eight scrupulously. Sometimes, not above twice a year, he had
to use a thick cudgel-like stick on account of a stiff-
ness in the hip—a slight touch of rheumatism, he supposed. Otherwise he knew nothing of the ills of the

flesh. At the ringing of the breakfast bell he went below to feed his canaries, wind up the chronometers, and take the head of the table. From there he had before his eyes the big carbon photographs of his daughter, her husband, and two fat-legged babies—his grandchildren —set in black frames into the maple-wood bulkheads of the cuddy. After breakfast he dusted the glass over these portraits himself with a cloth, and brushed the oil painting of his wife with a plummet*kept suspended from a small brass hook by the side of the heavy gold frame. Then with the door of his state-room shut, he would sit down on the couch under the portrait to read a chapter out of a thick pocket Bible—her Bible. But on some days he only sat there for half an hour with his finger between the leaves and the closed book resting on his knees. Perhaps he had remembered suddenly how fond of boat-sailing she used to be.

She had been a real shipmate and a true woman, too. It was like an article of faith with him that there never had been, and never could be, a brighter, cheerier home anywhere afloat or ashore than his home under the poop-deck of the *Condor*, with the big main cabin all white and gold, garlanded as if for a perpetual festival with an unfading wreath. She had decorated the centre of every panel with a cluster of home flowers. It took her a twelvemonth to go round the cuddy with this labour of love. To him it had remained a marvel of painting, the highest achievement of taste and skill; and as to old Swinburne, his mate, every time he came down to his meals he stood transfixed with admiration before the progress of the work. You could almost smell these roses, he declared, sniffing the faint flavour of turpentine which at that time pervaded the saloon, and (as he confessed afterwards) made him somewhat less hearty than usual in tackling his food. But there was nothing of the sort to interfere with his enjoyment of her singing. "Mrs. Whalley is a regular out-and-out nightingale, sir," he would pronounce with a judicial air after listening profoundly over the skylight to the very end of the piece. In fine weather, in the second dog-watch, the two. men could hear her trills and roulades*going on to the accompaniment of the piano in the cabin. On the very day they got engaged he had written to London for the instrument; but they had been married for over a year before it reached them, coming out round the Cape. The big case made part of the first direct general cargo landed in Hongkong harbour—an event that to the men who walked the busy quays of to-day seemed as hazily remote as the dark ages of history. But Captain Whalley could in a half-hour of solitude live again all his life, with its romance, its idyl, and its sorrow. He had to close her eyes himself. She went away from under the ensign like a sailor's wife, a sailor herself at heart. He had read the service over her, out of her own prayer-book, without a break in his voice. When he raised his eyes he could see old Swinburne facing him with his cap pressed to his breast, and his rugged, weather-beaten, impassive face streaming with drops of water like a lump of chipped red granite in a shower. It was all very well for that old sea-dog to cry. He had to read on to the end; but after the splash he did not remember much of what happened for the next few days. An elderly sailor of the crew, deft at needlework, put together a mourning frock for the child out of one of her black skirts.

He was not likely to forget; but you cannot dam up life like a sluggish stream. It will break out and flow over a man's troubles, it will close upon a sorrow like the sea upon a dead body, no matter how much love

has gone to the bottom. And the world is not bad.
People had been very kind to him; especially Mrs.
Gardner, the wife of the senior partner in Gardner,
Patteson & Co., the owners of the *Condor*. It was she
who volunteered to look after the little one, and in due
course took her to England (something of a journey
in those days, even by the overland mail route) with her
own girls to finish her education. It was ten years before he saw her again.

As a little child she had never been frightened of
bad weather; she would beg to be taken up on deck in
the bosom of his oilskin coat to watch the big seas
hurling themselves upon the *Condor*. The swirl and
crash of the waves seemed to fill her small soul with a
breathless delight. "A good boy spoiled," he used to
say of her in joke. He had named her Ivy because of
the sound of the word, and obscurely fascinated by a
vague association of ideas. She had twined herself
tightly round his heart, and he intended her to cling
close to her father as to a tower of strength; forgetting
while she was little, that in the nature of things she
would probably elect to cling to someone else. But he
loved life well enough for even that event to give him a
certain satisfaction, apart from his more intimate feeling of loss.

After he had purchased the *Fair Maid* to occupy his
loneliness, he hastened to accept a rather unprofitable
freight to Australia simply for the opportunity of seeing his daughter in her own home. What made him
dissatisfied there was not to see that she clung now to
somebody else, but that the prop she had selected
seemed on closer examination "a rather poor stick"—
even in the matter of health. He disliked his son-in-
law's studied civility perhaps more than his method of
handling the sum of money he had given Ivy at her

marriage. But of his apprehensions he said nothing. Only on the day of his departure, with the hall-door open all ready, holding her hands and looking steadily into her eyes, he had said, "You know, my dear, all I have is for you and the chicks. Mind you write to me openly." She had answered him by an almost imperceptible movement of her head. She resembled her mother in the colour of her eyes, and in character— and also in this, that she understood him without many words.

Sure enough she had to write; and some of these letters made Captain Whalley lift his white eye-brows. For the rest he considered he was reaping the true reward of his life by being thus able to produce on demand whatever was needed. He had not enjoyed himself so much in a way since his wife had died. Characteristically enough his son-in-law's punctuality in failure caused him at a distance to feel a sort of kindness towards the man. The fellow was so perpetually being jammed on a lee shore that to charge it all to his reckless navigation would be manifestly unfair. No, no! He knew well what that meant. It was bad luck. His own had been simply marvellous, but he had seen in his life too many good men—seamen and others—go under with the sheer weight of bad luck not to recognize the fatal signs. For all that, he was cogitating on the best way of tying up very strictly every penny he had to leave, when with a preliminary rumble of rumours (whose first sound reached him in Shanghai as it happened), the shock of the big failure came; and, after passing through the phases of stupor, of incredulity, of indignation, he had to accept the fact that he had nothing to speak of to leave.

Upon that, as if he had only waited for this catastrophe, the unlucky man, away there in Melbourne, gave

up his unprofitable game, and sat down—in an invalid's
bath-chair at that, too. "He will never walk again,"
wrote the wife. For the first time in his life Captain
Whalley was a bit staggered.

The *Fair Maid* had to go to work in bitter earnest
now. It was no longer a matter of preserving alive the
memory of Dare-devil Harry Whalley in the Eastern
Seas, or of keeping an old man in pocket-money and
clothes, with, perhaps, a bill for a few hundred first-
class cigars thrown in at the end of the year. He would
have to buckle-to, and keep her going hard on a scant
allowance of gilt for the ginger-bread scrolls at her stem
and stern.

This necessity opened his eyes to the fundamental
changes of the world. Of his past only the familiar
names remained, here and there, but the things and
the men, as he had known them, were gone. The name
of Gardner, Patteson & Co. was still displayed on the
walls of warehouses by the waterside, on the brass plates
and window-panes in the business quarters of more than
one Eastern port, but there was no longer a Gardner or
a Patteson in the firm. There was no longer for Captain Whalley an arm-chair and a welcome in the private
office, with a bit of business ready to be put in the way
of an old friend, for the sake of bygone services. The
husbands of the Gardner girls sat behind the desks in
that room where, long after he had left the employ,
he had kept his right of entrance in the old man's time.
Their ships now had yellow funnels with black tops,
and a time-table of appointed routes like a confounded
service of tramways. The winds of December and
June were all one to them; their captains (excellent
young men he doubted not) were, to be sure, familiar
with Whalley Island, because of late years the Government had established a white fixed light on the north

end (with a red danger sector over the Condor Reef), but most of them would have been extremely surprised to hear that a flesh-and-blood Whalley still existed—an old man going about the world trying to pick up a cargo here and there for his little barque.

And everywhere it was the same. Departed the men who would have nodded appreciatively at the mention of his name, and would have thought themselves bound in honour to do something for Dare-devil Harry Whalley. Departed the opportunities which he would have known how to seize; and gone with them the white-winged flock of clippers that lived in the boisterous uncertain life of the winds, skimming big fortunes out of the foam of the sea. In a world that pared down the profits to an irreducible minimum, in a world that was able to count its disengaged tonnage twice over every day and in which lean charters were snapped up by cable three months in advance, there were no chances of fortune for an individual wandering haphazard with a little barque—hardly indeed any room to exist.

He found it more difficult from year to year. He suffered greatly from the smallness of remittances he was able to send his daughter. Meantime he had given up good cigars, and even in the matter of inferior cheroots limited himself to six a day. He never told her of his difficulties, and she never enlarged upon her struggle to live. Their confidence in each other needed no explanations, and their perfect understanding endured without protestations of gratitude or regret. He would have been shocked if she had taken it into her head to thank him in so many words, but he found it perfectly natural that she should tell him she needed two hundred pounds.

He had come in with the *Fair Maid* in ballast to look for a freight in the *Sofala's* port of registry, and her

letter met him there.   Its tenor was that it was no use
mincing matters.   Her only resource was in opening a
boarding-house, for which the prospects, she judged,
were good.   Good enough, at any rate, to make her
tell him frankly that with two hundred pounds she
could make a start.   He had torn the envelope open,
hastily, on deck, where it was handed to him by the
ship-chandler's runner, who had brought his mail at
the moment of anchoring.   For the second time in his
life he was appalled, and remained stock-still at the
cabin door with the paper trembling between his fingers.
Open a boarding-house!   Two hundred pounds for a
start!   The only resource!   And he did not know where
to lay his hands on two hundred pence.

All that night Captain Whalley walked the poop
of his anchored ship, as though he had been about to
close with the land in thick weather, and uncertain of
his position after a run of many gray days without a
sight of sun, moon, or stars.   The black night twinkled
with the guiding lights of seamen and the steady
straight lines of lights on shore; and all around the *Fair
Maid* the riding lights of ships cast trembling trails
upon the water of the roadstead.   Captain Whalley
saw not a gleam anywhere till the dawn broke and he
found out that his clothing was soaked through with
the heavy dew.

His ship was awake.   He stopped short, stroked his
wet beard, and descended the poop ladder backwards,
with tired feet.   At the sight of him the chief officer,
lounging about sleepily on the quarterdeck, remained
open-mouthed in the middle of a great early-morning
yawn.

"Good morning to you," pronounced Captain Whalley, solemnly, passing into the cabin.   But he checked
himself in the doorway, and without looking back,

"By the bye," he said, "there should be an empty wooden case put away in the lazarette. It has not been broken up—has it?"

The mate shut his mouth, and then asked as if dazed, "What empty case, sir?"

"A big flat packing-case belonging to that painting in my room. Let it be taken up on deck and tell the carpenter to look it over. I may want to use it before long."

The chief officer did not stir a limb till he had heard the door of the captain's stateroom slam within the cuddy. Then he beckoned aft the second mate with his forefinger to tell him that there was something "in the wind."

When the bell rang Captain Whalley's authoritative voice boomed out through a closed door, "Sit down and don't wait for me." And his impressed officers took their places, exchanging looks and whispers across the table. What! No breakfast? And after apparently knocking about all night on deck, too! Clearly, there was something in the wind. In the skylight above their heads, bowed earnestly over the plates, three wire cages rocked and rattled to the restless jumping of the hungry canaries; and they could detect the sounds of their "old man's" deliberate movements within his stateroom. Captain Whalley was methodically winding up the chronometers, dusting the portrait of his late wife, getting a clean white shirt out of the drawers, making himself ready in his punctilious, unhurried manner to go ashore. He could not have swallowed a single mouthful of food that morning. He had made up his mind to sell the *Fair Maid*.

III

Just at that time the Japanese were casting far and wide for ships of European build, and he had no difficulty in finding a purchaser, a speculator who drove a hard bargain, but paid cash down for the *Fair Maid*, with a view to a profitable resale. Thus it came about that Captain Whalley found himself on a certain afternoon descending the steps of one of the most important post-offices of the East with a slip of bluish paper in his hand. This was the receipt of a registered letter enclosing a draft for two hundred pounds, and addressed to Melbourne. Captain Whalley pushed the paper into his waistcoat-pocket, took his stick from under his arm, and walked down the street.

It was a recently opened and untidy thoroughfare with rudimentary side-walks and a soft layer of dust cushioning the whole width of the road. One end touched the slummy street of Chinese shops near the harbour, the other drove straight on, without houses, for a couple of miles, through patches of jungle-like vegetation, to the yard gates of the new Consolidated Docks Company. The crude frontages of the new Government buildings alternated with the blank fencing of vacant plots, and the view of the sky seemed to give an added spaciousness to the broad vista. It was empty and shunned by natives after business hours, as though they had expected to see one of the tigers from the neighbourhood of the New Waterworks on the hill coming at a loping canter down the middle to get a Chinese shopkeeper for supper. Captain Whalley was not dwarfed by the solitude of the grandly planned street. He had too fine a presence for that. He was only a lonely figure walking purposefully, with a great white beard like a pilgrim, and with a thick stick that resembled a weapon. On one side the new Courts of Justice had a low and unadorned portico of squat columns half concealed by a few old trees left in the approach. On the other the pavilion wings of the new Colonial Treasury came out to the line of the street. But Captain Whalley, who had now no ship and no home, remembered in passing that on that very site when he first came out from England there had stood a fishing village, a few mat huts erected on piles between a muddy tidal creek and a miry pathway that went writhing into a tangled wilderness without any docks or waterworks.

No ship—no home. And his poor Ivy away there had no home either. A boarding-house is no sort of home though it may get you a living. His feelings were horribly rasped by the idea of the boarding-house. In his rank of life he had that truly aristocratic temperament characterized by a scorn of vulgar gentility and by prejudiced views as to the derogatory nature of certain occupations. For his own part he had always preferred sailing merchant ships (which is a straightforward occupation) to buying and selling merchandise of which the essence is to get the better of somebody in a bargain—an undignified trial of wits at best. His father had been Colonel Whalley (retired) of the H.E.I. Company's*service, with very slender means besides his pension, but with distinguished connections. He could remember as a boy how frequently waiters at the inns, country tradesmen and small people of that sort, used to "My lord" the old warrior on the strength of his appearance.

Captain Whalley himself (he would have entered the Navy if his father had not died before he was fourteen) had something of a grand air which would have suited an old and glorious admiral; but he became lost like a straw in the eddy of a brook amongst the swarm of brown and yellow humanity filling a thoroughfare, that by contrast with the vast and empty avenue he had left seemed as narrow as a lane and absolutely riotous with life. The walls of the houses were blue; the shops of the Chinamen yawned like cavernous lairs; heaps of nondescript merchandise overflowed the gloom of the long range of arcades, and the fiery serenity of sunset took the middle of the street from end to end with a glow like the reflection of a fire. It fell on the bright colours and the dark faces of the bare-footed crowd, on the pallid yellow backs of the half-naked jostling coolies, on the accoutrements of a tall Sikh trooper*with a parted beard and fierce moustaches on sentry before the gate of the police compound. Looming very big above the heads in a red haze of dust, the tightly packed car of the cable tramway navigated cautiously up the human stream, with the incessant blare of its horn, in the manner of a steamer groping in a fog.

Captain Whalley emerged like a diver on the other side, and in the desert shade between the walls of closed warehouses removed his hat to cool his brow. A certain disrepute attached to the calling of a landlady of a boarding-house. These women were said to be rapacious, unscrupulous, untruthful; and though he condemned no class of his fellow-creatures—God forbid!—these were suspicions to which it was unseemly that a Whalley should lay herself open. He had not expostulated with her, however. He was confident she shared his feelings; he was sorry for her; he trusted her judgment; he considered it a merciful dispensation that he could help her once more—but in his aristocratic heart of hearts he would have found it more easy to reconcile himself to the idea of her turning seamstress. Vaguely he remembered reading years ago a touching piece called the "Song of the Shirt." It was all very well making songs about poor women. The granddaughter of Colonel Whalley, the landlady of a boarding-house! Pooh! He replaced his hat, dived into two pockets, and stopping a moment to apply a flaring match to the end of a cheap cheroot, blew an embittered cloud of smoke at a world that could hold such surprises.

Of one thing he was certain—that she was the own child of a clever mother. Now he had got over the wrench of parting with his ship, he perceived clearly that such a step had been unavoidable. Perhaps he had been growing aware of it all along with an unconfessed knowledge. But she, far away there, must have had an intuitive perception of it, with the pluck to face that truth and the courage to speak out—all the qualities which had made her mother a woman of such excellent counsel.

It would have had to come to that in the end! It was fortunate she had forced his hand. In another year or two it would have been an utterly barren sale. To keep the ship going he had been involving himself deeper every year. He was defenceless before the insidious work of adversity, to whose more open assaults he could present a firm front; like a cliff that stands unmoved the open battering of the sea, with a lofty ignorance of the treacherous backwash undermining its base. As it was, every liability satisfied, her request answered, and owing no man a penny, there remained to him from the proceeds a sum of five hundred pounds put away safely. In addition he had

upon his person some forty odd dollars—enough to
pay his hotel bill, providing he did not linger too long
in the modest bedroom where he had taken refuge.

Scantily furnished, and with a waxed floor, it opened
into one of the side-verandahs. The straggling building of bricks, as airy as a bird-cage, resounded with the
incessant flapping of rattan screens worried by the wind
between the whitewashed square pillars of the sea-
front. The rooms were lofty, a ripple of sunshine
flowed over the ceilings; and the periodical invasions of
tourists from some passenger steamer in the harbour
flitted through the wind-swept dusk of the apartments
with the tumult of their unfamiliar voices and im-
permanent presences, like relays of migratory shades
condemned to speed headlong round the earth without
leaving a trace. The babble of their irruptions ebbed
out as suddenly as it had arisen; the draughty corridors
and the long chairs of the verandahs knew their sight-
seeing hurry or their prostrate repose no more; and Captain Whalley, substantial and dignified, left well nigh
alone in the vast hotel by each light-hearted skurry,
felt more and more like a stranded tourist with no aim
in view, like a forlorn traveller without a home. In
the solitude of his room he smoked thoughtfully, gazing
at the two sea-chests which held all that he could call
his own in this world. A thick roll of charts in a
sheath of sailcloth leaned in a corner; the flat packing-
case containing the portrait in oils and the three carbon
photographs had been pushed under the bed. He was
tired of discussing terms, of assisting at surveys, of all
the routine of the business. What to the other parties
was merely the sale of a ship was to him a momentous
event involving a radically new view of existence. He
knew that after this ship there would be no other; and
the hopes of his youth, the exercise of his abilities, every

feeling and achievement of his manhood, had been indissolubly connected with ships. He had served ships;
he had owned ships; and even the years of his actual
retirement from the sea had been made bearable by the
idea that he had only to stretch out his hand full of
money to get a ship. He had been at liberty to feel as
though he were the owner of all the ships in the world.
The selling of this one was weary work; but when she
passed from him at last, when he signed the last receipt,
it was as though all the ships had gone out of the world
together, leaving him on the shore of inaccessible oceans
with seven hundred pounds in his hands.

Striding firmly, without haste, along the quay, Captain Whalley averted his glances from the familiar
roadstead. Two generations of seamen born since his
first day at sea stood between him and all these ships
at the anchorage. His own was sold, and he had been
asking himself, What next?

From the feeling of loneliness, of inward emptiness—
and of loss, too, as if his very soul had been taken out
of him forcibly—there had sprung at first a desire to
start right off and join his daughter. "Here are the
last pence," he would say to her; "take them, my dear.
And here's your old father: you must take him, too."

His soul recoiled, as if afraid of what lay hidden at
the bottom of this impulse. Give up! Never! When
one is thoroughly weary all sorts of nonsense come into
one's head. A pretty gift it would have been for a poor
woman—this seven hundred pounds with the incum-
brance of a hale old fellow more than likely to last for
years and years to come. Was he not as fit to die in
harness as any of the youngsters in charge of these
anchored ships out yonder? He was as solid now as
ever he had been. But as to who would give him work
to do, that was another matter. Were he, with his

appearance and antecedents, to go about looking for a
junior's berth, people, he was afraid, would not take him
seriously; or else if he succeeded in impressing them, he
would maybe obtain their pity, which would be like
stripping yourself naked to be kicked. He was not
anxious to give himself away for less than nothing.
He had no use for anybody's pity. On the other hand,
a command—the only thing he could try for with
due regard for common decency—was not likely to be
lying in wait for him at the corner of the next street.
Commands don't go a-begging nowadays. Ever since
he had come ashore to carry out the business of the sale
he had kept his ears open, but had heard no hint of one
being vacant in the port. And even if there had been
one, his successful past itself stood in his way. He had
been his own employer too long. The only credential
he could produce was the testimony of his whole life.
What better recommendation could any one require?
But vaguely he felt that the unique document would
be looked upon as an archaic curiosity of the Eastern
waters, a screed traced in obsolete words—in a half-
forgotten language.

IV

REVOLVING these thoughts, he strolled on near the
railings of the quay, broad-chested, without a stoop,
as though his big shoulders had never felt the burden
of the loads that must be carried between the cradle
and the grave. No single betraying fold or line of care
disfigured the reposeful modelling of his face. It was
full and untanned; and the upper part emerged, massively quiet, out of the downward flow of silvery hair,
with the striking delicacy of its clear complexion and
the powerful width of the forehead. The first cast of
his glance fell on you candid and swift, like a boy's;
but because of the ragged snowy thatch of the eyebrows the affability of his attention acquired the
character of a keen and searching scrutiny. With age
he had put on flesh a little, had increased his girth like
an old tree presenting no symptoms of decay; and even
the opulent, lustrous ripple of white hairs upon his chest
seemed an attribute of unquenchable vitality and
vigour.

Once rather proud of his great bodily strength, and
even of his personal appearance, conscious of his worth,
and firm in his rectitude, there had remained to him,
like the heritage of departed prosperity, the tranquil
bearing of a man who had proved himself fit in every
sort of way for the life of his choice. He strode on
squarely under the projecting brim of an ancient
Panama hat. It had a low crown, a crease through its
whole diameter, a narrow black ribbon. Imperishable
and a little discoloured, this headgear made it easy to

pick him out from afar on thronged wharves and in the busy streets. He had never adopted the comparatively modern fashion of pipeclayed cork helmets. He disliked the form; and he hoped he could manage to keep a cool head to the end of his life without all these contrivances for hygienic ventilation. His hair was cropped close, his linen always of immaculate whiteness; a suit of thin gray flannel, worn threadbare but scrupulously brushed, floated about his burly limbs, adding to his bulk by the looseness of its cut. The years had mellowed the good-humoured, imperturbable audacity of his prime into a temper carelessly serene; and the leisurely tapping of his iron-shod stick accompanied his footfalls with a self-confident sound on the flagstones. It was impossible to connect such a fine presence and this unruffled aspect with the belittling troubles of poverty; the man's whole existence appeared to pass before you, facile and large, in the freedom of means as ample as the clothing of his body.

The irrational dread of having to break into his five hundred pounds for personal expenses in the hotel disturbed the steady poise of his mind. There was no time to lose. The bill was running up. He nourished the hope that this five hundred would perhaps be the means, if everything else failed, of obtaining some work which, keeping his body and soul together (not a matter of great outlay), would enable him to be of use to his daughter. To his mind it was her own money which he employed, as it were, in backing her father and solely for her benefit. Once at work, he would help her with the greater part of his earnings; he was good for many years yet, and this boarding-house business, he argued to himself, whatever the prospects, could not be much of a gold-mine from the first start. But what work? He was ready to lay hold of anything in an honest way so that it came quickly to his hand; because the five hundred pounds must be preserved intact for eventual use. That was the great point. With the entire five hundred one felt a substance at one's back; but it seemed to him that should he let it dwindle to four-fifty or even four-eighty, all the efficiency would be gone out of the money, as though there were some magic power in the round figure. But what sort of work?

Confronted by that haunting question as by an uneasy ghost, for whom he had no exorcising formula, Captain Whalley stopped short on the apex of a small bridge spanning steeply the bed of a canalized creek with granite shores. Moored between the square blocks a sea-going Malay prau floated half hidden under the arch of masonry, with her spars lowered down, without a sound of life on board, and covered from stem to stern with a ridge of palm-leaf mats. He had left behind him the overheated pavements bordered by the stone frontages that, like the sheer face of cliffs, followed the sweep of the quays; and an unconfined spaciousness of orderly and sylvan aspect opened before him its wide plots of rolled grass, like pieces of green carpet smoothly pegged out, its long ranges of trees lined up in colossal porticos of dark shafts roofed with a vault of branches.

Some of these avenues ended at the sea. It was a terraced shore; and beyond, upon the level expanse, profound and glistening like the gaze of a dark-blue eye, an oblique band of stippled purple lengthened itself indefinitely through the gap between a couple of verdant twin islets. The masts and spars of a few ships far away, hull down in the outer roads, sprang straight from the water in a fine maze of rosy lines pencilled on the clear shadow of the eastern board. Captain Whalley gave them a long glance. The ship, once his own, was anchored out there. It was staggering to think that it was open to him no longer to take a boat at the jetty and get himself pulled off to her when the evening came. To no ship. Perhaps never more. Before the sale was concluded, and till the purchase-money had been paid, he had spent daily some time on board the *Fair Maid*. The money had been paid this very morning, and now, all at once, there was positively no ship that he could go on board of when he liked; no ship that would need his presence in order to do her work—to live. It seemed an incredible state of affairs, something too bizarre to last. And the sea was full of craft of all sorts. There was that prau lying so still swathed in her shroud of sewn palm-leaves—she, too, had her indispensable man. They lived through each other, this Malay he had never seen, and this high-sterned thing of no size that seemed to be resting after a long journey. And of all the ships in sight, near and far, each was provided with a man, the man without whom the finest ship is a dead thing, a floating and purposeless log.

After his one glance at the roadstead he went on since there was nothing to turn back for, and the time must be got through somehow. The avenues of big trees ran straight over the Esplanade,* cutting each other at diverse angles, columnar below and luxuriant above. The interlaced boughs high up there seemed to slumber; not a leaf stirred overhead: and the reedy cast-iron lamp-posts in the middle of the road, gilt like sceptres diminished in a long perspective, with their globes of white porcelain atop, resembling a barbarous decoration of ostriches' eggs displayed in a row. The flaming sky kindled a tiny crimson spark upon the glistening surface of each glassy shell.

With his chin sunk a little, his hands behind his back,

and the end of his stick marking the gravel with a faint wavering line at his heels, Captain Whalley reflected that if a ship without a man was like a body without a soul, a sailor without a ship was of not much more account in this world than an aimless log adrift upon the sea. The log might be sound enough by itself, tough of fibre, and hard to destroy—but what of that! And a sudden sense of irremediable idleness weighted his feet like a great fatigue.

A succession of open carriages came bowling along the newly opened sea-road. You could see across the wide grass-plots the discs of vibration made by the spokes. The bright domes of the parasols swayed lightly outwards like full-blown blossoms on the rim of a vase; and the quiet sheet of dark-blue water, crossed by a bar of purple, made a background for the spinning wheels and the high action of the horses, whilst the turbaned heads of the Indian servants elevated above the line of the sea horizon glided rapidly on the paler blue of the sky. In an open space near the little bridge each turn-out trotted smartly in a wide curve away from the sunset; then pulling up sharp, entered the main alley in a long slow-moving file with the great red stillness of the sky at the back. The trunks of mighty trees stood all touched with red on the same side, the air seemed aflame under the high foliage, the very ground under the hoofs of the horses was red. The wheels turned solemnly; one after another the sunshades drooped, folding their colours like gorgeous flowers shutting their petals at the end of the day. In the whole half-mile of human beings no voice uttered a distinct word, only a faint thudding noise went on mingled with slight jingling sounds, and the motionless heads and shoulders of men and women sitting in couples emerged stolidly above the lowered hoods—as if

wooden.   But one carriage and pair coming late did not
join the line.

It fled along in a noiseless roll; but on entering the
avenue one of the dark bays snorted, arching his neck
and shying against the steel-tipped pole; a flake of foam
fell from the bit upon the point of a satiny shoulder,
and the dusky face of the coachman leaned forward
at once over the hands taking a fresh grip of the reins.
It was a long dark-green landau,* having a dignified and
buoyant motion between the sharply curved C-springs,*
and a sort of strictly official majesty in its supreme
elegance.   It seemed more roomy than is usual, its
horses seemed slightly bigger, the appointments a
shade more perfect, the servants perched somewhat
higher on the box.   The dresses of three women—two
young and pretty, and one, handsome, large, of mature
age—seemed to fill completely the shallow body of the
carriage.   The fourth face was that of a man, heavy
lidded, distinguished and sallow, with a sombre, thick,
iron-gray imperial and moustaches, which somehow
had the air of solid appendages.   His Excellency——

The rapid motion of that one equipage made all the
others appear utterly inferior, blighted, and reduced to
crawl painfully at a snail's pace.   The landau distanced
the whole file in a sort of sustained rush; the features
of the occupants whirling out of sight left behind an
impression of fixed stares and impassive vacancy; and
after it had vanished in full flight as it were, notwithstanding the long line of vehicles hugging the curb at a
walk, the whole lofty vista of the avenue seemed to lie
open and emptied of life in the enlarged impression of
an august solitude.

Captain Whalley had lifted his head to look, and his
mind, disturbed in its meditation, turned with wonder
(as men's minds will do) to matters of no importance.

It struck him that it was to this port, where he had just sold his last ship, that he had come with the very first he had ever owned, and with his head full of a plan for opening a new trade with a distant part of the Archipelago.* The then governor had given him no end of encouragement. No Excellency he—this Mr. Denham—this governor with his jacket off; a man who tended night and day, so to speak, the growing prosperity of the settlement with the self-forgetful devotion of a nurse for a child she loves; a lone bachelor who lived as in a camp with the few servants and his three dogs in what was called then the Government Bungalow: a low-roofed structure on the half-cleared slope of a hill, with a new flagstaff in front and a police orderly on the verandah. He remembered toiling up that hill under a heavy sun for his audience; the unfurnished aspect of the cool shaded room; the long table covered at one end with piles of papers, and with two guns, a brass telescope, a small bottle of oil with a feather stuck in the neck at the other—and the flattering attention given to him by the man in power. It was an undertaking full of risk he had come to expound, but a twenty minutes' talk in the Government Bungalow on the hill had made it go smoothly from the start. And as he was retiring Mr. Denham, already seated before the papers, called out after him, "Next month the *Dido* starts for a cruise that way, and I shall request her captain officially to give you a look in and see how you get on." The *Dido* was one of the smart frigates on the China station—and five-and-thirty years make a big slice of time. Five-and-thirty years ago an enterprise like his had for the colony enough importance to be looked after by a Queen's ship. A big slice of time. Individuals were of some account then. Men like himself; men, too, like poor

Evans, for instance, with his red face, his coal-black
whiskers, and his restless eyes, who had set up the first
patent slip for repairing small ships, on the edge of the
forest, in a lonely bay three miles up the coast. Mr.
Denham had encouraged that enterprise, too, and yet
somehow poor Evans had ended by dying at home
deucedly hard up. His son, they said, was squeezing
oil out of cocoa-nuts for a living on some God-forsaken
islet of the Indian Ocean; but it was from that patent
slip in a lonely wooded bay that had sprung the work-
shops of the Consolidated Docks Company, with its
three graving basins*carved out of solid rock, its wharves, its jetties, its electric-light plant, its steam-power
houses—with its gigantic sheer-legs,* fit to lift the
heaviest weight ever carried afloat, and whose head
could be seen like the top of a queer white monument
peeping over bushy points of land and sandy
promontories, as you approached the New Harbour
from the west.

There had been a time when men counted: there
were not so many carriages in the colony then, though
Mr. Denham, he fancies, had a buggy. And Captain
Whalley seemed to be swept out of the great avenue
by the swirl of a mental backwash. He remembered
muddy shores, a harbour without quays, the one
solitary wooden pier (but that was a public work)
jutting out crookedly, the first coal-sheds erected on
Monkey Point, that caught fire mysteriously and
smouldered for days, so that amazed ships came into a
roadstead full of sulphurous fog, and the sun hung
blood-red at midday. He remembered the things, the
faces, and something more besides—like the faint
flavour of a cup quaffed to the bottom, like a subtle
sparkle of the air that was not to be found in the atmosphere of to-day.

In this evocation, swift and full of detail like a flash of magnesium light into the niches of a dark memorial hall, Captain Whalley contemplated things once important, the efforts of small men, the growth of a great place, but now robbed of all consequence by the greatness of accomplished facts, by hopes greater still; and they gave him for a moment such an almost physical grip upon time, such a comprehension of our unchangeable feelings, that he stopped short, struck the ground with his stick, and ejaculated mentally, "What the devil am I doing here!" He seemed lost in a sort of surprise; but he heard his name called out in wheezy tones once, twice—and turned on his heels slowly.

He beheld then, waddling towards him autocratically, a man of an old-fashioned and gouty aspect, with hair as white as his own, but with shaved, florid cheeks, wearing a necktie—almost a neckcloth—whose stiff ends projected far beyond his chin; with round legs, round arms, a round body, a round face—generally producing the effect of his short figure having been distended by means of an air-pump as much as the seams of his clothing would stand. This was the Master-Attendant of the port. A master-attendant is a superior sort of harbour-master; a person, out in the East, of some consequence in his sphere; a Government official, a magistrate for the waters of the port, and possessed of vast but ill-defined disciplinary authority over seamen of all classes. This particular Master-Attendant was reported to consider it miserably inadequate, on the ground that it did not include the power of life and death. This was a jocular exaggeration. Captain Eliott was fairly satisfied with his position, and nursed no inconsiderable sense of such power as he had. His conceited and tyrannical disposition did not allow him to let it dwindle in his hands for want of use. The uproarious, choleric frankness of his comments on people's character and conduct caused him to be feared at bottom. Though in conversation many pretended not to mind him in the least, others would only smile sourly at the mention of his name, and there were even some who dared to pronounce him "a meddlesome old ruffian." But for almost all of them one of Captain Eliott's outbreaks was nearly as distasteful to face as a chance of annihilation.

V

As soon as he had come up quite close he said, mouthing in a growl—

"What's this I hear, Whalley? Is it true you're selling the *Fair Maid?*"

Captain Whalley, looking away, said the thing was done—money had been paid that morning; and the other expressed at once his approbation of such an extremely sensible proceeding. He had got out of his trap to stretch his legs, he explained, on his way home to dinner. Sir Frederick looked well at the end of his time. Didn't he?

Captain Whalley could not say; had only noticed the carriage going past.

The Master-Attendant, plunging his hands into the pockets of an alpaca jacket inappropriately short and tight for a man of his age and appearance, strutted with a slight limp, and with his head reaching only to the shoulder of Captain Whalley, who walked easily, staring straight before him. They had been good comrades years ago, almost intimates. At the time when Whalley commanded the renowned *Condor*, Eliott had charge of the nearly as famous *Ringdove**for the same owners; and when the appointment of Master-Attendant was created, Whalley would have been the only other serious candidate. But Captain Whalley, then in the prime of life, was resolved to serve no one but his own auspicious Fortune. Far away, tending his hot irons, he was glad to hear the other had been successful. There was a worldly suppleness in bluff

Ned Eliott that would serve him well in that sort of
official appointment. And they were so dissimilar at
bottom that as they came slowly to the end of the
avenue before the Cathedral, it had never come into
Whalley's head that he might have been in that man's
place—provided for to the end of his days.

The sacred edifice, standing in solemn isolation
amongst the converging avenues of enormous trees, as
if to put grave thoughts of heaven into the hours of
ease, presented a closed Gothic portal to the light and
glory of the west. The glass of the rosace above the
ogive* glowed like fiery coal in the deep carvings of a
wheel of stone. The two men faced about.

"I'll tell you what they ought to do next, Whalley,"
growled Captain Eliott suddenly.

"Well?"

"They ought to send a real live lord out here when
Sir Frederick's time is up. Eh?"

Captain Whalley perfunctorily did not see why a
lord of the right sort should not do as well as any one
else. But this was not the other's point of view.

"No, no. Place runs itself. Nothing can stop it
now. Good enough for a lord," he growled in short
sentences. "Look at the changes in our own time. We
need a lord here now. They have got a lord in Bombay."

He dined once or twice every year at the Government House—a many-windowed, arcaded palace upon
a hill laid out in roads and gardens. And lately he had
been taking about a duke in his Master-Attendant's
steam-launch to visit the harbour improvements.
Before that he had "most obligingly" gone out in person to pick out a good berth for the ducal yacht. Afterwards he had an invitation to lunch on board. The
duchess herself lunched with them. A big woman

with a red face. Complexion quite sunburnt. He should think ruined. Very gracious manners. They were going on to Japan. . . .

He ejaculated these details for Captain Whalley's edification, pausing to blow out his cheeks as if with a pent-up sense of importance, and repeatedly protruding his thick lips till the blunt crimson end of his nose seemed to dip into the milk of his moustache. The place ran itself; it was fit for any lord; it gave no trouble except in its Marine department—in its Marine department, he repeated twice, and after a heavy snort began to relate how the other day her Majesty's Consul-General in French Cochin-China*had cabled to him —in his official capacity—asking for a qualified man to be sent over to take charge of a Glasgow ship whose master had died in Saigon.

"I sent word of it to the officers' quarters in the Sailors' Home," he continued, while the limp in his gait seemed to grow more accentuated with the increasing irritation of his voice. "Place's full of them. Twice as many men as there are berths going in the local trade. All hungry for an easy job. Twice as many—and—What d'you think, Whalley? . . ."

He stopped short; his hands, clenched and thrust deeply downwards, seemed ready to burst the pockets of his jacket. A slight sigh escaped Captain Whalley.

"Hey? You would think they would be falling over each other. Not a bit of it. Frightened to go home. Nice and warm out here to lie about a verandah waiting for a job. I sit and wait in my office. Nobody. What did they suppose? That I was going to sit there like a dummy with the Consul-General's cable before me? Not likely. So I looked up a list of them I keep by me and sent word for Hamilton—the worst loafer of them all—and just made him go. Threatened to in-

struct the steward of the Sailors' Home to have him
turned out neck and crop. He did not think the berth
was good enough—if you—please. 'I've your little
record by me,' said I. 'You came ashore here eighteen
months ago, and you haven't done six months' work
since. You are in debt for your board now at the
Home, and I suppose you reckon the Marine Office
will pay in the end. Eh? So it shall; but if you
don't take this chance, away you go to England, assisted
passage, by the first homeward steamer that comes
along. You are no better than a pauper. We don't
want any white paupers here.' I scared him. But
look at the trouble all this gave me."

"You would not have had any trouble," Captain
Whalley said almost involuntarily, "if you had sent
for me."

Captain Elliott was immensely amused; he shook
with laughter as he walked. But suddenly he stopped
laughing. A vague recollection had crossed his mind.
Hadn't he heard it said at the time of the Travancore
and Deccan smash that poor Whalley had been cleaned
out completely. "Fellow's hard up, by heavens!"
he thought; and at once he cast a sidelong upwards
glance at his companion. But Captain Whalley was
smiling austerely straight before him, with a carriage
of the head inconceivable in a penniless man—and he
became reassured. Impossible. Could not have lost
everything. That ship had been only a hobby of his.
And the reflection that a man who had confessed to
receiving that very morning a presumably large sum
of money was not likely to spring upon him a demand
for a small loan put him entirely at his ease again. There
had come a long pause in their talk, however, and not
knowing how to begin again, he growled out soberly,
"We old fellows ought to take a rest now."

"The best thing for some of us would be to die at the oar," Captain Whalley said, negligently.

"Come, now. Aren't you a bit tired by this time of the whole show?" muttered the other, sullenly.

"Are you?"

Captain Eliott was. Infernally tired. He only hung on to his berth so long in order to get his pension on the highest scale before he went home. It would be no better than poverty, anyhow; still, it was the only thing between him and the workhouse. And he had a family. Three girls, as Whalley knew. He gave "Harry, old boy," to understand that these three girls were a source of the greatest anxiety and worry to him. Enough to drive a man distracted.

"Why? What have they been doing now?" asked Captain Whalley with a sort of amused absent-mindedness.

"Doing! Doing nothing. That's just it. Lawn-tennis and silly novels from morning to night. . . ."

If one of them at least had been a boy! But all three! And, as ill-luck would have it, there did not seem to be any decent young fellows left in the world. When he looked around in the club he saw only a lot of conceited popinjays too selfish to think of making a good woman happy. Extreme indigence stared him in the face with all that crowd to keep at home. He had cherished the idea of building himself a little house in the country—in Surrey—to end his days in, but he was afraid it was out of the question . . . and his staring eyes rolled upwards with such a pathetic anxiety that Captain Whalley charitably nodded down at him, restraining a sort of sickening desire to laugh.

"You must know what it is yourself, Harry. Girls are the very devil for worry and anxiety."

"Ay! But mine is doing well," Captain Whalley pronounced slowly, staring to the end of the avenue.

The Master-Attendant was glad to hear this. Uncommonly glad. He remembered her well. A pretty girl she was.

Captain Whalley, stepping out carelessly, assented as if in a dream:

"She was pretty."

The procession of carriages was breaking up.

One after another they left the file to go off at a trot, animating the vast avenue with their scattered life and movement; but soon the aspect of dignified solitude returned and took possession of the straight wide road. A syce*in white stood at the head of a Burmah pony harnessed to a varnished two-wheel cart; and the whole thing waiting by the curb seemed no bigger than a child's toy forgotten under the soaring trees. Captain Eliott waddled up to it and made as if to clamber in, but refrained; and keeping one hand resting easily on the shaft, he changed the conversation from his pension, his daughters, and his poverty back again to the only other topic in the world—the Marine Office, the men and the ships of the port.

He proceeded to give instances of what was expected of him; and his thick voice drowsed in the still air like the obstinate droning of an enormous bumble-bee. Captain Whalley did not know what was the force or the weakness that prevented him from saying goodnight and walking away. It was as though he had been too tired to make the effort. How queer. More queer than any of Ned's instances. Or was it that overpowering sense of idleness alone that made him stand there and listen to these stories? Nothing very real had ever troubled Ned Eliott; and gradually he seemed to detect deep in, as if wrapped up in the gross wheezy rumble, something of the clear hearty voice of the young captain of the *Ringdove*. He wondered if he, too, had changed to the same extent; and it seemed to him that the voice of his old chum had not changed so very much—that the man was the same. Not a bad fellow the pleasant, jolly Ned Eliott, friendly, well up to his business—and always a bit of a humbug. He remembered how he used to amuse his poor wife. She could read him like an open book. When the *Condor* and the *Ringdove* happened to be in port together, she would frequently ask him to bring Captain Eliott to dinner. They had not met often since those old days. Not once in five years, perhaps. He regarded from under his white eyebrows this man he could not bring himself to take into his confidence at this juncture; and the other went on with his intimate outpourings, and as remote from his hearer as though he had been talking on a hill-top a mile away.

He was in a bit of a quandary now as to the steamer *Sofala*. Ultimately every hitch in the port came into his hands to undo. They would miss him when he was gone in another eighteen months, and most likely some retired naval officer had been pitchforked into the appointment—a man that would understand nothing and care less. That steamer was a coasting craft having a steady trade connection as far north as Tenasserim; but the trouble was she could get no captain to take her on her regular trip. Nobody would go in her. He really had no power, of course, to order a man to take a job. It was all very well to stretch a point on the demand of a consul-general, but. . . .

"What's the matter with the ship?" Captain Whalley interrupted in measured tones.

"Nothing's the matter. Sound old steamer. Her

owner has been in my office this afternoon tearing his hair."

"Is he a white man?" asked Whalley in an interested voice.

"He calls himself a white man," answered the Master-Attendant scornfully; "but if so, it's just skin-deep and no more. I told him that to his face, too."

"But who is he, then?"

"He's the chief engineer of her. See *that*, Harry?"

"I see," Captain Whalley said, thoughtfully. "The engineer. I see."

How the fellow came to be a shipowner at the same time was quite a tale. He came out third in a home ship nearly fifteen years ago, Captain Eliott remembered, and got paid off after a bad sort of row both with his skipper and his chief. Anyway, they seemed jolly glad to get rid of him at all costs. Clearly a mutinous sort of chap. Well, he remained out here, a perfect nuisance, everlastingly shipped and unshipped, unable to keep a berth very long; pretty nigh went through every engine-room afloat belonging to the colony. Then suddenly, "What do you think happened, Harry?"

Captain Whalley, who seemed lost in a mental effort as of doing a sum in his head, gave a slight start. He really couldn't imagine. The Master-Attendant's voice vibrated dully with hoarse emphasis. The man actually had the luck to win the second great prize in the Manilla lottery. All these engineers and officers of ships took tickets in that gamble. It seemed to be a perfect mania with them all.

Everybody expected now that he would take himself off home with his money, and go to the devil in his own way. Not at all. The *Sofala*, judged too small and not quite modern enough for the sort of trade she was in, could be got for a moderate price from her owners, who

had ordered a new steamer from Europe. He rushed
in and bought her. This man had never given any
signs of that sort of mental intoxication the mere fact
of getting hold of a large sum of money may produce—
not till he got a ship of his own; but then he went off his
balance all at once: came bouncing into the Marine
Office on some transfer business, with his hat hanging
over his left eye and switching a little cane in his hand,
and told each one of the clerks separately that "Nobody could put him out now. It was his turn. There
was no one over him on earth, and there never would
be either." He swaggered and strutted between the
desks, talking at the top of his voice, and trembling like
a leaf all the while, so that the current business of the
office was suspended for the time he was in there, and
everybody in the big room stood open-mouthed looking
at his antics. Afterwards he could be seen during the
hottest hours of the day with his face as red as fire
rushing along up and down the quays to look at his
ship from different points of view: he seemed inclined
to stop every stranger he came across just to let them
know "that there would be no longer any one over him;
he had bought a ship; nobody on earth could put him
out of his engine-room now."

Good bargain as she was, the price of the *Sofala*
took up pretty near all the lottery-money. He had
left himself no capital to work with. That did not
matter so much, for these were the halcyon days of
steam coasting trade, before some of the home shipping
firms had thought of establishing local fleets to feed
their main lines. These, when once organized, took the
biggest slices out of that cake, of course; and by-and-by
a squad of confounded German tramps turned up east
of Suez Canal and swept up all the crumbs. They
prowled on the cheap to and fro along the coast and

between the islands, like a lot of sharks in the water ready to snap up anything you let drop. And then the high old times were over for good; for years the *Sofala* had made no more, he judged, than a fair living. Captain Eliott looked upon it as his duty in every way to assist an English ship to hold her own; and it stood to reason that if for want of a captain the *Sofala* began to miss her trips she would very soon lose her trade. There was the quandary. The man was too impracticable. "Too much of a beggar on horseback from the first," he explained. "Seemed to grow worse as the time went on. In the last three years he's run through eleven skippers; he had tried every single man here, outside of the regular lines. I had warned him before that this would not do. And now, of course, no one will look at the *Sofala*. I had one or two men up at my office and talked to them; but, as they said to me, what was the good of taking the berth to lead a regular dog's life for a month and then get the sack at the end of the first trip? The fellow, of course, told me it was all nonsense; there has been a plot hatching for years against him. And now it had come. All the horrid sailors in the port had conspired to bring him to his knees, because he was an engineer." Captain Eliott emitted a throaty chuckle.

"And the fact is, that if he misses a couple more trips he need never trouble himself to start again. He won't find any cargo in his old trade. There's too much competition nowadays for people to keep their stuff lying about for a ship that does not turn up when she's expected. It's a bad lookout for him. He swears he will shut himself on board and starve to death in his cabin rather than sell her—even if he could find a buyer. And that's not likely in the least. Not even the Japs would give her insured value for her. It isn't like selling sailing-ships. Steamers *do* get out of date, besides getting old."

"He must have laid by a good bit of money though," observed Captain Whalley, quietly.

The Harbour-master puffed out his purple cheeks to an amazing size.

"Not a stiver,* Harry. Not—a—single sti-ver."

He waited; but as Captain Whalley, stroking his beard slowly, looked down on the ground without a word, he tapped him on the forearm, tiptoed, and said in a hoarse whisper—

"The Manila lottery has been eating him up."

He frowned a little, nodding in tiny affirmative jerks. They all were going in for it; a third of the wages paid to ships' officers ("in my port," he snorted) went to Manila. It was a mania. That fellow Massy had been bitten by it like the rest of them from the first; but after winning once he seemed to have persuaded himself he had only to try again to get another big prize. He had taken dozens and scores of tickets for every drawing since. What with this vice and his ignorance of affairs, ever since he had improvidently bought that steamer he had been more or less short of money.

This, in Captain Eliott's opinion, gave an opening for a sensible sailor-man with a few pounds to step in and save that fool from the consequences of his folly. It was his craze to quarrel with his captains. He had had some really good men, too, who would have been too glad to stay if he would only let them. But no. He seemed to think he was no owner unless he was kicking somebody out in the morning and having a row with the new man in the evening. What was wanted for him was a master with a couple of hundred or so to take an interest in the ship on proper conditions. You don't discharge a man for no fault, only because of the fun of telling him to pack up his traps and go ashore, when you know that in that case you are bound to buy back his share. On the other hand, a fellow with an interest in the ship is not likely to throw up his job in a huff about a trifle. He had told Massy that. He had said: "'This won't do, Mr. Massy. We are getting very sick of you here in the Marine Office. What you must do now is to try whether you could get a sailor to join you as partner. That seems to be the only way.' And that was sound advice, Harry."

Captain Whalley, leaning on his stick, was perfectly still all over, and his hand, arrested in the act of stroking, grasped his whole beard. And what did the fellow say to that?

The fellow had the audacity to fly out at the Master-Attendant. He had received the advice in a most impudent manner. "I didn't come here to be laughed at," he had shrieked. "I appeal to you as an Englishman and a shipowner brought to the verge of ruin by an illegal conspiracy of your beggarly sailors, and all you condescend to do for me is to tell me to go and get a partner!" . . . The fellow had presumed to stamp with rage on the floor of the private office. Where was he going to get a partner? Was he being taken for a fool? Not a single one of that contemptible lot ashore at the "Home" had twopence in his pocket to bless himself with. The very native curs in the bazaar knew that much. . . . "And it's true enough, Harry," rumbled Captain Eliott, judicially. "They are much more likely one and all to owe money to the Chinamen in Denham Road for the clothes on their backs. 'Well,' said I, 'you make too much noise over it for my taste, Mr. Massy. Good morning.' He banged the door after him; he dared to bang my door, confound his cheek!"

The head of the Marine department was out of breath with indignation; then recollecting himself as it were, "I'll end by being late to dinner—yarning with you here . . . wife doesn't like it."

He clambered ponderously into the trap; leaned out side-ways, and only then wondered wheezily what on earth Captain Whalley could have been doing with himself of late. They had had no sight of each other for years and years till the other day when he had seen him unexpectedly in the office.

What on earth. . . .

Captain Whalley seemed to be smiling to himself in his white beard.

"The earth is big," he said, vaguely.

The other, as if to test the statement, stared all round from his driving-seat. The Esplanade was very quiet; only from afar, from very far, a long way from the sea-shore, across the stretches of grass, through the long ranges of trees, came faintly the toot—toot—toot of the cable car beginning to roll before the empty peristyle*of the Public Library on its three-mile journey to the New Harbour Docks.

"Doesn't seem to be so much room on it," growled the Master-Attendant, "since these Germans came along shouldering us at every turn. It was not so in our time."

He fell into deep thought, breathing stertorously, as though he had been taking a nap open-eyed. Perhaps he, too, on his side, had detected in the silent pilgrim-like figure, standing there by the wheel, like an arrested wayfarer, the buried lineaments of the features belonging to the young captain of the *Condor*. Good fellow—Harry Whalley—never very talkative. You never knew what he was up to—a bit too off-hand with people of consequence, and apt to take a wrong

view of a fellow's actions. Fact was he had a too
good opinion of himself. He would have liked to tell
him to get in and drive him home to dinner. But one
never knew. Wife would not like it.

"And it's funny to think, Harry," he went on in
a big subdued drone, "that of all the people on it there
seems only you and I left to remember this part of the
world as it used to be. . . ."

He was ready to indulge in the sweetness of a sentimental mood had it not struck him suddenly that Captain Whalley, unstirring and without a word, seemed to
be awaiting something—perhaps expecting. . . . He
gathered the reins at once and burst out in bluff hearty
growls—

"Ha! My dear boy. The men we have known—the
ships we've sailed—ay! and the things we've done. . . ."

The pony plunged—the syce skipped out of the way.
Captain Whalley raised his arm.

"Good-bye."

VI

THE sun had set. And when, after drilling a deep
hole with his stick, he moved from that spot the night
had massed its army of shadows under the trees. They
filled the eastern ends of the avenue as if only waiting
the signal for a general advance upon the open spaces
of the world; they were gathering low between the deep
stone-faced banks of the canal. The Malay prau, half
concealed under the arch of the bridge, had not altered
its position a quarter of an inch. For a long time Captain Whalley stared down over the parapet, till at last
the floating immobility of that beshrouded thing
seemed to grow upon him into something inexplicable
and alarming. The twilight abandoned the zenith; its
reflected gleams left the world below, and the water
of the canal seemed to turn into pitch. Captain Whalley crossed it.

The turning to the right, which was his way to his
hotel, was only a very few steps farther. He stopped
again (all the houses of the sea-front were shut up, the
quayside was deserted, but for one or two figures of
natives walking in the distance) and began to reckon the
amount of his bill. So many days in the hotel at so
many dollars a day. To count the days he used his
fingers: plunging one hand into his pocket, he jingled
a few silver coins. All right for three days more; and
then, unless something turned up, he must break into
the five hundred—Ivy's money—invested in her father.
It seemed to him that the first meal coming out of that
reserve would choke him—for certain. Reason was of

no use. It was a matter of feeling. His feelings had never played him false.

He did not turn to the right. He walked on, as if there still had been a ship in the roadstead to which he could get himself pulled off in the evening. Far away, beyond the houses, on the slope of an indigo promontory closing the view of the quays, the slim column of a factory-chimney smoked quietly straight up into the clear air. A Chinaman, curled down in the stern of one of the half-dozen sampans floating off the end of the jetty, caught sight of a beckoning hand. He jumped up, rolled his pigtail round his head swiftly, tucked in two rapid movements his wide dark trousers high up his yellow thighs, and by a single, noiseless, finlike stir of the oars, sheered the sampan alongside the steps with the ease and precision of a swimming fish.

"*Sofala*," articulated Captain Whalley from above; and the Chinaman, a new emigrant probably, stared upwards with a tense attention as if waiting to see the queer word fall visibly from the white man's lips. "*Sofala*," Captain Whalley repeated; and suddenly his heart failed him. He paused. The shores, the islets, the high ground, the low points, were dark: the horizon had grown sombre; and across the eastern sweep of the shore the white obelisk, marking the landing-place of the telegraph-cable, stood like a pale ghost on the beach before the dark spread of uneven roofs, intermingled with palms, of the native town. Captain Whalley began again:

"*Sofala*. Savee *So-fa-la*, John?"

This time the Chinaman made out that bizarre sound, and grunted his assent uncouthly, low down in his bare throat. With the first yellow twinkle of a star that appeared like the head of a pin stabbed deep into the smooth, pale, shimmering fabric of the sky, the edge of a keen chill seemed to cleave through the warm air of the earth. At the moment of stepping into the sampan to go and try for the command of the *Sofala* Captain Whalley shivered a little.

When on his return he landed on the quay again, Venus, like a choice jewel set low on the hem of the sky, cast a faint gold trail behind him upon the roadstead, as level as a floor made of one dark and polished stone. The lofty vaults of the avenues were black—all black overhead—and the porcelain globes on the lamp-posts resembled egg-shaped pearls, gigantic and luminous, displayed in a row whose farther end seemed to sink in the distance, down to the level of his knees. He put his hands behind his back. He would now consider calmly the discretion of it before saying the final word to-morrow. His feet scrunched the gravel loudly —the discretion of it. It would have been easier to appraise had there been a workable alternative. The honesty of it was indubitable: he meant well by the fellow; and periodically his shadow leaped up intense by his side on the trunks of the trees, to lengthen itself, oblique and dim, far over the grass—repeating his stride.

The discretion of it. Was there a choice? He seemed already to have lost something of himself; to have given up to a hungry spectre something of his truth and dignity in order to live. But his life was necessary. Let poverty do its worst in exacting its toll of humiliation. It was certain that Ned Eliott had rendered him, without knowing it, a service for which it would have been impossible to ask. He hoped Ned would not think there had been something underhand in his action. He supposed that now when he heard of it he would understand—or perhaps he would only think Whalley an eccentric old fool. What would

have been the good of telling him—any more than of
blurting the whole tale to that man Massy? Five
hundred pounds ready to invest. Let him make the
best of that. Let him wonder. You want a captain—
I want a ship. That's enough. B-r-r-r-r. What a
disagreeable impression that empty, dark, echoing
steamer had made upon him. . . .

A laid-up steamer was a dead thing and no mistake;
a sailing-ship somehow seems always ready to spring
into life with the breath of the incorruptible heaven; but
a steamer, thought Captain Whalley, with her fires out,
without the warm whiffs from below meeting you on her
decks, without the hiss of steam, the clangs of iron in her
breast—lies there as cold and still and pulseless as a
corpse.

In the solitude of the avenue, all black above and
lighted below, Captain Whalley, considering the discretion of his course, met, as it were incidentally, the
thought of death. He pushed it aside with dislike
and contempt. He almost laughed at it; and in the
unquenchable vitality of his age only thought with a
kind of exultation how little he needed to keep body
and soul together. Not a bad investment for the poor
woman this solid carcass of her father. And for the
rest—in case of anything—the agreement should be
clear: the whole five hundred to be paid back to her
integrally within three months. Integrally. Every
penny. He was not to lose any of her money whatever
else had to go—a little dignity—some of his self-respect.
He had never before allowed anybody to remain under
any sort of false impression as to himself. Well, let
that go—for her sake. After all, he had never *said*
anything misleading—and Captain Whalley felt himself
corrupt to the marrow of his bones. He laughed a
little with the intimate scorn of his worldly prudence.

Clearly, with a fellow of that sort, and in the peculiar relation they were to stand to each other, it would not have done to blurt out everything. He did not like the fellow. He did not like his spells of fawning loquacity and bursts of resentfulness. In the end— a poor devil. He would not have liked to stand in his shoes. Men were not evil, after all. He did not like his sleek hair, his queer way of standing at right angles, with his nose in the air, and glancing along his shoulder at you. No. On the whole, men were not bad—they were only silly or unhappy.

Captain Whalley had finished considering the discretion of that step—and there was the whole long night before him. In the full light his long beard would glisten like a silver breastplate covering his heart; in the spaces between the lamps his burly figure passed less distinct, loomed very big, wandering, and mysterious. No; there was not much real harm in men: and all the time a shadow marched with him, slanting on his left hand—which in the East is a presage of evil.

.   .   .   .

"Can you make out the clump of palms yet, Serang?" asked Captain Whalley from his chair on the bridge of the *Sofala* approaching the bar of Batu Beru.

"No, Tuan. By-and-by ·see." The old Malay, in a blue dungaree suit, planted on his bony dark feet under the bridge awning, put his hands behind his back and stared ahead out of the innumerable wrinkles at the corners of his eyes.

Captain Whalley sat still, without lifting his head to look for himself. Three years—thirty-six times. He had made these palms thirty-six times from the southward. They would come into view at the proper time. Thank God, the old ship made her courses and distances trip after trip, as correct as clockwork. At last he murmured again—

"In sight yet?"

"The sun makes a very great glare, Tuan."

"Watch well, Serang."

"Ya, Tuan."

A white man had ascended the ladder from the deck noiselessly, and had listened quietly to this short colloquy. Then he stepped out on the bridge and began to walk from end to end, holding up the long cherrywood stem of a pipe. His black hair lay plastered in long lanky wisps across the bald summit of his head; he had a furrowed brow, a yellow complexion, and a thick shapeless nose. A scanty growth of whisker did not conceal the contour of his jaw. His aspect was of brooding care; and sucking at a curved black mouthpiece, he presented such a heavy overhanging profile that even the Serang could not help reflecting sometimes upon the extreme unloveliness of some white men.

Captain Whalley seemed to brace himself up in his chair, but gave no recognition whatever to his presence. The other puffed jets of smoke; then suddenly—

"I could never understand that new mania of yours of having this Malay here for your shadow, partner."

Captain Whalley got up from the chair in all his imposing stature and walked across to the binnacle, holding such an unswerving course that the other had to back away hurriedly, and remained as if intimidated, with the pipe trembling in his hand. "Walk over me now," he muttered in a sort of astounded and discomfited whisper. Then slowly and distinctly he said—

"I—am—not—dirt." And then added defiantly, "As you seem to think."

The Serang jerked out—

"See the palms now, Tuan."

Captain Whalley strode forward to the rail; but his eyes, instead of going straight to the point, with the assured keen glance of a sailor, wandered irresolutely in space, as though he, the discoverer of new routes, had lost his way upon this narrow sea.

Another white man, the mate, came up on the bridge. He was tall, young, lean, with a moustache like a trooper, and something malicious in the eye. He took up a position beside the engineer. Captain Whalley with his back to them, inquired—

"What's on the log?"

"Eighty-five," answered the mate quickly, and nudged the engineer with his elbow.

Captain Whalley's muscular hands squeezed the iron rail with an extraordinary force; his eyes glared with an enormous effort; he knitted his eyebrows, the perspiration fell from under his hat—and in a faint voice he murmured, "Steady her, Serang—when she is on the proper bearing."

The silent Malay stepped back, waited a little, and lifted his arm warningly to the helmsman. The wheel revolved rapidly to meet the swing of the ship. Again the mate nudged the engineer. But Massy turned upon him.

"Mr. Sterne," he said, violently, "let me tell you —as a shipowner—that you are no better than a confounded fool."

VII

STERNE went down smirking and apparently not at
all disconcerted, but the engineer Massy remained on
the bridge, moving about with uneasy self-assertion.
Everybody on board was his inferior—everyone without exception. He paid their wages and found them
in their food. They ate more of his bread and pocketed
more of his money than they were worth; and they had
no care in the world, while he alone had to meet all the
difficulties of shipowning. When he contemplated his
position in all its menacing entirety, it seemed to him
that he had been for years the prey of a band of para-
sites; and for years he had scowled at everybody connected with the *Sofala* except, perhaps, at the Chinese
firemen who served to get her along. Their use was
manifest: they were an indispensable part of the machinery of which he was the master.

When he passed along his decks he shouldered those
he came across brutally; but the Malay deck hands had
learned to dodge out of his way. He had to bring himself to tolerate them because of the necessary manual
labour of the ship which must be done. He had to
struggle and plan and scheme to keep the *Sofala* afloat—
and what did he get for it? Not even enough respect.
They could not have given him enough of that if all
their thoughts and all their actions had been directed
to that end. The vanity of possession, the vainglory
of power, had passed away by this time, and there
remained only the material embarrassments, the fear
of losing that position which had turned out not worth

having, and an anxiety of thought which no abject
subservience of men could repay.

He walked up and down. The bridge was his own
after all. He had paid for it; and with the stem of the
pipe in his hand he would stop short at times as if to
listen with a profound and concentrated attention to
the deadened beat of the engines (his own engines)
and the slight grinding of the steering chains upon the
continuous low wash of water alongside. But for these
sounds, the ship might have been lying as still as if
moored to a bank, and as silent as if abandoned by every
living soul; only the coast, the low coast of mud and
mangroves with the three palms in a bunch at the back,
grew slowly more distinct in its long straight line; without a single feature to arrest attention. The native
passengers of the *Sofala* lay about on mats under the
awnings; the smoke of her funnel seemed the only sign
of her life and connected with her gliding motion in a
mysterious manner.

Captain Whalley on his feet, with a pair of binoculars
in his hand and the little Malay Serang at his elbow,
like an old giant attended by a wizened pigmy, was taking her over the shallow water of the bar.

This submarine ridge of mud, scoured by the stream
out of the soft bottom of the river and heaped up far
out on the hard bottom of the sea, was difficult to get
over. The alluvial coast having no distinguishing
marks, the bearings of the crossing-place had to be
taken from the shape of the mountains inland. The
guidance of a form flattened and uneven at the top like
a grinder tooth, and of another smooth, saddle-backed
summit, had to be searched for within the great un-
clouded glare that seemed to shift and float like a dry
fiery mist, filling the air, ascending from the water,
shrouding the distances, scorching to the eye. In this

veil of light the near edge of the shore alone stood out
almost coal-black with an opaque and motionless
solidity.   Thirty miles away the serrated range of the
interior stretched across the horizon, its outlines and
shades of blue, faint and tremulous like a background
painted on airy gossamer on the quivering fabric of an
impalpable curtain let down to the plain of alluvial
soil; and the openings of the estuary appeared, shining
white, like bits of silver let into the square pieces snipped
clean and sharp out of the body of the land bordered
with mangroves.

On the forepart of the bridge the giant and the pigmy
muttered to each other frequently in quiet tones.   Behind them Massy stood sideways with an expression of
disdain and suspense on his face.   His globular eyes
were perfectly motionless, and he seemed to have forgotten the long pipe he held in his hand.

On the fore-deck below the bridge, steeply roofed
with the white slopes of the awnings, a young lascar*
seaman had clambered outside the rail.   He adjusted
quickly a broad band of sail canvas under his armpits,
and throwing his chest against it, leaned out far over
the water.   The sleeve of his thin cotton shirt, cut off
close to the shoulder, bared his brown arm of full
rounded form and with a satiny skin like a woman's.
He swung it rigidly with the rotary and menacing action
of a slinger: the 14-lb. weight hurtled circling in the air,
then suddenly flew ahead as far as the curve of the
bow.   The wet thin line swished like scratched silk
running through the dark fingers of the man, and the
plunge of the lead close to the ship's side made a vanishing silvery scar upon the golden glitter; then after an
interval the voice of the young Malay uplifted and long-
drawn declared the depth of the water in his own
language.

"Tiga stengah," he cried after each splash and pause, gathering the line busily for another cast. "Tiga stengah," which means three fathom and a half. For a mile or so from seaward there was a uniform depth of water right up to the bar. "Half-three. Half-three. Half-three,"—and his modulated cry, returned leisurely and monotonous, like the repeated call of a bird, seemed to float away in sunshine and disappear in the spacious silence of the empty sea and of a lifeless shore lying open, north and south, east and west, without the stir of a single cloud-shadow or the whisper of any other voice.

The owner-engineer of the *Sofala* remained very still behind the two seamen of different race, creed, and colour; the European with the time-defying vigour of his old frame, the little Malay, old, too, but slight and shrunken like a withered brown leaf blown by a chance wind under the mighty shadow of the other. Very busy looking forward at the land, they had not a glance to spare; and Massy, glaring at them from behind, seemed to resent their attention to their duty like a personal slight upon himself.

This was unreasonable; but he had lived in his own world of unreasonable resentments for many years. At last, passing his moist palm over the rare lanky wisps of coarse hair on the top of his yellow head, he began to talk slowly.

"A leadsman, you want! I suppose that's your correct mail-boat style. Haven't you enough judgment to tell where you are by looking at the land? Why, before I had been a twelvemonth in the trade I was up to that trick—and I am only an engineer. I can point to you from here where the bar is, and I could tell you besides that you are likely as not to stick her in the mud in about five minutes from now; only you would

call it interfering, I suppose. And there's that written
agreement of ours, that says I mustn't interfere."

His voice stopped. Captain Whalley, without re-
laxing the set severity of his features, moved his lips to
ask in a quick mumble—

"How near, Serang?"

"Very near now, Tuan," the Malay muttered, rapidly.

"Dead slow," said the Captain aloud in a firm tone.

The Serang snatched at the handle of the telegraph.
A gong clanged down below. Massy with a scornful
snigger walked off and put his head down the engine-
room skylight.

"You may expect some rare fooling with the engines,
Jack," he bellowed. The space into which he stared
was deep and full of gloom; and the gray gleams of steel
down there seemed cool after the intense glare of the
sea around the ship. The air, however, came up
clammy and hot on his face. A short hoot on which it
would have been impossible to put any sort of interpre-
tation came from the bottom cavernously. This was
the way in which the second engineer answered his chief.

He was a middle-aged man with an inattentive manner, and apparently wrapped up in such a taciturn concern for his engines that he seemed to have lost the use
of speech. When addressed directly his only answer
would be a grunt or a hoot, according to the distance.
For all the years he had been in the *Sofala* he had never
been known to exchange as much as a frank Good-morn-
ing with any of his shipmates. He did not seem aware
that men came and went in the world; he did not seem
to see them at all. Indeed he never recognized his
shipmates on shore. At table (the four white men of
the *Sofala* messed together) he sat looking into his plate
dispassionately, but at the end of the meal would
jump up and bolt down below as if a sudden thought

had impelled him to rush and see whether somebody had not stolen the engines while he dined. In port at the end of the trip he went ashore regularly, but no one knew where he spent his evenings or in what manner. The local coasting fleet had preserved a wild and incoherent tale of his infatuation for the wife of a sergeant in an Irish infantry regiment. The regiment, however, had done its turn of garrison duty there ages before, and was gone somewhere to the other side of the earth, out of men's knowledge. Twice or perhaps three times in the course of the year he would take too much to drink. On these occasions he returned on board at an earlier hour than usual; ran across the deck balancing himself with his spread arms like a tight-rope walker; and locking the door of his cabin, he would converse and argue with himself the livelong night in an amazing variety of tones; storm, sneer and whine with an inexhaustible persistence. Massy in his berth next door, raising himself on his elbow, would discover that his second had remembered the name of every white man that had passed through the *Sofala* for years and years back. He remembered the names of men that had died, that had gone home, that had gone to America: he remembered in his cups the names of men whose connection with the ship had been so short that Massy had almost forgotten its circumstances and could barely recall their faces. The inebriated voice on the other side of the bulkhead commented upon them all with an extraordinary and ingenious venom of scandalous inventions. It seems they had all offended him in some way, and in return he had found them all out. He muttered darkly; he laughed sardonically; he crushed them one after another; but of his chief, Massy, he babbled with an envious and naïve admiration. Clever scoundrel! Don't meet the likes of him every day. Just look at him. Ha! Great! Ship of his own. Wouldn't catch *him* going wrong. No fear—the beast! And Massy, after listening with a gratified smile to these artless tributes to his greatness, would begin to shout, thumping at the bulkhead with both fists—

"Shut up, you lunatic! Won't you let me go to sleep, you fool!"

But a half smile of pride lingered on his lips; outside the solitary lascar told off for night duty in harbour, perhaps a youth fresh from a forest village, would stand motionless in the shadows of the deck listening to the endless drunken gabble. His heart would be thumping with breathless awe of white men: the arbitrary and obstinate men who pursue inflexibly their incomprehensible purposes—beings with weird intonations in the voice, moved by unaccountable feelings, actuated by inscrutable motives.

VIII

FOR a while after his second's answering hoot Massy hung over the engine-room gloomily. Captain Whalley who, by the power of five hundred pounds, had kept his command for three years, might have been suspected of never having seen that coast before. He seemed unable to put down his glasses, as though they had been glued under his contracted eyebrows. This settled frown gave to his face an air of invincible and just severity; but his raised elbow trembled slightly, and the perspiration poured from under his hat as if a second sun had suddenly blazed up at the zenith by the side of the ardent still globe already there, in whose blinding white heat the earth whirled and shone like a mote of dust.

From time to time, still holding up his glasses, he raised his other hand to wipe his streaming face. The drops rolled down his cheeks, fell like rain upon the white hairs of his beard, and brusquely, as if guided by an uncontrollable and anxious impulse, his arm reached out to the stand of the engine-room telegraph.

The gong clanged down below. The balanced vibration of the dead-slow speed ceased together with every sound and tremor in the ship, as if the great still-ness that reigned upon the coast had stolen in through her sides of iron and taken possession of her innermost recesses. The illusion of perfect immobility seemed to fall upon her from the luminous blue dome without a stain arching over a flat sea without a stir. The faint breeze she had made for herself expired, as if all at once

the air had become too thick to budge; even the slight
hiss of the water on her stem died out. The narrow,
long hull, carrying its way without a ripple, seemed to
approach the shoal water of the bar by stealth. The
plunge of the lead with the mournful, mechanical cry
of the lascar came at longer and longer intervals; and
the men on her bridge seemed to hold their breath. The
Malay at the helm looked fixedly at the compass card,
the Captain and the Serang stared at the coast.

Massy had left the skylight, and, walking flat-footed,
had returned softly to the very spot on the bridge he
had occupied before. A slow, lingering grin exposed
his set of big white teeth: they gleamed evenly in the
shade of the awning like the keyboard of a piano in a
dusky room.

At last, pretending to talk to himself in excessive
astonishment, he said not very loud—

"Stop the engines now. What next, I wonder?"

He waited, stooping from the shoulders, his head
bowed, his glance oblique. Then raising his voice a
shade—

"If I dared make an absurd remark I would say that
you haven't the stomach to. . . ."

But a yelling spirit of excitement, like some frantic
soul wandering unsuspected in the vast stillness of the
coast, had seized upon the body of the lascar at the lead.
The languid monotony of his sing-song changed to a
swift, sharp clamour. The weight flew after a single
whirr, the line whistled, splash followed splash in haste.
The water had shoaled, and the man, instead of the
drowsy tale of fathoms, was calling out the soundings in
feet.

"Fifteen feet. Fifteen, fifteen! Fourteen, fourteen. . . ."

Captain Whalley lowered the arm holding the glasses.

It descended slowly as if by its own weight; no other part of his towering body stirred; and the swift cries with their eager warning note passed him by as though he had been deaf.

Massy, very still, and turning an attentive ear, had fastened his eyes upon the silvery, close-cropped back of the steady old head. The ship herself seemed to be arrested but for the gradual decrease of depth under her keel.

"Thirteen feet. . . . Thirteen! Twelve!" cried the leadsman anxiously below the bridge. And suddenly the barefooted Serang stepped away noiselessly to steal a glance over the side.

Narrow of shoulder, in a suit of faded blue cotton: an old gray felt hat rammed down on his head, with a hollow in the nape of his dark neck, and with his slender limbs, he appeared from the back no bigger than a boy of fourteen. There was a childlike impulsiveness in the curiosity with which he watched the spread of the voluminous, yellowish convolutions rolling up from below to the surface of the blue water like massive clouds driving slowly upwards on the unfathomable sky. He was not startled at the sight in the least. It was not doubt, but the certitude that the keel of the *Sofala* must be stirring the mud now, which made him peep over the side.

His peering eyes, set aslant in a face of the Chinese type, a little old face, immovable, as if carved in old brown oak, had informed him long before that the ship was not headed at the bar properly. Paid off from the *Fair Maid*, together with the rest of the crew, after the completion of the sale, he had hung, in his faded blue suit and floppy gray hat, about the doors of the Harbour Office, till one day, seeing Captain Whalley coming along to get a crew for the *Sofala*, he had put himself quietly in the way, with his bare feet in the dust and an upward mute glance. The eyes of his old commander had fallen on him favourably—it must have been an auspicious day—and in less than half an hour the white men in the "Ofiss" had written his name on a document as Serang of the fire-ship *Sofala*. Since that time he had repeatedly looked at that estuary, upon that coast, from this bridge and from this side of the bar. The record of the visual world fell through his eyes upon his unspeculating mind as on a sensitized plate through the lens of a camera. His knowledge was absolute and precise; nevertheless, had he been asked his opinion, and especially if questioned in the downright, alarming manner of white men, he would have displayed the hesitation of ignorance. He was certain of his facts—but such a certitude counted for little against the doubt what answer would be pleasing. Fifty years ago, in a jungle village, and before he was a day old, his father (who died without ever seeing a white face) had had his nativity cast by a man of skill and wisdom in astrology, because in the arrangement of the stars may be read the last word of human destiny. His destiny had been to thrive by the favour of various white men on the sea. He had swept the decks of ships, had tended their helms, had minded their stores, had risen at last to be a Serang; and his placid mind had remained as incapable of penetrating the simplest motives of those he served as they themselves were incapable of detecting through the crust of the earth the secret nature of its heart, which may be fire or may be stone. But he had no doubt whatever that the *Sofala* was out of the proper track for crossing the bar at Batu Beru.

It was a slight error. The ship could not have been more than twice her own length too far to the northward; and a white man at a loss for a cause (since it was impossible to suspect Captain Whalley of blundering ignorance, of want of skill, or of neglect) would have been inclined to doubt the testimony of his senses. It was some such feeling that kept Massy motionless, with his teeth laid bare by an anxious grin. Not so the Serang. He was not troubled by any intellectual mistrust of his senses. If his captain chose to stir the mud it was well. He had known in his life white men indulge in outbreaks equally strange. He was only genuinely interested to see what would come of it. At last, apparently satisfied, he stepped back from the rail.

He had made no sound: Captain Whalley, however, seemed to have observed the movements of his Serang. Holding his head rigidly, he asked with a mere stir of his lips—

"Going ahead still, Serang?"

"Still going a little, Tuan," answered the Malay. Then added casually, "She is over."

The lead confirmed his words; the depth of water increased at every cast, and the soul of excitement departed suddenly from the lascar swung in the canvas belt over the *Sofala's* side. Captain Whalley ordered the lead in, set the engines ahead without haste, and averting his eyes from the coast directed the Serang to keep a course for the middle of the entrance.

Massy brought the palm of his hand with a loud smack against his thigh.

"You grazed on the bar. Just look astern and see if you didn't. Look at the track she left. You can see it plainly. Upon my soul, I thought you would! What made you do that? What on earth made you do that? I believe you are trying to scare me."

He talked slowly, as it were circumspectly, keeping

his prominent black eyes on his captain. There was also a slight plaintive note in his rising choler, for, primarily, it was the clear sense of a wrong suffered undeservedly that made him hate the man who, for a beggarly five hundred pounds, claimed a sixth part of the profits under the three years' agreement. Whenever his resentment got the better of the awe the person of Captain Whalley inspired he would positively whimper with fury.

"You don't know what to invent to plague my life out of me. I would not have thought that a man of your sort would condescend. . . ."

He paused, half hopefully, half timidly, whenever Captain Whalley made the slightest movement in the deck-chair, as though expecting to be conciliated by a soft speech or else rushed upon and hunted off the bridge.

"I am puzzled," he went on again, with the watchful, unsmiling baring of his big teeth. "I don't know what to think. I do believe you are trying to frighten me. You very nearly planted her on the bar for at least twelve hours, besides getting the engines choked with mud. Ships can't afford to lose twelve hours on a trip nowadays—as you ought to know very well, and do know very well to be sure, only. . . ."

His slow volubility, the sideways cranings of his neck, the black glances out of the very corners of his eyes, left Captain Whalley unmoved. He looked at the deck with a severe frown. Massy waited for some little time, then began to threaten plaintively.

"You think you've got me bound hand and foot in that agreement. You think you can torment me in any way you please. Ah! But remember it has another six weeks to run yet. There's time for me to dismiss you before the three years are out. You will do yet something that will give me the chance to dismiss you, and make you wait a twelvemonth for your money before you can take yourself off and pull out your five hundred, and leave me without a penny to get the new boilers for her. You gloat over that idea—don't you? I do believe you sit here gloating. It's as if I had sold my soul for five hundred pounds to be everlastingly damned in the end. . . ."

He paused, without apparent exasperation, then continued evenly—

". . . With the boilers worn out and the survey hanging over my head, Captain Whalley—— Captain Whalley, I say, what do you do with your money? You must have stacks of money somewhere—a man like you must. It stands to reason. I am not a fool, you know, Captain Whalley—partner."

Again he paused, as though he had done for good. He passed his tongue over his lips, gave a backward glance at the Serang conning the ship with quiet whispers and slight signs of the hand. The wash of the propeller sent a swift ripple, crested with dark froth, upon a long flat spit of black slime. The *Sofala* had entered the river; the trail she had stirred up over the bar was a mile astern of her now, out of sight, had disappeared utterly; and the smooth, empty sea along the coast was left behind in the glittering desolation of sunshine. On each side of her, low down, the growth of sombre twisted mangroves covered the semi-liquid banks; and Massy continued in his old tone, with an abrupt start, as if his speech had been ground out of him, like the tune of a music-box, by turning a handle.

"Though if anybody ever got the best of me, it is you. I don't mind saying this. I've said it—there! What more can you want? Isn't that enough for your pride, Captain Whalley? You got over me from the first.

It's all of a piece, when I look back at it. You allowed
me to insert that clause about intemperance without
saying anything, only looking very sick when I made
a point of it going in black on white. How could I tell
what was wrong about you? There's generally something wrong somewhere. And, lo and behold! when
you come on board it turns out that you've been in the
habit of drinking nothing but water for years and
years."

His dogmatic, reproachful whine stopped. He brooded
profoundly, after the manner of crafty and unintelligent
men. It seemed inconceivable that Captain Whalley
should not laugh at the expression of disgust that over-
spread the heavy, yellow countenance. But Captain
Whalley never raised his eyes—sitting in his arm-chair,
outraged, dignified, and motionless.

"Much good it was to me," Massy remonstrated,
monotonously, "to insert a clause of dismissal for intemperance against a man who drinks nothing but
water. And you looked so upset, too, when I read my
draft in the lawyer's office that morning, Captain
Whalley—you looked so crestfallen, that I made sure
I had gone home on your weak spot. A shipowner
can't be too careful as to the sort of skipper he gets.
You must have been laughing at me in your sleeve all
the blessed time. . . . Eh? What are you going
to say?"

Captain Whalley had only shuffled his feet slightly.
A dull animosity became apparent in Massy's sideways
stare.

"But recollect that there are other grounds of dismissal. There's habitual carelessness, amounting to
incompetence—there's gross and persistent neglect
of duty. I am not quite as big a fool as you try to make
me out to be. You have been careless of late—leaving

everything to that Serang. Why! I've seen you letting that old fool of a Malay take bearings for you, as if you were too big to attend to your work yourself. And what do you call that silly touch-and-go manner in which you took the ship over the bar just now? You expect me to put up with that."

Leaning on his elbow against the ladder abaft the bridge, Sterne, the mate, tried to hear, blinking the while from the distance at the second engineer, who had come up for a moment, and stood in the engine-room companion. Wiping his hands on a bunch of cotton waste, he looked about with indifference to the right and left at the river banks slipping astern of the *Sofala* steadily.

Massy turned full at the chair. The character of his whine became again threatening.

"Take care. I may yet dismiss you and freeze to your money for a year. I may. . . ."

But before the silent, rigid immobility of the man whose money had come in the nick of time to save him from utter ruin, his voice died out in his throat.

"Not that I want you to go," he resumed after a silence, and in an absurdly insinuating tone. "I want nothing better than to be friends and renew the agreement, if you will consent to find another couple of hundred to help with the new boilers, Captain Whalley. I've told you before. She must have new boilers; you know it as well as I do. Have you thought this over?"

He waited. The slender stem of the pipe with its bulky lump of a bowl at the end hung down from his thick lips. It had gone out. Suddenly he took it from between his teeth and wrung his hands slightly.

"Don't you believe me?" He thrust the pipe bowl into the pocket of his shiny black jacket.

"It's like dealing with the devil," he said. "Why

don't you speak? At first you were so high and mighty with me I hardly dared to creep about my own deck. Now I can't get a word from you. You don't seem to see me at all. What does it mean? Upon my soul, you terrify me with this deaf and dumb trick. What's going on in that head of yours? What are you plotting against me there so hard that you can't say a word? You will never make me believe that you—you—don't know where to lay your hands on a couple of hundred. You have made me curse the day I was born. . . ."

"Mr. Massy," said Captain Whalley, suddenly, without stirring.

The engineer started violently.

"If that is so I can only beg you to forgive me."

"Starboard," muttered the Serang to the helmsman; and the *Sofala* began to swing round the bend into the second reach.

"Ough!" Massy shuddered. "You make my blood run cold. What made you come here? What made you come aboard that evening all of a sudden, with your high talk and your money—tempting me? I always wondered what was your motive? You fastened yourself on me to have easy times and grow fat on my life blood, I tell you. Was that it? I believe you are the greatest miser in the world, or else why. . . ."

"No. I am only poor," interrupted Captain Whalley, stonily.

"Steady," murmured the Serang. Massy turned away with his chin on his shoulder.

"I don't believe it," he said in his dogmatic tone. Captain Whalley made no movement. "There you sit like a gorged vulture—exactly like a vulture."

He embraced the middle of the reach and both the banks in one blank, unseeing, circular glance, and left the bridge slowly.

IX

ON TURNING to descend Massy perceived the head of Sterne the mate loitering, with his sly, confident smile, his red moustaches and blinking eyes, at the foot of the ladder.

Sterne had been a junior in one of the larger shipping concerns before joining the *Sofala*. He had thrown up his berth, he said, "on general principles." The promotion in the employ was very slow, he complained, and he thought it was time for him to try and get on a bit in the world. It seemed as though nobody would ever die or leave the firm; they all stuck fast in their berths till they got mildewed; he was tired of waiting; and he feared that when a vacancy did occur the best servants were by no means sure of being treated fairly. Besides, the captain he had to serve under—Captain Provost—was an unaccountable sort of man and had taken a dislike to him for some reason or other. For doing rather more than his bare duty as likely as not. When he had done anything wrong he could take a talking to, like a man; but he expected to be treated like a man, too, and not to be addressed invariably as though he were a dog. He had asked Captain Provost plump and plain to tell him where he was at fault, and Captain Provost, in a most scornful way, had told him that he was a perfect officer, and that if he disliked the way he was being spoken to there was the gangway—he could take himself off ashore at once. But everybody knew what sort of man Captain Provost was. It was no use appealing to the office. Captain Provost had too much influence in the employ. All the same, they had to give him a good character. He made bold to say there was nothing in the world against him, and, as he had happened to hear that the mate of the *Sofala* had been taken to the hospital that morning with a sunstroke, he thought there would be no harm in seeing whether he would not do. . . .

He had come to Captain Whalley freshly shaved, red-faced, thin-flanked, throwing out his lean chest; and had recited his little tale with an open and manly assurance. Now and then his eyelids quivered slightly, his hand would steal up to the end of the flaming moustache; his eyebrows were straight, furry, of a chestnut colour, and the directness of his gaze seemed to tremble on the verge of impudence. Captain Whalley had engaged him temporarily; then, the other man having been ordered home by the doctors, he had remained for the next trip, and then the next. He had now attained permanency, and the performance of his duties was marked by an air of serious, single-minded application. Directly he was spoken to, he began to smile attentively, with a great deference expressed in his whole attitude; but there was in the rapid winking which went on all the time something quizzical, as though he had possessed the secret of some universal joke cheating all creation and impenetrable to other mortals.

Grave and smiling he watched Massy come down step by step; when the chief engineer had reached the deck he swung about, and they found themselves face to face. Matched as to height and utterly dissimilar, they confronted each other as if there had been something between them—something else than the bright strip of sunlight that, falling through the wide lacing of two awnings, cut crosswise the narrow planking of the

deck and separated their feet as it were a stream; something profound and subtle and incalculable, like an
unexpressed understanding, a secret mistrust, or some
sort of fear.

At last Sterne, blinking his deep-set eyes and sticking
forward his scraped, clean-cut chin, as crimson as the
rest of his face, murmured—

"You've seen? He grazed! You've seen?"

Massy, contemptuous, and without raising his yellow,
fleshy countenance, replied in the same pitch—

"Maybe. But if it had been you we would have been
stuck fast in the mud."

"Pardon me, Mr. Massy. I beg to deny it. Of
course a shipowner may say what he jolly well pleases on
his own deck. That's all right; but I beg to. . . ."

"Get out of my way!"

The other had a slight start, the impulse of sup-
pressed indignation perhaps, but held his ground.
Massy's downward glance wandered right and left,
as though the deck all round Sterne had been bestrewn
with eggs that must not be broken, and he had looked
irritably for places where he could set his feet in flight.
In the end he, too, did not move, though there was plenty
of room to pass on.

"I heard you say up there," went on the mate—"and
a very just remark it was, too—that there's always something wrong. . . ."

"Eavesdropping is what's wrong with *you*, Mr.
Sterne."

"Now, if you would only listen to me for a moment,
Mr. Massy, sir, I could. . . ."

"You are a sneak," interrupted Massy in a great
hurry, and even managed to get so far as to repeat, "a
common sneak," before the mate had broken in argu-
mentatively—

"Now, sir, what is it you want? You want. . . ."

"I want—I want," stammered Massy, infuriated and astonished— "I want? How do you know that I want anything? How dare you? . . . What do you mean? . . . What are you after—you. . . ."

"Promotion." Sterne silenced him with candid bravado. The engineer's round soft cheeks quivered still, but he said quietly enough—

"You are only worrying my head off," and Sterne met him with a confident little smile.

"A chap in business I know (well up in the world he is now) used to tell me that this was the proper way. 'Always push on to the front,' he would say. 'Keep yourself well before your boss. Interfere whenever you get a chance. Show him what you know. Worry him into seeing you.' That was his advice. Now I know no other boss than you here. You are the owner, and no one else counts for *that* much in my eyes. See, Mr. Massy? I want to get on. I make no secret of it that I am one of the sort that means to get on. These are the men to make use of, sir. You haven't arrived at the top of the tree, sir, without finding that out—I daresay."

"Worry your boss in order to get on," repeated Massy, as if awestruck by the irreverent originality of the idea. "I shouldn't wonder if this was just what the Blue Anchor people kicked you out of their employ for. Is that what you call getting on? You shall get on in the same way here if you aren't careful—I can promise you."

At this Sterne hung his head, thoughtful, perplexed, winking hard at the deck. All his attempts to ,enter into confidential relations with his owner had led of .late to nothing better than these dark threats of dismissal; and a threat of dismissal would check him at

once into a hesitating silence as though he were not
sure that the proper time for defying it had come.
On this occasion he seemed to have lost his tongue
for a moment, and Massy, getting in motion, heavily
passed him by with an abortive attempt at shouldering.
Sterne defeated it by stepping aside. He turned then
swiftly, opening his mouth very wide as if to shout
something after the engineer, but seemed to think better
of it.

Always—as he was ready to confess—on the lookout
for an opening to get on, it had become an instinct with
him to watch the conduct of his immediate superiors for
something "that one could lay hold of." It was his
belief that no skipper in the world would keep his command for a day if only the owners could be "made to
know." This romantic and naïve theory had led him
into trouble more than once, but he remained incor-
rigible; and his character was so instinctively disloyal
that whenever he joined a ship the intention of ousting
his commander out of the berth and taking his place was
always present at the back of his head, as a matter of
course. It filled the leisure of his waking hours with the
reveries of careful plans and compromising discoveries
—the dreams of his sleep with images of lucky turns
and favourable accidents. Skippers had been known to
sicken and die at sea, than which nothing could be better to give a smart mate a chance of showing what he's
made of. They also would tumble overboard sometimes: he had heard of one or two such cases. Others
again. . . . But, as it were constitutionally, he was
faithful to the belief that the conduct of no single one of
them would stand the test of careful watching by a man
who "knew what's what" and who kept his eyes "skinned pretty well" all the time.

After he had gained a permanent footing on board

the *Sofala* he allowed his perennial hope to rise high.
To begin with, it was a great advantage to have an old
man for captain: the sort of man besides who in the
nature of things was likely to give up the job before
long from one cause or another. Sterne was greatly
chagrined, however, to notice that he did not seem
anyway near being past his work yet. Still, these old
men go to pieces all at once sometimes. Then there
was the owner-engineer close at hand to be impressed
by his zeal and steadiness. Sterne never for a moment
doubted the obvious nature of his own merits (he was
really an excellent officer); only, nowadays, professional
merit alone does not take a man along fast enough. A
chap must have some push in him, and must keep his
wits at work, too, to help him forward. He made up
his mind to inherit the charge of this steamer if it
was to be done at all; not indeed estimating the command of the *Sofala* as a very great catch, but for the
reason that, out East especially, to make a start is
everything, and one command leads to another.

He began by promising himself to behave with great
circumspection; Massy's sombre and fantastic humours
intimidated him as being outside one's usual sea experience; but he was quite intelligent enough to realize
almost from the first that he was there in the presence
of an exceptional situation. His peculiar prying imagination penetrated it quickly; the feeling that there
was in it an element which eluded his grasp exasperated
his impatience to get on. And so one trip came to an
end, then another, and he had begun his third before
he saw an opening by which he could step in with any
sort of effect. It had all been very queer and very
obscure; something had been going on near him, as if
separated by a chasm from the common life and the
working routine of the ship, which was exactly like the

life and the routine of any other coasting steamer of that class.

Then one day he made his discovery.

It came to him after all these weeks of watchful observation and puzzled surmises, suddenly, like the long-sought solution of a riddle that suggests itself to the mind in a flash. Not with the same authority, however. Great heavens! Could it be that? And after remaining thunderstruck for a few seconds he tried to shake it off with self-contumely, as though it had been the product of an unhealthy bias toward the Incredible, the Inexplicable, the Unheard-of—the Mad!

This—the illuminating moment—had occurred the trip before, on the return passage. They had just left a place of call on the mainland called Pangu; they were steaming straight out of a bay. To the east a massive headland closed the view, with the tilted edges of the rocky strata showing through its ragged clothing of rank bushes and thorny creepers. The wind had begun to sing in the rigging; the sea along the coast, green and as if swollen a little above the line of the horizon, seemed to pour itself over, time after time, with a slow and thundering fall, into the shadow of the leeward cape; and across the wide opening the nearest of a group of small islands stood enveloped in the hazy yellow light of a breezy sunrise; still farther out the hummocky tops of other islets peeped out motionless above the water of the channels between, scoured tumultuously by the breeze.

The usual track of the *Sofala* both going and returning on every trip led her for a few miles along this reef-infested region. She followed a broad lane of water, dropping astern, one after another, these crumbs of the earth's crust resembling a squadron of dismasted hulks

run in disorder upon a foul ground of rocks and shoals.
Some of these fragments of land appeared, indeed, no
bigger than a stranded ship; others, quite flat, lay
awash like anchored rafts, like ponderous, black rafts of
stone; several, heavily timbered and round at the base,
emerged in squat domes of deep green foliage that
shuddered darkly all over to the flying touch of cloud
shadows driven by the sudden gusts of the squally
season. The thunderstorms of the coast broke frequently over that cluster; it turned then shadowy in its
whole extent; it turned more dark, and as if more still
in the play of fire; as if more impenetrably silent
in the peals of thunder; its blurred shapes vanished—
dissolving utterly at times in the thick rain—to reap-
pear clear-cut and black in the stormy light against the
gray sheet of the cloud—scattered on the slaty round
table of the sea. Unscathed by storms, resisting the
work of years, unfretted by the strife of the world, there
it lay unchanged as on that day, four hundred years ago,
when first beheld by Western eyes from the deck of a
high-pooped caravel.

It was one of these secluded spots that may be found
on the busy sea, as on land you come sometimes upon
the clustered houses of a hamlet untouched by men's
restlessness, untouched by their need, by their thought,
and as if forgotten by time itself. The lives of un-
counted generations had passed it by, and the multi-
tudes of seafowl, urging their way from all the points of
the horizon to sleep on the outer rocks of the group,
unrolled the converging evolutions of their flight in long,
sombre streamers upon the glow of the sky. The pal-
pitating cloud of their wings soared and stooped over
the pinnacles of the rocks, over the rocks slender
like spires, squat like martello towers;*over the pyra-
midal heaps like fallen ruins, over the lines of bald

boulders showing like a wall of stones battered to pieces and scorched by lightning—with the sleepy, clear glimmer of water in every breach. The noise of their continuous and violent screaming filled the air.

This great noise would meet the *Sofala* coming up from Batu Beru; it would meet her on quiet evenings, a pitiless and savage clamour enfeebled by distance, the clamour of seabirds settling to rest, and struggling for a footing at the end of the day. No one noticed it especially on board; it was the voice of their ship's unerring landfall, ending the steady stretch of a hundred miles. She had made good her course, she had run her distance till the punctual islets began to emerge one by one, the points of rocks, the hummocks of earth . . . and the cloud of birds hovered—the restless cloud emitting a strident and cruel uproar, the sound of the familiar scene, the living part of the broken land beneath, of the outspread sea, and of the high sky without a flaw.

But when the *Sofala* happened to close with the land after sunset she would find everything very still there under the mantle of the night. All would be still, dumb, almost invisible—but for the blotting out of the low constellations occulted in turns behind the vague masses of the islets whose true outlines eluded the eye amongst the dark spaces of the heaven: and the ship's three lights, resembling three stars—the red and the green with the white above—her three lights, like three companion stars wandering on the earth, held their unswerving course for the passage at the southern end of the group. Sometimes there were human eyes open to watch them come nearer, travelling smoothly in the sombre void; the eyes of a naked fisherman in his canoe floating over a reef. He thought drowsily: "Ha! The fire-ship that once in every moon goes in

and comes out of Pangu Bay." More he did not know
of her. And just as he had detected the faint rhythm
of the propeller beating the calm water a mile and a half
away, the time would come for the *Sofala* to alter her
course, the lights would swing off him their triple
beam—and disappear.

A few miserable, half-naked families, a sort of outcast
tribe of long-haired, lean, and wild-eyed people, strove
for their living in this lonely wilderness of islets, lying
like an abandoned outwork of the land at the gates of
the bay. Within the knots and loops of the rocks the
water rested more transparent than crystal under their
crooked and leaky canoes, scooped out of the trunk of a
tree: the forms of the bottom undulated slightly to the
dip of a paddle; and the men seemed to hang in the air,
they seemed to hang enclosed within the fibres of a
dark, sodden log, fishing patiently in a strange, unsteady, pellucid, green air above the shoals.

Their bodies stalked brown and emaciated as if dried
up in the sunshine; their lives ran out silently; the homes
where they were born, went to rest, and died—flimsy
sheds of rushes and coarse grass eked out with a few
ragged mats—were hidden out of sight from the open
sea. No glow of their household fires ever kindled for
a seaman a red spark upon the blind night of the group:
and the calms of the coast, the flaming long calms of the
equator, the unbreathing, concentrated calms like the
deep introspection of a passionate nature, brooded
awfully for days and weeks together over the unchangeable inheritance of their children; till at last the stones,
hot like live embers, scorched the naked sole, till the
water clung warm, and sickly, and as if thickened
about the legs of lean men with girded loins, wading
thigh-deep in the pale blaze of the shallows. And it
would happen now and then that the *Sofala*, through

some delay in one of the ports of call, would heave in sight making for Pangu Bay as late as noonday.

Only a blurring cloud at first, the thin mist of her smoke would arise mysteriously from an empty point on the clear line of sea and sky. The taciturn fishermen within the reefs would extend their lean arms toward the offing; and the brown figures stooping on the tiny beaches, the brown figures of men, women, and children grubbing in the sand in search of turtles' eggs, would rise up, crooked elbow aloft and hand over the eyes, to watch this monthly apparition glide straight on, swerve on—and go by. Their ears caught the panting of that ship; their eyes followed her till she passed between the two capes of the mainland going at full speed as though she hoped to make her way unchecked into the very bosom of the earth.

On such days the luminous sea would give no sign of the dangers lurking on both sides of her path. Everything remained still, crushed by the overwhelming power of the light; and the whole group, opaque in the sunshine,—the rocks resembling pinnacles, the rocks resembling spires, the rocks resembling ruins; the forms of islets resembling beehives, resembling mole-hills; the islets recalling the shapes of haystacks, the contours of ivy-clad towers—would stand reflected together upside down in the unwrinkled water, like carved toys of ebony disposed on the silvered plate-glass of a mirror.

The first touch of blowing weather would envelop the whole at once in the spume of the windward breakers, as if in a sudden cloudlike burst of steam; and the clear water seemed fairly to boil in all the passages. The provoked sea outlined exactly in a design of angry foam the wide base of the group; the submerged level of broken waste and refuse left over from the building of the coast near by, projecting its dangerous spurs, all

awash, far into the channel, and bristling with wicked
long spits often a mile long: with deadly spits made of
froth and stones.

And even nothing more than a brisk breeze—as on
that morning, the voyage before, when the *Sofala*
left Pangu Bay early, and Mr. Sterne's discovery was
to blossom out like a flower of incredible and evil aspect
from the tiny seed of instinctive suspicion—even such
a breeze had enough strength to tear the placid mask
from the face of the sea. To Sterne, gazing with indifference, it had been like a revelation to behold for
the first time the dangers marked by the hissing livid
patches on the water as distinctly as on the engraved
paper of a chart. It came into his mind that this was
the sort of day most favourable for a stranger attempting the passage: a clear day, just windy enough
for the sea to break on every ledge, buoying, as it were,
the channel plainly to the sight; whereas during a calm
you had nothing to depend on but the compass and the
practised judgment of your eye. And yet the successive
captains of the *Sofala* had had to take her through at
night more than once. Nowadays you could not afford to throw away six or seven hours of a steamer's
time. That you couldn't. But then use is everything,
and with proper care. . . . The channel was broad
and safe enough; the main point was to hit upon the
entrance correctly in the dark—for if a man got himself
involved in that stretch of broken water over yonder
he would never get out with a whole ship—if he ever got
out at all.

This was Sterne's last train of thought independent
of the great discovery. He had just seen to the securing
of the anchor, and had remained forward idling away
a moment or two. The captain was in charge on the
bridge. With a slight yawn he had turned away from

his survey of the sea and had leaned his shoulders against the fish davit.

These, properly speaking, were the very last moments of ease he was to know on board the *Sofala*. All the instants that came after were to be pregnant with purpose and intolerable with perplexity. No more idle, random thoughts; the discovery would put them on the rack, till sometimes he wished to goodness he had been fool enough not to make it at all. And yet, if his chance to get on rested on the discovery of "something wrong," he could not have hoped for a greater stroke of luck.

X

THE knowledge was too disturbing, really. There
was "something wrong" with a vengeance, and the
moral certitude of it was at first simply frightful to
contemplate. Sterne had been looking aft in a mood
so idle, that for once he was thinking no harm of any
one. His captain on the bridge presented himself
naturally to his sight. How insignificant, how casual
was the thought that had started the train of discovery
—like an accidental spark that suffices to ignite the
charge of a tremendous mine!

Caught under by the breeze, the awnings of the
foredeck bellied upwards and collapsed slowly, and
above their heavy flapping the gray stuff of Captain
Whalley's roomy coat fluttered incessantly around
his arms and trunk. He faced the wind in full light,
with his great silvery beard blown forcibly against his
chest; the eyebrows overhung heavily the shadows
whence his glance appeared to be staring ahead pierc-
ingly. Sterne could just detect the twin gleam of the
whites shifting under the shaggy arches of the brow.
At short range these eyes, for all the man's affable
manner, seemed to look you through and through.
Sterne never could defend himself from that feeling
when he had occasion to speak with his captain. He
did not like it. What a big heavy man he appeared
up there, with that little shrimp of a Serang in close at-
tendance—as was usual in this extraordinary steamer!
Confounded absurd custom that. He resented it.
Surely the old fellow could have looked after his ship

without that loafing native at his elbow. Sterne wriggled his shoulders with disgust. What was it? Indolence or what?

That old skipper must have been growing lazy for years. They all grew lazy out East here (Sterne was very conscious of his own unimpaired activity); they got slack all over. But he towered very erect on the bridge; and quite low by his side, as you see a small child looking over the edge of a table, the battered soft hat and the brown face of the Serang peeped over the white canvas screen of the rail.

No doubt the Malay was standing back, nearer to the wheel; but the great disparity of size in close association amused Sterne like the observation of a bizarre fact in nature. There were as queer fish out of the sea as any in it.

He saw Captain Whalley turn his head quickly to speak to his Serang; the wind whipped the whole white mass of the beard sideways. He would be directing the chap to look at the compass for him, or what not. Of course. Too much trouble to step over and see for himself. Sterne's scorn for that bodily indolence which overtakes white men in the East increased on reflection. Some of them would be utterly lost if they hadn't all these natives at their beck and call; they grew perfectly shameless about it, too. He was not of that sort, thank God! It wasn't in him to make himself dependent for his work on any shrivelled-up little Malay like that. As if one could ever trust a silly native for anything in the world! But that fine old man thought differently, it seems. There they were together, never far apart; a pair of them, recalling to the mind an old whale attended by a little pilot-fish.

The fancifulness of the comparison made him smile. A whale with an inseparable pilot-fish! That's what the old man looked like; for it could not be said he looked like a shark, though Mr. Massy had called him that very name. But Mr. Massy did not mind what he said in his savage fits. Sterne smiled to himself— and gradually the ideas evoked by the sound, by the imagined shape of the word pilot-fish; the ideas of aid, of guidance needed and received, came uppermost in his mind: the word pilot awakened the idea of trust, of dependence, the idea of the welcome, clear-eyed help brought to the seaman groping for the land in the dark: groping blindly in fogs: feeling his way in the thick weather of the gales that, filling the air with a salt mist blown up from the sea, contract the range of sight on all sides to a shrunken horizon that seems within reach of the hand.

A pilot sees better than a stranger, because his local knowledge, like a sharper vision, completes the shapes of things hurriedly glimpsed; penetrates the veils of mist spread over the land by the storms of the sea; defines with certitude the outlines of a coast lying under the pall of fog, the forms of landmarks half buried in a starless night as in a shallow grave. He recognizes because he already knows. It is not to his far-reaching eye but to his more extensive knowledge that the pilot looks for certitudes; for this certitude of the ship's position on which may depend a man's good fame and the peace of his conscience, the justification of the trust deposited in his hands, with his own life, too, which is seldom wholly his to throw away, and the humble lives of others rooted in distant affections, perhaps, and made as weighty as the lives of kings by the burden of the awaiting mystery. The pilot's knowledge brings relief and certitude to the commander of a ship; the Serang, however, in his fanciful suggestion of a pilot-fish attending a whale, could not in any way be credited with

a superior knowledge. Why should he have it? These
two men had come on that run together—the white
and the brown—on the same day: and of course a white
man would learn more in a week than the best native
would in a month. He was made to stick to the
skipper as though he were of some use—as the pilot-fish,
they say, is to the whale. But how—it was very
marked—how? A pilot-fish—a pilot—a. . . . But
if not superior knowledge then. . . .

Sterne's discovery was made. It was repugnant to
his imagination, shocking to his ideas of honesty,
shocking to his conception of mankind. This enormity
affected one's outlook on what was possible in this
world: it was as if for instance the sun had turned blue,
throwing a new and sinister light on men and nature.
Really in the first moment he had felt sickish, as though
he had got a blow below the belt: for a second the very
colour of the sea seemed changed—appeared queer to
his wandering eye; and he had a passing, unsteady
sensation in all his limbs as though the earth had started
turning the other way.

A very natural incredulity succeeding this sense of
upheaval brought a measure of relief. He had gasped;
it was over. But afterwards, during all that day, sudden
paroxysms of wonder would come over him in the midst
of his occupations. He would stop and shake his head.
The revolt of his incredulity had passed away almost
as quick as the first emotion of discovery, and for the
next twenty-four hours he had no sleep. That would
never do. At meal-times (he took the foot of the table
set up for the white men on the bridge) he could not
help losing himself in a fascinated contemplation of
Captain Whalley opposite. He watched the deliberate
upward movements of the arm; the old man put his
food to his lips as though he never expected to find any

taste in his daily bread, as though he did not know anything about it. He fed himself like a somnambulist. "It's an awful sight," thought Sterne; and he watched the long period of mournful, silent immobility, with a big brown hand lying loosely closed by the side of the plate, till he noticed the two engineers to the right and left looking at him in astonishment. He would close his mouth in a hurry then, and lowering his eyes, wink rapidly at his plate. It was awful to see the old chap sitting there: it was even awful to think that with three words he could blow him up sky-high. All he had to do was to raise his voice and pronounce a single short sentence, and yet that simple act seemed as impossible to attempt as moving the sun out of its place in the sky. The old chap could eat in his terrific mechanical way; but Sterne, from mental excitement, could not—not that evening, at any rate.

He had had ample time since to get accustomed to the strain of the meal-hours. He would never have believed it. But then use is everything; only the very potency of his success prevented anything resembling elation. He felt like a man who, in his legitimate search for a loaded gun to help him on his way through the world, chances to come upon a torpedo—upon a live torpedo with a shattering charge in its head and a pressure of many atmospheres in its tail. It is the sort of weapon to make its possessor careworn and nervous. He had no mind to be blown up himself; and he could not get rid of the notion that the explosion was bound to damage him, too, in some way.

This vague apprehension had restrained him at first. He was able now to eat and sleep with that fearful weapon by his side, with the conviction of its power always in his mind. It had not been arrived at by any reflective process; but once the idea had entered his head, the conviction had followed overwhelmingly in a multitude of observed little facts to which before he had given only a languid attention. The abrupt and faltering intonations of the deep voice; the taciturnity put on like an armour; the deliberate, as if guarded, movements; the long immobilities, as if the man he watched had been afraid to disturb the very air: every familiar gesture, every word uttered in his hearing, every sigh overheard, had acquired a special significance, a confirmatory import.

Every day that passed over the *Sofala* appeared to Sterne simply crammed full with proofs—with incontrovertible proofs. At night, when off duty, he would steal out of his cabin in pyjamas (for more proofs) and stand a full hour, perhaps, on his bare feet below the bridge, as absolutely motionless as the awning stanchion in its deck socket near by. On the stretches of easy navigation it is not usual for a coasting captain to remain on deck all the time of his watch. The Serang keeps it for him as a matter of custom; in open water, on a straight course, he is usually trusted to look after the ship by himself. But this old man seemed incapable of remaining quietly down below. No doubt he could not sleep. And no wonder. This was also a proof. Suddenly in the silence of the ship panting upon the still, dark sea, Sterne would hear a low voice above him exclaiming nervously—

"Serang!"

"Tuan!"

"You are watching the compass well?"

"Yes, I am watching, Tuan."

"The ship is making her course?"

"She is, Tuan. Very straight."

"It is well; and remember, Serang, that the order is, that you are to mind the helmsmen and keep a lookout with care, the same as if I were not on deck."

Then, when the Serang had made his answer, the low tones on the bridge would cease, and everything round Sterne seemed to become more still and more profoundly silent. Slightly chilled and with his back aching a little from long immobility, he would steal away to his room on the port side of the deck. He had long since parted with the last vestige of incredulity; of the original emotions, set into a tumult by the discovery, some trace of the first awe alone remained. Not the awe of the man himself—he could blow him up sky-high with six words—rather it was an awestruck indignation at the reckless perversity of avarice (what else could it be?), at the mad and sombre resolution that for the sake of a few dollars more seemed to set at nought the common rule of conscience and pretended to struggle against the very decree of Providence.

You could not find another man like this one in the whole round world—thank God. There was something devilishly dauntless in the character of such a deception which made you pause.

Other considerations occurring to his prudence had kept him tongue-tied from day to day. It seemed to him now that it would yet have been easier to speak out in the first hour of discovery. He almost regretted not having made a row at once. But then the very monstrosity of the disclosure. . . . Why! he could hardly face it himself, let alone pointing it out to somebody else. Moreover, with a desperado of that sort one never knew. The object was not to get him out (that was as well as done already), but to step into his place. Bizarre as the thought seemed he might have shown fight. A fellow up to working such a fraud would have enough cheek for anything; a fellow that, as it were, stood up against God Almighty Himself. He was a horrid marvel—that's what he was: he was perfectly capable of brazening out the affair scandalously till he got him (Sterne) kicked out of the ship and everlastingly damaged his prospects in this part of the East. Yet if you want to get on something must be risked. At times Sterne thought he had been unduly timid of taking action in the past; and what was worse, it had come to this, that in the present he did not seem to know what action to take.

Massy's savage moroseness was too disconcerting. It was an incalculable factor of the situation. You could not tell what there was behind that insulting ferocity. How could one trust such a temper? it did not put Sterne in bodily fear for himself, but it frightened him exceedingly as to his prospects.

Though of course inclined to credit himself with exceptional powers of observation, he had by now lived too long with his discovery. He had gone on looking at nothing else, till at last one day it occurred to him that the thing was so obvious that no one could miss seeing it. There were four white men in all on board the *Sofala*. Jack, the second engineer, was too dull to notice anything that took place out of his engine-room. Remained Massy—the owner—the interested person— nearly going mad with worry. Sterne had heard and seen more than enough on board to know what ailed him; but his exasperation seemed to make him deaf to cautious overtures. If he had only known it, there was the very thing he wanted. But how could you bargain with a man of that sort? It was like going into a tiger's den with a piece of raw meat in your hand. He was as likely as not to rend you for your pains. In fact, he was always threatening to do that very thing; and the urgency of the case, combined with the im-

possibility of handling it with safety, made Sterne in his
watches below toss and mutter open-eyed in his bunk,
for hours, as though he had been burning with fever.

Occurrences like the crossing of the bar just now
were extremely alarming to his prospects. He did not
want to be left behind by some swift catastrophe.
Massy being on the bridge, the old man had to brace
himself up, and make a show, he supposed. But it was
getting very bad with him, very bad indeed, now. Even
Massy had been emboldened to find fault this time;
Sterne, listening at the foot of the ladder, had heard the
other's whimpering and artless denunciations. Luckily
the beast was very stupid and could not see the why of
all this. However, small blame to him; it took a clever
man to hit upon the cause. Nevertheless, it was high
time to do something. The old man's game could not
be kept up for many days more.

"I may yet lose my life at this fooling—let alone my
chance," Sterne mumbled angrily to himself, after the
stooping back of the chief engineer had disappeared
round the corner of the skylight. Yes, no doubt—he
thought; but to blurt out his knowledge would not
advance his prospects. On the contrary, it would blast
them utterly as likely as not. He dreaded another
failure. He had a vague consciousness of not being
much liked by his fellows in this part of the world;
inexplicably enough, for he had done nothing to them.
Envy, he supposed. People were always down on a
clever chap who made no bones about his determination
to get on. To do your duty and count on the gratitude
of that brute Massy would be sheer folly. He was a
bad lot. Unmanly! A vicious man! Bad! Bad! A
brute! A brute without a spark of anything human
about him; without so much as simple curiosity even,
or else surely he would have responded in some way to

all these hints he had been given. . . . Such insensibility was almost mysterious. Massy's state of exasperation seemed to Sterne to have made him stupid beyond the ordinary silliness of shipowners.

Sterne, meditating on the embarrassments of that stupidity, forgot himself completely. His stony, unwinking stare was fixed on the planks of the deck.

The slight quiver agitating the whole fabric of the ship was more perceptible in the silent river, shaded and still like a forest path. The *Sofala*, gliding with an even motion, had passed beyond the coast-belt of mud and mangroves. The shores rose higher, in firm sloping banks, and the forest of big trees came down to the brink. Where the earth had been crumbled by the floods it showed a steep brown cut, denuding a mass of roots intertwined as if wrestling underground; and in the air, the interlaced boughs, bound and loaded with creepers, carried on the struggle for life, mingled their foliage in one solid wall of leaves, with here and there the shape of an enormous dark pillar soaring, or a ragged opening, as if torn by the flight of a cannon-ball, disclosing the impenetrable gloom within, the secular* inviolable shade of the virgin forest. The thump of the engines reverberated regularly like the strokes of a metronome beating the measure of the vast silence, the shadow of the western wall had fallen across the river, and the smoke pouring backwards from the funnel eddied down behind the ship, spread a thin dusky veil over the sombre water, which, checked by the flood-tide, seemed to lie stagnant in the whole straight length of the reaches.

Sterne's body, as if rooted on the spot, trembled slightly from top to toe with the internal vibration of the ship; from under his feet came sometimes a sudden clang of iron, the noisy burst of a shout below; to the

right the leaves of the tree-tops caught the rays of the
low sun, and seemed to shine with a golden green light
of their own shimmering around the highest boughs
which stood out black against a smooth blue sky that
seemed to droop over the bed of the river like the roof
of a tent. The passengers for Batu Beru, kneeling on
the planks, were engaged in rolling their bedding of
mats busily; they tied up bundles, they snapped the
locks of wooden chests. A pockmarked pedlar of small
wares threw his head back to drain into his throat
the last drops out of an earthenware bottle before
putting it away in a roll of blankets. Knots of travelling traders standing about the deck conversed in low
tones; the followers of a small Rajah*from down the
coast, broad-faced simple young fellows in white drawers
and round white cotton caps with their coloured sarongs
twisted across their bronze shoulders, squatted on their
hams on the hatch, chewing betel*with bright red mouths
as if they had been tasting blood. Their spears, lying
piled up together within the circle of their bare toes,
resembled a casual bundle of dry bamboos; a thin,
livid Chinaman, with a bulky package wrapped up
in leaves already thrust under his arm, gazed ahead
eagerly; a wandering Kling*rubbed his teeth with a bit
of wood, pouring over the side a bright stream of water
out of his lips; the fat Rajah dozed in a shabby deck-
chair—and at the turn of every bend the two walls of
leaves reappeared running parallel along the banks,
with their impenetrable solidity fading at the top to a
vaporous mistiness of countless slender twigs growing
free, of young delicate branches shooting from the topmost limbs of hoary trunks, of feathery heads of climb-
ers like delicate silver sprays standing up without a
quiver. There was not a sign of a clearing anywhere;
not a trace of human habitation, except when in one

place, on the bare end of a low point under an isolated group of slender tree-ferns, the jagged, tangled remnants of an old hut on piles appeared with that peculiar aspect of ruined bamboo walls that look as if smashed with a club. Farther on, half hidden under the drooping bushes, a canoe containing a man and a woman together with a dozen green cocoanuts in a heap, rocked helplessly after the *Sofala* had passed, like a navigating contrivance of venturesome insects, of travelling ants; while two glassy folds of water streaming away from each bow of the steamer across the whole width of the river ran with her upstream smoothly, fretting their outer ends into a brown whispering tumble of froth against the miry foot of each bank.

"I must," thought Sterne, "bring that brute Massy to his bearings. It's getting too absurd in the end. Here's the old man up there buried in his chair—he may just as well be in his grave for all the use he'll ever be in the world—and the Serang's in charge. Because that's what he is. In charge. In the place that's mine by rights. I must bring that savage brute to his bearings. I'll do it at once, too. . . ."

When the mate made an abrupt start, a little brown, half-naked boy, with large black eyes, and the string of a written charm round his neck, became panic-struck at once. He dropped the banana he had been munching, and ran to the knee of a grave dark Arab in flowing robes, sitting like a Biblical figure, incongruously, on a yellow tin trunk corded with a rope of twisted rattan. The father, unmoved, put out his hand to pat the little shaven poll protectingly.

XI

STERNE crossed the deck upon the track of the chief engineer. Jack, the second, retreating backwards down the engine-room ladder, and still wiping his hands, treated him to an incomprehensible grin of white teeth out of his grimy hard face; Massy was nowhere to be seen. Sterne scratched at the door softly, then, putting his lips to the rose of the ventilator, said—

"I must speak to you, Mr. Massy. Just give me a minute or two."

"I am busy. Go away from my door."

"But pray, Mr. Massy. . . ."

"You go away. D'you hear? Take yourself off altogether—to the other end of the ship—quite away. . . ." The voice inside dropped low. "To the devil."

Sterne paused: then very quietly—

"It's rather pressing. When do you think you will be at liberty, sir?"

The answer to this was an exasperated "Never"; and at once Sterne, with a very firm expression of face, turned the handle.

Mr. Massy's stateroom—a narrow, one-berth cabin —smelt strongly of soap, and presented to view a swept, dusted, unadorned neatness, not so much bare as barren, not so much severe as starved and lacking in humanity, like the ward of a public hospital, or rather (owing to the small size) like the clean retreat of a desperately poor but exemplary person. Not a single photograph frame ornamented the bulk-heads; not a

single article of clothing, not as much as a spare cap,
hung from the brass hooks. All the inside was painted
in one plain tint of pale blue; two big sea-chests in sailcloth covers and with iron padlocks fitted exactly in
the space under the bunk. One glance was enough to
embrace all the strip of scrubbed planks within the four
unconcealed corners. The absence of the usual settee
was striking; the teak-wood top of the washing-stand
seemed hermetically closed, and so was the lid of the
writing-desk, which protruded from the partition at the
foot of the bed-place, containing a mattress as thin as a
pancake under a threadbare blanket with a faded red
stripe, and a folded mosquito-net against the nights
spent in harbour. There was not a scrap of paper anywhere in sight, no boots on the floor, no litter of any
sort, not a speck of dust anywhere; no traces of pipe-ash
even, which, in a heavy smoker, was morally revolting,
like a manifestation of extreme hypocrisy; and the
bottom of the old wooden arm-chair (the only seat
there), polished with much use, shone as if its shabbi-
ness had been waxed. The screen of leaves on the
bank, passing as if unrolled endlessly in the round opening of the port, sent a wavering network of light and
shade into the place.

Sterne, holding the door open with one hand, had
thrust in his head and shoulders. At this amazing
intrusion Massy, who was doing absolutely nothing,
jumped up speechless.

"Don't call names," murmured Sterne, hurriedly.
"I won't be called names. I think of nothing but
your good, Mr. Massy."

A pause as of extreme astonishment followed. They
both seemed to have lost their tongues. Then the
mate went on with discreet glibness:

"You simply couldn't conceive what's going on on

board your ship. It wouldn't enter your head for a moment. You are too good—too—too upright, Mr. Massy, to suspect anybody of such a. . . . It's enough to make your hair stand on end."

He watched for the effect: Massy seemed dazed, uncomprehending. He only passed the palm of his hand on the coal-black wisps plastered across the top of his head. In a tone suddenly changed to confidential audacity Sterne hastened on:

"Remember that there's only six weeks left to run. . . ." The other was looking at him stonily. . . . "So anyhow you will require a captain for the ship before long."

Then only, as if that suggestion had scarified his flesh in the manner of red-hot iron, Massy gave a start and seemed ready to shriek. He contained himself by a great effort.

"Require—a—captain," he repeated with scathing slowness. "Who requires a captain? You dare tell me that I need any of you humbugging sailors to run my ship. You and your likes have been fattening on me for years. It would have hurt me less to throw my money overboard. Pam—pe—red us—e—less f-f-f-frauds. The old ship knows as much as the best of you." He snapped his teeth audibly and growled through them. "The silly law requires a captain."

Sterne had taken heart of grace meantime.

"And the silly insurance people, too, as well," he said, lightly. "But never mind that. What I want to ask is: Why shouldn't I do, sir? I don't say but you could take a steamer about the world as well as any of us sailors. I don't pretend to tell you that it is a very great trick. . . ." He emitted a short, hollow guffaw, familiarly. . . . I didn't make the law—but there it is; and I am an active young fellow; I quite hold with your ideas; I know your ways by this time, Mr. Massy. I wouldn't try to give myself airs like that—that—er—lazy specimen of an old man up there."

He put a marked emphasis on the last sentence, to lead Massy away from the track in case . . . but he did not doubt of now holding his success. The chief engineer seemed nonplussed, like a slow man invited to catch hold of a whirligig of some sort.

"What you want, sir, is a chap with no nonsense about him, who would be content to be your sailing-master. Quite right, too. Well, I am fit for the work as much as that Serang. Because that's what it amounts to. Do you know, sir, that a dam' Malay like a monkey is in charge of your ship—and no one else? Just listen to his feet pit-patting above us on the bridge —real officer in charge. He's taking her up the river while the great man is wallowing in the chair—perhaps asleep; and if he is, that would not make it much worse either—take my word for it."

He tried to thrust himself farther in. Massy, with lowered forehead, one hand grasping the back of the arm-chair, did not budge.

"You think, sir, that the man has got you tight in his agreement. . . ." Massy raised a heavy snarling face at this. . . . "Well, sir, one can't help hearing of it on board. It's no secret. And it has been the talk on shore for years; fellows have been making bets about it. No, sir! It's *you* who have got him at your mercy. You will say that you can't dismiss him for indolence. Difficult to prove in court, and so on. Why, yes. But if you say the word, sir, I can tell you something about his indolence that will give you the clear right to fire him out on the spot and put me in charge for the rest of this very trip—yes, sir, before we leave Batu Beru—and make him pay a dollar a day for his keep till we get back, if you like. Now, what do you think of that? Come, sir. Say the word. It's really well worth your while, and I am quite ready to take your bare word. A definite statement from you would be as good as a bond."

His eyes began to shine. He insisted. A simple statement—and he thought to himself that he would manage somehow to stick in his berth as long as it suited him. He would make himself indispensable; the ship had a bad name in her port; it would be easy to scare the fellows off. Massy would have to keep him.

"A definite statement from me would be enough," Massy repeated, slowly.

"Yes, sir. It would." Sterne stuck out his chin cheerily and blinked at close quarters with that unconscious impudence which had the power to enrage Massy beyond anything.

The engineer spoke very distinctly:

"Listen well to me, then, Mr. Sterne: I wouldn't —d'ye hear?—I wouldn't promise you the value of two pence for anything *you* can tell me."

He struck Sterne's arm away with a smart blow, and catching hold of the handle pulled the door to. The terrific slam darkened the cabin instantaneously to his eyes as if after the flash of an explosion. At once he dropped into the chair. "Oh, no! You don't!" he whispered faintly.

The ship had in that place to shave the bank so close that the gigantic wall of leaves came gliding like a shutter against the port; the darkness of the primeval forest seemed to flow into that bare cabin with the odour of rotting leaves, of sodden soil—the strong muddy smell of the living earth steaming uncovered after the passing of a deluge. The bushes swished loudly alongside: above there was a series of crackling sounds, with a sharp rain of small broken branches falling on the bridge; a creeper with a great rustle snapped on the head of a boat davit, and a long, luxuriant green twig actually whipped in and out of the open port, leaving behind a few torn leaves that remained suddenly at rest on Mr. Massy's blanket. Then, the ship sheering out in the stream, the light began to return, but did not augment beyond a subdued clearness: for the sun was very low already, and the river, wending its sinuous course through a multitude of secular trees as if at the bottom of a precipitous gorge, had been already invaded by a deepening gloom—the swift precursor of the night.

"Oh, no, you don't!" murmured the engineer again. His lips trembled almost imperceptibly; his hands, too, a little: and to calm himself he opened the writing-desk, spread out a sheet of thin grayish paper covered with a mass of printed figures and began to scan them attentively for the twentieth time this trip at least.

With his elbows propped, his head between his hands, he seemed to lose himself in the study of an abstruse problem in mathematics. It was the list of the winning numbers from the last drawing of the great lottery which had been the one inspiring fact of so many years of his existence. The conception of a life deprived of that periodical sheet of paper had slipped away from him entirely, as another man, according to his nature, would not have been able to conceive a world without fresh air, without activity, or without affection. A great pile of flimsy sheets had been growing for years in his desk, while the *Sofala*, driven by the faithful Jack, wore out her boilers in tramping up and down the Straits, from cape to cape, from river to river, from bay to bay; accumulating by that hard labour of an overworked, starved ship the blackened mass of these

documents.   Massy kept them under lock and key like
a treasure.   There was in them, as in the experience of
life, the fascination of hope, the excitement of a half-
penetrated mystery, the longing of a half-satisfied
desire.

For days together, on a trip, he would shut himself
up in his berth with them: the thump of the toiling
engines pulsated in his ear; and he would weary his
brain poring over the rows of disconnected figures,
bewildering by their senseless sequence, resembling the
hazards of destiny itself.   He nourished a conviction
that there must be some logic lurking somewhere in the
results of chance.   He thought he had seen its very
form.   His head swam; his limbs ached; he puffed
at his pipe mechanically; a contemplative stupor would
soothe the fretfulness of his temper, like the passive
bodily quietude procured by a drug, while the intellect
remains tensely on the stretch.   Nine, nine, nought,
four, two.   He made a note.   The next winning number of the great prize was forty-seven thousand and five.
These numbers of course would have to be avoided in
the future when writing to Manila for the tickets.   He
mumbled, pencil in hand   .   .   .   "and five. Hm . . .
hm."   He wetted his finger: the papers rustled.   Ha!
But what's this?   Three years ago, in the September
drawing, it was number nine, nought, four, two that
took the first prize.   Most remarkable.   There was a
hint there of a definite rule!   He was afraid of missing
some recondite principle in the overwhelming wealth
of his material.   What could it be? and for half an
hour he would remain dead still, bent low over the desk,
without twitching a muscle.   At his back the whole
berth would be thick with a heavy body of smoke, as
if a bomb had burst in there, unnoticed, unheard.

At last he would lock up the desk with the decision

of unshaken confidence, jump up and go out. He would walk swiftly back and forth on that part of the foredeck which was kept clear of the lumber*and of the bodies of the native passengers. They were a great nuisance, but they were also a source of profit that could not be disdained. He needed every penny of profit the *Sofala* could make. Little enough it was, in all conscience! The incertitude of chance gave him no concern, since he had somehow arrived at the conviction that, in the course of years, every number was bound to have its winning turn. It was simply a matter of time and of taking as many tickets as he could afford for every drawing. He generally took rather more; all the earnings of the ship went that way, and also the wages he allowed himself as chief engineer. It was the wages he paid to others that he begrudged with a reasoned and at the same time a passionate regret. He scowled at the lascars with their deck brooms, at the quartermasters rubbing the brass rails with greasy rags; he was eager to shake his fist and roar abuse in bad Malay at the poor carpenter—a timid, sickly, opium-fuddled China-man, in loose blue drawers for all costume, who invariably dropped his tools and fled below, with streaming tail and shaking all over, before the fury of that "devil." But it was when he raised up his eyes to the bridge where one of these sailor frauds was always planted by law in charge of his ship that he felt almost dizzy with rage. He abominated them all; it was an old feud, from the time he first went to sea, an unlicked cub with a great opinion of himself, in the engine-room. The slights that had been put upon him. The persecutions he had suffered at the hands of skippers—of absolute nobodies in a steamship after all. And now that he had risen to be a shipowner they were still a plague to him: he had absolutely to pay away precious money to the conceited useless loafers:—As if a fully qualified engineer—who was the owner as well—were not fit to be trusted with the whole charge of a ship. Well! he made it pretty warm for them; but it was a poor consolation. He had come in time to hate the ship, too, for the repairs she required, for the coal-bills he had to pay, for the poor beggarly freights she earned. He would clench his hand as he walked and hit the rail a sudden blow, viciously, as though she could be made to feel pain. And yet he could not do without her; he needed her; he must hang on to her tooth and nail to keep his head above water till the expected flood of fortune came sweeping up and landed him safely on the high shore of his ambition.

It was now to do nothing, nothing whatever, and have plenty of money to do it on. He had tasted of power, the highest form of it his limited experience was aware of—the power of shipowning. What a deception! Vanity of vanities! He wondered at his folly. He had thrown away the substance for the shadow. Of the gratification of wealth he did not know enough to excite his imagination with any visions of luxury. How could he—the child of a drunken boiler-maker—going straight from the workshop into the engine-room of a north-country collier! But the notion of the absolute idleness of wealth he could very well conceive. He revelled in it, to forget his present troubles; he imagined himself walking about the streets of Hull*(he knew their gutters well as a boy) with his pockets full of sovereigns.* He would buy himself a house; his married sisters, their husbands, his old workshop chums, would render him infinite homage. There would be nothing to think of. His word would be law. He had been out of work for a long time before he won his prize, and he remembered how Carlo Mariani (commonly known as Paunchy

Charley), the Maltese hotel-keeper at the slummy end of Denham Street, had cringed joyfully before him in the evening, when the news had come. Poor Charley, though he made his living by ministering to various abject vices, gave credit for the food to many a piece of white wreckage. He was naïvely overjoyed at the idea of his old bills being paid, and he reckoned confidently on a spell of festivities in the cavernous grogshop downstairs. Massy remembered the curious, respectful looks of the "trashy" white men in the place. His heart had swelled within him. Massy had left Charley's infamous den directly he had realized the possibilities open to him, with his nose in the air. Afterwards the memory of these adulations was a great sadness.

This was the true power of money—and no trouble with it, nor any thinking required either. He thought with difficulty and felt vividly; to his blunt brain the problems offered by any ordered scheme of life seemed in their cruel toughness to have been put in his way by the obvious malevolence of men. As a shipowner everyone had conspired to make him a nobody. How could he have been such a fool as to purchase that accursed ship? He had been abominably swindled; there was no end to this swindling, and as the difficulties of his improvident ambition gathered thicker round him, he really came to hate everybody he had ever come in contact with. A temper naturally irritable and an amazing sensitiveness to the claims of his own personality had ended by making of life for him a sort of inferno—a place where his lost soul had been given up to the torment of savage brooding.

But he had never hated any one so much as that old man who turned up one evening to save him from an utter disaster,—from the conspiracy of the wretched

sailors. He seemed to have fallen on board from the
sky. His footsteps echoed on the empty steamer, and
the strange deep-toned voice on deck repeating inter-
rogatively the words, "Mr. Massy, Mr. Massy there?"
had been startling like a wonder. And coming up from
the depths of the cold engine-room, where he had been
pottering dismally with a candle amongst the enormous
shadows, thrown on all sides by the skeleton limbs of
machinery, Massy had been struck dumb by astonishment in the presence of that imposing old man with a
beard like a silver plate, towering in the dusk rendered
lurid by the expiring flames of sunset.

"Want to see me on business? What business?
I am doing no business. Can't you see that this ship
is laid up?" Massy had turned at bay before the
pursuing irony of his disaster. Afterwards he could
not believe his ears. What was that old fellow getting
at? Things don't happen that way. It was a dream.
He would presently wake up and find the man vanished
like a shape of mist. The gravity, the dignity, the firm
and courteous tone of that athletic old stranger impressed Massy. He was almost afraid. But it was no
dream. Five hundreds pounds are no dream. At once
he became suspicious. What did it mean? Of course
it was an offer to catch hold of for dear life. But what
could there be behind?

Before they had parted, after appointing a meeting
in a solicitor's office early on the morrow, Massy was
asking himself, What is his motive? He spent the
night in hammering out the clauses of the agreement—
a unique instrument of its sort whose tenor got bruited
abroad somehow and became the talk and wonder of
the port.

Massy's object had been to secure for himself as
many ways as possible of getting rid of his partner with-

out being called upon at once to pay back his share. Captain Whalley's efforts were directed to making the money secure. Was it not Ivy's money—a part of her fortune whose only other asset was the time-defying body of her old father? Sure of his forbearance in the strength of his love for her, he accepted, with stately serenity, Massy's stupidly cunning paragraphs against his incompetence, his dishonesty, his drunkenness, for the sake of other stringent stipulations. At the end of three years he was at liberty to withdraw from the partnership, taking his money with him. Provision was made for forming a fund to pay him off. But if he left the *Sofala* before the term, from whatever cause (barring death), Massy was to have a whole year for paying. "Illness?" the lawyer had suggested: a young man fresh from Europe and not overburdened with business, who was rather amused. Massy began to whine unctuously, "How could he be expected? . . ."

"Let that go," Captain Whalley had said with a superb confidence in his body. "Acts of God," he added. In the midst of life we are in death, but he trusted his Maker with a still greater fearlessness— his Maker who knew his thoughts, his human affections, and his motives. His Creator knew what use he was making of his health—how much he wanted it. . . . "I trust my first illness will be my last. I've never been ill that I can remember," he had remarked. "Let it go."

But at this early stage he had already awakened Massy's hostility by refusing to make it six hundred instead of five. "I cannot do that," was all he had said, simply, but with so much decision that Massy desisted at once from pressing the point, but had thought to himself, "Can't! Old curmudgeon. *Won't!* He must have lots of money, but he would like to get hold of a soft berth and the sixth part of my profits for nothing if he only could."

And during these years Massy's dislike grew under the restraint of something resembling fear. The simplicity of that man appeared dangerous. Of late he had changed, however, had appeared less formidable and with a lessened vigour of life, as though he had received a secret wound. But still he remained incomprehensible in his simplicity, fearlessness, and rectitude. And when Massy learned that he meant to leave him at the end of the time, to leave him confronted with the problem of the boilers, his dislike blazed up secretly into hate.

It had made him so clear-eyed that for a long time now Mr. Sterne could have told him nothing he did not know. He had much ado in trying to terrorize that mean sneak into silence; he wanted to deal alone with the situation; and—incredible as it might have appeared to Mr. Sterne—he had not yet given up the desire and the hope of inducing that hated old man to stay. Why! there was nothing else to do, unless he were to abandon his chances of fortune. But now, suddenly, since the crossing of the bar at Batu Beru things seemed to be coming rapidly to a point. It disquieted him so much that the study of the winning numbers failed to soothe his agitation: and the twilight in the cabin deepened, very sombre.

He put the list away, muttering once more, "Oh, no, my boy, you don't. Not if I know it." He did not mean the blinking, eavesdropping humbug to force his action. He took his head again into his hands; his immobility confined in the darkness of this shut-up little place seemed to make him a thing apart infinitely removed from the stir and the sounds of the deck.

He heard them: the passengers were beginning to

jabber excitedly; somebody dragged a heavy box past his door. He heard Captain Whalley's voice above—

"Stations, Mr. Sterne." And the answer from somewhere on deck forward—

"Ay, ay, sir."

"We shall moor head upstream this time; the ebb has made."

"Head upstream, sir."

"You will see to it, Mr. Sterne."

The answer was covered by the autocratic clang of the engine-room gong. The propeller went on beating slowly: one, two, three; one, two three—with pauses as if hesitating on the turn. The gong clanged time after time, and the water churned this way and that by the blades was making a great noisy commotion alongside. Mr. Massy did not move. A shore-light on the other bank, a quarter of a mile across the river, drifted, no bigger than a tiny star, passing slowly athwart the circle of the port. Voices from Mr. Van Wyk's jetty answered the hails from the ship; ropes were thrown and missed and thrown again; the swaying flame of a torch carried in a large sampan coming to fetch away in state the Rajah from down the coast cast a sudden ruddy glare into his cabin, over his very person. Mr. Massy did not move. After a few last ponderous turns the engines stopped, and the prolonged clanging of the gong signified that the captain had done with them. A great number of boats and canoes of all sizes boarded the off-side of the *Sofala*. Then after a time the tumult of splashing, of cries, of shuffling feet, of packages dropped with a thump, the noise of the native passengers going away, subsided slowly. On the shore, a voice, cultivated, slightly authoritative, spoke very close alongside—

"Brought any mail for me this time?"

"Yes, Mr. Van Wyk." This was from Sterne, answering over the rail in a tone of respectful cordiality. "Shall I bring it up to you?"

But the voice asked again—

"Where's the captain?"

"Still on the bridge, I believe. He hasn't left his chair. Shall I. . . ."

The voice interrupted negligently—

"I will come on board."

"Mr. Van Wyk," Sterne suddenly broke out with an eager effort, "will you do me the favour. . . ."

The mate walked away quickly towards the gangway. A silence fell. Mr. Massy in the dark did not move.

He did not move even when he heard slow shuffling footsteps pass his cabin lazily. He contented himself to bellow out through the closed door—

"You—Jack!"

The footsteps came back without haste; the door-handle rattled, and the second engineer appeared in the opening, shadowy in the sheen of the skylight at his back, with his face apparently as black as the rest of his figure.

"We have been very long coming up this time," Mr. Massy growled, without changing his attitude.

"What do you expect with half the boiler tubes plugged up for leaks." The second defended himself loquaciously.

"None of your lip," said Massy.

"None of your rotten boilers—I say," retorted his faithful subordinate without animation, huskily.

"Go down there and carry a head of steam on them yourself—if you dare. I don't."

"You aren't worth your salt then," Massy said. The other made a faint noise which resembled a laugh but might have been a snarl.

"Better go slow than stop the ship altogether," he admonished his admired superior. Mr. Massy moved at last. He turned in his chair, and grinding his teeth—

"Dam' you and the ship! I wish she were at the bottom of the sea. Then you would have to starve."

The trusty second engineer closed the door gently.

Massy listened. Instead of passing on to the bathroom where he should have gone to clean himself, the second entered his cabin, which was next door. Mr. Massy jumped up and waited. Suddenly he heard the lock snap in there. He rushed out and gave a violent kick to the door.

"I believe you are locking yourself up to get drunk," he shouted.

A muffled answer came after a while.

"My own time."

"If you take to boozing on the trip I'll fire you out," Massy cried.

An obstinate silence followed that threat. Massy moved away, perplexed. On the bank two figures appeared, approaching the gangway. He heard a voice tinged with contempt—

"I would rather doubt your word. But I shall certainly speak to him of this."

The other voice, Sterne's, said with a sort of regretful formality—

"Thanks. That's all I want. I must do my duty."

Mr. Massy was surprised. A short, dapper figure leaped lightly on the deck and nearly bounded into him where he stood beyond the circle of light from the gangway lamp. When it had passed towards the bridge, after exchanging a hurried "Good evening," Massy said surlily to Sterne, who followed with slow steps—

"What is it you're making up to Mr. Van Wyk for, now?"

"Far from it, Mr. Massy. I am not good enough for Mr. Van Wyk. Neither are you, sir, in his opinion, I am afraid. Captain Whalley is, it seems. He's gone to ask him to dine up at the house this evening."

Then he murmured to himself darkly—

"I hope he will like it."

XII

MR. VAN WYK, the white man of Batu Beru, an ex-naval officer who, for reasons best known to himself, had thrown away the promise of a brilliant career to become the pioneer of tobacco-planting on that remote part of the coast, had learned to like Captain Whalley. The appearance of the new skipper had attracted his attention. Nothing more unlike all the diverse types he had seen succeeding each other on the bridge of the *Sofala* could be imagined.

At that time Batu Beru was not what it has become since: the centre of a prosperous tobacco-growing district, a tropically suburban-looking little settlement of bungalows in one long street shaded with two rows of trees, embowered by the flowering and trim luxuriance of the gardens, with a three-mile-long carriage-road for the afternoon drives and a first-class Resident with a fat, cheery wife to lead the society of married estate-managers and unmarried young fellows in the service of the big companies.

All this prosperity was not yet; and Mr. Van Wyk prospered alone on the left bank on his deep clearing carved out of the forest, which came down above and below to the water's edge. His lonely bungalow faced across the river the houses of the Sultan: a restless and melancholy old ruler who had done with love and war, for whom life no longer held any savour (except of evil forebodings) and time never had any value. He was afraid of death, and hoped he would die before the white men were ready to take his country from him. He crossed the river frequently (with never less than ten boats crammed full of people), in the wistful hope of extracting some information on the subject from his own white man. There was a certain chair on the verandah he always took: the dignitaries of the court squatted on the rugs and skins between the furniture: the inferior people remained below on the grass-plot between the house and the river in rows three or four deep all along the front. Not seldom the visit began at daybreak. Mr. Van Wyk tolerated these inroads. He would nod out of his bedroom window, toothbrush or razor in hand, or pass through the throng of courtiers in his bathing robe. He appeared and disappeared humming a tune, polished his nails with attention, rubbed his shaved face with eau-de-Cologne, drank his early tea, went out to see his coolies at work; returned, looked through some papers on his desk, read a page or two in a book or sat before his cottage piano leaning back on the stool, his arms extended, fingers on the keys, his body swaying slightly from side to side. When absolutely forced to speak he gave evasive, vaguely soothing answers out of pure compassion: the same feeling perhaps made him so lavishly hospitable with the aerated drinks that more than once he left himself without soda-water for a whole week. That old man had granted him as much land as he cared to have cleared: it was neither more nor less than a fortune.

Whether it was fortune or seclusion from his kind that Mr. Van Wyk sought, he could not have pitched upon a better place. Even the mail-boats of the subsidized company calling on the veriest clusters of palm-thatched hovels along the coast steamed past the mouth of Batu Beru river far away in the offing. The contract was old: perhaps in a few years' time, when it had expired, Batu Beru would be included in the service; meantime

all Mr. Van Dyk's mail was addressed to Malacca,
whence his agent sent it across once a month by the
Sofala. It followed that whenever Massy had run short
of money (through taking too many lottery tickets),
or got into a difficulty about a skipper, Mr. Van Wyk
was deprived of his letters and newspapers. In so far
he had a personal interest in the fortunes of the *Sofala*.
Though he considered himself a hermit (and for no
passing whim evidently, since he had stood eight years
of it already), he liked to know what went on in the
world.

Handy on the verandah upon a walnut *étagère**(it
had come last year by the *Sofala*—everything came by
the *Sofala*) there lay, piled up under bronze weights,
a pile of *The Times* weekly edition, the large sheets of the
Rotterdam Courant, the *Graphic* in its world-wide green
wrappers, an illustrated Dutch publication without a
cover, the numbers of a German magazine with covers
of the "Bismarck malade'"*colour.   There were also
parcels of new music—though the piano (it had come
years ago by the *Sofala*) in the damp atmosphere of the
forests was generally out of tune.   It was vexing to be
cut off from everything for sixty days at a stretch sometimes, without any means of knowing what was the
matter. And when the *Sofala* reappeared Mr. Van
Wyk would descend the steps of the verandah and stroll
over the grass-plot in front of his house, down to the
water-side, with a frown on his white brow.

"You've been laid up after an accident, I presume."

He addressed the bridge, but before anybody could
answer Massy was sure to have already scrambled
ashore over the rail and pushed in, squeezing the palms
of his hands together, bowing his sleek head as if gum-
med all over the top with black threads and tapes. And
he would be so enraged at the necessity of having to

offer such an explanation that his moaning would be
positively pitiful, while all the time he tried to compose
his big lips into a smile.

"No, Mr. Van Wyk. You would not believe it. I
couldn't get one of those wretches to take the ship out.
Not a single one of the lazy beasts could be induced, and
the law, you know, Mr. Van Wyk. . . ."

He moaned at great length apologetically; the words
conspiracy, plot, envy, came out prominently, whined
with greater energy. Mr. Van Wyk, examining with a
faint grimace his polished fingernails, would say, "H'm.
Very unfortunate," and turn his back on him.

Fastidious, clever, slightly sceptical, accustomed
to the best society (he had held a much-envied shore
appointment at the Ministry of Marine for a year
preceding his retreat from his profession and from
Europe), he possessed a latent warmth of feeling and a
capacity for sympathy which were concealed by a sort
of haughty, arbitrary indifference of manner arising
from his early training; and by a something an enemy
might have called foppish, in his aspect—like a distorted
echo of past elegancies. He managed to keep an almost military discipline amongst the coolies of the estate
he had dragged into the light of day out of the tangle
and shadows of the jungle; and the white shirt he put on
every evening with its stiff glossy front and high collar
looked as if he had meant to preserve the decent cere-
mony of evening-dress, but had wound a thick crimson
sash above his hips as a concession to the wilderness,
once his adversary, now his vanquished companion.
Moreover, it was a hygienic precaution. Worn wide
open in front, a short jacket of some airy silken stuff
floated from his shoulders. His fluffy, fair hair, thin
at the top, curled slightly at the sides; a carefully arranged moustache, an ungarnished forehead, the gleam

of low patent shoes peeping under the wide bottom
of trousers cut straight from the same stuff as the gossamer coat, completed a figure recalling, with its sash,
a pirate chief of romance, and at the same time the
elegance of a slightly bald dandy indulging, in seclusion,
a taste for unorthodox costume.

It was his evening get-up. The proper time for
the *Sofala* to arrive at Batu Beru was an hour before
sunset, and he looked picturesque, and somehow quite
correct, too, walking at the water's edge on the background of grass slope crowned with a low, long bungalow
with an immensely steep roof of palm thatch, and clad
to the eaves in flowering creepers. While the *Sofala*
was being made fast he strolled in the shade of the few
trees left near the landing-place, waiting till he could go
on board. Her white men were not of his kind. The
old Sultan (though his wistful invasions were a nuisance)
was really much more acceptable to his fastidious taste.
But still they were white; the periodical visits of the
ship made a break in the well-filled sameness of the day
without disturbing his privacy. Moreover, they were
necessary from a business point of view; and through
a strain of preciseness in his nature he was irritated when
she failed to appear at the appointed time.

The cause of the irregularity was too absurd, and
Massy, in his opinion, was a contemptible idiot. The
first time the *Sofala* reappeared under the new agreement swinging out of the bend below, after he had almost given up all hope of ever seeing her again, he felt
so angry that he did not go down at once to the landing-
place. His servants had come running to him with the
news, and he had dragged a chair close against the front
rail of the verandah, spread his elbows out, rested his
chin on his hands, and went on glaring at her fixedly
while she was being made fast opposite his house. He

could make out easily all the white faces on board. Who on earth was that kind of patriarch they had got there on the bridge now?

At last he sprang up and walked down the gravel path. It was a fact that the very gravel for his paths had been imported by the *Sofala*. Exasperated out of his quiet superciliousness, without looking at any one right or left, he accosted Massy straightway in so determined a manner that the engineer, taken aback, began to stammer unintelligibly. Nothing could be heard but the words: "Mr. Van Wyk. . . . Indeed, Mr. Van Wyk. . . . For the future, Mr. Van Wyk"—and by the suffusion of blood Massy's vast bilious face acquired an unnatural orange tint, out of which the disconcerted coal-black eyes shone in an extraordinary manner.

"Nonsense. I am tired of this. I wonder you have the impudence to come alongside my jetty as if I had it made for your convenience alone."

Massy tried to protest earnestly. Mr. Van Wyk was very angry. He had a good mind to ask that German firm—those people in Malacca—what was their name?—boats with green funnels. They would be only too glad of the opening to put one of their small steamers on the run. Yes; Schnitzler, Jacob Schnitzler, would in a moment. Yes. He had decided to write without delay.

In his agitation Massy caught up his falling pipe.

"You don't mean it, sir!" he shrieked.

"You shouldn't mismanage your business in this ridiculous manner."

Mr. Van Wyk turned on his heel. The other three whites on the bridge had not stirred during the scene. Massy walked hastily from side to side, puffed out his cheeks, suffocated.

"Stuck-up Dutchman!"

And he moaned out feverishly a long tale of griefs. The efforts he had made for all these years to please that man. This was the return you got for it, heh? Pretty. Write to Schnitzler—let in the green-funnel boats—get an old Hamburg Jew to ruin him. No, really he could laugh. . . . He laughed sobbingly. . . . Ha! ha! ha! And make him carry the letter in his own ship presumably.

He stumbled across a grating and swore. He would not hesitate to fling the Dutchman's correspondence overboard—the whole confounded bundle. He had never, never made any charge for that accommodation. But Captain Whalley, his new partner, would not let him probably; besides, it would be only putting off the evil day. For his own part he would make a hole in the water rather than look on tamely at the green funnels overrunning his trade.

He raved aloud. The China boys hung back with the dishes at the foot of the ladder. He yelled from the bridge down at the deck, "Aren't we going to have any chow this evening at all?" then turned violently to Captain Whalley, who waited, grave and patient, at the head of the table, smoothing his beard in silence now and then with a forbearing gesture.

"You don't seem to care what happens to me. Don't you see that this affects your interests as much as mine? It's no joking matter."

He took the foot of the table growling between his teeth.

"Unless you have a few thousands put away somewhere. I haven't."

Mr. Van Wyk dined in his thoroughly lit-up bungalow, putting a point of splendour in the night of his clearing above the dark bank of the river. Afterwards he sat down to his piano, and in a pause he became aware of slow footsteps passing on the path along the front. A plank or two creaked under a heavy tread; he swung half round on the music-stool, listening with his finger-tips at rest on the keyboard. His little terrier barked violently, backing in from the verandah. A deep voice apologized gravely for "this intrusion." He walked out quickly.

At the head of the steps the patriarchal figure, who was the new captain of the *Sofala* apparently (he had seen a round dozen of them, but not one of that sort), towered without advancing. The little dog barked unceasingly, till a flick of Mr. Van Wyk's handkerchief made him spring aside into silence. Captain Whalley, opening the matter, was met by a punctiliously polite but determined opposition.

They carried on their discussion standing where they had come face to face. Mr. Van Wyk observed his visitor with attention. Then at last, as if forced out of his reserve—

"I am surprised that you should intercede for such a confounded fool."

This outbreak was almost complimentary, as if its meaning had been, "That such a man as you should intercede!" Captain Whalley let it pass by without flinching. One would have thought he had heard nothing. He simply went on to state that he was personally interested in putting things straight between them. Personally. . . .

But Mr. Van Wyk, really carried away by his disgust with Massy, became very incisive—

"Indeed—if I am to be frank with you—his whole character does not seem to me particularly estimable or trustworthy. . . ."

Captain Whalley, always straight, seemed to grow

an inch taller and broader, as if the girth of his chest had suddenly expanded under his beard.

"My dear sir, you don't think I came here to discuss a man with whom I am—I am—h'm—closely associated."

A sort of solemn silence lasted for a moment. He was not used to asking favours, but the importance he attached to this affair had made him willing to try. . . . Mr. Van Wyk, favourably impressed, and suddenly mollified by a desire to laugh, interrupted—

"That's all right if you make it a personal matter; but you can do no less than sit down and smoke a cigar with me."

A slight pause, then Captain Whalley stepped forward heavily. As to the regularity of the service, for the future he made himself responsible for it; and his name was Whalley—perhaps to a sailor (he was speaking to a sailor, was he not?) not altogether unfamiliar. There was a lighthouse now, on an island. Maybe Mr. Van Wyk himself. . . .

"Oh, yes. Oh, indeed." Mr. Van Wyk caught on at once. He indicated a chair. How very interesting. For his own part he had seen some service in the last Acheen War,*but had never been so far East. Whalley Island? Of course. Now that was very interesting. What changes his guest must have seen since.

"I can look further back even—on a whole half-century."

Captain Whalley expanded a bit. The flavour of a good cigar (it was a weakness) had gone straight to his heart, also the civility of that young man. There was something in that accidental contact of which he had been starved in his years of struggle.

The front wall retreating made a square recess furnished like a room. A lamp with a milky glass shade,

suspended below the slope of the high roof at the end
of a slender brass chain, threw a bright round of light
upon a little table bearing an open book and an ivory
paper-knife.   And, in the translucent shadows beyond,
other tables could be seen, a number of easy-chairs of
various shapes, with a great profusion of skin rugs
strewn on the teakwood planking all over the verandah.
The flowering creepers scented the air.   Their foliage
clipped out between the uprights made as if several
frames of thick, unstirring leaves reflecting the lamplight in a green glow.   Through the opening at his elbow
Captain Whalley could see the gangway lantern of the
Sofala burning dim by the shore, the shadowy masses
of the town beyond the open lustrous darkness of the
river, and, as if hung along the straight edge of the
projecting eaves, a narrow black strip of the night sky
full of stars—resplendent.   The famous cigar in hand
he had a moment of complacency.

"A trifle.   Somebody must lead the way.   I just
showed that the thing could be done; but you men
brought up to the use of steam cannot conceive the vast
importance of my bit of venturesomeness to the Eastern
trade of the time.   Why, that new route reduced the
average time of a southern passage by eleven days for
more than half the year.   Eleven days!   It's on record.
But the remarkable thing—speaking to a sailor—I
should say was.   .   .   ."

He talked well, without egotism, professionally.   The
powerful voice, produced without effort, filled the
bungalow even into the empty rooms with a deep and
limpid resonance, seemed to make a stillness outside;
and Mr. Van Wyk was surprised by the serene quality
of its tone, like the perfection of manly gentleness.
Nursing one small foot, in a silk sock and a patent
leather shoe, on his knee, he was immensely enter-

tained. It was as if nobody could talk like this now, and the over-shadowed eyes, the flowing white beard, the big frame, the serenity, the whole temper of the man, were an amazing survival from the prehistoric times of the world coming up to him out of the sea.

Captain Whalley had been also the pioneer of the early trade in the Gulf of Pe-tchi-li. He even found occasion to mention that he had buried his "dear wife" there six-and-twenty years ago. Mr. Van Wyk, impassive, could not help speculating in his mind swiftly as to the sort of woman that would mate with such a man. Did they make an adventurous and well-matched pair? No. Very possibly she had been small, frail, no doubt very feminine—or most likely commonplace with domestic instincts, utterly insignificant. But Captain Whalley was no garrulous bore, and shaking his head as if to dissipate the momentary gloom that had settled on his handsome old face, he alluded conversationally to Mr. Van Wyk's solitude.

Mr. Van Wyk affirmed that sometimes he had more company than he wanted. He mentioned smilingly some of the peculiarities of his intercourse with "My Sultan." He made his visits in force. Those people damaged his grass-plot in front (it was not easy to obtain some approach to a lawn in the tropics), and the other day had broken down some rare bushes he had planted over there. And Captain Whalley remembered immediately that, in 'forty-seven, the then Sultan, "this man's grandfather," had been notorious as a great protector of the piratical fleets of praus from farther East. They had a safe refuge in the river at Batu Beru. He financed more especially a Balinini*chief called Haji Daman. Captain Whalley, nodding significantly his bushy white eyebrows, had very good reason to know something of that. The world had progressed since that time.

Mr. Van Wyk demurred with unexpected acrimony. Progressed in what? he wanted to know.

Why, in knowledge of truth, in decency, in justice, in order—in honesty, too, since men harmed each other mostly from ignorance. It was, Captain Whalley concluded quaintly, more pleasant to live in.

Mr. Van Wyk whimsically would not admit that Mr. Massy, for instance, was more pleasant naturally than the Balinini pirates.

The river had not gained much by the change. They were in their way every bit as honest. Massy was less ferocious than Haji Daman no doubt, but. . . .

"And what about you, my good sir?" Captain Whalley laughed a deep soft laugh. "*You* are an improvement, surely."

He continued in a vein of pleasantry. A good cigar was better than a knock on the head—the sort of welcome he would have found on this river forty or fifty years ago. Then leaning forward slightly, he became earnestly serious. It seems as if, outside their own sea-gipsy tribes, these rovers had hated all mankind with an incomprehensible, bloodthirsty hatred. Meantime their depredations had been stopped, and what was the consequence? The new generation was orderly, peaceable, settled in prosperous villages. He could speak from personal knowledge. And even the few survivors of that time—old men now—had changed so much, that it would have been unkind to remember against them that they had ever slit a throat in their lives. He had one especially in his mind's eye: a dignified, venerable headman of a certain large coast village about sixty miles sou'west of Tampasuk.* It did one's heart good to see him—to hear that man speak. He might have been a ferocious savage once. What men wanted was to be checked by superior intelligence, by superior knowledge, by superior force, too—yes, by force held in trust from God and sanctified by its use in accordance with His declared will. Captain Whalley believed a disposition for good existed in every man, even if the world were not a very happy place as a whole. In the wisdom of men he had not so much confidence.

The disposition had to be helped up pretty sharply sometimes, he admitted. They might be silly, wrong-headed, unhappy; but naturally evil—no. There was at bottom a complete harmlessness at least. . . .

"Is there?" Mr. Van Wyk snapped acrimoniously.

Captain Whalley laughed at the interjection, in the good humour of large, tolerating certitude. He could look back at half a century, he pointed out. The smoke oozed placidly through the white hairs hiding his kindly lips.

"At all events," he resumed after a pause, "I am glad that they've had no time to do you much harm as yet."

This allusion to his comparative youthfulness did not offend Mr. Van Wyk, who got up and wriggled his shoulders with an enigmatic half-smile. They walked out together amicably into the starry night towards the river-side. Their footsteps resounded unequally on the dark path. At the shore end of the gangway the lantern, hung low to the handrail, threw a vivid light on the white legs and the big black feet of Mr. Massy waiting about anxiously. From the waist upwards he remained shadowy, with a row of buttons gleaming up to the vague outline of his chin.

"You may thank Captain Whalley for this," Mr. Van Wyk said, curtly, to him before turning away.

The lamps on the verandah flung three long squares

of light between the uprights far over the grass. A bat
flitted before his face like a circling flake of velvety
blackness. Along the jasmine hedge the night air
seemed heavy with the fall of perfumed dew; flower-
beds bordered the path; the clipped bushes uprose in
dark, rounded clumps here and there before the house;
the dense foliage of creepers filtered the sheen of the
lamplight within in a soft glow all along the front;
and everything near and far stood still in a great immobility, in a great sweetness.

Mr. Van Wyk (a few years before he had had occasion
to imagine himself treated more badly than anybody
alive had ever been by a woman) felt for Captain
Whalley's optimistic views the disdain of a man who
had once been credulous himself. His disgust with the
world (the woman for a time had filled it for him completely) had taken the form of activity in retirement,
because, though capable of great depth of feeling, he was
energetic and essentially practical. But there was in
that uncommon old sailor, drifting on the outskirts of
his busy solitude, something that fascinated his scepticism. His very simplicity (amusing enough) was like
a delicate refinement of an upright character. The
striking dignity of manner could be nothing else, in a
man reduced to such a humble position, but the expression of something essentially noble in the character.
With all his trust in mankind he was no fool; the
serenity of his temper at the end of so many years, since
it could not obviously have been appeased by success,
wore an air of profound wisdom. Mr. Van Wyk was
amused at it sometimes. Even the very physical traits
of the old captain of the *Sofala*, his powerful frame, his
reposeful mien, his intelligent, handsome face, the big
limbs, the benign courtesy, the touch of rugged severity
in the shaggy eyebrows, made up a seductive person-

ality. Mr. Van Wyk disliked littleness of every kind, but there was nothing small about that man, and in the exemplary regularity of many trips an intimacy had grown up between them, a warm feeling at bottom under a kindly stateliness of forms agreeable to his fastidiousness.

They kept their respective opinions on all worldly matters. His other convictions Captain Whalley never intruded. The difference of their ages was like another bond between them. Once, when twitted with the uncharitableness of his youth, Mr. Van Wyk, running his eye over the vast proportions of his interlocutor, retorted in friendly banter—

"Oh. You'll come to my way of thinking yet. You'll have plenty of time. Don't call yourself old: you look good for a round hundred."

But he could not help his stinging incisiveness, and though moderating it by an almost affectionate smile, he added—

"And by then you will probably consent to die from sheer disgust."

Captain Whalley, smiling, too, shook his head. "God forbid!"

He thought that perhaps on the whole he deserved something better than to die in such sentiments. The time of course would have to come, and he trusted to his Maker to provide a manner of going out of which he need not be ashamed. For the rest he hoped he would live to a hundred if need be; other men had been known; it would be no miracle. He expected no miracles.

The pronounced, argumentative tone caused Mr. Van Wyk to raise his head and look at him steadily. Captain Whalley was gazing fixedly with a rapt expression, as though he had seen his Creator's favourable decree written in mysterious characters on the wall. He kept perfectly motionless for a few seconds, then got his vast bulk on to his feet so impetuously that Mr. Van Wyk was startled.

He struck first a heavy blow on his inflated chest: and, throwing out horizontally a big arm that remained steady, extended in the air like the limb of a tree on a windless day—

"Not a pain or an ache there. Can you see this shake in the least?"

His voice was low, in an awing, confident contrast with the headlong emphasis of his movements. He sat down abruptly.

"This isn't to boast of it, you know. I am nothing," he said in his effortless strong voice, that seemed to come out as naturally as a river flows. He picked up the stump of the cigar he had laid aside, and added peacefully, with a slight nod, "As it happens, my life is necessary; it isn't my own, it isn't—God knows."

He did not say much for the rest of the evening, but several times Mr. Van Wyk detected a faint smile of assurance flitting under the heavy moustache.

Later on Captain Whalley would now and then consent to dine "at the house." He could even be induced to drink a glass of wine. "Don't think I'm afraid of it, my good sir," he explained. "There was a very good reason why I should give it up."

On another occasion, leaning back at ease, he remarked, "You have treated me most—most humanely, my dear Mr. Van Wyk, from the very first."

"You'll admit there was some merit," Mr. Van Wyk hinted, slily. "An associate of that excellent Massy. . . . Well, well, my dear captain, I won't say a word against him."

"It would be no use your saying anything against

him," Captain Whalley affirmed a little moodily. "As I've told you before, my life—my work, is necessary, not for myself alone. I can't choose. . . ." He paused, turned the glass before him right round. . . . "I have an only child—a daughter."

The ample downward sweep of his arm over the table seemed to suggest a small girl at a vast distance. "I hope to see her once more before I die. Meantime it's enough to know that she has me sound and solid, thank God. You can't understand how one feels. Bone of my bone, flesh of my flesh; the very image of my poor wife. Well, she. . . ."

Again he paused, then pronounced stoically the words, "She has a hard struggle."

And his head fell on his breast, his eyebrows remained knitted, as by an effort of meditation. But generally his mind seemed steeped in the serenity of boundless trust in a higher power. Mr. Van Wyk wondered sometimes how much of it was due to the splendid vitality of the man, to the bodily vigour which seems to impart something of its force to the soul. But he had learned to like him very much.

XIII

THIS was the reason why Mr. Sterne's confidential communication, delivered hurriedly on the shore alongside the dark silent ship, had disturbed his equanimity. It was the most incomprehensible and unexpected thing that could happen; and the perturbation of his spirit was so great that, forgetting all about his letters, he ran rapidly up the bridge ladder.

The portable table was being put together for dinner to the left of the wheel by two pig-tailed "boys," who as usual snarled at each other over the job, while another, a doleful, burly, very yellow Chinaman, resembling Mr. Massy, waited apathetically with the cloth over his arm and a pile of thick dinner-plates against his chest. A common cabin lamp with its globe missing, brought up from below, had been hooked to the wooden framework of the awning; the side-screens had been lowered all round; Captain Whalley, filling the depths of the wicker-chair, seemed to sit benumbed in a canvas tent crudely lighted, and used for the storing of nautical objects; a shabby steering-wheel, a battered brass binnacle on a stout mahogany stand, two dingy life-buoys, an old cork fender lying in a corner, dilapidated deck-lockers with loops of tin rope instead of door-handles.

He shook off the appearance of numbness to return Mr. Van Wyk's unusually brisk greeting, but relapsed directly afterwards. To accept a pressing invitation to dinner "up at the house" cost him another very visible physical effort. Mr. Van Wyk, perplexed, folded his arms, and leaning back against the rail, with his little, black, shiny feet well out, examined him covertly.

"I've noticed of late that you are not quite yourself, old friend."

He put an affectionate gentleness into the last two words. The real intimacy of their intercourse had never been so vividly expressed before.

"Tut, tut, tut!"

The wicker-chair creaked heavily.

"Irritable," commented Mr. Van Wyk to himself; and aloud, "I'll expect to see you in half an hour, then," he said, negligently, moving off.

"In half an hour," Captain Whalley's rigid silvery head repeated behind him as if out of a trance.

Amidships, below, two voices, close against the engine-room, could be heard answering each other— one angry and slow, the other alert.

"I tell you the beast has locked himself in to get drunk."

"Can't help it now, Mr. Massy. After all, a man has a right to shut himself up in his cabin in his own time.

"Not to get drunk."

"I heard him swear that the worry with the boilers was enough to drive any man to drink," Sterne said, maliciously.

Massy hissed out something about bursting the door in. Mr. Van Wyk, to avoid them, crossed in the dark to the other side of the deserted deck. The planking of the little wharf rattled faintly under his hasty feet.

"Mr. Van Wyk! Mr. Van Wyk!"

He walked on: somebody was running on the path. "You've forgotten to get your mail."

Sterne, holding a bundle of papers in his hand, caught up with him.

"Oh, thanks."

But, as the other continued at his elbow, Mr. Van Wyk stopped short. The overhanging eaves, descending low upon the lighted front of the bungalow, threw their black straight-edged shadow into the great body of the night on that side. Everything was very still. A tinkle of cutlery and a slight jingle of glasses were heard. Mr. Van Wyk's servants were laying the table for two on the verandah.

"I am afraid you give me no credit whatever for my good intentions in the matter I've spoken to you about," said Sterne.

"I simply don't understand you."

"Captain Whalley is a very audacious man, but he will understand that his game is up. That's all that anybody need ever know of it from me. Believe me, I am very considerate in this, but duty is duty. I don't want to make a fuss. All I ask you, as his friend, is to tell him from me that the game's up. That will be sufficient."

Mr. Van Wyk felt a loathsome dismay at this queer privilege of friendship. He would not demean himself by asking for the slightest explanation; to drive the other away with contumely he did not think prudent— as yet, at any rate. So much assurance staggered him. Who could tell what there could be in it? he thought. His regard for Captain Whalley had the tenacity of a disinterested sentiment, and his practical instinct coming to his aid, he concealed his scorn.

"I gather, then, that this is something grave."

"Very grave," Sterne assented, solemnly, delighted at having produced an effect at last. He was ready to add some effusive protestations of regret at the "unavoidable necessity," but Mr. Van Wyk cut him short—very civilly, however.

Once on the verandah Mr. Van Wyk put his hands in his pockets, and, straddling his legs, stared down at a black panther skin lying on the floor before a rocking-chair. "It looks as if the fellow had not the pluck to play his own precious game openly," he thought.

This was true enough. In the face of Massy's last rebuff Sterne dared not declare his knowledge. His object was simply to get charge of the steamer and keep it for some time. Massy would never forgive him for forcing himself on; but if Captain Whalley left the ship of his own accord, the command would devolve upon him for the rest of the trip; so he hit upon the brilliant idea of scaring the old man away. A vague menace, a mere hint, would be enough in such a brazen case; and, with a strange admixture of compassion, he thought that Batu Beru was a very good place for throwing up the sponge. The skipper could go ashore quietly, and stay with that Dutchman of his. Weren't these two as thick as thieves together? And on reflection he seemed to see that there was a way to work the whole thing through that great friend of the old man's. This was another brilliant idea. He had an inborn preference for circuitous methods. In this particular case he desired to remain in the background as much as possible, to avoid exasperating Massy needlessly. No fuss! Let it all happen naturally.

Mr. Van Wyk all through the dinner was conscious of a sense of isolation that invades sometimes the closeness of human intercourse. Captain Whalley failed lamentably and obviously in his attempts to eat something. He seemed overcome by a strange absent-mindedness. His hand would hover irresolutely, as if left without guidance by a preoccupied mind. Mr. Van Wyk had heard him coming up from a long way off in the profound stillness of the river-side, and had noticed the

irresolute character of the footfalls. The toe of his boot
had struck the bottom stair as though he had come
along mooning with his head in the air right up to the
steps of the verandah. Had the captain of the *Sofala*
been another sort of man he would have suspected the
work of age there. But one glance at him was enough.
Time—after, indeed, marking him for its own—had
given him up to his usefulness, in which his simple faith
would see a proof of Divine mercy. "How could I
contrive to warn him?" Mr. Van Wyk wondered, as
if Captain Whalley had been miles and miles away, out
of sight and earshot of all evil. He was sickened by an
immense disgust of Sterne. To even mention his
threat to a man like Whalley would be positively in-
decent. There was something more vile and insulting
in its hint than in a definite charge of crime—the
debasing taint of blackmailing. "What could any one
bring against him?" he asked himself. This was a
limpid personality. "And for what object?" The
Power that man trusted had thought fit to leave him
nothing on earth that envy could lay hold of, except
a bare crust of bread.

"Won't you try some of this?" he asked, pushing a
dish slightly. Suddenly it occurred to Mr. Van Wyk
that Sterne might possibly be coveting the command
of the *Sofala*. His cynicism was quite startled by what
looked like a proof that no man may count himself safe
from his kind unless in the very abyss of misery. An
intrigue of that sort was hardly worth troubling about,
he judged; but still, with such a fool as Massy to deal
with, Whalley ought to and must be warned.

At this moment Captain Whalley, bolt upright, the
deep cavities of the eyes overhung by a bushy frown,
and one large brown hand resting on each side of his
empty plate, spoke across the table-cloth abruptly—

"Mr. Van Wyk, you've always treated me with the most humane consideration."

"My dear captain, you make too much of the simple fact that I am not a savage." Mr. Van Wyk, utterly revolted by the thought of Sterne's obscure attempt, raised his voice incisively, as if the mate had been hiding somewhere within earshot. "Any consideration I have been able to show was no more than the rightful due of a character I've learned to regard by this time with an esteem that nothing can shake."

A slight ring of glass made him lift his eyes from the slice of pine-apple he was cutting into small pieces on his plate. In changing his position Captain Whalley had contrived to upset an empty tumbler.

Without looking that way, leaning sideways on his elbow, his other hand shading his brow, he groped shadily for it, then desisted. Van Wyk stared blankly, as if something momentous had happened all at once. He did not know why he should feel so startled; but he forgot Sterne utterly for the moment.

"Why, what's the matter?"

And Captain Whalley, half-averted, in a deadened, agitated voice, muttered—

"Esteem!"

"And I may add something more," Mr. Van Wyk, very steady-eyed, pronounced slowly.

"Hold! Enough!" Captain Whalley did not change his attitude or raise his voice. "Say no more! I can make you no return. I am too poor even for that now. Your esteem is worth having. You are not a man that would stoop to deceive the poorest sort of devil on earth, or make a ship unseaworthy every time he takes her to sea."

Mr. Van Wyk, leaning forward, his face gone pink all over, with the starched table-napkin over his knees, was inclined to mistrust his senses, his power of comprehension, the sanity of his guest.

"Where? Why? In the name of God!—what's this? What ship? I don't understand who. . . ."

"Then, in the name of God, it is I! A ship's unseaworthy when her captain can't see. I am going blind."

Mr. Van Wyk made a slight movement, and sat very still afterwards for a few seconds; then, with the thought of Sterne's "The game's up," he ducked under the table to pick up the napkin which had slipped off his knees. This was the game that was up. And at the same time the muffled voice of Captain Whalley passed over him—

"I've deceived them all. Nobody knows."

He emerged flushed to the eyes. Captain Whalley, motionless under the full blaze of the lamp, shaded his face with his hand.

"And you had that courage?"

"Call it by what name you like. But you are a humane man—a—a—gentleman, Mr. Van Wyk. You may have asked me what I had done with my conscience."

He seemed to muse, profoundly silent, very still in his mournful pose.

"I began to tamper with it in my pride. You begin to see a lot of things when you are going blind. I could not be frank with an old chum even. I was not frank with Massy—no, not altogether. I knew he took me for a wealthy sailor fool, and I let him. I wanted to keep up my importance—because there was poor Ivy away there—my daughter. What did I want to trade on his misery for? I did trade on it—for her. And now, what mercy could I expect from him? He would trade on mine if he knew it. He would hunt the old fraud out, and stick to the money for a year. Ivy's money. And I haven't kept a penny for myself. How am I going to live for a year. A year! In a year there will be no sun in the sky for her father."

His deep voice came out, awfully veiled, as though he had been overwhelmed by the earth of a landslide and talking of the thoughts that haunt the dead in their graves. A cold shudder ran down Mr. Van Wyk's back.

"And how long is it since you have. . . ?" he began.

"It was a long time before I could bring myself to believe in this—this—visitation." Captain Whalley spoke with gloomy patience from under his hand.

He had not thought he had deserved it. He had begun by deceiving himself from day to day, from week to week. He had the Serang at hand there—an old servant. It came on gradually, and when he could no longer deceive himself. . . .

His voice died out almost.

"Rather than give her up I set myself to deceive you all."

"It's incredible," whispered Mr. Van Wyk. Captain Whalley's appalling murmur flowed on.

"Not even the sign of God's anger could make me forget her. How could I forsake my child, feeling my vigour all the time—the blood warm within me? Warm as yours. It seems to me that, like the blinded Samson, I would find the strength to shake down a temple upon my head. She's a struggling woman—my own child that we used to pray over together, my poor wife and I. Do you remember that day I as well as told you that I believed God would let me live to a hundred for her sake? What sin is there in loving your child? Do you see it? I was ready for her sake to live for ever. I half believed I would. I've been praying for death since. Ha! Presumptuous man—you wanted to live. . . ."

A tremendous, shuddering upheaval of that big frame, shaken by a gasping sob, set the glasses jingling all over the table, seemed to make the whole house tremble to the roof-tree. And Mr. Van Wyk, whose feeling of outraged love had been translated into a form of struggle with nature, understood very well that, for that man whose whole life had been conditioned by action, there could exist no other expression for all the emotions; that, to voluntarily cease venturing, doing, enduring, for his child's sake, would have been exactly like plucking his warm love for her out of his living heart. Something too monstrous, too impossible, even to conceive.

Captain Whalley had not changed his attitude, that seemed to express something of shame, sorrow, and defiance.

"I have even deceived you. If it had not been for that word 'esteem.' These are not the words for me. I would have lied to you. Haven't I lied to you? Weren't you going to trust your property on board this very trip?"

"I have a floating yearly policy," Mr. Van Wyk said almost unwittingly, and was amazed at the sudden cooping up of a commercial detail.

"The ship is unseaworthy, I tell you. The policy would be invalid if it were known. . . ."

"We shall share the guilt, then."

"Nothing could make mine less," said Captain Whalley.

He had not dared to consult a doctor; the man would have perhaps asked who he was, what he was doing; Massy might have heard something. He had lived on without any help, human or divine. The very prayers stuck in his throat. What was there to pray for? and death seemed as far as ever. Once he got into his cabin he dared not come out again; when he sat down he dared not get up; he dared not raise his eyes to anybody's face, he felt reluctant to look upon the sea or up to the sky. The world was fading before his great fear of giving himself away. The old ship was his last friend; he was not afraid of her; he knew every inch of her deck; but at her, too, he hardly dared to look, for fear of finding he could see less than the day before. A great incertitude enveloped him. The horizon was gone; the sky mingled darkly with the sea. Who was this figure standing over yonder? what was this thing lying down there? And a frightful doubt of the reality of what he could see made even the remnant of sight that remained to him an added torment, a pitfall always open for his miserable pretence. He was afraid to stumble inexcusably over something—to say a fatal Yes or No to a question. The hand of God was upon him, but it could not tear him away from his child. And, as if in a nightmare of humiliation, every featureless man seemed an enemy.

He let his hand fall heavily on the table. Mr. Van Wyk, arms down, chin on breast, with a gleam of white teeth pressing on the lower lip, meditated on Sterne's "The game's up."

"The Serang of course does not know."

"Nobody," said Captain Whalley, with assurance.

"Ah, yes. Nobody. Very well. Can you keep it up to the end of the trip? That is the last under the agreement with Massy."

Captain Whalley got up and stood erect, very stately, with the great white beard lying like a silver breastplate over the awful secret of his heart. Yes; that was the only hope there was for him of ever seeing her again, of securing the money, the last he could do for her, before he crept away somewhere—useless, a burden, a reproach to himself. His voice faltered.

"Think of it! Never see her any more: the only human being besides myself now on earth that can remember my wife. She's just like her mother. Lucky the poor woman is where there are no tears shed over those they loved on earth and that remain to pray not to be led into temptation—because, I suppose, the blessed know the secret of grace in God's dealings with His created children."

He swayed a little, said with austere dignity—

"I don't. I know only the child He has given me."

And he began to walk. Mr. Van Wyk, jumping up, saw the full meaning of the rigid head, the hesitating feet, the vaguely extended hand. His heart was beating fast; he moved a chair aside, and instinctively advanced as if to offer his arm. But Captain Whalley passed him by, making for the stairs quite straight.

"He could not see me at all out of his line," Van Wyk thought, with a sort of awe. Then going to the head of the stairs, he asked a little tremulously—

"What is it like—like a mist—like. . . ." Captain Whalley, half-way down, stopped, and turned round undismayed to answer:

"It is as if the light were ebbing out of the world. Have you ever watched the ebbing sea on an open stretch of sands withdrawing farther and farther away from you? It is like this—only there will be no flood to follow. Never. It is as if the sun were growing smaller, the stars going out one by one. There can't be many left that I can see by this. But I haven't had the courage to look of late. . . ." He must have been able to make out Mr. Van Wyk, because he checked him by an authoritative gesture and a stoical—

"I can get about alone yet."

It was as if he had taken his line, and would accept no help from men, after having been cast out, like a presumptuous Titan, from his heaven. Mr. Van Wyk, arrested, seemed to count the footsteps right out of earshot. He walked between the tables, tapping smartly with his heels, took up a paper-knife, dropped it after a vague glance along the blade; then happening upon the piano, struck a few chords, standing up before the keyboard with an attentive poise of the head like a piano-tuner; closing it, he pivoted on his heels brusquely, avoided the little terrier sleeping trustfully on crossed forepaws, came upon the stairs next, and, as though he had lost his balance on the top step, ran down headlong out of the house. His servants, beginning to clear the table, heard him mutter to himself (evil words no doubt) down there, and then after a pause go away with a strolling gait in the direction of the wharf.

The bulwarks of the *Sofala* lying alongside the bank made a low, black wall on the undulating contour of the shore. Two masts and a funnel uprose from behind it with a great rake, as if about to fall: a solid, square elevation in the middle bore the ghostly shapes of white boats, the curves of davits, lines of rail and stanchions, all confused and mingling darkly everywhere; but low down, amidships, a single lighted port stared out on the night, perfectly round, like a small, full moon, whose yellow beam caught a patch of wet mud, the edge of trodden grass, two turns of heavy cable wound round the foot of a thick wooden post in the ground.

Mr. Van Wyk, peering alongside, heard a muzzy[*] boastful voice apparently jeering at a person called Prendergast. It mouthed abuse thickly, choked; then pronounced very distinctly the word "Murphy," and chuckled. Glass tinkled tremulously. All these sounds came from the lighted port. Mr. Van Wyk hesitated, stooped; it was impossible to look through unless he went down into the mud.

"Sterne—of course. Look at him blink. Look at him! Sterne, Whalley, Massy. Massy, Whalley, Sterne. But Massy's the best. You can't come over him. He would just love to see you starve."

Mr. Van Wyk moved away, made out farther forward a shadowy head stuck out from under the awnings as if on the watch, and spoke quietly in Malay, "Is the mate asleep?"

"No. Here, at your service."

In a moment Sterne appeared, walking as noiselessly as a cat on the wharf.

"It's so jolly dark, and I had no idea you would be down to-night."

"What's this horrible raving?" asked Mr. Van Wyk, as if to explain the cause of a shudder that ran over him audibly.

"Jack's broken out on a drunk. That's our second. It's his way. He will be right enough by to-morrow afternoon, only Mr. Massy will keep on worrying up and down the deck. We had better get away."

He muttered suggestively of a talk "up at the house." He had long desired to effect an entrance there, but Mr. Van Wyk nonchalantly demurred: it would not, he feared, be quite prudent, perhaps; and the opaque black shadow under one of the two big trees left at the landing-place swallowed them up, impenetrably dense by the side of the wide river, that seemed to spin into threads of glitter the light of a few big stars dropped here and there upon its outspread and flowing stillness.

"The situation is grave beyond doubt," Mr. Van Wyk said. Ghost-like in their white clothes they could not distinguish each other's features, and their feet made no sound on the soft earth. A sort of purring was heard. Mr. Sterne felt gratified by such a beginning.

"I thought, Mr. Van Wyk, a gentleman of your sort would see at once how awkwardly I was situated."

"Yes, very. Obviously his health is bad. Perhaps he's breaking up. I see, and he himself is well aware —I assume I am speaking to a man of sense—he is well aware that his legs are giving out."

"His legs—ah!" Mr. Sterne was disconcerted, and then turned sulky. "You may call it his legs if you like; what I want to know is whether he intends to clear out quietly. That's a good one, too! His legs! Pooh!"

"Why, yes. Only look at the way he walks," Van Wyk took him up in a perfectly cool and undoubting tone. "The question, however, is whether your sense of duty does not carry you too far from your true interest. After all, I, too, could do something to serve you. You know who I am."

"Everybody along the Straits has heard of you, sir."

Mr. Van Wyk presumed that this meant something favourable. Sterne had a soft laugh at this pleasantry. He should think so! To the opening statement, that the partnership agreement was to expire at the end of this very trip, he gave an attentive assent. He was aware. One heard of nothing else on board all the blessed day long. As to Massy, it was no secret that he was in a jolly deep hole with these worn-out boilers. He would have to borrow somewhere a couple of hundred first of all to pay off the captain; and then he would have to raise money on mortgage upon the ship for the new boilers—that is, if he could find a lender at all. At best it meant loss of time, a break in the trade, short earnings for the year—and there was always the danger of having his connection filched away from him by the Germans. It was whispered about that he had already tried two firms. Neither would have anything to do with him. Ship too old, and the man too well known in the place. . . . Mr. Sterne's final rapid winking remained buried in the deep darkness sibilating with his whispers.

"Supposing, then, he got the loan," Mr. Van Wyk resumed in a deliberate undertone, "on your own showing he's more than likely to get a mortgagee's man thrust upon him as captain. For my part, I know that I would make that very stipulation myself if I had to find the money. And as a matter of fact I am thinking of doing so. It would be worth my while in many ways. Do you see how this would bear on the case under discussion?"

"Thank you, sir. I am sure you couldn't get anybody that would care more for your interests."

"Well, it suits my interest that Captain Whalley should finish his time. I shall probably take a passage with you down the Straits. If that can be done, I'll be on the spot when all these changes take place, and in a position to look after *your* interests."

"Mr. Van Wyk, I want nothing better. I am sure I am infinitely. . . ."

"I take it, then, that this may be done without any trouble."

"Well, sir, what risk there is can't be helped; but (speaking to you as my employer now) the thing is more safe than it looks. If anybody had told me of it I wouldn't have believed it, but I have been looking on myself. That old Serang has been trained up to the game. There's nothing the matter with his—his— limbs, sir. He's got used to do things on his own in a remarkable way. And let me tell you, sir, that Captain

Whalley, poor man, is by no means useless. Fact.
Let me explain to you, sir. He stiffens up that old
monkey of a Malay, who knows well enough what to do.
Why, he must have kept captain's watches in all sorts of
country ships off and on for the last five-and-twenty
years. These natives, sir, as long as they have a white
man close at the back, will go on doing the right thing
most surprisingly well—even if left quite to themselves.
Only the white man must be of the sort to put starch
into them, and the captain is just the one for that. Why,
sir, he has drilled him so well that now he needs hardly
speak at all. I have seen that little wrinkled ape made
to take the ship out of Pangu Bay on a blowy morning
and on all through the islands; take her out first-rate,
sir, dodging under the old man's elbow, and in such
quiet style that you could not have told for the life
of you which of the two was doing the work up there.
That's where our poor friend would be still of use to the
ship even if—if—he could no longer lift a foot, sir.
Providing the Serang does not know that there's anything wrong."

"He doesn't."

"Naturally not. Quite beyond his apprehension.
They aren't capable of finding out anything about us,
sir."

"You seem to be a shrewd man," said Mr. Van
Wyk in a choked mutter, as though he were feeling
sick.

"You'll find me a good enough servant, sir."

Mr. Sterne hoped now for a handshake at least, but
unexpectedly with a "What's this? Better not to be
seen together," Mr. Van Wyk's white shape wavered,
and instantly seemed to melt away in the black air
under the roof of boughs. The mate was startled. Yes.
There was that faint thumping clatter.

He stole out silently from under the shade. The lighted port-hole shone from afar. His head swam with the intoxication of sudden success. What a thing it was to have a gentleman to deal with! He crept aboard, and there was something weird in the shadowy stretch of empty decks, echoing with shouts and blows proceeding from a darker part amidships. Mr. Massy was raging before the door of the berth: the drunken voice within flowed on undisturbed in the violent racket of kicks.

"Shut up! Put your light out and turn in, you confounded swilling pig—you! D'you hear me, you beast?"

The kicking stopped, and in the pause the muzzy oracular voice announced from within—

"Ah! Massy, now—that's another thing. Massy's deep."

"Who's that aft there? You, Sterne? He'll drink himself into a fit of horrors." The chief engineer appeared vague and big at the corner of the engine-room skylight.

"He will be good enough for duty to-morrow. I would let him be, Mr. Massy."

Sterne slipped away into his berth, and at once had to sit down. His head swam with exultation. He got into his bunk as if in a dream. A feeling of profound peace, of pacific joy, came over him. On deck all was quiet.

Mr. Massy, with his ear against the door of Jack's cabin, listened critically to a deep, stertorous breathing within. This was a dead-drunk sleep. The bout was over: tranquillized on that score, he, too, went in, and with slow wriggles got out of his old tweed jacket. It was a garment with many pockets, which he used to put on at odd times of the day, being subject to sudden chilly fits, and when he felt warmed he would take it off and hang it about anywhere all over the ship. It would be seen swinging on belaying-pins, thrown over the heads of winches, suspended on people's very door-handles for that matter. Was he not the owner? But his favourite place was a hook on a wooden awning stanchion on the bridge, almost against the binnacle. He had even in the early days more than one tussle on that point with Captain Whalley, who desired the bridge to be kept tidy. He had been overawed then. Of late, though, he had been able to defy his partner with impunity. Captain Whalley never seemed to notice anything now. As to the Malays, in their awe of that scowling man not one of the crew would dream of laying a hand on the thing, no matter where or what it swung from.

With an unexpectedness which made Mr. Massy jump and drop the coat at his feet, there came from the next berth the crash and thud of a headlong, jingling, clattering fall. The faithful Jack must have dropped to sleep suddenly as he sat at his revels, and now had gone over chair and all, breaking, as it seemed by the sound, every single glass and bottle in the place. After the terrific smash all was still for a time in there, as though he had killed himself on the spot. Mr. Massy held his breath. At last a sleepy, uneasy groaning sigh was exhaled slowly on the other side of the bulkhead.

"I hope to goodness he's too drunk to wake up now," muttered Mr. Massy.

The sound of a softly knowing laugh nearly drove him to despair. He swore violently under his breath. The fool would keep him awake all night now for certain. He cursed his luck. He wanted to forget his maddening troubles in sleep sometimes. He could detect no movements. Without apparently making the slightest attempt to get up, Jack went on sniggering to himself where he lay; then began to speak, where he had left off as it were—

"Massy! I love the dirty rascal. He would like to see his poor old Jack starve—but just you look where he has climbed to. . . ." He hiccoughed in a superior, leisurely manner. . . . "Shipowning it with the best. A lottery ticket you want. Ha! ha! I will give you lottery tickets, my boy. Let the old ship sink and the old chum starve—that's right. He don't go wrong—Massy don't. Not he. He's a genius—that man is. That's the way to win your money. Ship and chum must go."

"The silly fool has taken it to heart," muttered Massy to himself. And, listening with a softened expression of face for any slight sign of returning drowsiness, he was discouraged profoundly by a burst of laughter full of joyful irony.

"Would like to see her at the bottom of the sea! Oh, you clever, clever devil! Wish her sunk, eh? I should think you would, my boy; the damned old thing and all your troubles with her. Rake in the insurance money—turn your back on your old chum—all's well—gentleman again."

A grim stillness had come over Massy's face. Only his big black eyes rolled uneasily. The raving fool. And yet it was all true. Yes. Lottery tickets, too. All true. What? Beginning again? He wished he wouldn't. . . .

But it was even so. The imaginative drunkard on the other side of the bulkhead shook off the deathlike stillness that after his last words had fallen on the dark ship moored to a silent shore.

"Don't you dare to say anything against George Massy, Esquire.   When he's tired of waiting he will do away with her. Look out! Down she goes—chum and all. He'll know how to. . . ."

The voice hesitated, weary, dreamy, lost, as if dying away in a vast open space.

". . . Find a trick that will work. He's up to it—never fear. . . ."

He must have been very drunk, for at last the heavy sleep gripped him with the suddenness of a magic spell, and the last word lengthened itself into an interminable, noisy, indrawn snore. And then even the snoring stopped, and all was still.

But it seemed as though Mr. Massy had suddenly come to doubt the efficacy of sleep as against a man's troubles; or perhaps he had found the relief he needed in the stillness of a calm contemplation that may contain the vivid thoughts of wealth, of a stroke of luck, of long idleness, and may bring before you the imagined form of every desire; for, turning about and throwing his arms over the edge of his bunk, he stood there with his feet on his favourite old coat, looking out through the round port into the night over the river. Sometimes a breath of wind would enter and touch his face, a cool breath charged with the damp, fresh feel from a vast body of water. A glimmer here and there was all he could see of it; and once he might after all suppose he had dozed off, since there appeared before his vision, unexpectedly and connected with no dream, a row of flaming and gigantic figures—three nought seven one two—making up a number such as you may see on a lottery ticket. And then all at once the port was no longer black: it was pearly gray, framing a shore crowded with houses, thatched roof beyond thatched roof, walls of mats and bamboo, gables of carved teak timber. Rows of dwellings raised on a forest of piles lined the steely bank of the river, brimful and still, with the tide on the turn. This was Batu Beru—and the day had come.

Mr. Massy shook himself, put on the tweed coat, and, shivering nervously as if from some great shock, made a note of the number. A fortunate, rare hint that. Yes; but to pursue fortune one wanted money —ready cash.

Then he went out and prepared to descend into the engine-room. Several small jobs had to be seen to, and Jack was lying dead drunk on the floor of his cabin, with the door locked at that. His gorge rose at the thought of work. Ay! But if you wanted to do nothing you had to get first a good bit of money. A ship won't save you. True, all true. He was tired of waiting for some chance that would rid him at last of that ship that had turned out a curse on his life.

XIV

THE deep, interminable hoot of the steam-whistle had, in its grave, vibrating note, something intolerable, which sent a slight shudder down Mr. Van Wyk's back. It was the early afternoon; the *Sofala* was leaving Batu Beru for Pangu, the next place of call. She swung in the stream, scantily attended by a few canoes, and, gliding on the broad river, became lost to view from the Van Wyk bungalow.

Its owner had not gone this time to see her off. Generally he came down to the wharf, exchanged a few words with the bridge while she cast off, and waved his hand to Captain Whalley at the last moment. This day he did not even go as far as the balustrade of the verandah. "He couldn't see me if I did," he said to himself. "I wonder whether he can make out the house at all." And this thought somehow made him feel more alone than he had ever felt for all these years. What was it? six or seven? Seven. A long time.

He sat on the verandah with a closed book on his knee, and, as it were, looked out upon his solitude, as if the fact of Captain Whalley's blindness had opened his eyes to his own. There were many sorts of heart-aches and troubles, and there was no place where they could not find a man out. And he felt ashamed, as though he had for six years behaved like a peevish boy.

His thought followed the *Sofala* on her way. On the spur of the moment he had acted impulsively, turning to the thing most pressing. And what else could

he have done? Later on he should see. It seemed
necessary that he should come out into the world, for a
time at least. He had money—something could be
arranged; he would grudge no time, no trouble, no loss
of his solitude. It weighed on him now—and Captain
Whalley appeared to him as he had sat shading his eyes,
as if, being deceived in the trust of his faith, he were
beyond all the good and evil that can be wrought by the
hands of men.

Mr. Van Wyk's thoughts followed the *Sofala* down
the river, winding about through the belt of the coast
forest, between the buttressed shafts of the big trees,
through the mangrove strip, and over the bar. The
ship crossed it easily in broad daylight, piloted, as it
happened, by Mr. Sterne, who took the watch from four
to six, and then went below to hug himself with delight
at the prospect of being virtually employed by a rich
man—like Mr. Van Wyk. He could not see how any
hitch could occur now. He did not seem able to get
over the feeling of being "fixed up at last." From six
to eight, in the course of duty, the Serang looked alone
after the ship. She had a clear road before her now till
about three in the morning, when she would close with the
Pangu group. At eight Mr. Sterne came out cheerily to
take charge again till midnight. At ten he was still
chirruping and humming to himself on the bridge, and
about that time Mr. Van Wyk's thought abandoned
the *Sofala*. Mr. Van Wyk had fallen asleep at last.

Massy, blocking the engine-room companion, jerked
himself into his tweed jacket surlily, while the second
waited with a scowl.

"Oh. You came out! You sot! Well, what have
you got to say for yourself?"

He had been in charge of the engines till then. A
sombre fury darkened his mind: a hot anger against the

ship, against the facts of life, against the men for their
cheating, against himself, too—because of an inward
tremor in his heart.

An incomprehensible growl answered him.

"What? Can't you open your mouth now? You
yelp out your infernal rot loud enough when you are
drunk. What do you mean by abusing people in that
way?—you old useless boozer, you!"

"Can't help it. Don't remember anything about
it. You shouldn't listen."

"You dare to tell me! What do you mean by going
on a drunk like this?"

"Don't ask me. Sick of the dam' boilers—you
would be. Sick of Life."

"I wish you were dead, then. You've made me
sick of you. Don't you remember the uproar you
made last night? You miserable old soaker!"

"No; I don't. Don't want to. Drink is drink."

"I wonder what prevents me from kicking you out.
What do you want here?"

"Relieve you. You've been long enough down there,
George."

"Don't you George me—you tippling old rascal,
you! If I were to die to-morrow you would starve.
Remember that. Say Mr. Massy."

"Mr. Massy," repeated the other, stolidly.

Dishevelled, with dull blood-shot eyes, a snuffy,
grimy shirt, greasy trousers, naked feet thrust into
ragged slippers, he bolted in head down directly Massy
had made way for him.

The chief engineer looked around. The deck was
empty as far as the taffrail. All the native passengers
had left in Batu Beru this time, and no others had
joined. The dial of the patent log tinkled periodically
in the dark at the end of the ship. It was a dead calm,

and, under the clouded sky, through the still air that seemed to cling warm, with a seaweed smell, to her slim hull, on a sea of sombre gray and unwrinkled, the ship moved on an even keel, as if floating detached in empty space. But Mr. Massy slapped his forehead, tottered a little, and caught hold of a belaying-pin at the foot of the mast.

"I shall go mad," he muttered, walking across the deck unsteadily. A shovel. was scraping loose coal down below—a fire-door clanged. Sterne on the bridge began whistling a new tune.

Captain Whalley, sitting on the couch, awake and fully dressed, heard the door of his cabin open. He did not move in the least, waiting to recognize the voice, with an appalling strain of prudence.

A bulkhead lamp blazed on the white paint, the crimson plush, the brown varnish of mahogany tops. The white wood packing-case under the bed-place had remained unopened for three years now, as though Captain Whalley had felt that, after the *Fair Maid* was gone, there could be no abiding-place on earth for his affections. His hands rested on his knees; his handsome head with big eyebrows presented a rigid profile to the doorway. The expected voice spoke out at last.

"Once more, then. What am I to call you?"

Ha! Massy. Again. The weariness of it crushed his heart—and the pain of shame was almost more than he could bear without crying out.

"Well. Is it to be 'partner' still?"

"You don't know what you ask."

"I know what I want. . . ."

Massy stepped in and closed the door.

". . . And I am going to have a try for it with you once more."

His whine was half persuasive, half menacing.

"For it's no manner of use to tell me that you are poor. You don't spend anything on· yourself, that's true enough; but there's another name for that. You think you are going to have what you want out of me for three years, and then cast me off without hearing what I think of you. You think I would have submitted to your airs if I had known you had only a beggarly five hundred pounds in the world. You ought to have told me."

"Perhaps," said Captain Whalley, bowing his head. "And yet it has saved you. . . ." Massy laughed scornfully. . . . "I have told you often enough since."

"And I don't believe you now. When I think how I let you lord it over my ship! Do you remember how you used to bullyrag me about my coat and *your* bridge? It was in his way. *His* bridge! 'And I won't be a party to this—and I couldn't think of doing that.' Honest man! And now it all comes out. 'I am poor, and I can't. I have only this five hundred in the world.'"

He contemplated the immobility of Captain Whalley, that seemed to present an inconquerable obstacle in his path. His face took a mournful cast.

"You are a hard man."

"Enough," said Captain Whalley, turning upon him. "You shall get nothing from me, because I have nothing of mine to give away now."

"Tell that to the marines!"

Mr. Massy, going out, looked back once; then the door closed, and Captain Whalley, alone, sat as still as before. He had nothing of his own—even his own past of honour, of truth, of just pride, was gone. All his spotless life had fallen into the abyss. He had said his last good-bye to it. But what belonged to *her*, that he meant to save. Only a little money. He would take it to her in his own hands—this last gift of a man that had lasted too long. And an immense and fierce impulse, the very passion of paternity, flamed up with all the unquenched vigour of his worthless life in a desire to see her face.

Just across the deck Massy had gone straight to his cabin, struck a light, and hunted up the note of the dreamed number whose figures had flamed up also with the fierceness of another passion. He must contrive somehow not to miss a drawing. That number meant something. But what expedient could he contrive to keep himself going?

"Wretched miser!" he mumbled.

If Mr. Sterne could at no time have told him anything new about his partner, he could have told Mr. Sterne that another use could be made of a man's affliction than just to kick him out, and thus defer the term of a difficult payment for a year. To keep the secret of the affliction and induce him to stay was a better move. If without means, he would be anxious to remain; and that settled the question of refunding him his share. He did not know exactly how much Captain Whalley was disabled; but if it so happened that he put the ship ashore somewhere for good and all, it was not the owner's fault—was it? He was not obliged to know that there was anything wrong. But probably nobody would raise such a point, and the ship was fully insured. He had had enough self-restraint to pay up the premiums. But this was not all. He could not believe Captain Whalley to be so confoundedly destitute as not to have some more money put away somewhere. If he, Massy, could get hold of it, that would pay for the boilers, and everything went on as before. And if she got lost in the end, so much the better. He hated her: he loathed the troubles that took his mind off the chances of fortune. He wished her at the bottom of the sea, and the insurance money in his pocket. And as, baffled, he left Captain Whalley's cabin, he enveloped in the same hatred the ship with the worn-out boilers and the man with the dimmed eyes.

And our conduct after all is so much a matter of outside suggestion, that had it not been for his Jack's drunken gabble he would have there and then had it out with this miserable man, who would neither help, nor stay, nor yet lose the ship. The old fraud! He longed to kick him out. But he restrained himself. Time enough for that—when he liked. There was a fearful new thought put into his head. Wasn't he up to it after all? How that beast Jack had raved! "Find a safe trick to get rid of her." Well, Jack was not so far wrong. A very clever trick had occurred to him. Ay! But what of the risk?

A feeling of pride—the pride of superiority to common prejudices—crept into his breast, made his heart beat fast, his mouth turn dry. Not everybody would dare; but he was Massy, and he was up to it!

Six bells were struck on deck. Eleven! He drank a glass of water, and sat down for ten minutes or so to calm himself. Then he got out of his chest a small bull's-eye lantern of his own and lit it.

Almost opposite his berth, across the narrow passage under the bridge, there was, in the iron deck-structure covering the stokehold fiddle and the boiler-space, a storeroom with iron sides, iron roof, iron-plated floor, too, on account of the heat below. All sorts of rubbish was shot there: it had a mound of scrap-iron in a corner; rows of empty oil-cans; sacks of cotton-waste, with a heap of charcoal, a deck-forge, fragments of an old hen-coop, winch-covers all in rags, remnants of lamps, and

a brown felt hat, discarded by a man dead now (of a
fever on the Brazil coast), who had been once mate of
the *Sofala,* had remained for years jammed forcibly
behind a length of burst copper pipe, flung at some
time or other out of the engine-room. A complete
and impervious blackness pervaded that Capharnaum*
of forgotten things. A small shaft of light from Mr.
Massy's bull's-eye fell slanting right through it.

His coat was unbuttoned; he shot the bolt of the door
(there was no other opening), and, squatting before the
scrap-heap, began to pack his pockets with pieces of
iron. He packed them carefully, as if the rusty nuts,
the broken bolts, the links of cargo chain, had been so
much gold he had that one chance to carry away. He
packed his side-pockets till they bulged, the breast-
pocket, the pockets inside. He turned over the pieces.
Some he rejected. A small mist of powdered rust began
to rise about his busy hands. Mr. Massy knew something of the scientific basis of his clever trick. If you
want to deflect the magnetic needle of a ship's compass,
soft iron is the best; likewise many small pieces in the
pockets of a jacket would have more effect than a few
large ones, because in that way you obtain a greater
amount of surface for weight in your iron, and it's
surface that tells.

He slipped out swiftly—two strides sufficed—and
in his cabin he perceived that his hands were all red
—red with rust. It disconcerted him, as though he
had found them covered with blood: he looked himself over hastily. Why, his trousers, too! He had been
rubbing his rusty palms on his legs.

He tore off the waistband button in his haste, brushed
his coat, washed his hands. Then the air of guilt left
him, and he sat down to wait.

He sat bolt upright and weighted with iron in his

chair. He had a hard, lumpy bulk against each hip, felt the scrappy iron in his pockets touch his ribs at every breath, the downward drag of all these pounds hanging upon his shoulders. He looked very dull, too, sitting idle there, and his yellow face, with motionless black eyes, had something passive and sad in its quietness.

When he heard eight bells struck above his head, he rose and made ready to go out. His movements seemed aimless, his lower lip had dropped a little, his eyes roamed about the cabin, and the tremendous tension of his will had robbed them of every vestige of intelligence.

With the last stroke of the bell the Serang appeared noiselessly on the bridge to relieve the mate. Sterne overflowed with good nature, since he had nothing more to desire.

"Got your eyes well open yet, Serang? It's middling dark; I'll wait till you get your sight properly."

The old Malay murmured, looked up with his worn eyes, sidled away into the light of the binnacle, and, clasping his hands behind his back, fixed his eyes on the compass-card.

"You'll have to keep a good lookout ahead for land, about half-past three. It's fairly clear, though. You have looked in on the captain as you came along—eh? He knows the time? Well, then, I am off."

At the foot of the ladder he stood aside for the captain. He watched him go up with an even, certain tread, and remained thoughtful for a moment. "It's funny," he said to himself, "but you can never tell whether that man has seen you or not. He might have heard me breathe this time."

He was a wonderful man when all was said and done. They said he had had a name in his day. Mr. Sterne could well believe it; and he concluded serenely that

Captain Whalley must be able to see people more or less—as himself just now, for instance—but not being certain of anybody, had to keep up that unnoticing silence of manner for fear of giving himself away. Mr. Sterne was a shrewd guesser.

This necessity of every moment brought home to Captain Whalley's heart the humiliation of his falsehood. He had drifted into it from paternal love, from incredulity, from boundless trust in divine justice meted out to men's feelings on this earth. He would give his poor Ivy the benefit of another month's work; perhaps the affliction was only temporary. Surely God would not rob his child of his power to help, and cast him naked into a night without end. He had caught at every hope; and when the evidence of his misfortune was stronger than hope, he tried not to believe the manifest thing.

In vain. In the steadily darkening universe a sinister clearness fell upon his ideas. In the illuminating moments of suffering he saw life, men, all things, the whole earth with all her burden of created nature, as he had never seen them before.

Sometimes he was seized with a sudden vertigo and an overwhelming terror; and then the image of his daughter appeared. Her, too, he had never seen so clearly before. Was it possible that he should ever be unable ·to do anything whatever for her? Nothing. And not see her any more? Never.

Why? The punishment was too great for a little presumption, for a little pride. And at last he came to cling to his deception with a fierce determination to carry it out to the end, to save her money intact, and behold her once more with his own eyes. Afterwards—what? The idea of suicide was revolting to the vigour of his manhood. He had prayed for death till the prayers had stuck in his throat. All the days of his life he had prayed, for daily bread, and not to be led into temptation, in a childlike humility of spirit. Did words mean anything? Whence did the gift of speech come? The violent beating of his heart reverberated in his head—seemed to shake his brain to pieces.

He sat down heavily in the deck-chair to keep the pretence of his watch. The night was dark. All the nights were dark now.

"Serang," he said, half aloud.

"Ada, Tuan. I am here."

"There are clouds on the sky?"

"There are, Tuan."

"Let her be steered straight. North."

"She is going north, Tuan."

The Serang stepped back. Captain Whalley recognized Massy's footfalls on the bridge.

The engineer walked over to port and returned, passing behind the chair several times. Captain Whalley detected an unusual character as of prudent care in this prowling. The near presence of that man brought with it always a recrudescence of moral suffering for Captain Whalley. It was not remorse. After all, he had done nothing but good to the poor devil. There was also a sense of danger—the necessity of a greater care.

Massy stopped and said—

"So you still say you must go?"

"I must indeed."

"And you couldn't at least leave the money for a term of years?"

"Impossible."

"Can't trust it with me without your care, eh?"

Captain Whalley remained silent. Massy sighed deeply over the back of the chair.

"It would just do to save me," he said in a tremulous voice.

"I've saved you once."

The chief engineer took off his coat with careful movements, and proceeded to feel for the brass hook screwed into the wooden stanchion. For this purpose he placed himself right in front of the binnacle, thus hiding completely the compass-card from the quartermaster at the wheel. "Tuan!" the lascar at last murmured softly, meaning to let the white man know that he could not see to steer.

Mr. Massy had accomplished his purpose. The coat was hanging from the nail, within six inches of the binnacle. And directly he had stepped aside the quartermaster, a middle-aged, pock-marked, Sumatra Malay, almost as dark as a negro, perceived with amazement that in that short time, in this smooth water, with no wind at all, the ship had gone swinging far out of her course. He had never known her get away like this before. With a slight grunt of astonishment he turned the wheel hastily to bring her head back north, which was the course. The grinding of the steering-chains, the chiding murmurs of the Serang, who had come over to the wheel, made a slight stir, which attracted Captain Whalley's anxious attention. He said, "Take better care." Then everything settled to the usual quiet on the bridge. Mr. Massy had disappeared.

But the iron in the pockets of the coat had done its work; and the *Sofala*, heading north by the compass made untrue by this simple device, was no longer making a safe course for Pangu Bay.

The hiss of water parted by her stem, the throb of her engines, all the sounds of her faithful and laborious life, went on uninterrupted in the great calm of the sea joining on all sides the motionless layer of cloud over the sky. A gentle stillness as vast as the world seemed to wait upon her path, enveloping her lovingly in a supreme caress. Mr. Massy thought there could be no better night for an arranged shipwreck.

Run up high and dry on one of the reefs east of Pangu—wait for daylight—hole in the bottom—out boats—Pangu Bay same evening. That's about it. As soon as she touched he would hasten on the bridge, get hold of the coat (nobody would notice in the dark), and shake it upside down over the side, or even fling it into the sea. A detail. Who could guess? Coat been seen hanging there from that hook hundreds of times. Nevertheless, when he sat down on the lower step of the bridge-ladder his knees knocked together a little. The waiting part was the worst of it. At times he would begin to pant quickly, as though he had been running, and then breathe largely, swelling with the intimate sense of a mastered fate. Now and then he would hear the shuffle of the Serang's bare feet up there: quiet, low voices would exchange a few words, and lapse almost at once into silence. . . .

"Tell me directly you see any land, Serang."

"Yes, Tuan. Not yet."

"No, not yet," Captain Whalley would agree.

The ship had been the best friend of his decline. He had sent all the money he had made by and in the *Sofala* to his daughter. His thought lingered on the name. How often he and his wife had talked over the cot of the child in the big stern-cabin of the *Condor;* she would grow up, she would marry, she would love them, they would live near her and look at her happiness—it would go on without end. Well, his wife was dead, to the child he had given all he had to give; he wished he could come near her, see her, see her face once, live in the sound of her voice, that could make the darkness of the living grave ready for him supportable. He had been starved of love too long. He imagined her tenderness.

The Serang had been peering forward, and now and then glancing at the chair. He fidgeted restlessly, and suddenly burst out close to Captain Whalley—

"Tuan, do you see anything of the land?"

The alarmed voice brought Captain Whalley to his feet at once. He! See! And at the question, the curse of his blindness seemed to fall on him with a hundredfold force.

"What's the time?" he cried.

"Half-past three, Tuan."

"We are close. You *must* see. Look, I say. Look."

Mr. Massy, awakened by the sudden sound of talking from a short doze on the lowest step, wondered why he was there. Ah! A faintness came over him. It is one thing to sow the seed of an accident and another to see the monstrous fruit hanging over your head ready to fall in the sound of agitated voice. "There's no danger," he muttered thickly to himself.

The horror of incertitude had seized upon Captain Whalley, the miserable mistrust of men, of things—of the very earth. He had steered that very course thirty-six times by the same compass—if anything was certain in this world it was its absolute, unerring correctness. Then what had happened? Did the Serang lie? Why lie? Why? Was he going blind, too?

"Is there a mist? Look low on the water. Low down, I say."

"Tuan, there's no mist. See for yourself."

Captain Whalley steadied the trembling of his limbs by an effort. Should he stop the engines at once and give himself away? A gust of irresolution swayed all sorts of bizarre notions in his mind. The unusual had

come, and he was not fit to deal with it. In this passage
of inexpressible anguish he saw her face—the face of a
young girl—with an amazing strength of illusion. No,
he must not give himself away after having gone so far
for her sake. "You steered the course? You made it?
Speak the truth."

"Ya, Tuan. On the course now. Look."

Captain Whalley strode to the binnacle, which to him
made such a dim spot of light in an infinity of shapeless
shadow. By bending his face right down to the glass
he had been able before. . . .

Having to stoop so low, he put out, instinctively,
his arm to where he knew there was a stanchion to
steady himself against. His hand closed on something
that was not wood but cloth. The slight pull adding
to the weight, the loop broke, and Mr. Massy's coat
falling, struck the deck heavily with a dull thump,
accompanied by a lot of clicks.

"What's this?"

Captain Whalley fell on his knees, with groping
hands extended in a frank gesture of blindness. They
trembled, these hands feeling for the truth. He saw
it. Iron near the compass. Wrong course. Wreck
her! His ship. Oh, no. Not that.

"Jump and stop her!" he roared out in a voice not
his own.

He ran himself—hands forward, a blind man, and
while the clanging of the gong echoed still all over the
ship, she seemed to butt full tilt into the side of a
mountain.

It was low water along the north side of the strait.
Mr. Massy had not reckoned on that. Instead of
running aground for half her length, the *Sofala* butted
the sheer ridge of a stone reef which would have been
awash, at high water. This made the shock absolutely

terrific. Everybody in the ship that was standing was thrown down headlong: the shaken rigging made a great rattling to the very trucks. All the lights went out; several chain-guys, snapping, clattered against the funnel; there were crashes, pings of parted wire-rope, splintering sounds, loud cracks; the masthead lamp flew over the bows, and all the doors about the deck began to bang heavily. Then, after having hit, she rebounded, hit the second time the very same spot like a battering-ram. This completed the havoc: the funnel, with all the guys gone, fell over with a hollow sound of thunder, smashing the wheel to bits, crushing the frame of the awnings, breaking the lockers, filling the bridge with a mass of broken wood. Captain Whalley picked himself up and stood knee-deep in wreckage, torn, bleeding, knowing the nature of the danger he had escaped mostly by the sound, and holding Mr. Massy's coat in his arms.

By this time Sterne (he had been flung out of his bunk) had set the engines astern. They worked for a few turns, then a voice bawled out, "Get out of the damned engine-room, Jack!"—and they stopped; but the ship had gone clear of the reef and lay still, with a heavy cloud of steam issuing from the broken deck-pipes, and vanishing in wispy shapes into the night. Notwithstanding the suddenness of the disaster there was no shouting, as if the very violence of the shock had half-stunned the shadowy lot of people swaying here and there about her decks. The voice of the Serang pronounced distinctly above the confused murmurs—

"No bottom." He had heaved the lead.

Mr. Sterne cried out next in a strained pitch—

"Where the devil has she got to? Where are we?"

Captain Whalley replied in a calm bass—

"Amongst the reefs to the eastward."

"You know it, sir? Then she will never get out again."

"She will be gone in five minutes. Boats, Sterne. Even one will save you all in this calm."

The Chinaman stokers went in a disorderly rush for the port boats. Nobody tried to check them. The Malays, after a moment of confusion, became quiet, and Mr. Sterne showed a good countenance. Captain Whalley had not moved. His thoughts were darker than this night in which he had lost his first ship.

"He made me lose a ship."

Another tall figure standing before him amongst the litter of the smash on the bridge whispered insanely—

"Say nothing of it."

Massy stumbled closer. Captain Whalley heard the chattering of his teeth.

"I have the coat."

"Throw it down and come along," urged the chattering voice. "B-b-b-b-boat!"

"You will get five years for this."

Mr. Massy had lost his voice. His speech was a mere dry rustling in his throat.

"Have mercy!"

"Had you any when you made me lose my ship? Mr. Massy, you shall get five years for this!"

"I wanted money! Money! My own money! I will give you some money. Take half of it. You love money yourself."

"There's a justice. . . ."

Massy made an awful effort, and in a strange, half-choked utterance—

"You blind devil! It's you that drove me to it."

Captain Whalley, hugging the coat to his breast, made no sound. The light had ebbed for ever from the world—let everything go. But this man should not escape scot-free.

Sterne's voice commanded—

"Lower away!"

The blocks rattled.

"Now then," he cried, "over with you. This way. You, Jack, here. Mr. Massy! Mr. Massy! Captain! Quick, sir! Let's get——"

"I shall go to prison for trying to cheat the insurance, but you'll get exposed; you, honest man, who has been cheating me. You are poor. Aren't you? You've nothing but the five hundred pounds. Well, you have nothing at all now. The ship's lost, and the insurance won't be paid."

Captain Whalley did not move. True! Ivy's money. Gone in this wreck. Again he had a flash of insight. He was indeed at the end of his tether.

Urgent voices cried out together alongside. Massy did not seem able to tear himself away from the bridge. He chattered and hissed despairingly—

"Give it up to me! Give it up!"

"No," said Captain Whalley; "I could not give it up. You had better go. Don't wait, man, if you want to live. She's settling down by the head fast. No; I shall keep it, but I shall stay on board."

Massy did not seem to understand; but the love of life, awakened suddenly, drove him away from the bridge.

Captain Whalley laid the coat down, and stumbled amongst the heaps of wreckage to the side.

"Is Mr. Massy with you?" he called out into the night.

Sterne from the boat shouted—

"Yes; we've got him. Come along, sir. It's madness to stay longer."

Captain Whalley felt along the rail carefully, and,

without a word, cast off the painter. They were expecting him still down there. They were waiting, till a voice suddenly exclaimed—

"We are adrift! Shove off!"

"Captain Whalley! Leap! . . . pull up a little . . . leap! You can swim."

In that old heart, in that vigorous body, there was, that nothing should be wanting, a horror of death that apparently could not be overcome by the horror of blindness. But after all, for Ivy he had carried his point, walking in his darkness to the very verge of a crime. God had not listened to his prayers. The light had finished ebbing out of the world; not a glimmer. It was a dark waste; but it was unseemly that a Whalley who had gone so far to carry a point should continue to live. He must pay the price.

"Leap as far as you can, sir; we will pick you up."

They did not hear him answer. But their shouting seemed to remind him of something. He groped his way back, and sought for Mr. Massy's coat. He could swim indeed; people sucked down by the whirlpool of a sinking ship do come up sometimes to the surface, and it was unseemly that a Whalley, who had made up his mind to die, should be beguiled by chance into a struggle. He would put all these pieces of iron into his own pockets.

They, looking from the boat, saw the *Sofala*, a black mass upon a black sea, lying still at an appalling cant. No sound came from her. Then, with a great bizarre shuffling noise, as if the boilers had broken through the bulkheads, and with a faint muffled detonation, where the ship had been there appeared for a moment something standing upright and narrow, like a rock out of the sea. Then that, too, disappeared.

When the *Sofala* failed to come back to Batu Beru

at the proper time, Mr. Van Wyk understood at once
that he would never see her any more. But he did not
know what had happened till some weeks afterwards,
when, in a native craft lent him by his Sultan, he had
made his way to the *Sofala's* port of registry, where already her existence and the official inquiry into her loss
were beginning to be forgotten.

It had not been a very remarkable or interesting case,
except for the fact that the captain had gone down with
his sinking ship. It was the only life lost; and Mr.
Van Wyk would not have been able to learn any details
had it not been for Sterne, whom he met one day on the
quay near the bridge over the creek, almost on the very
spot where Captain Whalley, to preserve his daughter's
five hundred pounds intact, had turned to get a sampan
which would take him on board the *Sofala*.

From afar Mr. Van Wyk saw Sterne blink straight
at him and raise his hand to his hat. They drew into
the shade of a building (it was a bank), and the mate
related how the boats with the crew got into Pangu Bay
about six hours after the accident, and how they had
lived for a fortnight in a state of destitution before
they found an opportunity to get away from that
beastly place. The inquiry had exonerated everybody
from all blame. The loss of the ship was put down to
an unusual set of the current. Indeed, it could not have
been anything else: there was no other way to account
for the ship being set seven miles to the eastward of her
position during the middle watch.

"A piece of bad luck for me, sir."

Sterne passed his tongue on his lips and glanced aside.
"I lost the advantage of being employed by you, sir.
I can never be sorry enough. But here it is: one man's
poison, another man's meat. This could not have been
handier for Mr. Massy if he had arranged that ship-

wreck himself. The most timely total loss I've ever heard of."

"What became of that Massy?" asked Mr. Van Wyk.

"He, sir? Ha! ha! He would keep on telling me that he meant to buy another ship; but as soon as he had the money in his pocket he cleared out for Manila by mail-boat early in the morning. I gave him chase right aboard, and he told me then he was going to make his fortune dead sure in Manila. I could go to the devil for all he cared. And yet he as good as promised to give me the command if I didn't talk too much."

"You never said anything. . . ." Mr. Van Wyk began.

"Not I, sir. Why should I? I mean to get on, but the dead aren't in my way," said Sterne. His eyelids were beating rapidly, then drooped for an instant. "Besides, sir, it would have been an awkward business. You made me hold my tongue just a bit too long."

"Do you know how it was that Captain Whalley remained on board? Did he really refuse to leave? Come now! Or was it perhaps an accidental. . . .?"

"Nothing!" Sterne interrupted with energy. "I tell you I yelled for him to leap overboard. He simply *must* have cast off the painter of the boat himself. We all yelled to him—that is, Jack and I. He wouldn't even answer us. The ship was as silent as a grave to the last. Then the boilers fetched away, and down she went. Accident! Not it! The game was up, sir, I tell you."

This was all that Sterne had to say.

Mr. Van Wyk had been of course made the guest of the club for a fortnight, and it was there that he met the lawyer in whose office had been signed the agreement between Massy and Captain Whalley.

"Extraordinary old man," he said. "He came into
my office from nowhere in particular as you may say,
with his five hundred pounds to invest, and that engineer fellow following him anxiously. And now he is
gone out a little inexplicably, just as he came. I could
never understand him quite. There was no mystery
at all about that Massy, eh? I wonder whether Whalley refused to leave the ship. It would have been
foolish. He was blameless, as the court found."

Mr. Van Wyk had known him well, he said, and he
could not believe in suicide. Such an act would not
have been in character with what he knew of the man.

"It is my opinion, too," the lawyer agreed. The
general theory was that the captain had remained too
long on board trying to save something of importance.
Perhaps the chart which would clear him, or else something of value in his cabin. The painter of the boat
had come adrift of itself, it was supposed. However,
strange to say, some little time before that voyage
poor Whalley had called in his office and had left with
him a sealed envelope addressed to his daughter, to be
forwarded to her in case of his death. Still it was nothing very unusual, especially in a man of his age. Mr.
Van Wyk shook his head. Captain Whalley looked
good for a hundred years.

"Perfectly true," assented the lawyer. "The old
fellow looked as though he had come into the world full
grown and with that long beard. I could never, somehow, imagine him either younger or older—don't you
know. There was a sense of physical power about
that man, too. And perhaps that was the secret of that
something peculiar in his person which struck everybody who came in contact with him. He looked indestructible by any ordinary means that put an end
to the rest of us. His deliberate, stately courtesy of

manner was full of significance. It was as though he
were certain of having plenty of time for everything.
Yes, there was something indestructible about him;
and the way he talked sometimes you might have
thought he believed it himself. When he called on me
last with that letter he wanted me to take charge of,
he was not depressed at all. Perhaps a shade more
deliberate in his talk and manner. Not depressed in
the least. Had he a presentiment, I wonder? Perhaps!
Still it seems a miserable end for such a striking figure."

"Oh, yes! It was a miserable end," Mr. Van Wyk
said, with so much fervour that the lawyer looked up
at him curiously; and afterwards, after parting with
him, he remarked to an acquaintance—

"Queer person that Dutch tobacco-planter from Batu
Beru. Know anything of him?"

"Heaps of money," answered the bank manager.
"I hear he's going home by the next mail to form a
company to take over his estates. Another tobacco
district thrown open. He's wise, I think. These
good times won't last for ever."

In the southern hemisphere Captain Whalley's
daughter had no presentiment of evil when she opened
the envelope addressed to her in the lawyer's hand-
writing. She had received it in the afternoon; all the
boarders had gone out, her boys were at school, her
husband sat upstairs in his big arm-chair with a book,
thin-faced, wrapped up in rugs to the waist. The house
was still, and the grayness of a cloudy day lay against
the panes of the windows.

In a shabby dining-room, where a faint cold smell of
dishes lingered all the year round, sitting at the end of a
long table surrounded by many chairs pushed in with
their backs close against the edge of the perpetually

laid table-cloth, she read the opening sentences: "Most profound regret—painful duty—your father is no more —in accordance with his instructions—fatal casualty— consolation—no blame attached to his memory. . . ."

Her face was thin, her temples a little sunk under the smoother bands of black hair, her lips remained resolutely compressed, while her dark eyes grew larger, till at last, with a low cry, she stood up, and instantly stooped to pick up another envelope which had slipped off her knees on to the floor.

She tore it open, snatched out the enclosure. . . .

"My dearest child," it said, "I am writing this while I am able yet to write legibly. I am trying hard to save for you all the money that is left; I have only kept it to serve you better. It is yours. It shall not be lost; it shall not be touched. There's five hundred pounds. Of what I have earned I have kept nothing back till now. For the future, if I live, I must keep back some—a little—to bring me to you. I must come to you. I must see you once more.

"It is hard to believe that you will ever look on these lines. God seems to have forgotten me. I want to see you—and yet death would be a greater favour. If you ever read these words, I charge you to begin by thanking a God merciful at last, for I shall be dead then, and it will be well. My dear, I am at the end of my tether."

The next paragraph began with the words: "My sight is going. . . ."

She read no more that day. The hand holding up the paper to her eyes fell slowly, and her slender figure in a plain black dress walked rigidly to the window. Her eyes were dry: no cry of sorrow or whisper of thanks went up to heaven from her lips. Life had been too hard, for all the efforts of his love. It had silenced her emotions. But for the first time in all these years its sting had departed, the carking care of poverty, the meanness of a hard struggle for bread. Even the image of her husband and of her children seemed to glide away from her into the gray twilight; it was her father's face alone that she saw, as though he had come to see her, always quiet and big, as she had seen him last, but with something more august and tender in his aspect.

She slipped his folded letter between the two buttons of her plain black bodice, and leaning her forehead against a window-pane remained there till dusk, perfectly motionless, giving him all the time she could spare. Gone! Was it possible? My God, was it possible? The blow had come softened by the spaces of the earth, by the years of absence. There had been whole days when she had not thought of him at all— had no time. But she had loved him, she felt she had loved him after all.

THE END

EXPLANATORY NOTES

The following notes do not tie Conrad's experiences in Malaysia and Africa to the events in his fiction. He believed that explicitness would be fatal to his endeavours. Indeed, he never mentions Sumatra, Belgium or Singapore in 'Youth', 'Heart of Darkness', or 'The End.of the Tether'. For those who need the information that ties the life to the art there are three books ready at hand: Roger Tennant, *Joseph Conrad* (New York, 1981) for all three stories; Norman Sherry, *Conrad's Eastern World* (Cambridge, 1966) *passim* for 'Youth' and pp. 173–207 for 'The End of the Tether'; N. Sherry, *Conrad's Western World* (Cambridge, 1971) pp. 9–133 for 'Heart of Darkness'.

3 *Conway boy*: the *Conway* was a Naval Training Vessel moored in the Thames.

  P. & O. Service: the Peninsular and Oriental Steam Navigation Company had a Royal Mail contract.

6 *Yarmouth*: seaport in Norfolk, where Breydon Water (the combined waters of the Yare, Waveney and Bure) enters the North Sea.

  Dogger Bank: submerged sandbank in the North Sea, sixty miles off the English coast.

7 *the Tyne*: river flowing into the North Sea below Newcastle, in Northumberland.

  tier: a row of moored or anchored ships.

  Sartor Resartus: (1833) by Thomas Carlyle, Victorian philosopher (1795–1881).

  Burnaby's Ride to Khiva: Colonel Frederick Gustavas Burnaby (1842–85), British soldier and traveller, wrote *Ride to Khiva* (1876) describing his winter ride across the Russian steppes.

10 *the Lizards*: the Lizard Peninsula, terminating in Lizard point (Lizard Head), Cornwall.

14 *Falmouth*: English Channel seaport and holiday resort, Cornwall.

15 *Geordie*: slang for a coal-carrying sailing vessel.

  messes: meals.

16 *grog-blossoms*: enlarged blood vessels and small tuberosities on the nose or face of persons who drink alcohol to excess.

17 *Land's End*: westernmost peninsula of Cornwall; also, the western-most point of England.

Forelands: North Foreland and the South Foreland, Kent, eastern-most point of the English Channel.

18 *Java Head*: the western tip of the Indonesian island of Java in the Indian Ocean; it was a famous landmark for ships engaged in the China trade because it marked the Sunda Strait between Sumatra and Java.

27 *Calashes*: native sailors of the Far East.

Malay seamen: from Southeast Asia, including the east coast of Sumatra and the coast of Borneo.

Batavia: former Dutch name of Djakarta, Java.

Anjer: Anjer Lor, Java.

33 *Erebus*: in Greek mythology, the darkness of the western region where the house of Hades and the sunless Cimmerian land were located.

45 *Gravesend*: last major town in the Thames estuary, twenty-six miles east of London, on the south shore (in Kent) where Essex forms the north shore.

47 *Drake... Franklin*: Sir Francis Drake (1540–96) sailed the *Golden Hind* in the service of Elizabeth I; Sir John Franklin (1786–1849), in 1845, led an exploring party in the *Erebus* and *Terror* in search of the North-West Passage, but by the winter of 1848–9 all hands were dead.

Deptford... Greenwich... Erith: three ports between London and Gravesend.

'Change: the 'Wall Street' of London.

"interlopers": ships that trespassed on the rights of trade monopolies such as the East India Company, with its large transports engaged in regular general trade.

49 *Falernian wine*: famous ancient wine from Campania; should not be confused with Neapolitan Falerno.

Ravenna: now inland, was the chief Roman naval base in northern Italy on the upper Adriatic.

57 *Ave!*: 'Hail!'

Morituri te salutant: 'Those who are about to die salute you!'

58 *alienist*: a precursor of the modern psychiatrist.

61 *drooped*: all versions of the story except the manuscript read *dropped*.

67 *worsted*: wool.

68 *sent*: most printed versions of the story retain the typographical error *set*.

70 *Deal*: English Channel port, Kent.

71 *Zanzibaris*: the natives of Zanzibar were used as mercenaries throughout Africa.

sixteen stone: 224 pounds.

77 *assegais*: slender South African throwing spears.

86 *serviette*: French form for napkin.

ichthyosaurus: a huge prehistoric kind of crocodile.

100 *float*: each blade of the paddle-wheel; *Youth* (1902) reads *boat*.

108 *serried*: crowded, compact, dense, pressed together.

109 *Martini-Henry*: a breech-action military rifle that takes a cartridge with an especially large powder charge.

141 *ulster*: long loose overcoat, worn by both sexes, originally made in Ulster, Ireland.

148 *secular*: ancient.

160 *back*: *Youth* (1902) reads *black*.

165 *Sofala*: after '*do*', '*re*', '*me*', the fifth, fourth, and sixth word-notes in the seven-note, diatonic scale, followed by '*ti*'. The *Sofala* runs its trade-route from Singapore, at the southern tip of the Malay Peninsula, 800 miles up through the Strait of Malacca, along the west coast of the Peninsula as far north as Tenasserim in Lower Burma, and back down 800 miles again: up and down, up and down, just like practising the scales over and over and over. Sofala is also the name of a one-time Trade District in south central Mozambique (old Portuguese East Africa), and the port of Beira was sometimes called Sofala unofficially.

Serang: the boatswain of an East Indian crew; also the skipper of a small native boat.

167 *Condor*: a powerful, majestic bird, all black with a white 'collar'.

168 *General Directory*: probably the *China Sea Directory* published by the British Admiralty in 1868.

170 *Fair Maid*: from the popular sailor's drinking song, 'I'll go no more a-rovin' from you, fair maid'.

172 *plummet*: a small feather-duster (plume-ette or plumeau).

173 *roulades*: in vocal music, an ornament consisting of a quick run, arpeggio, or other figure, sung to one syllable; a vocal flourish; a diversion.

181 *H.E.I. Company*: Honourable East India Company.

182 *Sikh trooper*: adherents of the Hindu sect of Sikhism, Sikhs were soldiers in the colonial British-Indian army.

190 *Esplanade*: a clear level space or stretch of ground, usually along a shore for public walks or drives.

192 *landau*: a four-wheeled carriage invented in Germany, seating four people on two facing seats with an elevated front seat for the driver, and two folding hoods, one at each end, which met at the top to form a box-like enclosure with side windows.

C-springs: a leaf spring, the ends of which are formed in a large curve roughly resembling the letter C.

193 *Archipelago*: the islands of Indonesia and the Philippines, between the continents of Asia and Australia.

194 *graving basins*: where ships could be dry-docked to have their hulls scraped clean.

sheer-legs: colloquial term for hoisting shears, made of two tall spars joined at the tops, bottoms spread, like a huge compass or pair of scissors.

197 *Ringdove*: a common European pigeon, white with a black 'collar'.

198 *rosace above the ogive*: the circular rose-window above the high arch of the door.

199 *French Cochin-China*: until 1949, a French protectorate; from 1954 to 1974, as South Vietnam, an American protectorate; now, the southern part of Vietnam.

202 *syce*: an Indian groom.

207 *stiver*: Dutch coin of little worth.

209 *peristyle*: a courtyard surrounded by a colonnade.

220 *lascar*: an East Indian sailor.

242 *martello towers*: masonry turrets on forts.

257 *secular*: ancient.

258 *Rajah*: originally an Indian prince or king, but also applied to Malay chiefs.

betel: the nutlike seed of the betel palm; masticatory of the East Indies; a pungent astringent stimulant, which stains the teeth black.

Kling: from one of the ancient tribes of India, formerly held in low esteem by other Indians; familiar in the seaports of eastern India and Malaysia; some texts carry the misprint *King*.

259 *rattan*: a portion of the stem of the rattan palm that is used for walking sticks, wickerwork, and cordage.

267 *lumber*: miscellaneous gear.

268 *Hull*: officially Kingston-Upon-Hull (Yorkshire), on the north bank of the Humber Estuary, twenty-two miles from the North Sea.

 sovereigns: gold coin of Great Britain, worth one pound sterling or twenty shillings.

279 *étagère*: a cabinet with open shelves.

 "*Bismarck malade*": yellowish red-yellow, of medium saturation, and low brilliance.

285 *Acheen War*: the Dutch conquered the province of Acheen in northwestern Sumatra in 1874, but the Achinese waged guerilla warfare throughout the rest of the century.

287 *Balinini*: (?) from Baling in Malay, or from the island of Bali.

288 *Tampasuk*: in North Borneo.

305 *muzzy*: dull-spirited; muddled or confused; stupid with drink.

321 *bull's-eye lantern*: a lantern with a simple lens of large numerical aperture, used for concentrating rays of light.

322 *Capharnaum*: ancient city on the north-western shore of the Sea of Galilee: modern excavations did not begin until 1905.

GLOSSARY OF NAUTICAL TERMS

aft (after), near the stern

astern, in the direction of the stern; the opposite of ahead/forward

athwart (across), therefore, 'athwart-ships' means across the length of a vessel. The opposite of fore-and-aft.

ballast, heavy material—iron, lead, or stone—placed in the bottom of the hold, to keep a vessel steady

barque, a small ship, square-sterned, without head-rails; also, a three-masted vessel with fore-and-aft sails on her mizzen mast (i.e. no square sails)

belay, to make a rope or line fast by turns around a piece of wood or iron without hitching it

belaying-pins, a short piece of wood or iron to 'belay' ropes to

binnacle, a case or box that holds the compass; it is fitted with a lamp for use at night

boatswain ('bo'sun'), a ship's petty officer who has charge of the rigging and who calls the crew to duty

bow, the front of a ship

breaker, small barrel for containing water or other liquids

bulkheads, walls forming rooms or compartments below deck that also serve to prevent water from filling all areas of any deck level all at once

bulwarks, a kind of low wooden fence around the main deck, with openings to allow water to run off during heavy weather

bunts, the middle part of a square sail; the part of a furled sail that is gathered up in a bunched roll at the centre of the yard; hence, rarely, the middle part of a yard

caravel, a small vessel with broad bow, high, narrow poop, three or four masts, and usually lateen sails on the two or three after masts

cat-heads, tackle used to raise or suspend the anchor

chandler, person in charge of supplies and equipment

chronometer, an accurate navigational clock indicating Greenwich Mean Time, used to determine the longitude at sea by means of a timepiece and observation of the heavenly bodies

clipper, a fast sailing vessel, especially a full-rigged ship of a type developed by American builders about 1840, characterized by fine lines, an overhanging bow, tall raking masts, and a large sail area

coasters, ships engaged in taking on and off cargo at many ports of call along a coast

companion-hatchway, a covered square opening cut in the deck to get below to quarters or storage holds by means of the companion, or ladder

compass card, the circular card attached to the needles of a ship's compass on which are marked the 32 points of the compass and 360 degrees of the circle

counter, the portion of a ship from the waterline to the angle of the stern

cruising yawl, a fore-and-aft rigged vessel with a mainmast stepped a little farther forward than in a sloop and carrying a mainsail and one or more jibs, with a mizzenmast far aft, usually placed abaft the rudder post

cuddy, a small cabin, or the saloon, under the poop deck

davits, a pair of small projecting cranes on the sides or stern of the ship for suspending, lowering, and hoisting a ship's boats

dock, large basin either permanently filled with water (wet dock) or capable of being filled and drained (dry dock)

fathom, a rough measure of length (5–6 feet); the distance a man can extend his arms

fife-rail, a rail surrounding the mast for use in holding the pins, to which some of the rigging is attached

fore (foreward), at or toward the bow

forespeak, the part of the hold of a ship that is farthest forward, in the angle of the ship's bow

fore-rigging, sails at or toward the bow

furl, to roll up and bind a sail neatly on its respective yard or boom

gasket, a line or band used to lash a furled sail securely

gunwale ('gun'l'), the upper rail of a boat or vessel

head, front or top

hove to, sails adjusted to counteract each other in order to stay, as nearly as possible, in one place

hulk, a vessel condemned as unfit for the risks of the sea; the masts are removed and it is used for storage or as a barge

hull, the body of a ship exclusive of masts, sails, yards, and rigging

kedge-anchor, small anchor used in mooring or warping

keel, the lowest and principal timber of a vessel, running fore-and-aft its whole length, and supporting the whole frame. It is composed of several pieces, placed lengthwise, and scarfed and bolted together.

knot, a unit of speed per hour, based on a nautical mile (6,076.1 feet)

lazarette, space between decks used as a store room

leadsman, the man who handles the sounding equipment

lee, the side opposite to that from

which the wind blows; if a vessel has the wind on her starboard side, that will be the 'weather side' and port will be the 'lee' side

Mates, the officers along with the Captain: Chief (First), Second, and Third (if a large ship)

mizzen-mast, the aftermost mast of a three-masted ship

patent log, dial of, apparatus trailed behind a vessel to measure the rate of progress

pile, a pillar, literally; or, figuratively, a pier

poop, a raised deck running from the mizzenmast to the stern, containing accommodation for the master and officers

prau, the Indonesian name for an undecked native boat, dugout, or plank-built craft that is rowed, paddled, or sailed

quartermaster, a petty officer who attends to a ship's helm, binnacle, and signals under the master or navigator

quay, a wharf

reach, a straight portion between the curves of a body of water

rigging, the general term for all the ropes of a vessel. Also, the common term for the shrouds with their ratlines; as: the main rigging, mizzen rigging, etc.

sampan, a skiff, used in the river and harbour traffic of China, Japan and neighbouring islands, propelled usually with a scull.

It sometimes has a sail, and usually a mat roofing over its cabin.

scow, a large flat-bottomed boat, having broad, square ends

scuttle, among other meanings, short for scuttle-butt, the fresh water cask for a day's use

shoal, a place where a sea, river, etc., is shallow; a shallow

shrouds, a set of ropes reaching from the mast-heads to the vessel's sides, to support the masts

sounding-pole/rod, a pole used to measure water depth

spar, a stout, rounded wood or metal piece; hence (plural), the general term for masts, yards, booms, etc.

sprit, pole or spar extended diagonally upward from a mast to the topmost corner of a fore-and-aft sail, serving to extend the sail

square-rigged, literally, a ship with square sails, but usually means a big, fully outfitted ship

stanchions, upright posts of wood or iron, placed so as to support the beams of a vessel. Also, upright pieces of timber, placed at intervals along the sides of a vessel, to support the bulwarks and rail. Also, any fixed upright support.

starboard, right side, right-hand side

steam-collier, a steam-driven, coal-carrying ship

stern, rear of a ship

sticks, slang for masts

stun' sail, a light sail, sometimes set on the exterior of a hull and extended by horizontal spars or poles when the wind is fair

taffrail, a curved railing on the captain's balcony over the stern of a ship

thwart, one of the planks that extend crosswise in an open boat for lateral stiffening and which serve as seats for the oarsmen (from athwart)

tons/tonnage, a ton is both 100 cubic feet and 2240 pounds. GROSS TONNAGE is the enclosed space (internal capacity) of a ship. NET TONNAGE is the space left for cargo after the ship's supplies and crew's gear have been stowed. DISPLACE-MENT TONNAGE is the weight of the ship calculated by the sea water displaced when afloat. DEAD-WEIGHT TONNAGE is the difference between loaded and unloaded, hence indicates the weight of cargo that can be shipped.

top-gallant-mast, mast for the third sail up from the deck

truck, a circular or square piece of wood fixed on the head of a mast or the top of a flagstaff, usually containing small holes for signal halyards

trireme, a Roman galley with three ranks of oars, one above another

watch, a division of time on board ship. Also, a certain portion of ship's company, appointed to 'stand watch' (be on duty) a given length of time, usually four hours. In the merchant service all hands are divided into two watches, 'port' and 'starboard', with an officer to command each. First night-watch, 20.00–24.00 hours; second night-watch, 00.01–04.00 hours.

windlass, a machine used in merchant ships to heave up the anchors from the bottom

yard, a long piece of timber, tapering slightly toward the ends, and hung at the centre of a mast, to spread the square sails upon (in square-rigged ships). To 'trim the yards' is to adjust the yards with reference to the direction of the wind and the course of the ship.

yard-arm, either end of a yard

THE WORLD'S CLASSICS

A Select List

ARTHUR CONAN DOYLE
Sherlock Holmes: Selected Stories
With an introduction by S. C. Roberts

MARIA EDGEWORTH: Castle Rackrent
Edited by George Watson

GEORGE ELIOT: The Mill on the Floss
Edited by Gordon S. Haight

GUSTAVE FLAUBERT: Madame Bovary
Translated by Gerard Hopkins
With an introduction by Terence Cave

JOHN GALT: The Provost
Edited by Ian A. Gordon

WILLIAM GODWIN: Caleb Williams
Edited by David McCracken

OLIVER GOLDSMITH: The Vicar of Wakefield
Edited by Arthur Friedman

KENNETH GRAHAME: The Wind in the Willows
Edited by Peter Green

ALEXANDER HERZEN: Childhood, Youth and Exile
With an introduction by Isaiah Berlin

JAMES HOGG: The Private Memoirs and
Confessions of a Justified Sinner
Edited by John Carey

HOMER: The Iliad
Translated by Robert Fitzgerald
With an introduction by G. S. Kirk

The Odyssey
Translated by Walter Shewring
With an introduction by G. S. Kirk

HENRIK IBSEN: Four Major Plays
Translated by James McFarlane and Jens Arup
With an introduction by James McFarlane

MARY WOLLSTONECRAFT:
Mary *and* The Wrongs of Woman
Edited by Gary Kelly